HELL BENT

Also by Leigh Bardugo

Ninth House

The Shadow and Bone Trilogy
Shadow and Bone

Siege and Storm

Ruin and Rising

The Six of Crows Duology
Six of Crows

Crooked Kingdom

The King of Scars Duology
King of Scars

Rule of Wolves

The Language of Thorns

The Lives of Saints

HELL BENT

Leigh Bardugo

FLATIRON
BOOKS
NEW YORK

HELL BENT. Copyright © 2022 by Leigh Bardugo. All rights reserved. Printed in the United States of America. For information, address Flatiron Books, 120 Broadway, New York, NY 10271.

www.flatironbooks.com

Designed by Donna Sinisgalli Noetzel

Map by Rhys Davies and WB

Endpaper illustration by Travis DeMello

Library of Congress Cataloging-in-Publication Data

Names: Bardugo, Leigh, author.
Title: Hell bent / Leigh Bardugo.
Description: First edition. | New York, NY : Flatiron Books, 2023. |
Series: Alex Stern ; 2
Identifiers: LCCN 2022034375 | ISBN 9781250313102 (hardcover) | ISBN 9781250894274 (international, sold outside the U.S., subject to rights availability) | ISBN 9781250313119 (ebook)
Subjects: LCGFT: Paranormal fiction. | Novels.
Classification: LCC PS3602.A775325 H45 2023 | DDC 813/.6—dc23/eng/20220725
LC record available at https://lccn.loc.gov/2022034375

Our books may be purchased in bulk for promotional, educational, or business use. Please contact your local bookseller or the Macmillan Corporate and Premium Sales Department at 1-800-221-7945, extension 5442, or by email at MacmillanSpecialMarkets@macmillan.com.

First U.S. Edition: 2023

First International Edition: 2023

10 9 8 7 6 5 4 3 2 1

For Miriam Pastan,
who read my fortune in a cup of coffee

Ignorant they of all things till I came
And told them of the rising of the stars
And their dark settings, taught them numbers, too,
The queen of knowledge. I instructed them
How to join letters, making them their slaves
To serve the memory, mother of the muse.

Aeschylus, *Prometheus Bound*
Inscribed above the entrance to
Sterling Memorial Library, Yale University

Culebra que no mir morde, que viva mil anos.
May the snake that doesn't bite me live a thousand
    years.

Sephardic proverb

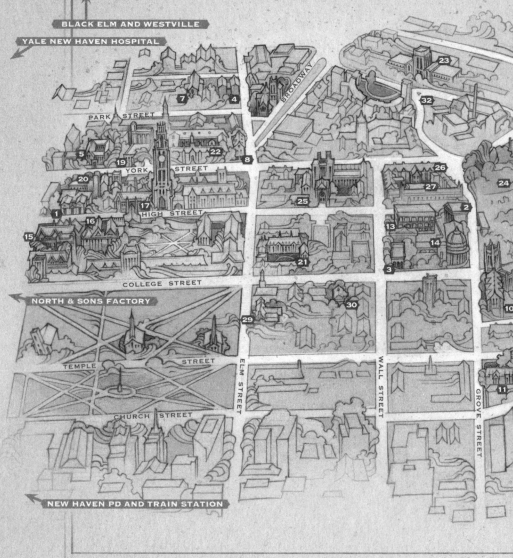

YALE UNIVERSITY
NEW HAVEN, CT

BLACK ELM AND WESTVILLE

YALE NEW HAVEN HOSPITAL

BROADWAY

PARK STREET

YORK STREET

STREET

HIGH STREET

COLLEGE STREET

NORTH & SONS FACTORY

ELM STREET

WALL STREET

GROVE STREET

TEMPLE STREET

CHURCH STREET

NEW HAVEN PD AND TRAIN STATION

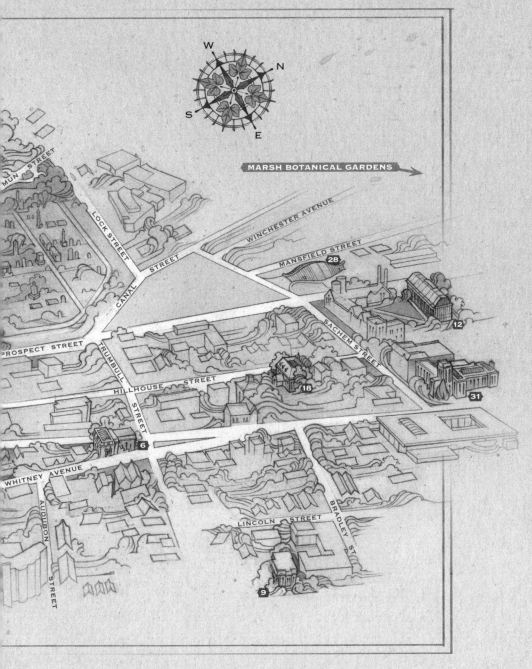

PART I

As Above

November

Alex approached Black Elm as if she were sidling up to a wild animal, cautious in her walk up the long, curving driveway, careful not to show her fear. How many times had she made this walk? But today was different. The house appeared through the bare branches of the trees, as if it had been waiting for her, as if it had heard her footsteps and anticipated her arrival. It didn't crouch like prey. It stood, two stories of gray stone and peaked roofs, a wolf with paws planted and teeth bared. Black Elm had been tame once, glossy and preening. But it had been left on its own too long.

The boarded-up windows on the second floor made it all so much worse, a wound in the wolf's side that, left untended, might turn it mad.

She slotted her key into the old back door and slipped into the kitchen. It was chillier inside than out—they couldn't afford to keep the place heated, and there was no reason to. But despite the cold and the mission she'd come here to fulfill, the room still felt welcoming. Copper pans hung in neat rows above the big vintage stove, bright and ready, eager to be used. The slate floor was spotless, the counters wiped clean and set with a milk bottle full of holly branches that Dawes had arranged just so. The kitchen was the most functional room of Black Elm, alive with regular care, a tidy temple of light. This was how Dawes dealt with all they'd done, with the thing lurking in the ballroom.

Alex had a routine. Well, Dawes had a routine and Alex tried to follow it, and it felt like a rock to cling to now as fear tried to drag her under. Unlock the door, sort the mail and set it on the counter, fill Cosmo's bowls with fresh food and water.

They were usually empty, but today Cosmo had tipped the food on its side, scattering the floor with fish-shaped pellets, as if in protest.

Darlington's cat was mad at being left alone. Or frightened by not being quite so alone anymore.

"Or maybe you're just a picky little shit," Alex muttered, cleaning up the food. "I'll pass your comments along to the chef."

She didn't like the sound of her voice, brittle in the quiet, but she made herself finish slowly, methodically. She filled the water and food bowls, tossed out the junk mail addressed to Daniel Arlington, and tucked a water bill into her bag that she would take back to Il Bastone. Steps in a ritual, performed with care, but they offered no protection. She considered making coffee. She could sit outside in the winter sunlight and wait for Cosmo to come find her, when he saw fit to leave off prowling the messy tangle of the hedge maze for mice. She could do that. Push her worry and anger aside, and try to solve this puzzle, even though she didn't want to complete the picture emerging with every new and nasty piece.

Alex glanced up at the ceiling as if she were able to see through the floorboards. No, she couldn't just sit on the porch and pretend everything was as it should be, not when her feet wanted to climb those stairs, not when she knew she should run the other way, lock the kitchen door behind her, pretend she'd never heard of this place. Alex had come here for a reason, but now she wondered at her stupidity. She wasn't up to this task. She'd talk to Dawes, maybe even Turner. For once she'd make a plan instead of rushing headlong into disaster.

She washed her hands at the sink, and it was only when she turned to reach for a towel that she saw the open door.

Alex dried her hands, trying to ignore the way her heart had leapt into a run. She had never noticed that door in the butler's pantry, a gap between the pretty glass cupboards and shelves. She'd never seen it open before. It shouldn't be open now.

Dawes might have left it that way. But Dawes was licking her wounds from the ritual and hiding behind her rows of index cards. She hadn't been here in days, not since she had set those holly branches on the kitchen counter, making a picture of what life should be. Clean and easy. An antidote to the rest of their days and nights, to the secret above.

She and Dawes never bothered with the butler's pantry, its rows of dusty dishes and glassware, its soup terrine the size of a small bathtub. It was one of the many vestigial limbs of the old house, disused and forgotten, left to atrophy since Darlington's disappearance. And they certainly never bothered with the basement. Alex had never even thought about it. Not until now, standing at the kitchen sink, surrounded by tidy blue tiles painted with windmills and tall ships, staring at that black gap, a perfect rectangle, a sudden void. It looked as if someone had simply peeled away part of the kitchen. It looked like the mouth of a grave.

Call Dawes.

Alex leaned against the counter.

Back out of the kitchen and call Turner.

She set down the towel and drew a knife from the block beside the sink. She wished there were a Gray nearby, but she didn't want to risk calling one to her.

The size of the house, its deep silence, sat heavy around her. She glanced up again, thought of the golden shimmer of the circle, the heat it gave off. *I have appetites.* Had those words excited her when they should have only made her afraid?

Alex walked quietly toward the open door, the absence of a door. How deep had they dug when they'd built this house? She could count three, four, five stone steps leading down into the basement, and then they faded into the dark. Maybe there were no more stairs. Maybe she would take a step, fall, keep falling into the cold.

She felt along the wall for a light switch, then looked up and saw a ratty piece of twine dangling from an exposed bulb. She yanked on it, and the stairs were flooded with warm yellow light. The bulb made a comforting hum.

"Shit," Alex said on a breath. Her terror dissolved, leaving nothing but embarrassment in its place. Just stairs, a wooden railing, shelves stacked with rags, cans of paint, tools lining the wall. A faint, musty smell rose up from the dark below, a vegetable stink, the hint of rot. She heard the drip of water and the shuffle of what might have been a rat.

She couldn't quite make out the base of the stairs, but there had to be another switch or bulb below. She could go down there, make sure no one had been rooting around, see if she and Dawes needed to set out traps.

But why was the door open?

Cosmo could have nudged it on one of his ratting expeditions. Or maybe Dawes really had popped by and gone down to the basement for something ordinary—weed killer, paper towels. She'd forgotten to close up properly.

So Alex would shut the door. Lock it tight. And if, by chance, there was something down there that wasn't meant to be down there, it could stay right where it was until she called for reinforcements.

She reached for the twine and paused there, hand gripping the string, listening. She thought she heard—there, again, a soft hiss.

The sound of her name. *Galaxy.*

"Fuck this." She knew how this particular movie ended, and there was no way she was going down there.

She yanked on the twine and heard the pop of the bulb, then felt a hard shove between her shoulder blades.

Alex fell. The knife clattered from her hands. She fought the urge to reach out to break her fall and covered her head instead, letting her shoulder take the brunt of it. She half-slid, half-tumbled to the base of the stairs, and hit the floor hard, her breath flooding out of her like a draft through a window. The door above her slammed. She heard the lock click. She was in the dark.

Her heart was racing now. What was down here with her? Who had locked her in with it? *Get up, Stern. Get your shit together. Get ready to fight.*

Was it her voice she was hearing? Darlington's?

Hers, of course. Darlington would never swear.

She pushed herself to her feet, bracing her back against the wall. At least nothing could come at her from that direction. It was hard to breathe. Once bones broke, they learned the habit. Blake Keely had cracked two of her ribs less than a year ago. She thought they might be broken again. Her hands were slippery. The floor was wet from some old leak in the walls, and the air smelled fetid and wrong. She wiped her palms on her jeans and waited, her breath coming in ragged gasps. From somewhere in the dark, she heard what might have been a whimper.

"Who's there?" she rasped, hating the fear in her voice. "Come at me, you cowardly fuck."

Nothing.

She fumbled for her phone, for light, the blue glow vibrant and startling. She directed the beam over shelves of old paint thinner, tools, boxes labeled in a jagged hand she knew was Darlington's, dusty crates emblazoned with a circular logo: *Arlington & Co. Rubber Boots.* Then the light glinted off two pairs of eyes.

Alex choked on a scream, nearly dropping her phone. Not people, Grays, a man and a woman, clinging to each other, trembling with fear. But it wasn't Alex they were afraid of.

She'd gotten it wrong. The floor wasn't wet from a leak or rainwater or some old burst pipe. The floor was slick with blood. Her hands were covered in it. She'd smeared it on her jeans.

Two bodies lay heaped on the old brick. They looked like castoff clothing, piles of rags. She knew those faces. *Heaven, to keep its beauty, cast them out.*

There was so much blood. New blood. Fresh.

The Grays hadn't abandoned their bodies. Even in her panic, she knew that was strange.

"Who did this?" she asked them and the woman moaned.

The man pressed a finger to his lips, eyes full of fear as they darted around the basement. His whisper drifted through the dark.

"We're not alone."

1

October,
One Month Before

Alex wasn't far from Tara's apartment. She'd driven these streets with Darlington at the start of her freshman year, walked them when she was hunting Tara's killer. It had been winter then, the branches bare, the tiny yards crusted with dirty mounds of snow. This neighborhood looked better in the still-warm days of early October, clouds of green leaves softening the edges of the rooflines, ivy climbing over the chain-link fences, all of it made gentle and dreamy by the glint of streetlights carving golden circles into the soft hours of dusk.

She was standing in the well of shadow between two row houses, watching the street that fronted the Taurus Cafe, a windowless lump of brick decorated by signs promising keno and lotto and Corona. Alex could hear the thump of music from somewhere inside. Small rings of people smoked and chatted beneath the lights, despite the sign beside the door that read *No loitering police take notice*. She was glad of the noise, but less happy at the prospect of so many witnesses seeing her come and go. Better to come back in the daytime when the street would be deserted, but she didn't have that luxury.

She knew the bar would be packed with Grays, drawn by sweat, bodies pressed together, the damp clink of beer bottles; she wanted someone closer to hand.

There—a Gray in a parka and a beanie, hovering by an arguing couple, undisturbed by the heavy heat of a too-long summer. She made eye contact with him, his baby face an uncomfortable jolt. He'd died young.

"*Come on along*," she sang under her breath, then gave a disgusted snort. She had that goofy song in her head. Some a cappella group had been practicing in the courtyard when Alex was getting ready to leave the dorm.

"How are they already starting that shit?" Lauren had complained, sorting through her crates of vinyl, her blond hair even brighter after a summer spent lifeguarding.

"It's Irving Berlin," Mercy had noted.

"I don't care."

"It's also racist."

"That shit is racist!" Lauren had called out of the window and put AC/DC on her record player, turning the volume all the way up.

Alex loved every minute of it. She'd been surprised at how much she'd missed Lauren and Mercy over the summer, their easy talk and gossip, the shared worry over classes, the arguments about music and clothes, all of it like a tether she could grasp to bring her back to the ordinary world. *This is my life*, she'd told herself, curled up on the couch in front of a noisy fan, watching Mercy hang a garland of stars over the fireplace in their new common room, quite a change from their cramped rooms on Old Campus. The couch and recliner had made it into their new suite, the coffee table they'd all assembled together at the start of freshman year, the toaster and its seemingly inexhaustible supply of Pop-Tarts sent courtesy of Lauren's mom. Alex had asked Lethe for a bike and a printer and a new tutor at the end of last year. They'd been happy to agree, and she wished she'd asked for more.

Their freshman dorm on Old Campus had been the most beautiful place Alex had ever lived, but the residential college—JE proper—felt real, solid and elegant, permanent. She liked the stained glass windows, the stonework faces in every corner of the courtyard, the scuffed wood floors, the heavily carved fireplace that didn't work but that they'd decorated with candles and a vintage globe. She even liked the little Gray in an old-fashioned dress, a child with hair done up in crisp curls who liked to linger in the branches above the tree swing.

She and Mercy were sharing a double because Lauren had won the single in their draw. Alex was sure she'd cheated, but she didn't much mind. It would have been easier to come and go if she had a room to herself, but there was also something comforting about lying in bed at night and hearing Mercy snore across the room. And at least they weren't stuck in bunks anymore.

Alex had planned on hanging out with Mercy and Lauren for a few hours before she had to leave to oversee a ritual at Book and Snake, listening to records and trying to ignore the annoying *mmmm ooh* of a singing group punishing "Alexander's Ragtime Band."

Come on along. Come on along. Let me take you by the hand.

But then the text from Eitan had appeared.

So now she was eyeing the Taurus Cafe. She was about to step out of the shadows when a black-and-white drove by, a new cruiser, sleek and quiet as a deep-sea predator. It flashed its lights and gave a brief belch of the siren, a warning that the New Haven PD did indeed take notice.

"Yeah, fuck you," someone growled, but the crowd dispersed, drifting into the club or weaving down the sidewalk to find their cars. It wasn't properly late yet. There was still plenty of time to find another party, another chance at something good.

Alex didn't want to think about the cops or getting caught or what Turner might say if she got dragged in on a B&E or, worse, an assault charge. She hadn't heard from the detective since the end of her freshman year, and she doubted he'd be glad to see her under the best of circumstances.

Once the cruiser was gone, Alex made sure the sidewalk was clear of possible witnesses and crossed the street to an ugly white duplex, just a couple doors down from the bar. Funny how all sad places looked the same. Trash cans overflowing. Weed-choked yards and junked-up porches. *I'll get around to it or I won't.* But there was a new truck in the driveway of this particular house, complete with personalized license plate: ODMNOUT. At least she knew she had the right spot.

Alex drew a mirrored compact from the pocket of her jeans. When she hadn't been mapping New Haven's infinite churches for Dawes, she'd spent the summer digging through the drawers of Il Bastone's armory. She told herself it was a good way to waste time, get familiar with Lethe, maybe eye up what might be worth stealing if it came to that, but the truth was that when she was rummaging in the armory cabinets, reading the little handwritten cards—*the Carpet of Ozymandias*; *Monsoon Rings for calling rain, incomplete set*; *Palillos del Dios*—she could feel Darlington with her, peering over her shoulder. *Those castanets will banish a poltergeist, Stern, if one plays the correct rhythm. But you'll still walk away with your fingers burned black.*

It was comforting and troubling at the same time. Invariably, that steady scholar's voice turned accusing. *Where are you, Stern? Why haven't you come?*

Alex rolled her shoulders, trying to shrug off her guilt. She needed to stay focused. That morning, she'd held the pocket mirror up to the TV to see if she could capture a glamour from the screen. She hadn't been sure it would work, but it had. Now she popped it open and let the illusion fall over her. She jogged up the steps to the porch and knocked.

The man who answered the door was huge and heavily muscled, his neck thick and pink as a cartoon ham. She didn't need to consult the image on her phone. This was Chris Owens, also known as Oddman, record as long as he was and twice as wide.

"Holy shit," he said when he saw Alex at the door, his eyes trained on the space a foot above her head. The glamour had added twelve inches to her height.

She raised her hand and waved.

"I . . . Can I help you?" Oddman asked.

Alex bobbed her chin toward the apartment interior.

Oddman shook his head as if waking from a dream. "Yeah, of

course." He stepped aside, sweeping his arm out in a grand gesture of welcome.

The living room was surprisingly neat: a halogen lamp tucked into the corner, a big leather couch with a matching recliner arranged to face a massive flat-screen tuned to ESPN. "You want something to drink or . . ." He hesitated, and Alex knew the calculation he was making. There was only one reason a celebrity would turn up on his doorstep on a Thursday night—any night really. "You looking to score?"

Alex hadn't really needed confirmation, but now she had it. "You owe twelve large."

Oddman took a lurching step back as if he'd suddenly lost his balance. Because he was hearing Alex's voice. She hadn't bothered to try to disguise it, and the dissonance between her voice and the glamour of Tom Brady created by the mirror had caused the illusion to waver. It didn't matter. Alex had only needed the magic to get inside Oddman's apartment without a fuss.

"What the fuck—"

"Twelve large," Alex repeated.

Now he saw her as she was, a tiny girl standing in his living room, black hair parted in the middle, so skinny she might slip straight through the floorboards.

"I don't know who the fuck you are," he bellowed, "but you're in the wrong damn house."

He was already striding toward her, his bulk making the room shake.

Alex's arm shot out, reaching toward the window, toward the sidewalk in front of the Taurus Cafe. She felt the Gray in the beanie rush into her, tasted green apple Jolly Ranchers, smelled the skunk smoke of weed. His spirit felt unfinished and frantic, a bird slamming itself against a windowpane again and again. But his strength was pure and ferocious. She put up her hands, and her palms struck Oddman square in the chest.

The big man went flying. His body slammed into the TV, shattering the screen and knocking it to the floor. Alex couldn't pretend it didn't feel good to steal the Gray's strength, to be dangerous just for a moment.

She crossed the room and stood over Oddman, waited for his dazed eyes to clear.

"Twelve large," she said again. "You have a week to get it or I come back and break bones." Though it was possible she'd cracked his sternum already.

"I don't have it," Oddman said on a groan, his hand rubbing his chest. "My sister's kid—"

Alex knew the excuses; she'd made them herself. *My mom is in the hospital. My check is late. My car needs a new transmission and I can't pay you if I can't get to work.* It didn't really matter if they were true or not.

She squatted down. "I feel for you. I really do. But I have my job, you have yours. Twelve thousand dollars by next Friday or he'll make me come back and turn you into an example for every dime bag hump in the neighborhood. And I don't want to do that."

She really didn't.

Oddman seemed to believe her. "He . . . got something on you?"

"Enough to bring me here tonight and to bring me back again." Alex's temples gave a sudden throb, and the oversweet tang of apple candy burst into her mouth. "Shit, man. You look bad."

It took Alex a second to realize she was the one speaking—with someone else's voice.

Oddman's eyes widened. "Derrik?"

"Yeah!" That wasn't her voice, wasn't her laugh.

Oddman reached out to touch her shoulder, something between wonder and fear making his hand shake. "You . . . I went to your wake."

Alex stood, nearly losing her footing. She caught a glimpse of herself in the reflection from the broken TV, but the person looking back at her wasn't a scrawny girl in a tank top and jeans. It was a boy in a beanie and a parka.

She shoved the Gray out of her. For a moment, they stared at each other—Derrik, apparently. She didn't know what had killed him and she didn't want to know. He'd somehow pushed to the forefront of her consciousness, taken over her face, her voice. And she wanted none of that.

"*Bela Lugosi's dead*," she snarled at him. They'd become her favorite death words over the summer. He vanished.

Oddman had pressed himself against the wall as if he could disappear into it. His eyes were full of tears. "What the fuck is happening?"

"Don't worry about it," she said. "Just get the money and all this goes away."

Alex only wished she had it that easy.

Rete Mirabile
Provenance: Galway, Ireland; 18th century
Donor: Book and Snake, 1962

The "wonderful net" was procured by the Lettermen c. 1922. Specific date of origin and maker are unknown, but oral histories suggest it was created through Celtic song magic or possibly seidh (see the Norse sea giantess Rán). Analysis indicates the net itself is ordinary cotton, braided with human tendon. After a loved one had been lost at sea, the net could be thrown into the ocean while attached to a stake on shore. The next morning, the body would be returned, which some found comforting and others distressing, given the possible state of remains.

Gifted by Book and Snake when their attempts to recall specific corpses failed.

— from the Lethe Armory Catalogue as revised
and edited by Pamela Dawes, Oculus

Why is it the boys at Book and Snake don't seem to be able to cook up anything that works the way it should? First they resurrect a bunch of sailors who can only speak Irish. Next they empty their not insubstantial coffers to get their hands on an authenticated letter from the Egyptian Middle Kingdom before Wolf's Head can drum up the cash. A letter for the resurrection of a king. But who do they get when they light that thing up in their tomb? Not Amenhotep or good ol' Tutankhamun, not even a headless Charles I at their door, but Elvis Presley—tired, bloated, and hungry for a peanut butter and banana sandwich. They had a hell of a time getting him back to Memphis with no one the wiser.

—Lethe Days Diary of Dez Carghill
(Branford College '62)

2

The walk back to campus was long, and the heat felt like an animal dogging her steps, its breath moist against the nape of her neck. But Alex didn't slow her pace. She wanted distance between herself and that Gray. What had happened back there? And how was she supposed to keep it from happening again? Sweat trickled down her back. She wished she'd worn shorts, but it didn't feel right to wear cutoffs to a beatdown.

She paralleled the canal trail, counting down her long strides, trying to get her head straight before she was back on campus. She'd walked part of that trail last year, with Mercy, to see the leaves turn, a flood of red and gold, fireworks captured in their fullest bloom. She'd thought how different it was from the LA River with its concrete banks, and she'd remembered how she had floated in those dirty waters, flush with Hellie's strength, wishing they could both drift out to the open sea, become their own island. She'd wondered where Hellie was buried and hoped it was someplace beautiful, someplace nothing like that sad, scraping-along river, that collapsed vein.

The canal trail would be green now, choked with summer growth, but Grays loved it and Alex didn't want to be anywhere near them just this minute, so she stuck to the dull parking lots and faceless office buildings of Science Park, hurried past the industrial lofts, and on to Prospect. Only Darlington's ghost chased her here. His voice telling stories of the Winchester family and how their descendants had mixed and married with the Yale elite, or the hulking mass of

Sarah Winchester's grave across town—an eight-foot lump of rough-hewn rock, a cross pressed into it like a child's school project. Alex wondered if Mrs. Winchester had chosen to be buried at Evergreen instead of Grove Street because she knew she wouldn't rest easy right down the road from the factory where her husband had produced barrel after barrel, gun after gun.

Alex didn't slow down until she'd passed the new colleges and crossed Trumbull. It was comforting to be back near campus where the trees grew over the streets in shady canopies. How had she become someone who felt more at home here than on the streets outside the Taurus? Comfort was the drug she hadn't understood until it was too late and she was hooked on cups of tea and book-lined shelves, nights uninterrupted by the wail of sirens and the ceaseless churning of helicopters overhead. Her Tom Brady glamour had shaken loose completely when she'd let the Gray enter her, so at least she didn't need to worry about causing a stir on campus.

Students were out enjoying the warm night, waddling along with couches jammed between them, handing out flyers for parties. A girl on roller skates coasted down the middle of the street, fearless, in a bikini top and tiny shorts, her skin gleaming against the blue night. This was their dream time, the magical early days of fall semester, the happy haze of meeting once again, old friendships rekindling in firefly sparks before the real work of the year began. Alex wanted to wallow in it too, to remember that she was safe, she was okay. But there wasn't time.

The Hutch was only a few blocks away, and she stopped to try to get her head together, leaning against the low wall in front of Sterling Library. How had that Gray overtaken her? She knew her connection to the dead had been deepened by what she'd had to do in her fight with Belbalm. She'd called them to her and offered them her name. They'd answered. They'd saved her. And of course rescue had come at a price. All her life, she'd been able to see Grays; now she could hear them too. They were that much closer, that much harder to ignore.

But maybe she hadn't really understood what salvation would cost her at all. Something very bad had happened in Oddman's house, something she couldn't explain. She was meant to control the dead, to use them. Not the other way around.

She pulled out her phone and saw two texts from Dawes, both exactly fifteen minutes apart and in all caps. *URGENT CALL IN.*

Alex ignored the messages and scrolled down, then typed out a quick *It's done.*

The reply was immediate: *When I have my money*

She really hoped Oddman got his house in order. She deleted Eitan's messages, then called Dawes.

"Where are you?" Dawes answered breathlessly.

Something big must be happening if Dawes was ignoring protocol. Alex could picture her pacing the parlor at Black Elm, her knot of red hair sliding to one side, headphones clamped around her neck.

"Sterling. On my way back to the Hutch."

"You're going to be late to—"

"If I stand here talking to you, I will be. What's up?"

"They've selected a new Praetor."

"Damn. Already?" The Praetor was the faculty liaison for Lethe, who served as a go-between with the university administration. Only Yale's president and dean knew about the real activities of the secret societies, and it was Lethe's job to make sure it stayed that way. The Praetor was a kind of den mother. The responsible adult in the room. At least he was supposed to be. Dean Sandow had turned out to be a murderer.

Alex knew a Lethe Praetor had to be a former Lethe deputy and had to be a member of the Yale faculty or at least reside in New Haven. That couldn't be easy to find. Alex and Dawes had assumed it would take the board at least another semester to find someone to replace the very dead Dean Sandow. They'd counted on it.

"Who is he?" Alex asked.

"It could be a woman."

"Is it?"

"No. But Anselm didn't give me a name."

"Did you ask?" Alex pushed.

A long pause. "Not exactly."

There was no point needling Dawes. Much like Alex, she didn't like people, but unlike Alex, she avoided confrontation. And really, it wasn't her job. Oculus kept Lethe running smoothly—fridge and armory stocked, rituals scheduled, properties kept in order. She was the research arm of Lethe, not the harass-board-members arm.

Alex sighed. "When are they bringing him in?"

"Saturday. Anselm wants to set up a meeting, maybe a tea."

"Nope. No way. I need more than a couple of days to prepare." Alex turned away from the passing students, staring up at the stone scribes that guarded the Sterling Library doors. Darlington was with her here, picking away at Yale's mysteries. "Egyptian, Mayan, Hebrew, Chinese, Arabic, engravings of cave paintings from Les Combarelles. They covered all their bases."

"What do they mean?" Alex had asked.

"Quotes from libraries, holy texts. The Chinese quote is from a dead judge's mausoleum. The Mayan comes from the Temple of the Cross, but they chose it at random because no one knew how to translate it until twenty years later."

Alex had laughed. "Like a drunk dude getting a kanji tattoo."

"To use one of your turns of phrase, they half-assed it. But it certainly looks impressive, doesn't it, Stern?"

It had. It still did.

Now Alex hunched over her phone and whispered to Dawes, knowing she probably looked like a girl in the middle of a breakup. "We need a delay."

"What good is that going to do us?"

Alex didn't have an answer for that. They'd been searching for the Gauntlet all summer and come up empty. "I went to First Presbyterian."

"And?"

"Nothing. At least as far as I can tell. I'll send you the photos."

"Gateways to hell aren't just lying around for people to walk through," Michelle Alameddine had warned when they'd all sat down together at Blue State after Dean Sandow's funeral. "That would be way too dangerous. Think of the Gauntlet as a secret passage that appears when you say the magic words. But in this case, the magic words are a series of steps, a path you have to walk. You take your first steps in the labyrinth, and only then does the path become clear."

"So we're hunting for something we can't even see?" Alex had asked.

"There would be signs, symbols." Michelle had shrugged. "Or at least that's one theory. That's all hell and the afterlife are. Theories. Because the people who get to see the other side don't come back to tell about it."

She was right. Alex had only been to the borderlands when she'd made her bargain with the Bridegroom, and she'd barely survived that. People weren't meant to move between this life and the next and back again. But that was exactly what they'd have to do to get Darlington home.

"There are rumors of a Gauntlet on Station Island in Lough Derg," Michelle continued. "There might have been one in the Imperial Library of Constantinople before it was destroyed. And according to Darlington, a bunch of society boys built one right here."

Dawes had nearly spit out her tea. "Darlington said that?"

Michelle gave her a bemused look. "His little pet project was creating a magical map of New Haven, of all the places where power ebbed and flowed. He said some society members had done it on a dare and that he intended to find it."

"And?"

"I told him he was an idiot and that he should spend more time worrying about his future and less time digging into Lethe's past."

Alex found herself smiling. "How'd that go over?"

"How do you think?"

"I actually don't know," she'd said at the time, too tired and too raw to pretend. "Darlington loved Lethe, but he also would have wanted to listen to his Virgil. He took that seriously."

Michelle studied the leavings of her scone. "I liked that about him. He took me seriously. Even when I didn't."

"Yes," Dawes had said quietly.

But Michelle had only returned to New Haven once over the summer. All June and July Dawes had been researching from her sister's place in Westport, sending Alex into the Lethe House library with requests for books and treatises. They'd tried to come up with the right series of words to frame their requests in the Albemarle Book, but all that came back were old accounts of mystics and martyrs having visions of hell—Charles the Fat, Dante's two towers in Bologna, caves in Guatemala and Belize said to lead to Xibalba.

Dawes took the train from Westport a few times so they could sit together and try to find someplace to start. They always invited Michelle, but she only took them up on it that one time, on a weekend when she was off from her job in gifts and acquisitions at the Butler Library. They'd spent all day poring over society records and books on the monk of Evesham, then had lunch in the parlor. Dawes made chicken salad and lemon bars wrapped in checkered napkins, but Michelle had only picked at her food and kept checking her phone, eager to be gone.

"She doesn't want to help," Dawes had said when Michelle left and the door to Il Bastone was shut firmly behind her.

"She does," said Alex. "But she's afraid to."

Alex couldn't really blame her. The Lethe board had made it clear they believed Darlington was dead, and they weren't interested in hearing otherwise. There had been too much mess the previous year, too much noise. They wanted that chapter closed. But two weeks after Michelle's visit, Alex and Dawes had gotten their big break: a single, lonely paragraph in a Lethe Days Diary from 1938.

Now Alex pushed off from the wall outside of Sterling and hurried up Elm onto York. "Tell them I can't meet on Saturday. Tell them I have . . . orientation or something."

Dawes groaned. "You know I'm a terrible liar."

"How are you going to get better if you don't practice?"

Alex dodged down the alley and entered the Hutch, welcoming the cool dark of the back stairs, that sweet autumn smell of clove and currants. The rooms were spotless but lonely, the battered plaid couches and scenes of shepherds tending their flocks trapped in gloom. She didn't like spending real time at the Hutch. She didn't want to be reminded of the lost days when she'd hidden in these secret rooms, wounded and hopeless. Pathetic. She wasn't going to let that happen to her this year. She was going to find a way to keep control. She snatched up the backpack she'd loaded with supplies earlier—graveyard dirt, bone dust chalk, and something labeled a Phantom Loop, a kind of fancy lacrosse stick she'd pilfered from the Lethe armory.

For once, she'd done the homework.

Alex loved the Book and Snake tomb because it was across from Grove Street Cemetery and that meant she wouldn't have to see many Grays, particularly at night. Sometimes they were drawn there by funerals if the deceased had been especially loved or loathed, and Alex had once been treated to the grim sight of a Gray trying to lick the cheek of a weeping woman. But at night the cemetery was nothing but cold stone and decay—the last place Grays wanted to be when there was a campus right next door, full of students flirting and sweating, drinking too much beer or too much coffee, alive with nerves and ego.

The tomb itself looked like something between a Greek temple and an oversized mausoleum—no windows or doors, all white marble fronted by towering columns. "It's meant to look like the Erechtheion," Darlington had told her. "At the Acropolis. Or some people say the Temple of Nike."

"So which is it?" Alex had asked. She'd felt like she was in moderately safe territory. She remembered learning about the Acropolis and the Agora and how much she'd loved the stories of the Greek gods.

"Neither. It was built as a necromanteion, a house to welcome and commune with the dead."

And Alex had laughed because by then she knew how much Grays hated any reminder of death. "So they built a big mausoleum?

They should have built a casino and put a sign out front that said *Ladies drink free*."

"Crude, Stern. But you're not wrong."

That had been almost a year ago exactly. Tonight she was alone. Alex climbed the steps and knocked on the big bronze doors. This was the second ritual she'd observed this semester. The first—a rite of renewal at Manuscript—had been easy enough. The new delegation had stripped down to nothing and rolled a grizzled news anchor into a ditch lined with rosemary and hot coals. He'd emerged two hours later looking red-faced, sweaty, and about ten years younger.

The door swung open on a girl in a black robe, her face covered by a sheer veil embroidered with black snakes. She pulled it up over her head.

"Virgil?"

Alex nodded. The societies never asked about Darlington anymore. To the new delegates, she was Virgil, an expert, an authority. They'd never met the gentleman of Lethe. They didn't know they were getting a half-trained pretender. As far as they were concerned, Alex was Lethe and always had been. "You're Calista?"

The girl beamed. "The delegation president." She was a senior, probably only a year older than Alex, but she seemed like a different species—smooth-skinned, bright-eyed, her hair a soft halo of curls. "We're almost ready to start. I'm so nervous!"

"Don't be," said Alex. Because that was what she was supposed to say. Virgil was calm, knowledgeable; she'd seen it all before.

They passed beneath a stone carving that read, *Omnia mutantur, nihil interit*. Everything changes, nothing perishes.

Darlington had rolled his eyes as he gave the translation on one of their visits. "Don't ask me why a society built around Greek necromancy thinks it's appropriate to quote a Roman poet. *Omnia dicta fortiori si dicta Latina*."

"I know you want me to ask, so I'm not going to."

He'd actually smiled. "Everything sounds more impressive in Latin."

They'd been getting along well then, and Alex had felt something like hope, a kind of ease between them that might have grown into trust.

If she hadn't let him die.

Inside, the tomb was cold and lit by torches, the smoke gusted away by small vents high above. Most of the rooms were ordinary, but the central temple was perfectly round and painted with brightly colored frescoes of naked men in laurel crowns.

"Why are they climbing ladders?" Alex had asked when she'd first seen the murals.

"Not *Why are they all naked?* Symbolism, Stern. They're ascending to greater knowledge. On the backs of the dead. Look at the bases."

The ladders were propped on the bowed backs of kneeling skeletons.

At the center of the room stood two towering statues of veiled women, stone snakes at their feet. A lamp hung from their clasped hands, the fire burning a soft blue. Beneath it two older men were huddled in conversation. One wore robes of black and gold, an alum who would serve as high priest. The other looked like someone's very strict dad, his gray hair in a tight crew cut, his button-down tucked neatly into pressed khaki trousers.

Two more robed figures entered, carrying a large crate. Alex doubted it was a couch from Ikea. They set it down between two brass symbols on the floor—Greek letters that fanned out in a spiral over the marble slabs.

"Why did you lobby so hard to have a ritual sanctioned this week?" Alex asked Calista, eyeing the crate as the Lettermen used a crowbar to jimmy the top open. Most of the time societies took the evenings assigned to them in the calendar or occasionally petitioned for an emergency dispensation that invariably threw the whole schedule into upheaval. But the Lettermen had been very clear that Book and Snake needed *this* Thursday night for their ritual.

"It was the only day . . ." Calista hesitated, torn between pride and the demand for discretion. "A certain four-star general has a very tight schedule."

"Got it," said Alex, glancing at the stern-faced man with the crew cut. She took out her chalk and her notes and began to draw the circle of protection—carefully, precisely. She didn't realize how hard she was gripping the chalk until it snapped in two and she had to work with one of the stubs. She was nervous, but she didn't have that panicked, never-studied-for-the-test feeling. She had reviewed her notes, drawn the symbols again and again in the shadowy comfort of Il Bastone's parlor, New Order on the tinny sound system. She'd felt like the house approved of her newfound diligence, its doors locked and secured, its heavy curtains drawn to keep the sun out.

"Are we ready?" The high priest was approaching, rubbing his hands together. "We have a schedule to keep."

Alex couldn't remember his name, some alum she'd met the previous year. He'd oversee the ritual with the new delegation. Behind him, she saw the Lettermen lifting a corpse out of the crate. They laid it on the floor, naked and white. The smell of roses filled the air, and the priest must have seen Alex's surprise because he said, "That's how we prepare the body."

Alex didn't think of herself as squeamish; she'd been too close to death her whole life to shy away from severed limbs or gunshot wounds—at least when it came to Grays. But it was always different with an actual body, stiff and silent, more alien in its stillness than a ghost could ever be. It was as if she could feel the void where the person should be.

"Who is he?" she asked.

"No one anymore. He *was* Jacob Yeshevsky, Silicon Valley darling and friend to Russian hackers everywhere. Died on a yacht less than twenty-four hours ago."

"Twenty-four hours," Alex echoed. Book and Snake had requested this night for their ritual back in August.

"We have our sources." He bobbed his head toward the cemetery. "The dead knew his time was coming."

"And predicted it to the day. Thoughtful of them."

Jacob Yeshevsky had been murdered. She felt sure of that. And even if Book and Snake hadn't planned it, they'd known it was going to happen. But she wasn't here to cause trouble, and Jacob Yeshevsky was beyond her help.

"The circle is ready," said Alex. The ritual had to be protected by the circle, but she'd set a gate at each compass point, and one would be kept open to allow magic to flow in. That was where Alex would stand guard, in case any Grays tried to crash the party, drawn by longing, greed, any powerful emotion. Though unless things got really exciting, she doubted Grays would want to be this close to a fresh corpse and all of this grand funereal gloom.

"You're a lot cuter than that girl Darlington used to run around with," the priest said.

Alex didn't return his smile. "Michelle Alameddine is way out of your league."

His grin only deepened. "Absolutely no one is out of my league."

"Stop trying to fuck the help and let's go," barked the general.

The priest departed with another smile.

Alex wasn't sure if it was ballsy or creepy to hit on someone within spitting distance of a dead body, but she intended to get well away from Book and Snake as soon as she could. She had to remain the good girl. Do the job. Do it right. She and Dawes didn't want any trouble, didn't want to give Lethe any reason to split them up or interfere with what they had planned. A new Praetor getting in their way was going to be messy enough.

A deep gong sounded. The Lettermen stood outside the perimeter of the circle, their veils drawn over their faces, mourners in black, leaving only the general, the high priest, and the dead man at the circle's center.

"*There studious let me sit*," intoned the priest, his voice echoing through the chamber, "*and hold high converse with the mighty dead.*"

"For what it's worth, that quote is about libraries, not necromancy," Darlington had whispered to her once. It marked the start of every Book and Snake ritual. "It's written in stone at Sterling."

Alex hadn't wanted to confess that she spent most of her time at Sterling Library dozing off in one of the reading rooms with her boots propped on a heating vent.

The priest tossed something into the lamp above them, and bluish smoke billowed up from the flames, then seemed to settle, sinking onto the bare feet of the statues. One of the stone snakes began to move, its white scales iridescent in the firelight. It slithered toward the corpse, undulating across the marble floor, then paused, as if scenting the body. Alex choked back a gasp when it lunged, jaws wide, and latched on to the corpse's calf.

The corpse began to twitch, muscles spasming, bouncing off the iron floor like hot kernels in a pan. The snake released its grip and Yeshevsky's body sprang into a deep crouch, feet wide, hands cupping its knees, waddling like a crab but with a speed that made Alex's skin crawl. Its face—*his* face—was stretched into a grimace, eyes wide and panicked, mouth pulling down like a theatrical mask of tragedy.

"I need passwords," said the general as the corpse capered around the temple, "solid intel, not . . ." He waved his hand through the air, damning the domed crypt, the students in their robes, and poor, dead Jacob Yeshevsky in a single gesture. "Fortune-telling."

"We'll get you what you need," the priest replied smoothly. "But if you're asked to reveal your sources—"

"You think I want oversight sniffing around this Illuminati bullshit?"

Alex couldn't see the priest's face beneath his veil, but his scorn was clear. "We are *not* the Illuminati."

"Posers," muttered one of the Lettermen standing near Alex.

"Just get him talking," said the general.

It's a front, Alex thought. That brusque, grunting, all-business act was cover. The general hadn't known what he was walking into when he'd hatched his agreement with Book and Snake, connected by some high-powered alumnus. What had he imagined? Some muttered words, a voice from the beyond? Had he thought there would be dignity in this? But this was what real magic looked like— indecent, decadent, perverse. *Welcome to Yale. Sir, yes, sir.*

A string of drool hung from Jacob Yeshevsky's mouth as he waited in that deep, unnatural crouch, rocking slowly side to side, toes wiggling slightly, eyes rolling in his head, a grotesque, a gargoyle.

"Is the scribe ready?" asked the priest.

"I am," replied one of the Lettermen, veiled and perched in a small balcony above.

"Speak then," boomed the priest, "while you may. Answer our questions and return to your rest."

He nodded at the general, who cleared his throat.

"Who was your primary contact at the FSB?"

Yeshevsky's body crab-walked left, right, left, with that unnerving speed. Alex had done some research into golems and *glumae* last year, but she had no idea how she'd fight that thing if it came running at her. It was moving from brass letter to brass letter on the floor, as if the whole room was a Ouija board, the corpse skittering over it like a planchet, the scribe documenting each pause from above.

Every so often, the body would slow and the priest would add something to the fire, producing that same blue smoke. The snake would rouse itself, slither across the floor, and bite Yeshevsky again, juicing him with whatever strange venom it possessed in its fangs.

It's just a body, Alex reminded herself. But that wasn't entirely true. Some part of Yeshevsky's consciousness had been drawn back into it to answer questions for the blustering general. Would it vanish beyond the Veil when this sick bit of business was done? Would it be whole, or would it return to the afterlife damaged by the horror of being crammed back into a lifeless corpse?

This was why Grays steered clear of Book and Snake. Not because their tomb looked like a mausoleum, but because the dead weren't meant to be treated this way.

Alex considered the veiled and bowed heads of the Lettermen, the scribe. *You're right to hide your faces*, she thought. *When your time comes, someone's going to be waiting for payback on the other side.*

3

It turned out taking dictation letter by letter from a reanimated corpse took a long time, and it was 2 a.m. when they finally finished the ritual.

Alex wiped away the chalk circle and made sure to stay far from the eyeline of the high priest. She didn't think it would be good for her new and improved make-no-waves policy if she kneed some esteemed alum in the nuts.

"Calista," she said quietly, flagging down the delegation president.

"Thank you *so* much, Alex! I mean Virgil." She giggled. "It all went *so* well."

"Jacob Yeshevsky might disagree."

She laughed again. "True."

"What happens to him now?"

"The family thinks he's being cremated, so they'll still get his ashes. No harm done."

Alex cast a glance at the crate where Yeshevsky's body had been stowed. When the general had gotten his answers and the ritual concluded with a final strike of the gong, the body hadn't simply collapsed. They'd had to wait for it to tire, clambering over the letters. Whatever it was saying, no one was bothering to transcribe it, and the sight of that corpse dancing frantically over the floor, building word after word, maybe gibberish or a cry from beyond the grave or the recipe for his grandmother's banana bread, had somehow been worse than anything that had come before.

"No harm done," Alex echoed. "What was he spelling out there, at the end?"

"Something about mother's milk or the Milky Way."

"It doesn't mean anything," the high priest said. He'd removed his veil and robes and was dressed in a white linen shirt and pants as if he'd just sauntered off of a beach in Santorini. "Just a glitch. It happens. Worse when the corpse isn't fresh."

Alex slung her backpack over her shoulder, eager to be gone. "Sure."

"Maybe it was a reference to the space program," Calista said, glancing at the alum as if for approval.

"We're having drinks in the—" the high priest began.

But Alex was already shoving her way out of the temple room and down the hall. She didn't slow her steps until she was free of the Book and Snake tomb and the stink of roses, the air still warm with the last gasp of summer, beneath a starless New Haven sky.

Alex was surprised to find Dawes waiting at the Hutch, sitting cross-legged and barefoot on the rug in cargo shorts and a white T-shirt, her index cards arranged in neat piles around her, her hair tucked into a lopsided bun. She'd placed her Tevas neatly by the door.

"Well?" she asked. "How did it go?"

"The body got free and I had to bring it down with the Phantom Loop."

"Oh God."

"Yup," Alex said as she headed into the bathroom. "Lassoed that thing and rode it all the way to Stamford."

"Alex," Dawes scolded.

"It went fine. But . . ." Alex stripped off her clothes, eager to be rid of the smell of the uncanny. "I don't know. The corpse kind of ran down at the end. Started in about the Milky Way or mother's milk or milk for his undead cereal. It was fucking grim." She turned on the shower. "Did you tell Anselm we can't meet with the new Praetor on

Saturday?" When Dawes didn't answer, Alex repeated the question. "I can't meet with the new Praetor on Saturday, okay?"

A long moment later, Dawes said, "I told Anselm. But that only buys us a week. Maybe . . . Maybe the Praetor will have an open mind."

Alex doubted it. There were plenty of rogues in Lethe's history—Lee De Forest, who had caused a campus-wide blackout and been suspended as a result; hell, one of the founders, Hiram Bingham III, hadn't known anything about archaeology and had still scurried off to Peru to steal a few artifacts—but there was no chance Lethe had chosen some kind of maverick to serve as Praetor now, not after what had happened last year. And not with Alex in the mix. She was too much of an unknown, an experiment they were still waiting to see play out.

"Dawes, trust me. Whoever this guy is, he's not going to sanction a field trip to hell."

She lit the censer filled with cedar and palo santo and stepped under the water, using verbena to wash away the stink of the uncanny.

In their months of searching, she and Dawes had found exactly one clue to the location of the Gauntlet, a cramped bit of text in the *Lethe Days Diary of Nelson Hartwell*, DC '38.

Bunchy got drunk and tried to convince us some of Johnny and Punter's friends built a Gauntlet so they could open a door to the fiery furnace, if you please. Naturally I demanded proof. "No, no," says Bunch. "Far too chancy to leave any record." They swore each other to secrecy and all they let slip was that it was built on hallowed ground. A bit too convenient, I say. Bet they all just skipped chapel and ended up well sauced in a crypt somewhere.

Hallowed ground. That was all she and Dawes had to go on, a single paragraph about a drunk named Bunchy. But that hadn't stopped them from trying to visit every graveyard, cemetery, synagogue, and church built before 1938 in New Haven, hunting for signs. They'd come up empty, and now they'd have the new Praetor looking over their shoulder.

"What if we say fuck the Gauntlet and try Sandow's hound-dog casting instead?" she called over the rush of the water.

"That didn't go very well last time."

No, it hadn't. They'd almost been eaten by a hellbeast for their trouble.

"But Sandow wasn't really trying, was he?" Alex said, rinsing the soap from her hair. "He thought Darlington was gone forever, that there was no way he could survive a trip to hell. He thought the casting would just prove Darlington was dead."

It had been a horrible night, but the ritual *had* brought back Darlington, or at least his voice, to accuse Sandow.

Alex turned off the water and grabbed a towel off the rack. The apartment seemed impossibly quiet.

She almost thought she imagined it when she heard a faint "Okay."

Alex paused, wringing the water from her hair. "What?"

"Okay."

Alex had expected Dawes to protest, start throwing up obstacles— it wasn't the right time, they needed to plan, it was too dangerous. Had she spread her tarot cards out in front of her in the living room? Was she reading something other than calamity?

Alex pulled on a clean pair of shorts and a tank top. Dawes was in the same spot on the floor, but she'd pulled her knees up to her chest and wrapped her arms around them.

"What do you mean, 'okay'?" Alex asked.

"Do you know what the Greeks called the Milky Way?"

"You know I don't."

"*Galaxias.*"

Alex sat down on the edge of the couch, trying to ignore the sliver of cold in her gut.

Galaxias. Galaxy. Was that the word the corpse had been spelling out again and again?

"He was trying to reach you," said Dawes. "To reach us."

"You don't know that." But it had happened before. During the prognostication ritual the night that Tara was murdered, and again during the new moon ritual when Darlington had tried to warn them about Sandow. Was that what he was trying to do now? Warn her? Blame her? Or was he crying out to her from the other side of the Veil, begging for her help?

"There's . . . something . . . we could try." Dawes's words came in stutter stops, Morse code, a distress signal. "I have an idea."

Alex wondered how many catastrophes had begun with those words. "I hope it's a good one."

"But if the Lethe board finds out—"

"They won't."

"I can't lose this job. And neither can you."

Alex didn't intend to think about that right now. "Do we go to Black Elm?"

"No. We need the table at Scroll and Key. We need to open a portal."

"To hell."

"I can't think of anything else." Dawes sounded desperate.

They'd been trying all summer and had nothing to show for it. But had Alex really been trying? Or had she felt safe tucked away with her research at Il Bastone? Walking the streets of New Haven, searching for churches and sacred places, seeking out signs of the Gauntlet and finding nothing? Had she let herself forget that some-where Darlington was lost and suffering?

"Good," Alex said. "Then we open a portal."

"How do we get into Scroll and Key?"

"I'll get us in."

Dawes chewed on her lower lip.

"I'm not going to hit anyone, Dawes."

Dawes tugged at a strand of her red hair, gone curly in the heat.

Alex rolled her eyes. "Or threaten anyone. I'm going to be real polite."

And she would be. She had to find a way back to the game of pretend she'd played last year, had to find a new sea level. They would bring Darlington back. They would make everything right again. As far as the Lethe board knew, she was just a student who'd had a very bad freshman year. They didn't know about the grade bump Sandow had granted her, or the part she'd played in his death, or the kills she'd racked up one awful night in Van Nuys.

But Darlington did. And if he wanted to make a case against her, that would be the end of it. What would she do then? What she always did. Locate the exits. Get out before the real trouble sticks. Nab a few expensive artifacts on the way out. That litany had become a kind of comfort, a chant to keep her fear of the future at bay. But it was all more complicated now. Her options had been bleak before, but now they were downright ugly, and she was all out of places to run. Because of Eitan. Because whether Gauntlet or gate or bus to the beyond, there was always hell to pay.

4

Last Summer

She would have stayed in New Haven for the summer. If not for Eitan.

Alex told her mother she'd gotten a job on campus, and that was enough for Mira. She thought Los Angeles was temptation for Alex, that she'd step off a plane and fall back into her old life with her old friends.

There was no chance of that, but *They're all dead, Mama* wasn't going to put Mira's mind at ease, and the truth was that Alex didn't want to go home. She didn't want to sleep in her old bedroom with the sounds of the 101 like an angry ocean in the distance. She didn't want to hear about her mother's latest obsession—gemstone massage, aura cleansing, essential oils, an endless hunt for easy miracles. Leaving Yale felt perilous, a little too much like a fairy tale, a cruel one where once she left the enchanted castle, she'd have no way back.

She thought she'd spend the summer with Dawes and Michelle Alameddine, hatching a plan to rescue Darlington. But Dawes had to nanny for her sister in Westport, and Michelle had been difficult to reach, so Alex was mostly left alone at Il Bastone. She'd wondered if the house would reject her after all the bloodshed of the previous semester, the stained glass window that would never be quite as perfect as it had been, the floor still stained with Blake Keely's blood and now hidden by a new carpet. What if she showed up at the front door and the knob simply wouldn't turn for her?

But on that spring day, when Alex stowed their common room

furniture in the basement of Jonathan Edwards, and said goodbye to Mercy and Lauren, Il Bastone's doorknob had rattled happily beneath her hand, the door springing open like a pair of welcoming arms.

She really had meant to find a job for the summer, but business around campus had slowed too much. So eventually, she just stopped looking. She had a small summer stipend from Lethe, and she spent it on junk food, frozen egg rolls, and pigs-in-a-blanket she could heat up in the toaster oven. She hadn't even asked if she could stay at Il Bastone. She just did. Who else had bled for this place?

Alex spent her days examining the course catalogue and talking to Mercy. They'd pieced together as much of Alex's schedule as possible so that she could get ahead on the reading. She read paperbacks too, one after the next like she was chain-smoking—romance, science fiction, old pulp fantasy. All she wanted to do was sit, unbothered in a circle of lamplight, and live someone else's life. But every evening was spent in the library. She'd write down Dawes's suggestions in the Albemarle Book or come up with some of her own, then wait to see what the library would provide. One book had a spine of actual vertebrae, another released a cloud of soft mist every time she opened it, and another was so hot to the touch she'd had to scrounge around in the kitchen and return with oven mitts.

Only the armory was climate-controlled, to protect the artifacts, so when the weather got too hot, she took a heap of blankets and pillows from the Dante bedroom, and made a nest for herself at the bottom of Hiram's Crucible. Darlington would have been scandalized, but the air-conditioning was worth it. Sometimes when she slept there, she dreamed of a mountaintop covered in green. She'd been there before, knew her way up staircases and through tight passages that smelled of damp stone. There was a room with three windows and a round basin in which to watch the stars. She saw her own face reflected in the water. But when she woke, she knew she'd never been to Peru, only seen it in books.

Alex was lying on her side on one of the velvet sofas in the parlor of Il Bastone, reading a beat-up copy of *The Illustrated Man* she'd found at the Young Men's Institute library, when her phone rang. She didn't recognize the number, so she hadn't bothered to answer. She'd purged all of her old contacts when she'd left Los Angeles. But the second time the phone rang, she picked up.

She recognized Eitan's voice instantly, that heavy accent. "Alex Stern. We need to have conversation. You understand?"

"No," she said, her heart jackrabbiting in her chest. It had rained that day, and she'd pushed open all the curtains so she could watch the storm, bright gasps of lightning crackling across the gray sky. She sat up, marking her place in her book with a receipt. She had the uneasy sensation she'd never get to finish this particular story.

"I don't want to discuss on the phone. You come see me at the house."

He thought she was in LA. *That's good,* Alex told herself. He didn't know he couldn't get hands on her easily. But why was he calling? Eitan had been Len's supplier, an Israeli gangster who operated out of a sleek mansion that floated on an Encino hilltop above the 405. She'd thought he had long since forgotten about her.

"I'm not going up to Mulholland," she said. "I don't have a car." Even if she had been in LA, there was no way she was driving into the hills to Eitan's house just so he could put a bullet in her brain with no one there to watch.

"Your mother has car. Old Jetta. Not reliable." Of course Eitan knew where to find her mom. Men like Eitan knew all about where to look for leverage. "Shlomo watches your house for so long, but only your mama comes and goes. Never you. Where are you, Alex?"

"Right now?" Alex looked around the parlor, at the dusty rugs, the summer light turned soft by the rain-spattered windowpanes. She heard the ice maker rumble from the fridge in the kitchen. Later she'd go make a sandwich with the bread and lunch meat Dawes had ordered when she discovered how much of Alex's diet consisted of chicken fingers, and that arrived every week as if by magic. "Crashing with friends in Topanga Canyon. I'll come this weekend."

"Not Saturday. Come tomorrow. Friday before five."

Eitan kept kosher and kept the Sabbath holy. Killing and extortion were for the other six days of the week.

"I've got work," she said. "I can come Sunday."

"Good girl."

She hung up and clutched the phone to her chest, staring up at the coffered ceiling. The lights flickered, and she knew the house was picking up her fear. She reached down and pressed her palm against the polished floorboards. The night Alex had almost bled to death in the hallway above, Il Bastone had been wounded too, one of its lovely windows smashed, its carpets ruined with blood. Alex had helped to clean it all up. She'd hovered beside the man Dawes had hired to restore the window. She'd steamed and scrubbed the blood from the floors and the carpets in the hallway. Her blood, Dean Sandow's, Blake Keely's. Both of them dead but not Alex. Alex had survived, and so had Il Bastone.

She couldn't tell if the vibration through the floor was real or imagined, but she felt calmer for it. This had been her safe place as the campus emptied—warded, dark, and cool. She ventured out only occasionally, went for walks up the hill and out to the covered bridge by the Eli Whitney Museum, its red barn spanning the river like something out of a painting Mercy would laugh at. She took her new bike down to Edgerton Park, rode through the flower beds and looked at the old gatehouse, and every other morning, she rode all the way to Black Elm, fed Cosmo, wandered the overgrown hedge maze. But always she returned to the house on Orange, to Il Bastone. She'd thought she would feel lonely here, without Dawes or Darlington, but instead she'd sipped sodas straight from the old-fashioned icebox, napped in the fancy bedroom with its moon-and-sun stained glass, snooped around the armory. The house always had something new to show her.

Alex didn't want to leave. She didn't want to go back to her mother's miserable apartment in Van Nuys. And she didn't want to talk to Eitan. Did he have unfinished business with Len that had been put on hold for a year? Or did he somehow know what Alex had done? Had he connected her to his cousin's death?

It didn't much matter. She had to go. She toggled through the numbers on her phone and found Michael Anselm. He was the Lethe board member who had stepped into the authority-shaped hole left by Dean Sandow. He'd graduated fifteen years before, and Alex and Dawes had looked up his Lethe Days Diary but found it particularly boring. Names and dates of rituals and little else. That was how he seemed on the phone too. Dry, dull, eager to get back to his job in finance or banking or whatever passed for printing money. But he'd gotten Alex a bike and a laptop, so she wasn't going to complain.

Anselm picked up on the second ring. "Alex?" He sounded worried and she couldn't blame him. She might very well be calling to tell him that the law school library had caught fire or an undead army was amassing in Commons. She didn't know much about Anselm but she pictured him wearing striped ties and going home to a yellow Lab, two kids involved with Habitat for Humanity, and a wife who stayed in shape.

"Hi, Michael, sorry to bother you in the middle of the day—"

"Is everything okay?"

"Everything is fine. But I need to go home for the weekend. To see my mom."

"Oh, I'm sorry to hear that," he said, as if she'd told him her mother was ill. Which Alex had been perfectly prepared to do.

"Can you, I mean, can Lethe help me out with the fare?" Alex knew she was supposed to be embarrassed, but since nearly dying in this house, she hadn't hesitated to ask Lethe for anything and everything she might need. They owed her, and Dawes, and Darlington. Dawes wasn't asking and Darlington sure as hell wasn't going to collect, so it was up to Alex to clear the ledger.

"Of course!" Michael said. "Whatever you need. I'll put you on with my assistant."

And that was that. Anselm's assistant arranged for a car to the airport and the return flight. Alex wondered if she would be on it or if she would die at the top of Mulholland Drive. She packed underwear and a toothbrush in her backpack, and made a stop in the armory, but then realized she had no idea what to bring with her. She felt like she was walking into a trap, but Lethe didn't traffic in the kinds of objects that could stop men like Eitan. At least not anything she could bring on a plane.

"I'll be back," she murmured to the house as the front door locked behind her. She paused to listen to the soft whining of the jackals beneath the porch and she hoped it was true.

Alex had made good on that promise. She'd even finished that Ray Bradbury paperback. She just hadn't known she would return with fresh blood on her hands.

The Coat of Many Foxes
Provenance: Goslar, Germany; 15th century
Donor: Scroll and Key, 1993

Believed to be the work of Alaric Förstner, who was subsequently burned at the stake for his decimation of the local fox population. The coat changed hands multiple times, and there are records that indicate it belonged to an Oxford don around the same time that C. S. Lewis was teaching there, but this has never been fully substantiated. There is speculation that at one time, hanging the coat in a closet, armoire, or wardrobe would create a portal, but whatever magic the coat may or may not have possessed is long gone. Yet another example of the instability of portal magic. See Tayyaara for a rare exception.

—*from the Lethe Armory Catalogue as revised*
and edited by Pamela Dawes, Oculus

5

October

On Friday morning, Alex went to Modern Poets and EE101 with Mercy and did her best to pay attention. It was too early in the year for her to be short on sleep.

She wanted to stay in that night, catch up on rest, finish hanging posters in her room. Mercy's side was already elaborately turned out in art prints and strips of poetry in Chinese characters collaged with fashion illustrations. She'd created a kind of makeshift canopy over her bed in blue tulle that made the whole place feel glamorous.

But Mercy and Lauren wanted to go out, so they went out. Alex even put on a dress, short and black, held up by cobweb straps, identical in all but color to Mercy's and Lauren's. Alex felt like they were a tiny army, three sleepwalkers in dainty nightgowns. Mercy and Lauren wore strappy sandals, but Alex didn't have any and she stuck to her battered black boots. Easier to run in.

They paused by the swing to take pictures and Alex chose one to send to her mom, the one where she looked happiest, the one where she looked all right. Lauren on her left—thick honey-blond hair and teeth brighter than a flashlight beam. Mercy on her right—hair in a shiny black bob, big vintage earrings in the shape of daisies, caution in her eyes.

Were Eitan's people still watching Mira? Or had he decided to leave her mother alone now that Alex was doing what she was told? California seemed less like another coast than another age, a hazy time before that Alex wanted to keep blurry, the details too painful to draw into focus.

The party was at a house on Lynwood, not far from St. Elmo's sad slump of an apartment, its hopeful weather vanes spinning slowly on the roof. Alex drank water the whole night and was bored out of her skull, but she didn't mind. She liked standing with a red Solo cup in her hand, flanked by her friends, pretending to be buzzed. Well, not quite pretending. She'd dosed herself with basso belladonna. She'd told herself she was going to get through the year clean, but the year was being a dick, so she'd do what she had to.

Saturday morning, she slipped out while Mercy was still asleep and called over to Scroll and Key. As promised, she was nothing but polite; then she curled up in bed and went back to sleep until Mercy woke her.

They ate breakfast late in the dining hall, and Alex piled her plate high as she always did. They were about to try to open a portal to hell; she should be too nervous to eat. Instead, she felt like she couldn't get full. She wanted more syrup, more bacon, more everything. Grays loved this place, the smells of the food, the gossip. Alex could have warded it, the same way she had set up protections on her dorm room. But if something came after her, she wanted a Gray close enough to use—just not near enough to bother her. And here, they seemed to blend into the crowd. There was something peaceable about all of it, the dead breaking bread with the living.

Alex knew there were more beautiful rooms at Yale, but this was her favorite, the dark wood of the rafters floating high above, the great stone fireplace. She loved to sit here and let the clatter of trays, the roar of chatter wash over her. She had expected Darlington to smirk when she'd told him how much she loved JE's dining hall, but he'd only nodded and said, "It's too grand to be the common room of a tavern or an inn, but that's how it feels. As if you could put up your feet here and wait for any storm to pass." Maybe that was true for some weary traveler, for the student she was pretending to be. But the real Alex belonged in the storm, a lightning rod for trouble. That would change when Darlington returned. It wouldn't just be her and Dawes trying to bar the door against the dark anymore.

"Where are you going?" Mercy asked as Alex rose and shoved a piece of buttered toast in her mouth. "We've got reading."

"I finished 'The Knight's Tale.'"

"And 'The Wife of Bath'?"

"Yup."

Lauren leaned back in her chair. "Hold up. Alex, you're *ahead* on the reading?"

"I'm very scholarly now."

"We have to memorize the first eighteen lines," said Mercy. "And it isn't easy."

Alex set down her bag. "What? Why?"

"So we know how it all sounds? They're in Middle English."

"I had to learn them in high school," said Lauren.

"That's because you went to a fancy prep school in Brookline," said Mercy. "Alex and I were stuck in public school, honing our street smarts."

Lauren nearly spit out her juice laughing.

"Best be careful," Alex said with a grin. "Mercy will fuck you up."

"You didn't say where you were going!" Lauren called after her as she strode out of the dining hall. Alex had almost forgotten how tiring it was to come up with excuses.

Dawes was waiting in front of the music school, its pink-and-white facade like a heavily decorated cake. Alex had never seen Venice, probably never would, but she knew this was the style. Darlington had loved this building too.

"They said yes?"

No *Hello*, no *How are you*. Dawes looked impossibly awkward in long frumpy cargo shorts and a white V-neck, a canvas satchel slung across her body. Something seemed off about her, and Alex realized she was so used to seeing Dawes with headphones fastened around her neck, she appeared oddly naked without them.

"In a way," said Alex. "I told them I was doing an inspection."

"Oh, good . . . Wait, why are you doing an inspection?"

"Dawes." Alex cast her a look. "What would I be inspecting?"

"You said you'd talk to them, not lie to them."

"Lying is a kind of talking. A very useful kind. And it didn't take much." After the shit Scroll and Key had pulled last year—not the drugs, of course; that was perfectly acceptable according to the rules of Lethe. But they'd let outsiders, *townies*, into their tomb and made them part of their rituals. It had all ended in murder and scandal. And of course there had been no repercussions except a firm warning and a fine.

Robbie Kendall was waiting on the steps of the tomb in madras shorts and a light blue polo shirt, his blond hair worn just long enough to suggest surfer without actually looking disreputable. The afternoon heat didn't seem to be getting to him. He looked like he'd never sweat in his life.

"Hi," he said, smiling nervously. "Alex? Or, uh . . . do I call you Virgil?"

Alex felt Dawes stiffen beside her. She hadn't been with Alex on the first two ritual nights. She hadn't heard that name since Darlington vanished.

"That's right," Alex said, surreptitiously wiping her palms before she shook his hand. "This is Oculus. Pamela Dawes."

"Cool. What is it you guys wanted to see?"

Alex regarded Robbie coolly. "Give me the keys. You can wait outside."

Robbie hesitated. He was the new delegation president, a senior, eager to get everything right. A perfect mark really.

"I don't know if—"

Alex glanced over her shoulder and lowered her voice. "Is this how you want to start the year?"

Robbie's mouth popped open. "I . . . No."

"Your fellow Locksmiths' callous disregard for the rules nearly got me and Oculus killed last year. Two deputies of Lethe. You're lucky all of your privileges weren't suspended."

"Suspended?"

It was as if he'd never even considered it, as if such a thing were impossible.

"That's right. A semester, maybe a whole year missed. I advocated for leniency, but . . ." She shrugged. "Maybe that was a mistake."

"No, no. Definitely not." Robbie fumbled with his keys. "Definitely not."

Alex almost felt bad for him. He'd had his first taste of magic when he was initiated the previous semester, his first glimpse at the world beyond the Veil. He'd been promised a year of wild journeys and mystery. He would do anything he could to keep his supply coming.

The heavy door opened on an elaborate stone entry, the cool dark a welcome relief from the heat. A Gray in pin-striped trousers hummed happily to himself in the hallway, gazing at a glass case full of black-and-white photos. The interior of Scroll and Key was strangely heavy in contrast to its graceful exterior, rough rock punctuated by elaborate Moorish arches. It felt as if they'd stepped into a cave.

Alex snatched the keys from Robbie's hand before he could reconsider. "Wait outside, please."

This time he didn't protest, just said an eager "Sure! Take your time."

When the door was closed behind them, Alex expected a lecture or at least a disapproving scowl, but Dawes only looked thoughtful.

"What is it?" Alex asked as they headed down the hall to the sanctum.

Dawes shrugged, and it was as if she were still wearing one of her heavy sweatshirts. "You sound like him."

Had Alex been doing her Darlington act? She guessed she had. Every time she spoke with the authority of Lethe, it was with his voice really—assured, confident, knowledgeable. Everything she wasn't.

She opened the door to the ritual room. It was a vast star-shaped chamber at the heart of the tomb, a statue of a knight in each of its six pointed corners, a circular table at its center. But the table wasn't really a table at all; it was a doorway, a passage to anywhere you wanted to go. And some places you didn't.

Alex smoothed her hand over the inscription on its edge. *Have power on this dark land to lighten it, and power on this dead world to make it live.* Tara had stood at this table before she'd been murdered. She'd been an intruder here, just like Alex.

"Is this going to work?" Alex asked. "The nexus has a wobble." It was why the Locksmiths had resorted to psychedelics, why they'd had to rely on a town girl and her drug dealer boyfriend to mix up a special concoction that would help open portals and ease their passage to other lands. "We don't have any of Tara's special sauce."

"I don't know," Dawes said, chewing on her lip. "I . . . I don't know what else to try. We could wait. We should."

Their eyes met over the big round table, supposedly made from planks of the same table where King Arthur's knights had once gathered.

"We should," Alex agreed.

"But we're not going to, are we?"

Alex shook her head. More than three months had passed since Sandow's funeral, since Alex had shared her theory that Darlington wasn't dead but trapped somewhere in hell, the gentleman demon who had so terrified the dead and whatever monsters gathered beyond the Veil. Nothing Alex and Dawes had learned in the time since had given them cause to believe that it was anything more than wishful thinking. But that hadn't stopped them from trying to piece together a way to reach him. *Galaxias.* Galaxy. A cry from the other side of the Veil. What would it mean to be an apprentice once more? To be Dante again? Months of seeking clues to the Gauntlet had added up to nothing, and this might too, but they at least had to try. Anselm had been an absentee parent, checking in dutifully from New York but leaving them to their own devices. They couldn't count on the new Praetor doing the same.

"Let's set the protections," Alex said.

She and Dawes worked together, pouring out salt in a Solomon's Knot formation—an ordinary circle wouldn't do. They were, in theory, opening a portal to hell, or at least a corner of it, and if Darlington was more demon than man these days, they didn't want him cavorting all over campus with his demon buddies.

Every line of the knot touched another line, making it impossible to tell where the design began. Alex consulted the image she'd copied from a book on spiritual containment. Apparently demons loved puzzles and games and the knot would keep them occupied until they could be banished, or, in Darlington's case, clapped into chains of pure silver. At least Alex hoped they were pure silver. She'd found them in a drawer in the armory, and she sure hoped Lethe hadn't scrimped. And if the hellbeast tried to come through again? They placed gems at each compass point: amethyst, carnelian, opal, tourmaline. Little glittering trinkets to bind a monster.

"They don't look like much, do they?" asked Alex.

All Dawes did was chew her lip harder.

"It's going to be fine," Alex said, not believing a word of it. "What's next?"

They set lines of salt every few feet down the hall, more safeguards in case something got past the knot. The final line they poured out was pale brown. It had been mixed with their own blood, a last line of defense.

Dawes pulled a tiny toy trumpet out of her satchel.

Alex couldn't hide her disbelief. "You're going to call Darlington out of hell with that?"

"We don't have the bells from Aurelian, and the ritual just calls for 'an instrument of action or alarm.' You have the note?"

They'd used the deed to Black Elm during the failed new moon ritual, a contract Darlington had signed with full hope and intent. They didn't have anything like that this time around, but they did have a note, written by Michelle Alameddine, that they'd found in the desk of the Virgil bedroom at Lethe, just a few lines of a poem and a note:

There was a monastery that produced Armagnac so refined, its monks were forced to flee to Italy when Louis XIV joked about killing them to protect their secrets. This is the last bottle. Don't drink it on an empty stomach, and don't call unless you're dead. Good luck, Virgil!

It wasn't much, but they had the bottle of Armagnac too. It was far less grand than Alex had imagined, murkily green, the old label illegible.

"He hasn't opened it," Dawes observed as Alex set the bottle on the floor at the center of the knot, her expression disapproving.

"We're not looking through his underwear drawer. It's just alcohol."

"It isn't meant for us."

"And we're not drinking it," Alex snapped. Because Dawes was right. They had no business stealing things that had been meant for Darlington, that were precious to him.

We'll bring him back and he'll forgive us, she told herself as she drew a small glass from her bag and filled it, the liquid warm and orange as late sun. *He'll forgive me. For all of it.*

"We should really have four people for this," said Dawes. "One for each compass point."

They should have four people. They should have found the Gauntlet. They should have taken the time to put together something other than this patchwork mess of a ritual.

But here they were at the edge of the cliff, and Alex knew Dawes wasn't looking to be talked off the ledge. She wanted someone to drag her over.

"Come on," Alex said. "He's waiting on the other side."

Dawes drew in a deep breath, her brown eyes too bright. "Okay." She drew a small bottle full of sesame oil from her pocket and began to anoint the table with it, tracing the rim with her finger as she walked first clockwise, then counterclockwise, chanting in stilted Arabic.

When she caught up to her starting point, she met Alex's gaze, then drew her finger through the oil, closing the circle.

The table seemed to drop away to nothing. Alex felt like she was

looking down into forever. She looked up and saw a circle of darkness above where there had been a glass skylight a moment before.
The night was thick with stars, but it was the middle of the day. She
had to shut her eyes as a wave of vertigo washed over her.

"Burn it," said Dawes. "Call him."

Alex struck a match and held it to the note, then tossed the flaming paper into the nothingness where the table had been. It seemed
to float there, edges curling, and before it could fall, she threw a
handful of iron filings into the blaze. The words began to peel up
from the paper and into the air.

Good
luck
you're
dead

"Stand back," said Dawes. She raised the trumpet to her lips. The
sound that emerged should have been thin and tinny. Instead, a rich
bellow echoed off the walls, the triumphant blast of a horn calling
riders to the hunt.

In the distance Alex heard the soft patter of paws.

"It's working!" Dawes whispered.

They leaned over the space where the table had been and Dawes
blew the trumpet again, it echoed back to them from somewhere in
the distance.

Come home, Darlington. Alex picked up the glass of Armagnac
and tipped it into that star-filled abyss. *Come back and drink from this
fancy bottle, raise a toast.* She could still hear that old song playing in
her head. *Come on along. Come on along. Let me take you by the hand.*

The patter grew, but it didn't sound like the soft thud of paws. It
was too loud and growing louder.

Alex looked around the room for a clue to what was happening.
"Something's wrong."

The sound rose from somewhere in the darkness. From somewhere below.

It shook the stone floor in a swelling rumble Alex could feel
through her boots. She peered down into nothing and smelled sulfur.

"Dawes, close it up."

"But—"

"Close the portal!"

She saw flecks of red in the dark now, and a moment later, she understood—they were eyes.

"Dawes!"

Too late. Alex stumbled back against the wall as a herd of stampeding horses thundered out of the table, bursting into the room in a seething mass of black horseflesh. They were the color of coal, their eyes red and glowing. Each beat of their hooves against the floor exploded into flame. They crashed through the temple room door, scattering salt and stones, and roared down the hall. The herd of hellhorses blew through the lines of salt one by one.

"They're not going to stop!" Dawes cried.

They were going to smash through the front door and onto the street.

But when the stampede struck the line of salt they'd mixed with their blood, it was like a wave crashing against the rocks. The herd spilled left and right, a messy roiling tide. One of the horses fell on its side, its high whinny like a human scream. It righted itself and then the stampede was clamoring back toward the temple room.

"Dawes!" Alex shouted. She knew plenty of death words. She had silver chains, a rope full of elaborate knots, a damned Rubik's Cube because demons liked puzzles. But she had no idea how to deal with a herd of horses snorting sulfur that had been summoned from the depths of hell.

"Get out of the way!" Dawes yelled.

Alex pressed herself against the wall. Dawes stood on the far side of the table, her red hair streaming around her face, shouting words Alex didn't understand. She raised the trumpet to her lips, and the sound was like a thousand horns, an orchestra of command.

They're going to crush her, Alex thought. *She'll break into nothing, dissolve into ash.*

The horses leapt, a black tide of heavy bodies and blue flame, and Dawes hurled the trumpet into the abyss. The horses dove after it, arcing impossibly in the air, less like horses than tumbling sea foam. They flowed like water and dissolved into darkness.

"Close it!" Alex shouted.

Dawes held up her empty palms and swiped them together, as if washing her hands of it all. "*Ghalaqa al-baab! Al-tariiq muharram lakum!*"

Then a voice echoed through the room—from somewhere below or somewhere above, it was impossible to tell. But Alex knew that voice, and the word he spoke was clear and pleading.

Wait.

"No!" Dawes screamed. But it was too late. There was an enormous boom, like the sound of a heavy door slamming shut. Alex was thrown off her feet.

6

Alex didn't remember much of what happened next. Her ears were ringing, her eyes watering, and the stink of sulfur was so sharp, she barely had time to roll onto her hands and knees before she vomited. She heard Dawes retching too and she wanted to weep with happiness. If Dawes was puking, she wasn't dead.

Robbie ran into the room, waving away the smoke and shouting, "What the fuck? What the fuck?" Then he was vomiting too.

The room was covered in black soot. Alex and Dawes were coated in it. And the table—the table King Arthur's knights had supposedly gathered around—was cracked down the middle.

Wait.

She couldn't even pretend she hadn't heard it because Dawes had too. Alex had seen the anguish in her eyes as the portal slammed shut.

Alex crawled over to Dawes. She was curled up against the wall shaking. "Don't say a goddamn word," Alex whispered. "It was an inspection, that's all."

"I heard him—" Tears filled her eyes.

"I know, but right now we've got to cover our asses. Say it with me. It was an inspection."

"It was an inspec—inspection."

The rest was a blur—shouting from the Scroll and Key delegates; calls from their board and alumni; more shouting from Michael Anselm, who arrived on the Metro-North and offered the use of

Hiram's Crucible to restore the table and make it whole. Dawes and Alex did their best to wipe the soot off themselves and then faced Anselm in the entry hall of the Scroll and Key tomb.

"This isn't on us," Alex said. Best to come out swinging. "We wanted to make sure they hadn't been opening portals or performing unsanctioned rituals, so I constructed a revelation casting."

She'd prepared a cover story. She hadn't anticipated she'd have to cover a massive explosion, but it was all she had.

Anselm was pacing back and forth, his cell in one hand, and a Scroll and Key alumnus could be heard screaming on the other end. He covered the phone with his palm. "You knew the nexus was unstable. Someone could have been killed."

"The table is in two pieces!" shrieked the alum on the phone. "The entire temple room is ruined!"

"We'll arrange for cleaning." Again Anselm covered the phone and whispered furiously, "Il Bastone."

"Don't worry," Alex said to Dawes as they passed a wrathful group of Locksmiths and headed down the stairs to the sidewalk. Robbie Kendall looked like he'd fallen down a chimney, and he'd lost one of his loafers. "Anselm is going to blame me, not you. Dawes?"

She wasn't listening. She had a startled, faraway look in her eyes. It was that word. *Wait.*

"Dawes, you have to keep it together. We can't tell them what happened, no matter how shell-shocked you are."

"Okay."

But Dawes was silent all the way to Il Bastone.

A single word. Darlington's voice. Desperate, demanding. *Wait.* They'd almost done it, almost reached him. They'd been so close.

He would have gotten it right. He always did.

It took the better part of an hour washing with parsley and al-mond oil to get the stink off of them. Dawes had gone to the Dante bathroom, and Alex had stripped down in the beautiful Virgil suite with its big claw-foot tub.

Her clothes were ruined.

"This damn job should have a stipend for replacements," she grumbled to the house as she pulled on a pair of Lethe sweats and went down to the parlor.

Anselm was still on his phone. He was younger than she'd thought at first, early thirties, and not bad-looking in a corporate kind of way. He held up a finger when he saw her, and she went to find Dawes in the kitchen. She had laid out plates of smoked salmon and cucumber salad, tucked a bottle of white wine into a bucket of ice. Alex was tempted to roll her eyes, but she was hungry and this was the Lethe way. Maybe they should just invite the hellbeast to a cold supper.

Dawes was standing in front of a sink full of dishes and soap suds, staring out the window, the water running, her freshly washed hair hanging loose. Alex had never seen it down before.

Alex reached out and shut off the water. "You okay?"

Dawes kept her eyes on the window. There wasn't much to see—the alley, the side of a neatly upkept Victorian.

"Dawes? Anselm isn't done with us. I—"

"Lethe set up a security system at Black Elm when . . . when we knew it might be empty for a while. Just a couple of cameras."

Alex felt an unpleasant flutter in her stomach. "I know. Front door, back door." Sandow had made sure the windows were boarded up, and the old Mercedes had been repaired on Lethe's dime. Dawes occasionally used it to run errands, just to keep it from sitting idle.

Dawes tucked her chin into her neck. "I put one in the ballroom."

In the ballroom. Where they'd attempted the new moon ritual.

"And?" Alex could hear Anselm talking in the parlor, the crackle of soap bubbles in the sink.

"Something . . . I got a notification." She bobbed her head at her phone resting on the counter.

Alex made herself pick it up, swipe the screen. Nothing but a dark blur was visible, a faint light dancing at the edges.

"That's all the camera is picking up," said Dawes.

Alex stared at the screen as if she could find some pattern in the dark. "It might just be Cosmo. He could have knocked the camera over."

Darlington's cat had rejected all attempts to rehome him to Il Bastone or Dawes's apartment up near the divinity school. All they could do was offer tributes of food and water and hope he'd watch over Black Elm, and that the old house would watch over him.

"Don't get your hopes up, Dawes."

"Of course not."

Of course not.

But Dawes still had that startled look and Alex knew what she was thinking.

Wait. The plea had come too late, but what if, when the portal at Scroll and Key had slammed shut, Darlington had somehow still found a way through? What if they'd somehow gotten it right? What if they'd brought him back?

And what if we got it very wrong? What if whatever was waiting at Black Elm wasn't Darlington at all?

"Alex?" Anselm called from the other room. "A word. Just you, please." But Dawes hadn't budged. She had her hands clenched around the edge of the sink, like she was clinging to the safety bar on a roller coaster, like she was getting ready to scream on the way down. Had Alex really ever understood what Darlington meant to Pamela Dawes? Quiet, closed-off Dawes, who had mastered the art of disappearing into the furniture? The girl only he'd called Pammie?

"We'll get rid of Anselm and then go take a look," Alex said. Her voice was steady, but her heart had taken off at a sprint.

It's nothing, Alex told herself as she joined Anselm in the parlor. A cat. A squatter. A wayward tree branch. A wayward boy. She needed to keep a clear head if she was going to figure out how to appease Anselm and the Lethe board.

"I've spoken with the new Praetor. He was already reluctant to take the position, and I doubt today's activities will fill him with confidence, so I've made every effort to downplay this little disaster."

Thanks didn't seem appropriate, so Alex stayed quiet.

"What were you really doing at Scroll and Key?"

Alex had been hoping Anselm wouldn't be so direct. Lethe liked to dance around trouble, and they were expert at finding dusty rugs to sweep the truth under. She took a closer look at Anselm—tan from some kind of summer vacation, slightly rumpled from the night's adventures. He'd loosened his collar and poured himself a scotch. He looked like an actor playing a man whose wife had just asked him for a divorce.

"I smelled sulfur," he continued wearily. "Everyone within two miles probably smelled it. So tell me what went wrong with a revelation casting to cause something like that? To smash a centuries-old table?"

"You said it yourself: Their nexus is unstable."

"Not fire-and-brimstone unstable." He lifted his glass, pointing a finger as if ordering another. "You were trying to open a portal to hell. I thought I made myself clear. Daniel Arlington isn't—"

Alex considered. He wasn't going to let her get away with saying this was an accident or a revelation casting gone wrong. But she wasn't about to admit to trying to find Darlington, not when he might be back, not when something far worse might be waiting at Black Elm.

"It wasn't an accident," she lied. "I did it on purpose."

Anselm blinked. "You intended to destroy the table?"

"That's right. They shouldn't have gotten away with what they did last year."

"Alex," he scolded gently, "our job is to protect. Not dole out punishment."

Don't kid yourself. Our job is to make sure the kids keep the noise down and tidy up after.

"They shouldn't get to do rituals," she said. "They shouldn't get to pick up right where they left off." The anger in her voice was real.

Anselm sighed. "Maybe not. But that table is a priceless artifact and we're lucky the crucible can piece it back together. I appreciate your . . . sense of fairness, but Dawes, at least, should know better."

"Dawes was just along for the ride. I told her I needed a second person for the ritual, but not what I had planned."

"She is not a stupid woman. I don't believe that for a second." Anselm studied her. "What spell did you use?"

He was testing her, and as usual, she hadn't done the reading.

"I put it together myself." Anselm winced. Good. He already thought she was incompetent. That could work for her. "I used an old stink bomb casting I found in one of the Lethe Days Diaries. Some guy used it as a prank."

"That was the blow you struck for justice? A stink bomb?"

"It got out of hand."

Anselm shook his head and downed the rest of his scotch. "The level of stupid we all got up to here. I'm amazed anyone survived."

"So I'm in keeping with a grand tradition."

Anselm did not look amused. He wasn't like Darlington or even Sandow. Lethe and its mysteries were just something that had happened to him.

"You're lucky no one was killed." He set down his glass and met her eyes. Alex did her best to look innocent, but she hadn't had much practice. "I'm going to put forward a theory. You weren't trying to wreck the table tonight. You were trying to open a portal to hell and somehow reach Daniel Arlington."

Why couldn't he be one of the dim ones?

"Interesting theory," said Alex. "But not what happened."

"Just like your theory that Darlington is in hell? Pure speculation?"

"You a lawyer?"

"I am."

"You talk like one."

"I don't consider that an insult."

"It's not an insult. If I wanted to insult you, I'd call you two pounds of shit in a one-pound bag. For example." Alex knew she should rein in her anger, but she was tired and frustrated. The board had made it clear they didn't believe Alex's theory on Darlington's whereabouts and that there would be no heroic attempts to set him free. But if Anselm was bothered, he didn't show it. He just looked worn out. "We owe Darlington a little effort. If it weren't for Dean Sandow, he wouldn't be down there."

If it weren't for me.

"Down there," Anselm repeated, bemused. "Do you really think hell is a big pit somewhere under the sewer lines? That if you just dig deep enough, you'll get there?"

"That's not what I meant." Though that had been exactly what she'd been picturing. She hadn't worried too much about the logistics, about what opening a portal or walking the Gauntlet might entail. That was Dawes's job. Alex's job was to be the cannonball once Dawes figured out where to point the cannon.

"I don't want to be cruel, Alex. But you don't even understand the possibilities of the trouble you could cause. And for what? A chance to expiate your guilt? A theory you can barely articulate?"

Darlington could have articulated it just fine if he'd been there. Dawes could if she weren't scared of speaking above a whisper.

"Then get someone with the right résumé to convince you. I know he's . . ." She'd almost said *down there.* "He's not dead." He might well be resting comfortably in the Black Elm ballroom.

"You lost a mentor and a friend." Anselm's blue eyes were steady, kind. "Believe it or not, I understand. But you want to open a door that isn't meant to be opened. You have no idea what might come through."

Why didn't these people ever get it? Protect your own. Pay your debts. There was no other way to live, not if you wanted to live right.

She crossed her arms. "We owe him."

"He's gone, Alex. It's time to accept that. Even if you were right, whatever survived in hell wouldn't be the Darlington you know. I appreciate your loyalty. But if you take a chance like this again, you and Pamela Dawes will no longer be welcome at Lethe."

He lifted his empty glass as if he expected to find it full, then pushed it aside. He folded his hands, and she could see him thinking through what to say. Anselm was eager to be gone, to get back to New York and his life. There were people who carried Lethe with them forever, who took jobs hunting down magical artifacts or did dissertations on the occult, who locked themselves in libraries or traveled the globe seeking new magic. But not Michael Anselm. He'd gone into law, found a job that required suits and results. He had none of the ambling, gentle scholarship of Dean Sandow, none of Darlington's greedy curiosity. He had built an ordinary life propped up by money and rules.

"Do you understand me, Alex? You're out of second chances."

She understood. Dawes would lose her job. Alex would lose her scholarship. That would be the end of it. "I understand."

"I need your word that this will be the last of it, that we can get back to business as usual and that you'll be prepared to supervise rituals every Thursday night. I know you didn't have the training you should have, but you have Dawes and you seem to be a . . . resourceful young woman. Michelle Alameddine is available if you feel—"

"We'll manage. Dawes and I can handle it."

"I won't cover for you again. No more trouble, Alex."

"No more trouble," Alex promised. "You can trust me." The big lies were as easy as the small ones.

7

Alex had thought they'd be free to speed straight to Black Elm as soon as Anselm was gone, but he left them on the phone with his assistant, who rolled one call after another to Scroll and Key alumni and members of the Lethe board so that Alex and Dawes could explain themselves and apologize contritely, again and again.

Alex pressed the mute button. "This isn't healthy. I can only feign sincerity for so long before I rupture something."

"Well then, try meaning it," Dawes scolded and stabbed the mute button as if she were skewering a cocktail shrimp. "Madame Secretary, I'd like to discuss the harm we caused tonight . . ."

It was midnight before they were free of the apology chain and headed for the old Mercedes parked behind Il Bastone. Alex wasn't sure if it was right or wrong to be in Darlington's car in this moment. It felt uncomfortably like they were just on their way to pick him up, like he'd be waiting at the end of Black Elm's long driveway with a duffel slung over his shoulder, ready to slide into the back seat, like they'd drive and keep driving until the car gave up or sprouted wings.

Dawes was a nervous driver at the best of times, and tonight it was as if she were afraid the Mercedes would combust if she pushed it over forty miles per hour. Eventually they reached the stone columns that marked the entry to Black Elm.

The woods that surrounded the house were still thick with summer leaves, so when they came upon the brick walls and gables, the house appeared too suddenly, an unpleasant surprise. A light was on in the kitchen, but they'd set that to a timer.

"Look," said Dawes, her voice barely a breath.

Alex was already looking. They'd boarded up the windows on the second floor after Dean Sandow had deliberately botched his ritual to bring Darlington home. A faint light shone through the edges, soft, flickering amber.

Dawes parked the car outside of the garage. Her hands gripped the steering wheel, white-knuckled. "It might be nothing."

"Then it's nothing," said Alex, pleased with how steady she sounded. "Stop trying to strangle the steering wheel and let's go."

They both shut their car doors gently, and Alex realized it was because they were afraid to disturb what might be waiting upstairs. There was a chill in the air, the first hint of the end of summer and the autumn to come. There would be no more fireflies, no more drinks on the porch or sounds of tag played late into the night.

Alex unlocked the kitchen door, and Dawes gasped as Cosmo sprang from behind the cupboards, screeching past them into the yard.

Alex thought her heart might leap straight out of her rib cage. "For fuck's sake, cat."

Dawes held her satchel to her chest as if it were some kind of talisman. "Did you see his fur?"

One side of Cosmo's white fur looked like it had been singed black. Alex wanted to make some kind of excuse. Cosmo was always getting into trouble, showing up with a new scar or covered in brambles, jaws clamped around a poor murdered mouse. But she couldn't force her mouth to make the words.

Before they'd left Il Bastone, they'd stopped in the Lethe armory for more salt, and they'd brought the silver chains. They seemed silly and useless, toys for children, old wives' tales.

Dawes hovered at the kitchen door as if it were the actual portal to hell. "We could call Michelle or . . ."

"Anselm? If we summoned some kind of monster, do you really want to tell him?"

"It's pretty quiet for a monster."

"Maybe it's a giant snake."

"Why did you have to say that?"

"It's not a snake," Alex said. "It could still be nothing. Or . . . an electrical fire or something."

"I don't smell smoke."

So what was making that dancing light?

It didn't matter. If Darlington were here, standing at this threshold, he wouldn't hesitate. He'd be the knight. He'd be a lot better prepared, but he'd walk up those stairs. *Protect your own. Pay your debts.*

"I'm going up, Dawes. You can stay here. I won't hold it against you."

She meant it. But Dawes followed anyway.

They plunged past the brightly lit kitchen and into the dark. Alex never explored Black Elm's other rooms when she came to feed Cosmo or pick up the mail. They were too silent, too still. It felt like walking through a bombed-out church.

Dawes paused at the bottom of the grand staircase. "Alex—"

"I know."

Sulfur. Not as powerful as it had been at Scroll and Key but unmistakable.

Alex felt a cold bead of sweat roll down her neck. They could turn back, try to arm themselves better, get help, call Michelle Alameddine and tell her they'd gone ahead and done something stupid. But Alex felt like she couldn't stop herself. She was the cannonball. She was the bullet. And the gun had gone off when Dawes had told her there'd been some kind of disturbance at the house. *You want to open a door that isn't meant to be opened.* There was nothing to do but keep going.

At the top of the stairs, they paused again. That same golden light flickered in the hallway, filtering out from beneath the closed ballroom door. She could hear Dawes breathing—in through the nose, out through the mouth—trying to calm herself as they approached the door. Alex reached for the handle and yanked her hand back with a hiss. It was hot to the touch.

"What did we do?" Dawes asked on a trembling breath.

Alex wrapped her shirt around her hand, grasped the handle, and pulled open the door.

The heat hit them in a gust, an oven door opening. The smell here wasn't sulfuric; it was almost sweet, like wood burning.

The room was dusty, its boarded-up windows as sad as ever, the walls littered with weights and workout equipment. They hadn't bothered to clean up the chalk circle they'd created for Sandow's failed new moon ritual. No one had wanted to return to the ball-room, to remember the hellbeast looming above them, the cries of murder, the horrible finality of it all.

Now Alex was grateful they'd all been such cowards. The chalk circle glowed golden, less a circle than a shimmering wall, and at its center, Daniel Tabor Arlington V sat cross-legged, naked as a baby in the bath. Two horns curled back from his forehead, their ridges gleaming as if shot through with molten gold, and his body was covered in bright markings. A wide golden collar ringed his neck, ornamented with rows of garnet and jade.

"Oh," said Dawes, her eyes darting around the room as if afraid to let her gaze land anywhere, but finally settling in the far corner— the place most distant from the sight of Darlington's cock, which was very erect and shining like a supercharged, oversized glowstick.

His eyes were closed and his hands rested lightly atop his knees, palms down, as if he were meditating.

"Darlington?" Alex choked out.

Nothing. The heat seemed to be radiating directly from him.

"Daniel?"

Dawes took a shuffling step forward, her Tevas smacking against the dusty floorboards, but Alex blocked her with an outstretched arm.

"Don't," she said. "We don't even know if that's him." *Whatever survived in hell wouldn't be the Darlington you know.*

Dawes looked helpless. "His hair grew out."

It took a second for Alex to catch up, but Dawes was right. Darlington's hair had always been kept tidy but not too tidy, as effortless as the rest of him. Now it curled around his neck. Apparently there were no barbers in hell.

"He . . . he doesn't look hurt," Alex ventured. No scars, no bruises, all his limbs intact. But she knew that she and Dawes were thinking the same thing: that while they'd been trying to solve the mystery of how to get into hell and living their lives, watching TV, eating ice cream, and planning for the school year, Darlington had been alive and trapped, maybe being tortured, in hell.

Had she not quite believed it? Despite her talk of the gentleman demon? Despite the arguments she'd made to Anselm and the board? Had some of her thought everyone else was right and that this ridiculous quest was just another opportunity to throw herself into harm's way and appease her own guilt over his death?

But here he was. Or someone who looked very much like him.

"The circle is binding him," Dawes said. "It's Sandow's old casting."

Hear the silence of an empty home. No one will be made welcome. When Sandow had realized Darlington might be alive on the other side, he'd used the last moments of the ritual to ban him from Black Elm and the living world.

Dawes tilted her head to one side. "I think he's trapped." Then it was as if she had woken from sleep. She looked almost panicked. "We have to find a way to get him out."

Alex cast a glance at the horned and naked creature sitting in what her mother would have praised as a very fine sukhasana pose. "I'm not sure that's a good idea."

But Dawes was already striding toward the circle. She reached for it.

"Dawes—"

As soon as her hand broke the perimeter of the circle, Dawes screamed. She stumbled backward, clutching her fingers to her chest.

Alex lunged for her, pulling her away. The smell of sulfur overwhelmed her again and she had to struggle not to gag. She crouched beside Dawes and forced her to release her wrist. Dawes's fingertips were singed black. Alex remembered Cosmo howling out of the kitchen. He'd tried to cross the circle too. He'd tried to get to Darlington.

"Come on," Alex said. "I'm getting you back to Il Bastone. There's got to be some kind of potion or balm or something there, right?"

"We can't leave him," Dawes protested as Alex dragged her to her feet.

Darlington sat silent and unmoving like some kind of golden idol.

"He's not going anywhere."

"It's our fault. If I had finished the ritual, if the portal—"

"Dawes," Alex said, giving her a shake. "That's not how this works. Sandow sent the hellbeast—"

A low growl rumbled through the room. Darlington hadn't moved, but there was no question that sound had come from him. Alex felt a shiver pass over her.

"I don't think he likes that," whispered Dawes.

Is it you? Alex wanted to ask. She wanted to try charging straight through that circle. Would she end in a heap of cinders? A pile of salt? And what was waiting on the other side of that shimmering veil? Darlington? Or something wearing his skin?

"Come on," she said, herding Dawes out of the ballroom and down the stairs. She didn't want to leave him, but she didn't want to be in that room a minute longer.

Alex was locking up the kitchen door when her phone buzzed. She drew it from her pocket, keeping one eye on Dawes, one on the light from the boarded-up windows above. She hesitated when she saw the name on her screen.

"It's Turner," she said, pushing Dawes toward the car.

"Detective Turner?"

Call me.

Alex scowled and replied: *You call me. Remember how?*

She didn't know why she was bitter. She hadn't heard from Turner in months. She'd understood he was angry after the dean's death, but she'd thought he liked her and that they'd managed some pretty good investigating together. To her surprise her phone rang almost immediately. She'd been sure Turner would ignore her. He didn't like to be told.

Alex put the detective on speaker.

"You do remember," she said. She nudged Dawes toward the passenger seat and whispered, "I'm driving." Dawes really must have been hurting because she didn't protest.

"I've got a body at the med school," said Turner.

"I'm guessing there are a lot of bodies at the med school."

"I need you or someone to come take a look."

That stung too. Turner knew better than most what she'd been through last year, but apparently she was just a Lethe deputy now.

"Why?"

"There's something that isn't sitting right. Just come by, tell me I'm seeing things, and we can go back to not talking."

Alex didn't want to go. She didn't want Turner to just be able to call her up when he wanted to and not before. But he was Centurion and she was Dante. *Virgil.*

"Fine. But you owe me."

"I don't owe you shit. This is your actual job."

He hung up. Alex was tempted to stand him up on principle. But better to worry about a dead body than whatever was sitting in the ballroom at Black Elm. She reversed too fast and the tires kicked up a spray of gravel.

You're not fleeing a crime scene, Stern. Calm down.

She refused to look in the rearview mirror. She didn't want to see that flickering golden light.

Dawes huddled against the passenger-side door. She looked like she might be ill. "Another murder?"

"He didn't actually say. Just a body."

"You don't . . . Could it be related to what we did?"

Damn. Alex hadn't even considered that. It seemed unlikely, but rituals had all kinds of magical blowback, particularly when they went wrong.

"I doubt it," she said with more confidence than she felt.

"Do you want me to come with you?"

Part of her did. Dawes was a better representative of Lethe than Alex would ever be. She would know what to look for, what to say.

But Dawes was injured inside and out. She needed a chance to heal and wallow a little in her guilt and grief. Alex knew the feeling.

"No, you're Oculus. This is Dante business."

Dawes looked absurdly comforted by that. She wasn't giving in to fear. She was following protocol.

They drove with the windows down, the night cool around them. They could be anywhere right now. They could be anyone, free of fear or duty, headed someplace good. Vacation. A night out. A house somewhere up the coast. Darlington could be sprawled out in the back, duffel tucked under the seat, hands folded beneath his head. They could be all right.

"Was it him?" Dawes whispered in the dark, the night air snatching her words, casting them out into the sleeping city, the houses and fields beyond.

Alex didn't know what to say, so she turned on the radio and drove toward campus, waiting to see the lights of Il Bastone that would tell her she was home.

Darlington managed the challenge of the jackals easily—no surprise. He's got Lethe written all over him and it's nice to see someone genuinely enjoying all Il Bastone has to offer. When I explained the particulars of Hiram's elixir, he recited Yeats to me. "The world is full of magic things, patiently waiting for our senses to grow sharper." I didn't have the heart to tell him I know the quote and I've always hated it. It's too easy to believe that we're being watched and studied by something with infinite patience, as we rush unknowing toward an irreversible moment of revelation.

My new Dante is eager and I suspect my primary task will be to keep that enthusiasm from killing him. How easily he speaks of magic, as if it is not forbidden, as if it does not always ask a terrible price.

—Lethe Days Diary of Michelle Alameddine
(Hopper College)

8

Once they were back at the armory, Dawes walked Alex through a curative for the burns on her fingers, all the while insisting that she was fine and that she was happy to be left alone. Alex could see that she most definitely wasn't fine, but if Dawes wanted to clap on her headphones and spend two hours not working on her dissertation, Alex wasn't going to stand in her way. She left the Mercedes parked behind Il Bastone so Dawes wouldn't get twitchy about her driving it solo and called a car to take her to the med school.

Turner had texted her an address, but she didn't know this part of campus well. She'd been to the medical library only once, when Darlington had escorted her to the basement and into a pretty paneled room lined with glass jars, each with a black lid and a square label, each with a full or partial human brain floating inside.

"Cushing's personal collection," he'd said, then opened one of the drawers beneath the shelves to reveal a row of tiny infant skulls. He donned nitrile gloves, then selected two for a mid-quarter prognostication Skull and Bones wanted to perform.

"Why those?" Alex had asked.

"The skulls aren't finished forming. They show all possible futures. Don't worry, we bring them back intact."

"I'm not worried." After all, they were just bones. But she'd let Darlington make the return visit to the Cushing collection on his own.

The building at 300 George was nothing like the beautiful old library with its star-strewn ceiling. The Department of Psychiatry stretched most of the block, big, gray, and modern. She'd expected to see police cars, crime scene tape, maybe even reporters. But everything was quiet. Turner's Dodge was parked out front beside a dark van.

She stood on the sidewalk a long moment. Last year she'd begged Turner to involve her in his investigation, but now she hesitated, thinking of the creature that might or might not be Darlington sitting in that golden circle. She had too much to worry about already and too many secrets to keep. She couldn't afford to get involved in a murder. And some paranoid part of her wondered if this was all some elaborate setup, if Turner had found out about the jobs she was doing for Eitan.

But her choices were to go home or walk through the fire, and Alex didn't really know how to not get burned. She texted Turner, and a minute later, the front door opened.

He waved her inside. Turner looked good, but he always did. The man knew how to dress and his khaki, summer-weight suit was all sharp lines and clean creases.

"You look like you escaped from juvie," he said when he saw her Lethe House sweats.

"I'm getting my cardio in. I jogged here."

"Really?"

"No. What's going on?"

Turner shook his head. "Probably an ordinary death that has nothing to do with . . . hocus-pocus. But after the buffoonery you got up to last year, I wanted an expert opinion."

"I got up to solving crime, Turner. What did you get up to?"

"I'm already sorry I called you."

"Makes two of us."

Inside, the lobby was quiet and dark, lit only by the streetlights filtering through the windows. They took an elevator to the third floor, and Alex followed Turner down a stark hallway bright with overhead fluorescents. She saw a gurney and two men in blue windbreakers from the coroner's office leaning against the wall, absorbed in their phones.

They were waiting to take the body.

"Where is everyone?" Alex asked. She couldn't help but think about the circus that had surrounded Tara's murder.

"Right now it's looking like natural causes, so we're trying to keep this quiet."

Turner led her into a small, messy office with a big window that probably had a nice view during the day. Now it was just a glossy black mirror, and the reflection gave Alex the uneasy feeling she'd slipped into a different version of her life. She'd done stints in juvie and it was only dumb luck she'd never gotten jammed up when she was an adult. Seeing herself in her sad sweats beside Turner in his fine suit made her feel small, and she didn't like it.

"Who is she?" Alex asked.

The woman was slumped at her desk, as if she'd laid her head down on her extended arm to take a short nap. Her long salt-and-pepper hair lay over one shoulder in a braid, and her glasses hung from a colorful chain around her neck.

"Were you at a bonfire?" Turner asked. "You smell like . . ." He hesitated, and Alex knew it was because whatever scent was on her was not quite smoke.

"Ritual stuff," she said and predictably Turner scowled.

But he was still a detective. "It's not Thursday."

"I'm trying to brush up before the semester really gets going."

He looked like he knew she was lying, and that was fine. She didn't have any interest in explaining that she and Dawes had attempted to yank Darlington out of hell with what could only be described as unexpected results. Turner didn't even know they were trying.

"Someone found her here?" she asked.

"Her name is Marjorie Stephen, she's a tenured psych professor. Nearly twelve years with the department, runs one of the labs. The night cleaner found the body and called me."

"Called you? Not 9-1-1?"

He shook his head. "I know him from the neighborhood, friend of my mom's. He didn't want trouble with the cops."

"Neither do I."

Turner raised a brow. "Then act like it."

Every contrary bone in Alex's body wanted to tell him to fuck off. "Why am I here?"

"Have a look. Crime scene's come and gone."

Alex wasn't really sure she wanted to. She'd seen way too many corpses since she'd joined Lethe, and this was the second in three days.

She walked around the body, giving it a wide berth, trying to avoid that cold absence. "Jesus," she gasped when she reached the other side. The woman's eyes were wide and staring, their pupils a milky gray. "What did that? Poison?"

"We don't know yet. Could be nothing. An aneurysm, a stroke."

"That's not what happens when you have a stroke."

"No," Turner admitted. "I've never seen it."

Alex leaned in, wary. "There's . . ."

"No smell yet. We're estimating time of death sometime between 8 and 10 p.m. tonight, but we'll know more after the autopsy."

Alex tried not to show her relief. Some part of her had wondered if Dawes was right and their ritual had been the cause of this. She knew stray magic could do real damage. But this woman had died hours later.

The professor had her hand on a book. "The Bible?" Alex asked, surprised.

"It's possible she was in pain and seeking comfort," said Turner. Reluctantly he added, "It's also possible this was staged."

"Seriously?"

"Look closer."

Marjorie Stephen's hand was gripped around the book, and one of her fingers was tucked between the pages, as if she had been trying to keep her place when she lay down to die.

"Where did she stop reading?"

Turner pushed up the pages with a gloved hand. Alex forced herself to lean in.

"Judges?"

"You know your Bible?" Turner asked.

"Do you?"

"Well enough."

"Is that part of police training?"

"That's six years of Sunday school when I could have been playing baseball."

"Were you any good?"

"Nope. But I'm not any good at scripture either."

"So what am I missing?"

"I don't know. Judges is boring as hell. Lists of names, not much else."

"And you pulled security footage or whatever?"

"We did. Plenty of people in the building at that time, but we'll have to sort through the lobby tapes to see if anyone wasn't supposed to be here." He tapped the desk calendar with his gloved finger. On the Saturday of Marjorie Stephen's death, she—or someone—had written, *Hide the outcasts.* "Ring any bells?"

Alex hesitated, then shook her head. "Maybe. I don't think so."

"It's also from the Bible."

"Judges?"

"Isaiah. The destruction of Moab."

Turner was watching her closely, waiting to see if any of this would spark. Alex had the distinct sensation of letting him down.

"What about the professor's family?" she asked.

"We informed the husband. We'll talk to him tomorrow. Three kids, all grown. They're driving and flying in."

"Did he say if she was religious?"

"According to him, the closest she got to church was yoga every Sunday."

"That Bible says otherwise." Alex knew the look of a well-loved book, spine broken, pages dog-eared and marked up.

Now Turner's lips quirked in a smile. "It sure does. But look again. Look at her."

Alex didn't want to. She was still reeling from what she'd seen at Black Elm and now Turner was testing her. But then she saw it.

"Her rings are loose."

"That's right. And look at her face."

No way was Alex gazing into those milky eyes again. "She looks like a dead woman."

"She looks like an eighty-year-old dead woman. Marjorie Stephen just turned fifty-five."

Alex's stomach lurched, as if she'd missed a step. That was why Turner thought the societies were involved.

"She hadn't been ill," he continued. "This lady liked to hike East Rock and Sleeping Giant. She ran every morning. We spoke to two people with offices on this hallway who saw her earlier today. They said she looked normal, perfectly healthy. When we showed them a photo of the body, they barely recognized her."

It smacked of the uncanny. But what about the Bible? The societies weren't the type to quote scripture. Their texts were far rarer and more arcane.

"I don't know," said Alex. "It doesn't quite add up."

Turner rubbed a hand over his low fade. "Good. So tell me I'm jumping at shadows."

Alex wanted to. But there was something wrong here, something more than a woman left to die alone with a Bible in her hand, something in those milky gray eyes.

"I can search the Lethe library," Alex said. "But I'm going to require some reciprocity."

"That's not actually the way this works, *Dante*."

"I'm Virgil now," Alex said, though maybe not for long. "It works the way Lethe says it does."

"There's something different about you, Stern."

"I cut my hair."

"No, you didn't. But something's off about you."

"I'll make you a list."

He led her into the hall and waved the coroner staff through to the office, where they'd zip Marjorie Stephen into a body bag and wheel her away. Alex wondered if they'd close her eyes first.

"Tell me what you find in the library," Turner said at the elevator.

"Send me the tox report," Alex replied. "That would be the likeliest link to the societies. But you're right. It's probably nothing except a waste of my night."

Before the doors could close, Turner shoved his hand in and they pinged back open. "I've got it," he said. "You always looked like you had trouble chasing you."

Alex jabbed the door-close button. "So?"

"Now you look like it caught up."

9

Last Summer

Alex touched down at LAX at 9 a.m. on Sunday. Michael Anselm and Lethe had sprung for first class, so she'd ordered two shots of gratis whiskey to knock herself out and slept through the flight. She dreamed of her last night at Ground Zero, Hellie lying cold beside her, the feel of the bat in her hand. This time, Len spoke before she took her first swing.

Some doors don't stay locked, Alex.

And then he'd stopped talking.

She woke drenched in sweat, Los Angeles sun beating through the muddy glass of the airplane window.

It was too hot to wear a hoodie, but just in case Eitan was watching arrivals, she put it on, zipped it up, and caught a cab to the 7-Eleven near her mom's apartment. The bill ran her nearly one hundred bucks. The city looked hazy and bleak, the dull yellow-gray of an overcooked yolk.

She bought an iced coffee and Doritos, and set up about a half block away from the apartment. She wanted to see her mother, make sure she was okay. She had thought about just knocking on the door, but Mira would panic if she showed up unannounced. And how would Alex explain where she'd gotten the money to fly home?

She still felt a pang when she saw her mother's friend Andrea at the intercom. A minute later, Mira emerged in yoga pants and an oversized T-shirt emblazoned with an ornate hamsa, reusable shopping bags slung over her shoulder. They strode off together, arms and legs pumping in a power walk, and Alex followed for a while. She knew they were headed to the farmers' market, where they'd buy bone broth or spirulina or organic alfalfa. Her mother looked happy and golden, her blond hair freshly highlighted, her soft arms tanned. She looked like a stranger. The Mira Alex knew lived in a constant state of worry for her angry, crazy daughter. This woman's daughter went to Yale. She had a summer job. She texted photos of her roommates and new spring flowers and noodle bowls.

Alex sat down on a bench at the edge of the park, and watched her mother and Andrea disappear into the white tents of the market. She felt breathless and teary and like she wanted to hit something. Mira had been a crap mother, too caught up in her own storms to be any kind of an anchor. For a while Alex had hated her, and some part of her still did. She hadn't been born with her mother's gift for forgiving or forgetting. She didn't have Mira's sunshine hair and soft blue eyes, her love for peace, her bookshelves lined with ways to be kinder, more empathetic, a gentler being in the world, a force for good. The awful truth was that if she could have stopped loving her mother, she would have. She would have let Eitan make his threats and stayed away forever. But she couldn't shake the habit of loving Mira, and she couldn't untangle the longing she felt for the mother she might have had from the desire to protect the one she did have.

She called Eitan. He didn't answer, but a minute later she received a text.

Come after 10 tonight.

I could come now. That felt safer than *You said lunch, you manipulative asshole.*

The minutes ticked by. No answer. And there wouldn't be one. The king did what the king liked. But if he wanted to kill her, he didn't have a reason to wait for nightfall. That was almost reassuring. So what was this? Some kind of trap? An attempt to pump Alex for information on Len or his cousin's death? Alex had to believe she could talk her way out of it. Eitan thought she was a junkie, a joke, and as long as he didn't take her seriously, she was safe.

Alex sat watching the market a while longer, then hopped a bus down Ventura Boulevard. She told herself she was just killing time, but it didn't stop her from getting off at her old stop, or walking the old route to Ground Zero. Why? She hadn't been back since she'd been taken away in an ambulance, and she wasn't sure she was ready to see that ugly old apartment building with its stained stucco and its sad balconies looking out at nothing.

But it was gone, not a scrap or sign of it left, just a big dirt hole and a lot of rebar going up for whatever new thing would replace it, all of it surrounded by a chain-link fence.

It made sense. No one wanted to rent an apartment where a multiple murder had taken place. A crime that was still unsolved. And no one was going to put up a monument here or even one of those flimsy white crosses surrounded by cheap flowers and stuffed animals and handwritten notes. Nobody cared about the people who had died here. Criminals. Dealers. Losers.

Alex wished she'd brought something pretty for Hellie, a rose or some shitty grocery store carnations or one of the cards from Hellie's old tarot deck. The Star. The Sun. Hellie had been both of those things.

Had she expected to find her here? A Gray haunting this miserable spot? No. If Hellie came back through the Veil, she would go to the ocean, to the boardwalk, drawn by the clatter of skateboards and syrupy snow cones, the sweet clouds of heat coming off those big drums of kettle corn, couples kissing at the tattoo parlor, surfers daring the water. Alex was tempted to go look for her, to spend the afternoon in Venice, heart leaping after every blond head. It would be a kind of penance.

"I should have found a way to save us both," she said to no one. She stood sweating in the sun for as long as she could bear it, and then walked back to the bus stop. This whole town felt like a graveyard.

Alex spent her remaining hours up at the Getty, watching the sun set through the smog, eating a stack of chocolate chip cookies from the café. She made herself walk through the galleries because she felt she should. There was a Gérôme exhibit up. She'd never heard of him, but she read the typed descriptions beside each painting and stood for a long time in front of *The Grief of the Pasha*, looking at the tiger's dead body laid gently on a bed of flowers, and thinking about the hole where Ground Zero had been.

A little before ten, she had a car take her up to Eitan's house on Mulholland. She could see the rush of the 405 below, red blood cells, white blood cells, a flood of tiny lights. She might die here tonight and no one would know.

"You want me to wait?" the driver asked when they reached the security gate.

"I'm good." Maybe if she said it enough times it would be true.

She thought about just hopping the fence, but Eitan had dogs. She thought about texting Dawes so that someone would know she'd been here. But what was the point? Was Dawes going to avenge her? Would Turner pull a few strings, get someone to look into her case, have Eitan brought in for questioning with one of his expensive lawyers?

Alex was about to press the buzzer on the intercom when the gate began to open on silent hinges. She looked up and waved at the camera perched on the wall. *I'm harmless. I'm nobody and nothing worth bothering with.*

She walked up the long path, sneakers crunching on the gravel. She could hear the sound of the freeway far below. It was the sound of your own blood moving through your veins when you cupped your hands over your ears. Olive trees lined the path, and there were six cars parked in the circular driveway. A Bentley, a Range Rover, a Lambo, two Chevy Suburbans, and a bright yellow Mercedes.

The house was all lit up, its windows shining like gold bars, its pool a bright slab of turquoise. She glimpsed a few people gathered around the water. Men with careful hair dressed in untucked shirts and expensive jeans; long, liquid women who looked like they'd been poured from some expensive bottle, dressed in bikinis and scraps of silk that flowed around them as they walked. She could see a Gray in a slinky sequined dress beside them, her hair feathered, drawn by the quick thrill that came with cocaine or ketamine, the pulse of lust that always seemed to surround this house, whether twenty people were gathered or two hundred. Alex had only ever been to Eitan's big parties, noisy, messy events fueled by throbbing bass that shook the hillside, half-naked bodies in the pool, crates of Israeli vodka. She and Hellie would trail after Len as he exclaimed, every single time, as if he'd never seen the place before, "This is it. This is what we need a piece of. Shit. It's not like Eitan's that smart. Right place, right time."

But Eitan was smart. Smart enough not to trust Len with any real weight. Smart enough to know something wasn't right about Alex.

She glanced at the partiers by the pool and wondered if she should have dressed more nicely, not because she was invited but as some kind of show of respect. Too late now.

"Hi, Tzvi," she said to the bodyguard at the door. He wasn't built like a bouncer. He was tall but wiry, and there were rumors he was former Mossad. Alex had only seen him in action once, when someone's rowdy buddy had shot off a gun in the middle of a party. Tzvi had the gun out of his hands and the guy out the door while the sound of the bullet was still ricocheting off the hillside. Later she found out he'd broken the guy's arm in two places.

Tzvi bobbed his chin at her and gestured for her to raise her arms. She endured the pat-down—swift and efficient, no titty grabs or slow squeezes like you got from some of Eitan's staff—and followed the bodyguard into the house. Eitan's place was all marble floors, chandeliers, high echoing ceilings. Things that had once meant wealth to Alex, luxury, a trove of treasures costly and desirable. But Yale had made her a snob. Now the gold, the recessed lighting, the veined marble just seemed showy and crass. They screamed new money.

Eitan was seated on a big white leather couch, R&B filtering through the enormous glass doors from outside.

"Alex!" he said warmly. "You take me by surprise. I wasn't sure you would come."

"Why wouldn't I come?" she asked. Harmless, easy, a little rabbit not even worth catching.

He laughed. "True, true. I don't think you want me to come get you. Hungry? Thirsty?"

Always. "Not really."

"Alex," he chided, like a doting grandmother. "It's good to eat."

Fuck it. The Alex she needed him to believe in had no reason to be nervous. She had nothing to hide. "Sure, thank you."

"You are always polite. Not like Len. Alitza made pie." He waved to another armed man, who disappeared into the kitchen.

"How is Alitza?" She was Eitan's cook, and she'd never seemed to approve of any of what went on at his house.

Eitan shrugged. "Always she complains. I buy her . . . what is it? Disney Annual Pass. She goes every week now."

The guard returned with a huge slice of cherry pie, topped with a scoop of vanilla ice cream.

Through the glass door, Alex could see the glittery Gray in her slinky dress gyrating on the dance floor, hands raised over her head, her phantom body pressed against oblivious partiers.

Alex made herself take a bit of pie.

"Jesus," she muttered, her mouth still full. "This might be the best thing I've ever eaten."

"I know," said Eitan. "This is why I keep her." For a while, Eitan watched her eat. When the silence was too much, Alex set the plate on the big glass coffee table, wiped her mouth.

"I thought you would be dead by now," he said.

It wasn't a bad bet.

"I thought you die of overdose," he continued. "Or maybe you meet another bad boyfriend?"

That did sound convincing. "Yeah, I met someone. He's nice. We're going to move to the East Coast."

"New York?"

"We'll see."

"Very expensive. Even Queens is expensive now. I never find the men who kill Ariel. I never even hear a whisper. A night like that doesn't happen without talk. I listen. I ask everyone else to listen. Nothing."

"Sorry to hear that."

Again Eitan shrugged. "Strange, you know? Because is not a clean crime. Is ugly. Amateur. People like this, they don't cover their tracks."

"I don't know what happened that night," Alex said. "If I did, I wouldn't be protecting the people who killed my friends."

"Was Len your friend?"

The question startled her. "Something like that."

"I don't think so." He gestured to the backyard. "These are not my friends. They like my food, my house, my drugs. Vampires. You know, like the Tom Petty song?"

"Sure."

"I love that song." He touched a few buttons on his phone and the strumming of a guitar filled the room. "Tzvi rolls his eyes." Alex glanced over her shoulder at the stone-faced bodyguard. "He thinks I need new music. But I like it. I don't think Len was your friend."

Alex had spent years of her life with Len, lived with him, slept with him, run errands for him, run drugs for him. She'd stolen and shoplifted for him, fucked strangers for him. She'd let him fuck her even when she hadn't wanted to be fucked. He'd never made her come, not once, but he'd made her laugh on occasion, which might be worth more. She was glad he was dead, and she'd never bothered to ask where he was buried or even if his parents had come to get the body. She didn't feel guilt or remorse or any of the things she was supposed to feel for a friend.

"Maybe not," Alex conceded.

"Good," Eitan said, as if he was her therapist and they'd made some kind of breakthrough. "The problem with the police is they only look—" He held his hand up in front of his face. "Right there. Only what's expected. So they check the traffic cameras, look for cars. Who comes to a house to do a crime like this walking?" He made his fingers scissor back and forth, a headless man on a stroll across nothing. "On foot. Stupid to think about it. But there's such a thing as a wise fool."

Sophomore. From the Greek *sophos* meaning wise, and *moros* meaning fool. A little joke one of her professors had made. Alex stayed quiet.

"So I think, why not look. What can it hurt?"

Quite a bit, Alex suspected. Did Eitan know she'd killed Ariel? Had he really brought her here to even the score? And had she walked right up to his house like an ass?

"You know the pawn shop on Vanowen?"

Alex knew it. All Valley Pawn and Trading. She'd pawned her grandfather's kiddush cup there when she was desperate for cash.

"They have a camera on the sidewalk out front all the time," said Eitan. "They don't look at the footage if there's no trouble. But I had trouble. Ariel had trouble. So I look."

He held out his phone. Alex knew what she was going to see, but she took it anyway.

The sidewalk was faintly green, the street nearly empty of cars and black as a river. A girl crossed the frame. She wore nothing but a tank top and underwear, and she had something clutched in her hands. Alex knew it was the broken remnants of Len's wooden bat. The one she'd used to kill him, and Betcha, and Corker, and Cam. And Eitan's cousin Ariel.

She slid her finger over the screen, rewinding. She felt Eitan watching her, calculating, but Alex couldn't stop staring at the girl on the screen. She seemed too bright, like she was glowing, her eyes strange in the green light of a night vision camera. *Hellie was with me*, she thought. *Inside me.* On that last night, Hellie had kept her strong, helped her get rid of the evidence, made her wash herself clean in the Los Angeles River. Hellie had protected her to the end.

"Little girl," said Eitan. "So much blood."

There was no point denying it was her on the video. "I was high. I don't remember any of—"

She didn't get the last word out. A meaty arm clamped across her throat, cutting off her air. Tzvi.

Alex tried to pry his arm free, clawing at the bodyguard's skin. She felt herself lifted off the couch as her feet kicked out at nothing. She couldn't even scream. She saw Eitan on the white cushions, watching her with calm interest, the partiers through the window, gathered around the pool, oblivious. The dead girl in sequins was still dancing.

Alex didn't think. Her hand shot out as her mind reached for the Gray, demanding her strength. Her mouth flooded with the taste of cigarettes and cherry lip gloss, the back of her throat itched as if she'd just snorted a bump. She could smell perfume and sweat. Power burst through her.

Alex seized Tzvi's arm and squeezed. He grunted in surprise. She felt his bones bend beneath her palms. He released her and Alex tumbled backward over the couch. She scrambled to her feet and grabbed a big lump of sculpture from the side table, swung. But he was fast, and no matter the strength inside her she was untrained. All she had was brute force. He dodged the blow easily, and the momentum carried the sculpture into the wall, hitting with so much force it plunged straight through. She felt Tzvi's fist connect with her gut, knocking the wind from her. Alex went to one knee and grabbed Tzvi's leg, using the Gray's strength to knock him off his feet.

"Enough, enough," shouted Eitan, clapping his hands.

Instantly Tzvi backed away, hands up as if gentling a wild animal, eyes narrowed. Alex crouched on the floor, ready to run, struggling for breath. She could see marks from her fingers on his forearm, already starting to bruise.

Eitan was still sitting on the couch, but now he was smiling. "When I saw what happen to Ariel, I think, it's impossible. This little girl could never do so much damage."

And Alex understood she'd made a terrible mistake. He hadn't brought her here to kill her. If he had, Tzvi would have used a knife or a garrote instead of his hands. He would have attacked to kill instead of just punching her in the stomach.

"So," said Eitan. "Now I know better. You and I have business, Alex Stern."

It had all been a game. No, an audition. She'd been looking for a trap, just not the one he'd had waiting for her. And she'd walked right into it. The wise fool.

10

October

Alex took a car the short distance back to the dorms from the crime scene. She probably should have walked, but the area around the med school wasn't safe and she was too tired for a tussle.

By the time she got washed up and tucked into bed, it was 3 a.m. Mercy was fast asleep, and Alex was glad she didn't have to answer any questions. She slept and dreamed she was climbing the stairs at Black Elm. She entered the ballroom, slid past the barrier of the golden circle, its warmth a comfort, like slipping into a hot bath. Darlington was waiting for her.

Alex didn't remember waking. One moment she was asleep and standing inside the circle of protection with Darlington; the next she was alone beneath an autumn sky at the door to Black Elm. At first she thought she was still dreaming. The house was dark except for the gold light bleeding from beneath the boarded windows on the second floor. She could hear the wind in the trees, shaking the leaves, a warning whisper, *Summer is over, summer is over.*

She looked down at her feet. They were covered in mud and blood.

Am I here, or am I dreaming? She'd gone back to her dorm room after she'd left Turner at the psych department, brushed her teeth, climbed into bed. Maybe she was still there now.

But her feet *hurt.* Her arms had broken out in gooseflesh. She was wearing nothing but the shorts and tank top she slept in.

Real awareness crept in. She was cold, alone, and in the dark. She had *walked* here. Barefoot. No phone. No money.

She had never sleepwalked in her life.

Alex put her hand to the kitchen door. She could see herself reflected in the glass, bone white against the dark. She didn't want to go in. She didn't want to walk up those stairs. That was a lie. She could feel the dream pulling at her. She'd been standing with Darlington inside the golden circle. She wanted to be there now.

She looked up at the windows. Did he know she was here? Did he want her here?

"For fuck's sake," she said, her voice too loud, dying too abruptly in the woods that surrounded the house, as if no sound could be permitted to carry to the outside world.

She needed to get back to the dorms. She could try to find a Gray to summon and use its strength to get her home, but her feet already hurt like hell. Besides, after that little incident at Oddman's place, she wasn't sure she wanted to invite another Gray in. She could try limping to a gas station. Or she could break a window and use the landline to call Dawes. Assuming the landline worked.

Then she remembered: the cameras. Dawes would have gotten an alert someone was at the door. She waved frantically at the doorbell, feeling like a fool. "Dawes," she said, "are you there?"

"Alex?"

Alex placed her head against the cold stone. She'd never been more grateful to hear Dawes's voice. "I think I sleepwalked. Can you come get me?"

"You *walked* to Black Elm?"

"I know. And I'm half naked and freezing my ass off."

"There's a key under the hydrangea pot. Get in and warm up. I'll be there as soon as I can."

"Okay," said Alex. "Thanks."

She tilted the pot up, grabbed the key. And then she was standing in the dining room.

She didn't remember unlocking the door or passing through the kitchen. She hadn't even turned the light on. An old sheet had been placed over the dining room table to keep it from collecting dust. She snatched it up and wound it around her body, desperate for warmth.

Wait for Dawes. She had every intention of doing just that, but she'd also had every intention of staying in the kitchen by the stove.

She felt as if she were still asleep, still dreaming, as if there had been no key, no conversation with Dawes. Her feet wanted to move. The house had opened to her because he was waiting.

Goddamn it, Darlington. Alex clutched the banister. She was at the base of the stairs. She looked back and saw the dark stretch of the living room, the windows to the garden beyond. She tried to anchor herself to the banister with both hands, but she was a bad marionette, yanking at her strings. She had to keep climbing. Up the stairs and down the hallway to the ballroom. There were no carpets to soften her steps.

She knew of only one Gray who frequented Black Elm. An old man, his bathrobe forever half open, a cigarette hanging from his lips. He came and went, as if he couldn't decide whether or not to stay, and right now he was nowhere to be found. She had no salt in her pockets, no graveyard dust, no protection at all.

She willed herself not to push the door open, but she did anyway. She hooked her fingers over the door jamb. "Dawes!" she shouted.

But Dawes wasn't at Black Elm yet. No one was in the old house except for Alex, and the demon that had once been Darlington was staring at her from the center of the circle with bright golden eyes.

He was still sitting cross-legged, hands on his knees, palms down. But now his eyes were open and they glowed with the same golden light as the markings on his skin.

"Stern."

The shock of his voice was enough to loosen her grip on the door. But she didn't stumble forward. Whatever force he'd been using to control her had abated.

"What the hell was that?"

"Good afternoon to you too, Stern. Or is it morning? Hard to tell in here."

Alex had to force herself to stay still, not to run, not to weep. That voice. It was *Darlington*. Fully human, fully him. It had only the faintest echo, as if he were speaking from the depths of a cave.

"It's the middle of the night," she managed, her voice rough. "I'm not sure what time."

"I'd like you to bring me some books, if you would."

"Books?"

"Yes, I'm bored. I realize that speaks a lazy mind, but . . ." He shrugged lightly, the markings on his body glimmering.

"Darlington . . . You know you're naked, right?"

Like some perverse statue, hands resting on knees, horns alight, cock erect and glowing.

"I'm a demon, not a dullard, Stern. But my dignity has long since been left in tatters. And you didn't dress for the occasion either."

Alex clutched the sheet tighter. "Which books do you want?"

"You choose."

"Is that why you dragged me up here?"

"I didn't drag you anywhere."

"I didn't walk barefoot across New Haven in the dead of night for kicks. I was compelled." But that wasn't quite right. It hadn't felt like the coin of compulsion or Astrumsalinas or any of the other strange magic she'd encountered. It had felt deeper.

"Interesting," he said in a voice that didn't sound interested at all.

Alex backed away, wondering at every moment if her feet would simply stop obeying and she'd be forced to stay. Once she was in the hallway, she took a moment to catch her breath.

It's him. He's alive.

And he wasn't angry. Unless this was some kind of con. He hadn't come back bent on revenge or ready to punish Alex for failing him. But what was this? What had brought her here?

She considered making a run for it. Dawes would be here soon. She might be turning onto this street right now. But what was Alex going to say when she came running out of the house? *The monster demanded that I do his bidding! He bade me select reading material for him!*

If she was honest, she didn't want to go. She didn't want to leave him. She wanted to know what came next.

She took the stairs up to the third floor and Darlington's tiny, round tower room. She hadn't been here since the night of the new moon ritual, when she'd been searching for information on the Bridegroom's death.

She peered out the window. The driveway curved into the trees, the road invisible from here. No sign of Dawes. She wasn't sure if she was worried or glad.

But choosing reading material for Darlington was its own nightmare assignment. What might entertain a demon with a taste for the finer things? She finally opted for a book on modernism in urban planning, a spiral-bound biography of Bertram Goodhue, and a paperback copy of *Dogsbody* by Diana Wynne Jones.

"Aren't these just going to catch fire?" she asked when she returned to the ballroom.

"Try one."

Alex put the paperback on the floor and gave it a hard shove. It slid through the barrier, seemingly unharmed.

Darlington's hand shot out and captured the book. The collar at his neck glinted, the garnets like red eyes, watching.

"That's quite a piece of jewelry," she said. It was really too big to be called a collar. It stretched from his throat out to his shoulders, like something a pharaoh might wear.

"The yoke. Thinking of pawning it?"

"It's not doing you much good."

He ran a fond hand over the paperback. The letters seemed to shimmer and change to unfamiliar symbols. "Would that I might make thee love books more than thy mother," he murmured.

His fingers were tipped in golden claws, and a memory came to her, the feeling of his body wrapped around hers. *I will serve you 'til the end of days.*

She shivered despite the heat of the room.

"Why did that work?" she asked. "Why didn't it burn?"

"Stories exist in all worlds. They are immutable. Like gold."

She wasn't sure what to make of that. She slid the rest of the books across the boundary of the circle.

"Okay?" she asked. Her whole body was humming, trapped between the desire to run and the hunger to remain. It felt dangerous to stand in this room, alone with him, this person who wasn't quite a person, this creature she knew and didn't know.

Darlington perused the titles. "These will do for now. Though *Fire and Hemlock* seems more apropos than *Dogsbody*. Here," he said. "Catch."

He tossed the paperback in the air. Without thinking, Alex reached for it, realizing too late that she was going to breach the circle. She hissed as her outstretched arm struck the boundary.

But nothing happened. The book landed in her palm with a loud smack. Alex stared at it, at her arm on the other side of that golden veil.

Why hadn't she burned the way Dawes had?

Her tattoos had changed. They glowed golden and they seemed to be alive: the Wheel spinning; the lion atop it prowling over her forearm; the peonies blossoming, then losing their petals, then blooming once more. She drew her hand back, dropping the book.

"What the fuck?"

The demon was staring at her, and Alex rocked back on her heels, the reality of what had happened sinking in. If she could get in, then could he . . .

"I can't get out," he said.

"Prove it."

"I don't think that would be wise."

"Why not?"

A small furrow formed between his brows, and she felt a pinch in her heart. Despite the horns, the markings, that was Darlington.

"Because every time I try to breach the circle, I feel a little less human."

"What *are* you, Darlington?"

"What are *you*, Wheelwalker?"

The word hit Alex like a hard slap. How did he know? What did he know? Belbalm had called her Wheelwalker. She'd claimed to be one too, but Alex hadn't found any mention of their kind in Lethe's collection.

"How do you know that word?" she asked.

"Sandow." That name emerged as a growl that shook the floor.

"You saw him . . . behind the Veil?"

Darlington looked at her with those strange golden eyes.

"Are you afraid to say it, Stern? You know where I've been, far beyond the borderlands, far beyond the Veil. My host was happy to welcome Sandow to his realm, a murderer who killed for gain. Greed is a sin in every language." Two expressions flickered across his face, at war, one of distaste, the other of almost obscene satisfaction. Some part of him had liked punishing Sandow. And some part of him was disgusted by it.

"A little revenge can be good for the soul, Darlington."

"Not a word to bandy about casually, Stern."

She didn't think he meant *revenge*.

"Alex?" Dawes's voice floated up from the bottom floor.

"It's best if she doesn't find you here."

"What is this, Darlington?" Alex whispered. "How do we help you? How do we get you out?"

"Find the Gauntlet."

"Believe me, we're trying. You don't have any idea where it is?"

"Would that I did," he said, and there was desperation in his voice, even as he released a laugh that raised the hair on Alex's arms. "But I am just a man, heir to nothing. Find the Gauntlet, make the descent. I can't exist between two worlds for long. Eventually the tether will snap."

"And you'll be trapped in hell forever?"

Again his expression seem to flicker. Hopelessness. Anticipation. "Or whatever I am will be unleashed upon the world." He was close to the edge of the circle now. Alex hadn't seen him move, hadn't even seen him stand. "I have appetites, Stern. They are not entirely . . . wholesome."

His clawed fingertips pierced the golden circle, and Alex stumbled backward, a high-pitched yelp emerging from her lips.

Darlington seemed to shift. He was taller, broader; his horns looked sharper. He had fangs. *I feel a little less human.*

Then he seemed to yank himself back to the center of the circle. He was sitting once more, hands on knees, as if he'd never moved. Maybe he really was meditating, trying to keep his demon self in check.

"Find the Gauntlet, make the descent. Come get me, Stern." He paused then, and his golden eyes flashed open. "Please."

That word, raw and human, was all she could bear. Alex ran, down the hall, down the steps. She slammed into Dawes at the foot of the stairs.

"Alex!" Dawes cried as they fought to keep their balance.

"Come on," Alex said, dragging Dawes back through the house.

"What happened?" Dawes was saying as she let herself be pulled along. "You shouldn't have gone up there—"

"I know."

"We can't be sure what we're dealing—"

"I know, Dawes. Just get me out of here and I'll explain everything."

Alex threw open the kitchen door, grateful for the clean burst of cold air. She could hear Belbalm's voice: *All worlds are open to us. If we are bold enough to enter.* Did that mean the underworld too? She had passed through the boundary unscathed, just like in the dream. What would happen if she entered the circle?

Alex grunted and stumbled when her feet hit the gravel.

Dawes caught her by the elbow.

"Alex, *slow down*. Here." She held up soft white tube socks and a pair of Tevas. "I brought these for you. They're too big, but better than going barefoot."

Alex sat down on the doormat to pull on the socks and shoes.

She wasn't going back inside. Her head was buzzing. Her body felt alien.

"What were you doing up there?" Dawes asked.

Alex could hear the accusation in her voice and she didn't quite know how to reply. She thought about lying, but there was too much to explain. Like how she'd ended up at Black Elm in her pajamas.

"I woke up here," she said, trembling in the cold now that her panic had eased. "I dreamed . . . I dreamed I was here and then I was."

"You sleepwalked?"

"I guess so. And then it was like I was still sleepwalking. I don't quite know how I ended up in the ballroom. But . . . he talked."

"He talked to you?" Dawes's voice was too loud.

"Yeah."

"I see." Dawes seemed to close in on herself, the concerned friend receding, the mother hen emerging. "Let's get you warm."

Alex let herself be helped to her feet and shepherded into the car, where Dawes cranked the heater up, the faint smell of brimstone emerging as it always had since the night of the new moon ritual. Dawes rested her hands on the wheel as if making a decision.

Then she put the car into gear and they were driving back toward campus. The streets were nearly empty, and Alex wondered who had seen her walking, if anyone had stopped to ask if she needed help, a half-naked girl, barefoot and wandering in the dark, just like that night with Hellie.

It was only once they were back at Il Bastone, with Alex's feet coated in healing balm and propped on a towel-covered cushion, a cup of tea by her side, that Dawes sat down, opened her notebook, and said, "Okay, tell me."

Alex had expected more emotion, lip chewing, maybe tears. But Dawes was Oculus now, in research mode, ready to document and investigate, and Alex was grateful for it.

"He said he doesn't have much time," Alex began, then did her best to explain the rest, that he had nearly breached the circle, that he'd begged them to find the Gauntlet, but that he didn't know where it was.

Dawes made a small humming noise.

"He'd have no reason not to tell us," said Alex.

"He might not be able to. It depends . . . it depends how much demon he's become. Demons love puzzles, remember? They never move in a straight line."

"He talked about Sandow too. He saw him on the other side. He said his host had welcomed him."

"That's what I mean," said Dawes. "He could have named his host, whatever god or demon or hellbeast he's in service to, but he didn't. What did he say about the host?"

"Nothing. Just that Sandow had killed for gain. He said greed was a sin in any language."

"So Darlington may be bound to Mammon or Plutus or Gullveig or some other god of greed. That might help us if we can figure out where the Gauntlet is and how to reveal it. What else?"

"Nothing. He wanted books and I brought him books. He said he was bored."

"That's it?"

"That's it. He said something about loving books more than his mother."

Dawes's lips softened in a smile. "It's an Egyptian proverb. Suits him well."

Egyptian. Alex sat up straighter, her feet sliding from the pillow. Dawes yelped. "Please don't get that on the rug!"

"When the books didn't burn, he said stories were immutable."

"So?" Dawes asked, bustling into the kitchen for a towel.

Alex remembered walking beneath the entry to Sterling with Darlington. There were four stone scribes over the entrance. One of them was Egyptian.

"When was Sterling Library built?"

"1931, I think?" Dawes said from the kitchen. "People really hated it at the time. I think the term used was *cathedral orgy*. They said it looked too much like . . ." Dawes halted in the doorway, wet towel in her hands. "They said it looked like a church."

"Hallowed ground."

She and Dawes had taken what long-dead Bunchy said too literally. They'd been looking in the wrong places.

Dawes drifted slowly back into the parlor, the towel still dripping in her hands. "John Sterling donated the money for the library." She sat down. "He was in Skull and Bones."

"That doesn't mean much," Alex said cautiously. "There are a lot of rich guys in Skull and Bones."

Dawes nodded, still slow, as if she were underwater. "The architect died suddenly and someone else had to take over."

Alex waited.

"James Gamble Rogers took the job. He was in Scroll and Key. *Punter* is another word for a gambler."

Johnny and Punter's friends built a Gauntlet. On hallowed ground.

Dawes was clutching the towel with both hands now, as if it were a microphone she was about to sing into. "*Would that I might make thee love books more than thy mother.* That quote is above the entry, above the scribe. It's written in hieroglyphs."

Stories were immutable. And what was a library but a house full of stories?

"It's Sterling," Alex said. "The library is the portal to hell."

Erected in memory of

JOHN WILLIAM STERLING

BORN 12 MAY 1844

DIED 5 JULY 1918

B.A. 1864 : M.A. 1874

LL.D. 1893 : LAWYER

LOYAL FRIEND

TRUSTED ADVISER

AGGRESSIVE LEADER

DEVOTED ALUMNUS

James Gamble Rogers Architect

—Memorial inscription, entrance
to Sterling Memorial Library

If I must be a prisoner I would desire to have no other prison than that library.

—James I, engraved above the entrance to the
exhibition corridor of Sterling Memorial Library

11

Alex had every intention of helping Dawes research, but the next thing she knew she was waking up in the parlor at Il Bastone, morning light drifting through the windows. A copy of the 1931 *Yale Gazette* article detailing Sterling's decoration rested open on her chest as though she'd tried to use the book to tuck herself in.

She felt warm and easy, as if she'd imagined everything at Black Elm, and this morning could just be simple, an ordinary Sunday. She touched her hand to the floorboards and they seemed to hum.

"Did you do that?" she asked Il Bastone, staring up at the coffered ceiling and the pendant lamp that hung high above her from a brass chain. The bulb flickered softly behind its frosted glass globe. The house had known she needed rest. It was looking out for her. At least, that was what it felt like and maybe what Alex needed to believe.

Dawes had left a note on the coffee table: *Going to Beinecke. Breakfast on the counter. Call me when you're up. Bad news.*

When wasn't it bad news? When was Dawes going to leave her a note that said, *All good. Go work on that paper so you don't fall further behind. Left you fresh scones and a couple of puppies?*

Alex needed to get home, but she was famished and it would be a shame to waste a breakfast, so she shuffled into the kitchen in Dawes's giant Tevas.

"Shit," she said, when she saw the plates of pancakes, the vat of scrambled eggs strewn with chives, heaps of bacon, hollandaise warm in its flowered pitcher, and, yes, a pile of strawberry scones. There was enough food to feed an entire a cappella group if they would stop humming for a minute. Dawes cooked to soothe herself and that meant the news was very bad indeed.

Alex piled her plate with two of everything and called Dawes, but she didn't answer. *You're freaking me out*, she texted. *And everything is fucking delicious.*

When she was done, she filled a go-cup with coffee and tucked three chocolate chip pancakes into a plastic bag for later. She thought about making a detour to the Lethe library to see if the Albemarle Book could find anything on Turner's Bible quote or poisons that aged their victims, but that would have to wait. She needed a hot shower and some real clothes. On her way out, she patted the door jamb and briefly wondered if she was making friends with a house or losing her mind.

She had crossed campus and was halfway up the stairs to her room at JE when her phone finally buzzed.

Sterling at noon. We need four murderers.

Alex stared at Dawes's message and replied, *I'll stop at the store. Should I get half a dozen to be safe?*

Her phone rang. "This isn't a joke."

"Why four, Dawes?"

"To get into hell. I think that's why Darlington mentioned Sandow. He was giving us directions. It takes four people for the ritual once the Gauntlet is activated, four pilgrims for the four compass points."

"Do we really have to—"

"You saw what happened when we tried to cut corners at Scroll and Key. I'm not going to blow up the library. And I think . . ."

Dawes's voice trailed off.

"And?" Alex prompted, all the optimism of the morning bleeding out of her.

"If we get this wrong, I don't think we're coming back."

Alex leaned against the wall, listening to the echo of voices up and down the stone stairwell, the sounds of the college waking, the ancient pipes gurgling with water, someone singing an old song about

Bette Davis's eyes. She couldn't pretend to be surprised. Talk of Gauntlets and boys named Bunchy made it all feel like a game and that was the danger. Power could become too easy. There were too many opportunities to try just because you could.

"I get it, Dawes. But we're in it now." From the moment they'd met up in the cemetery and Alex had floated her wild theory of the gentleman demon, they'd known they couldn't turn their backs on the chance that Darlington was still alive. But the stakes were different than they had been last spring. She remembered her dream, Len saying, *Some doors don't stay locked.* Well, they'd blown this door wide open when they'd botched that ritual at Scroll and Key, and now something half man, half monster was trapped in the ballroom at Black Elm. "We save him," she said. "And if we can't save him, we stop him."

"What . . . what does that mean?" Dawes asked, her fear like a spotlight searching for answers.

It meant that if they couldn't free Darlington, they couldn't risk freeing the demon, and that might mean destroying them both. *Whatever I am will be unleashed upon the world.* But Dawes wasn't ready to hear that.

"I'll see you at Sterling," Alex said, and hung up.

She trudged up the remaining stairs, feeling tired all over again. Maybe she could nap before she met Dawes at the library. She pushed open the door to their common room expecting to see Mercy curled up in the recliner with her laptop and a cup of tea. But Mercy was sitting upright on the couch, back straight, in her hyacinth robe—directly across from Michelle Alameddine. Darlington's mentor, his Virgil.

Alex hadn't seen her since Michelle had practically fled their summer research session. She was wearing a plaid dress, a cardigan, and woven flats, her thick hair bound in a braid, a jaunty scarf tied at her neck. She looked quality. She looked like a grown-up.

"Hey," Alex said, her surprise rendering her incapable of much more. "I . . . How long have you been waiting?"

"Not long, but I have a train to make. *What* are you wearing?"

Alex had forgotten she was still in her pajama shorts, a Lethe sweatshirt, and Dawes's bunchy socks and Tevas. "Let me change."

Who is she? Mercy mouthed as Alex hurried into their bedroom. But that was not a conversation Alex intended to have in mime.

She shut the door behind her and shoved open the window, letting the crisp morning air clear her head. Just like that, summer had gone. She yanked on black jeans and a black Henley, traded the Tevas for her boots, and rubbed some toothpaste over her teeth.

"Is there somewhere we can talk?" Michelle asked when Alex emerged from the bedroom.

"I can give you guys privacy," Mercy offered.

"No," said Alex. She wasn't going to kick Mercy out of their room. "Come on."

She led Michelle downstairs. She'd thought they could talk in the JE library, but there were already people staking out tables.

"Let's go to the sculpture garden," Michelle suggested, pushing through the doors. Alex sometimes forgot it was here, an empty sprawl of gravel and the occasional art installation that sat just outside the reading room. It wasn't much to look at, a pocket of quiet and trees sandwiched between buildings.

"So you fucked that up," Michelle said. She sat down on a bench and crossed her arms. "I told you not to try it."

"People tell me that a lot. Anselm called you?"

"He wanted to know if you and Dawes had reached out to me, if you were still trying to get Darlington back."

"How did he—"

"We were spotted together at the funeral. And I was Darlington's Virgil."

"And?" Alex asked.

"I didn't . . . rat you out."

She sounded like she was quoting an episode of *Law & Order*.

"But you're not going to help us."

"Help you with what?" Michelle asked.

Alex hesitated. Anything she said to Michelle might make it straight back to Michael Anselm. But Darlington had considered

Michelle one of Lethe's best. She might still be able to help them, even if she wasn't willing to get down in the dirt.

"We found the Gauntlet."

Michelle sat up straighter. "Darlington was right?"

Alex couldn't help smiling. "Of course he was. The Gauntlet is real and it's here on campus. We can—"

But Michelle held up a hand. "Don't tell me. I don't want to know."

"But—"

"Alex, I came to Yale on a scholarship. Lethe knew that. It's part of what made me appealing to them. I needed their money and I was happy to do what they asked. My Virgil was Jason Barclay Cartwright, and he was lazy because he could afford to be. I couldn't. You can't either. I want you to think about what this could cost you."

Alex had. But that didn't change the math. "I owe him."

"Well, I don't."

Simple enough. "I thought you liked Darlington."

"I did. He was a good kid." She was only three years older, but that was how Michelle saw him, the little boy playing knight. "He wanted to believe."

"In what?"

"In everything. Has Dawes told you what you're in for? What this kind of ritual entails?"

"She mentioned we're going to need four murderers." Well, *two more* murderers, since she and Dawes had half of that particular equation covered.

"That's only the beginning. The Gauntlet isn't some magic portal. You don't just walk through it. You're going to have to die to make it to the underworld."

"I've died before," said Alex. "I made it to the borderlands. I'll make it back from this too."

Michelle shook her head. "You don't care, do you? You're just going to rush right at it."

I'm the Wheelwalker, Alex wanted to say. *It has to be me.* Except not even she knew what that meant. It sounded foolish, childish—

I'm special, I have a quest—when the truth was much closer to what Michelle had said. Of course Alex was going to just rush right at it. She was a cannonball. She wasn't good for much at rest, but give her a hard enough shove, let her build up enough momentum, and she'd punch a hole through anything.

"It's not that bad," Alex said. "Dying."

"I know." Michelle hesitated, then pulled up her sleeve, and Alex saw her tattoo for the first time. A semicolon. She knew that symbol.

"You tried to kill yourself."

Michelle nodded. "In high school. Lethe didn't know. Otherwise they never would have tapped me. Too much of a risk. I've been to the other side. I don't remember it, but I know this isn't hopping a bus, and I am never going back. Alex . . . I didn't come here to play Anselm's stooge. I came to warn you. Whatever is out there, on the other side of the Veil, it isn't just Grays."

Alex remembered the waters of the borderlands, the strange shapes she'd seen on the far shore, the way the current had yanked her off her feet. She thought of the force that had drawn her to Black Elm, that had wanted her in that room, maybe inside of that circle. "They tried to keep me there."

Michelle nodded. "Because they're hungry. Have you ever read *Kittscher's Daemonologie*?"

Of course she hadn't. "No, but I hear it's a real page-turner."

Michelle cast her eyes heavenward. "What Darlington must have made of you. Lethe has a copy. Before you do anything crazy, read it. Death isn't just a place you visit. I fought my way back once. I'm not going to risk it again."

Alex couldn't argue with that. Even Dawes had hesitations about what they were about to attempt, and Michelle had the right to live and be done with Lethe. It still made Alex angry, little-kid angry, don't-leave-me-here angry. She and Dawes weren't enough to take this on.

"I understand," she said, embarrassed by how sullen she sounded.

"I hope you do." Michelle sighed deeply, glad to be rid of whatever burden she'd been carrying. She closed her eyes and breathed in, scenting that first hint of fall. "This was one of Darlington's favorite spots."

"Is," Alex corrected.

Michelle's smile was soft and sad. It terrified Alex. *She thinks we're going to fail. She knows it.*

"Have you seen the plaque?" she asked.

Alex shook her head.

Michelle led her over to one of the window casements. "George Douglas Miller was a Bonesman. He had a whole plan for expanding the Skull and Bones tomb, building a dormitory." She pointed to the towers that loomed over the stairs that led to the sculpture garden. *Crenellated*, Alex could hear Darlington whisper. *Cod-medieval.* Alex had never noticed them before. "Those towers were from the old alumni hall. Miller had them moved here when Yale knocked it down in 1911, the first step in his grand vision. But he ran out of money. Or maybe he ran out of will."

She tapped a plaque at the base of the casement. It read: *The original part of Weir Hall, purchased by Yale University in 1917, was begun in 1911 by George Douglas Miller, B.A. 1870, in partial fulfillment of his vision "to build, in the heart of New Haven, a replica of an Oxford quadrangle."* But it was the second sentence that surprised Alex. *In accordance with his wishes, this tablet has been erected to commemorate his only son, Samuel Miller 1881–1883, who was born and died on these premises.*

"I never noticed it," Michelle continued. "I never knew about any of this until Darlington. I hope you bring him back, Alex. But just remember Lethe doesn't care about people like you and me. No one is looking out for us but us."

Alex traced her fingers over the letters. "Darlington was. He'd go to hell for me, for you, for anyone who needed saving."

"Alex," Michelle said, dusting off her skirt, "he'd go to hell just to take notes on the climate."

Alex hated the condescension in her voice, but Michelle wasn't wrong. Darlington had wanted to know everything, no matter the cost. She wondered if the creature he'd become felt the same.

"You came up on the train?" Alex asked.

"Yes, and I need to get back for dinner with my boyfriend's parents."

Perfectly sensible. But Alex had the feeling Michelle was holding something back. She waved as Michelle descended the stairs beneath the arch that would take her to High Street, where she'd catch a cab to the train station.

"That's me," said a voice beside Alex, and she had to fight not to react. The little Gray with crisp curls had perched in the window beside the plaque. "I'm glad they put my name on it."

Alex ignored him. She didn't want Grays to know she could hear their stories and complaints. It was bad enough having to listen to the living.

Mercy was waiting in the common room. She'd dressed in a pumpkin-colored sweater and a corduroy skirt, as if the barest suggestion of autumn in the air had signaled the need for a costume change. She had her laptop open but closed it when Alex came in.

"So, is this going to be like last year?" Mercy asked. "You disappearing and then nearly getting killed?"

Alex sat down in the recliner. "Yes to the first part . . . I hope not to the second part?"

"I like having you around."

"I like being around."

"Who was that anyway?"

Alex hesitated. "Who did she say she was?"

"A friend of your cousin's."

Lies came easy to Alex. They always had. She'd been lying since she'd learned she saw things other people didn't, since she'd understood how easy it was to slap the words *crazy* or *unstable* on a girl and make them stick. She could feel all those friendly lies ready to unfurl from her tongue, scarves from a cheap magician. That was what Lethe and the societies demanded. Secrecy. Loyalty.

Well, fuck them.

"Darlington isn't my cousin. And he isn't in Spain. And I need to talk to you about what happened last year."

Mercy fiddled with the laptop cord. "When you had a giant bite mark in your side and I had to call your mom?"

"No," Alex said. "I want to talk about what happened to you."

She wasn't sure how Mercy would react. She was ready to back off if she needed to.

Mercy set her computer aside, then said, "I'm hungry."

Alex hadn't expected that. "I can make you a Pop-Tart or . . ." She reached into her satchel and took out Dawes's chocolate chip pancakes.

"Do you just walk around with breakfast food in your bag?"

"Honestly? All the time."

Mercy ate most of a pancake and Alex made coffee for both of them, and then she started talking. About the societies, Darlington, the mess of their freshman year. Mercy's eyebrows rose slowly higher as Alex's story spilled out. Occasionally she would nod, but Alex wasn't sure if she was just encouraging her to continue or actually taking it all in.

Eventually Alex didn't so much stop as wind down, as if there just weren't enough words for all the secrets she'd been keeping. Everything around them felt too ordinary for a story like this. The sounds of doors opening and closing in the echoing stairwells, shouts from the courtyard, the rush of cars somewhere on York Street. Alex knew she was risking being late to meet Dawes, but she didn't want to look down at her phone.

"So," Mercy said slowly, "is that where you got the tattoos?"

Alex almost laughed. No one had mentioned her sleeves of peonies and snakes and stars that had suddenly appeared at the end of the school year. It was as if they hadn't been able to grasp that such a thing was possible, so their minds had made the necessary corrections.

"Not where I got them, but Darlington helped me hide them for a while."

"Using magic?" Mercy asked.

"Yup."

"Which is real."

"Yup."

"And super deadly."

"It is," said Alex.

"And kind of gross."

"Very gross."

"I prayed a lot this summer."

Alex tried not to show her surprise. "Did it help?"

"Some. I went to therapy too. I used this app and I talked to someone for a while, about what happened. It helped me stop thinking about it all the time. I tried talking to our pastor too. But I'm just not sorry Blake's dead."

"Should you be?"

Mercy laughed. "Alex! Yes. Forgiveness is supposed to be healing."

But Blake hadn't asked for grace. He hadn't asked for anything. He'd just moved through the world taking what he wanted until something got in his way.

"I don't know how to forgive," Alex admitted. "And I don't think I want to learn."

Mercy rubbed the hem of her sweater between her fingers, studying the weave as if it were a text to be translated. "Tell me how he died."

Alex did. She didn't talk about the new moon ritual or Darlington. She began with Blake breaking into Il Bastone, the fight, the way he'd controlled her, made her stay still while he beat her, the moment when Dawes had crushed his skull with the marble bust of Hiram Bingham III. She talked about the way Blake had wept, and how she'd discovered the coin of compulsion he'd clutched in his hand. He'd been under Dean Sandow's control when he tried to kill her.

Mercy kept her eyes on that bit of pumpkin-colored wool, fingers moving back and forth, back and forth. "It's not just that I'm not sorry . . ." she said at last. Her voice was low, shaking, almost a growl. "I'm glad he's dead. I'm glad he got to feel what it was like to be out of control, to be frightened. I'm . . . glad he died scared."

She looked up, her eyes full of tears. "Why am I like this? Why am I still so angry?"

"I don't know," said Alex. "But I'm like that too."

"I've gone through every moment that led up to the party so many times. What I wore, what I said. Why did he pick me that night? What did he see?"

Alex had no idea how to answer those questions. *Forgive yourself for going to the party. Forgive yourself for assuming the world isn't full of beasts at the door.* But she knew it was never that easy.

"He didn't see you at all," Alex said. "People like that . . . they don't see us. They just see opportunities. Something to grab." Michelle was right about that at least.

Mercy wiped the tears from her eyes. "You make it sound like shoplifting."

"A little."

"Don't lie to me again, okay?"

"I'll try." It was the best Alex could offer without lying all over again.

12

Mercy had peppered Alex with questions for the rest of the hour, all of them about magic and Lethe. It felt like an oral exam, but Alex figured Mercy was owed, and as she did her best to explain, she had to sit with the unpleasant truth that Mercy would have been a better candidate for Lethe. She was brilliant, she spoke fluent French, and she wasn't bad on Latin either. But she hadn't committed homicide, so Alex supposed that put her behind the curve on this assignment.

"Good luck," Mercy said when Alex left to meet Dawes. "Try not to die or anything."

"Not today at least."

"Is Darlington why you don't date?"

Alex paused with her hand on the doorframe. "What does he have to do with it?"

"I mean, he's not your cousin and he's one of the more beautiful humans I've seen."

"He's a friend. A mentor."

"So?"

"He's . . . expensive." Darlington was too beautiful, too well-read, too well-traveled. He wasn't just cut from a different cloth; he was too finely made and tailored.

Mercy grinned. "I like expensive things."

"He's not a cashmere scarf, Mercy. He has horns."

"I have a birthmark shaped like Wisconsin."

"I'm leaving."

"Don't forget you have to pick a book for our HumBrit section!" Mercy called after her.

Humor in the Modern British Novel. Alex had hoped for Monty Python but had gotten *Lucky Jim* and *Novel on Yellow Paper*. It wasn't a bad trade. She left Mercy with a promise to meet up for dinner, glad to flee the inquisition. She'd been too busy trying not to die to think about dating or even hooking up. Darlington had nothing to do with it, no matter how good he looked with his clothes off.

Dawes was waiting at the entrance to Sterling, slouching by the sculptural slab of the Women's Table as if she might doze off at any second. Alex felt an unwelcome rush of guilt. Dawes wasn't made for this kind of work. She was supposed to stay safe at Il Bastone, tending to her thesis like a slow-growing garden. She was support staff, an indoor cat. Their ritual at Scroll and Key had been well outside her comfort zone, and it hadn't exactly rewarded either of them with a feeling of accomplishment. Now Dawes looked almost like she'd been roughed up. She had dark smudges beneath her eyes from lack of sleep, her hair was unwashed, and Alex was fairly certain she was still in the clothes she'd worn last night, though with Dawes it could be tough to be sure.

Alex wanted to tell her to go home and get some rest, that she could handle this herself. But she absolutely couldn't, and she didn't know how much time they had before the bomb that was Darlington went off.

"Have you slept at all?" she asked.

Dawes gave a sharp shake of her head, fingers tight around the 1931 *Yale Gazette* Alex had fallen asleep with and a black moleskin notebook. "I was in the Lethe library all night, trying to find stories of people who walked Gauntlets."

"Any luck?"

"There were a few."

"That's good, right?"

Dawes was so pale her freckles looked like they were floating above her skin. "I found less than five records that can be substantiated in any way and that left any trace of a ritual."

"Is it enough to get us started?"

Dawes shot her an annoyed glance. "You're not listening. These rituals aren't on record, they aren't discussed, because they were failures, because the participants tried to hide the results. People went mad, they vanished, they died horribly. It's possible a Gauntlet was responsible for the destruction of Thonis. This is not something we should be messing around with."

"Michelle said as much."

Dawes blinked her bloodshot eyes. "I . . . You told her about the Gauntlet?"

"She came to see me. She was trying to warn us off trying."

"With good reason."

"So you want to stop?"

"It's not that simple!"

Alex pulled Dawes over to the wall and lowered her voice. "It is. Unless you want to try breaking into Scroll and Key and opening another half-baked portal, this is all we have. We do it or we have to destroy him. There aren't any other choices."

"The ritual starts with us being buried alive." Dawes was shaking.

Alex rested an awkward hand on her shoulder. "Let's see what we find, okay? We don't have to go through with it. This is just research."

It was as if Alex had whispered a transformation spell.

Dawes released a jagged breath, nodded. Research she understood.

"Tell me about the scribe," Alex said, eager to get her talking about something that wasn't death or destruction.

"There are eight scribes," Dawes said, taking a few steps back and pointing at the stonework above the Sterling doors. "All from different parts of the world. The more recent civilizations are on the right: Mayan, Chinese, Greek, Arabic. There's the Athenian owl. And on the left, the four ancient scribes: Cro-Magnon cave drawings, an Assyrian inscription from the library at Nineveh, the Hebrew is from Psalms, and the Egyptian . . . the hieroglyphs were chosen by Dr. Ludlow Seguine Bull."

Would that I might make thee love books more than thy mother. An apt inscription for a library but maybe something more.

Dawes smiled, her fear eaten up by the thrill of discovery. "Dr. Bull was a Locksmith. He was a member of Scroll and Key. He started out studying law but then switched to Egyptology."

Quite a change. Alex felt a prickle of excitement. "This is the first step in the Gauntlet."

"Maybe. If it is, we'll have to wake the Gauntlet by anointing the first passage with blood."

"Why is it always blood? Why can't it ever be jam or blue crayon?"

And if this was the first step in the Gauntlet, what came next? She studied the scribe bent to his work, the hieroglyphs, the oars of the Phoenician ship, the wings of the Babylonian bull, the medieval scholar standing at the center of it all, as if making note of the clutter around him. Was the answer somewhere in all of this stonework? There were too many possibilities, too many symbols to decipher.

Without a word, they passed through the arched entrance and inside. But the interior of the library was even more overwhelming.

"How big is this place?"

"Over four thousand square feet," said Dawes. "And every inch of it is covered in stonework and stained glass. Each room was themed. Even the lunchroom. There's a carved bucket and mop above the janitor's closet. They pulled from everything for the decoration— medieval manuscripts, Aesop's fables, the *Ars Moriendi.*" Dawes stopped in the middle of the wide aisle, her smile evaporating.

"What?"

"*Ars Moriendi.* It . . . It literally means the art of dying. They were instructions on how to die well."

"Research, remember?" Alex urged, that guilt washing over her again. Dawes really was terrified, and Alex knew if she stopped to think hard enough, she might have the sense to be scared too. She craned her neck, looking up at the vaulted ceilings, the repeating patterns of flowers and stone, the lights of the chandeliers like roses themselves. "It really does look like a church."

"A grand cathedral," Dawes agreed, a little steadier now. "At the time, there was a lot of controversy over Yale building in such a theatrical style. I pulled some of the articles. They aren't kind. But the assumption was that Goodhue—the original architect—was continuing in the Gothic tradition set by the rest of the campus."

Goodhue. Alex remembered his spiral-bound biography on the stack of books in Darlington's bedroom. Had he sent her up there deliberately?

"But Goodhue died," Alex said. "Suddenly."

"He was very young."

"And he had no connection to the societies."

"Not that we know of. James Gamble Rogers stepped in, and Sterling's money paid for all of it. There's a plaque dedicated to him by the entrance. It was the largest gift ever given to a university at the time. It paid for the Sterling Hall of Medicine, the Sterling Law Building, and the div school." Dawes hesitated. "There's a labyrinth in the courtyard. It's supposed to encourage meditation, but—"

"But maybe it's really meant to be a maze?" A puzzle to trap any interested demons.

Dawes nodded. "Sterling didn't have children. He never married. He lived with a friend for forty years. James Bloss. They shared a room, traveled together. His biographer referred to him as Sterling's longtime chum, but they were most likely in love, lifelong partners. Sterling's will called for all his papers and correspondence to be burned at his death. The speculation is he was protecting himself and Bloss, but maybe he had something else he wanted to hide."

Like a plan to build a gateway to the underworld.

Alex looked back at the entrance. "If the scribe is the start, what's the next step?"

"Darlington didn't allude to just any scribe to lead us to Sterling," Dawes said, waving the *Gazette.* "He quoted the Egyptian. There are two rooms with stained glass windows referencing the Egyptian *Book of the Dead.* Thematically . . ."

But Alex had stopped listening. She was looking down the long nave to the reception desk and the mural above it, the colors clean and bright, at odds with the gloom of the building.

"Dawes," she said, interrupting, excited but also afraid of making a fool of herself. "What if the next step is right in front of us? That's Mary, right? Mother Mary?" *Would that I might make thee love books more than thy mother.*

Dawes blinked, staring at the mural and the golden-haired, white-gowned woman at its center. "It's not Mary."

"Oh." Alex tried to hide her disappointment.

"It's called *Alma Mater*," said Dawes, her excitement making the words vibrate. "Nourishing mother."

They took off at a brisk walk. It was hard not to break into a run.

The mural was massive and set into a Gothic arch. It showed a graceful woman with an open book in one hand, an orb in the other. She was framed by a golden window, the towers of some city floating above her. But maybe it wasn't a window. Maybe it was a doorway.

"She sure looks like Mary," Alex noted. The mural could have been an altar piece right out of a church. "There's even a monk next to her."

There were eight figures gathered around her. Eight figures, eight houses of the Veil? That seemed like a reach.

"Light and Truth are the two women on the left," said Dawes. "The rest of the figures represent art, religion, literature, and so on."

"But none of them are holding up a sign to what's next. I guess we either go left or right."

"Or up," Dawes said. "The elevators lead to the stacks and offices."

"Literature is pointing to the left."

Dawes nodded. "But Light and Truth are facing right to . . . the tree." She grabbed Alex's arm. "It's the same as the one in the mural. The Tree of Knowledge."

Above Alma Mater's head, amid the arches of a building that might well be a library, were the branches of a tree—perfectly echoed in stone over the archway to their right. Another entrance. Maybe another step in the Gauntlet.

"I know this quote," Alex said as they approached the archway. "*There studious let me sit and hold high converse with the mighty dead.*"

"Thomson?" Dawes asked. "I don't know much about him. He was Scottish, but he's not widely read anymore."

"But Book and Snake use it at the start of their rituals." Beneath the arch was a stone hourglass, another memento mori. It might be a signpost. It might be nothing at all. Except . . . "Dawes, look."

The arch beneath the Tree of Knowledge led into a corridor. There were glass display cases on the left, and on the right, a series of windows emblazoned with yellow and blue stained glass. Each column between them was decorated with a stone grotesque, students bent over their books. Most were playful—some kid drinking a jug of beer and looking at a centerfold instead of his work, another listening to music, another sleeping. One of the open books read *U R A JOKE*. Alex had just walked right by them without noticing, focused on the papers she had to write, the reading yet unread. Until Darlington had pointed them out.

"I feel like he's here with us," she said.

"I wish he was," Dawes replied, trying to find the correct page in her old *Gazette* article. "Architecture is his specialty, not mine. But this . . ." She gestured to the particular grotesque Alex had pointed out. "The only description is 'reading an exciting book.'"

And yet they were staring straight at Death, skull peeking from his cloak, one skeletal hand resting on the stone student's shoulder. *There studious let me sit and hold high converse with the mighty dead.*

"I think we're being led down the corridor," Alex said. "Where does it go?"

Dawes frowned. "Nowhere really. It dead-ends in Manuscripts and Archives. There's an exit there that would take us out of the building."

They walked to the end of the corridor. There was an odd vestibule with a high ceiling. Ironwork mermen with split tails gazed down at them from the windows. Were they chasing phantoms? If demons loved games, maybe Darlington had given them just enough clues to get them stuck wandering Sterling, hunting secret messages in the stone.

There was another archway ahead, but it was strangely bare of decoration. To their right there were two doors and a panel of small square windows that looked they belonged in a pub. Some of them were decorated with illustrations on the glass—the Barrel Maker, the Baker, the Organ Player.

"What are these?" she asked.

Dawes was flipping through the *Gazette*. "Whoever wrote this made it impossible to find anything. If it isn't deliberate, it's a crime." She blew a stray strand of red hair off her forehead. "Okay, they're woodcuts by someone called Jost Amman."

As soon as the words were out of Dawes's mouth they both went still. "Let me see that." Dawes handed over the *Gazette*. Dawes had pronounced *Jost* as *Yost*, but seeing it spelled out on the page, there was no mistaking it. She remembered begging Darlington to tell her if he knew where to find the Gauntlet—and the odd desperation in his voice when he'd answered: *Would that I did. But I am just a man, heir to nothing.* He'd wanted to tell her, but he couldn't. He'd had to play the demon's game and hope that they would solve his puzzle.

Just a man. Jost Amman. They were in the right place.

So show me the next step, Darlington. To their left was a little stone mouse nibbling at the wall. To their right, a tiny stone spider. Was that a nod to fire-and-brimstone Jonathan Edwards? Alex only knew the sermon because it was a joke in her residential college. *The God that holds you over the pit of hell, much as one holds a spider or some loathsome insect over the fire, abhors you, and is dreadfully provoked.* It was why their intramural teams were called the JE Spiders. *How's that for Sunday school, Turner?*

"Where do these doors go?" Alex asked. There were two of them, awkwardly wedged into a corner.

"This one goes to the courtyard," Dawes said, pointing to a door with *Lux et Veritas* engraved in stone above it. Light and Truth, Yale's motto, just like the figures embodied in the mural that had led them here. "That one goes to a bunch of offices."

"What are we missing?"

Dawes said nothing, gnawing on her lip.

"Dawes?"

"I . . . well, it's just a theory."

"We can't spend years hammering this one out like a thesis. Give me anything."

She tugged on a strand of her hair, and Alex could see Dawes fighting herself, always seeking perfection. "In the records of the Gauntlets I could find, four pilgrims enter together—the soldier, the scholar, the priest, and the prince. They make a circuit, each locating a doorway and taking up their posts. The soldier is the last and completes the circuit on his—or her—own."

"Okay," said Alex, though she was struggling to see what that had to do with anything.

"At first I thought . . . well, there are four doors that lead out into the Selin Courtyard. One at each corner. I thought maybe the clues were leading us around the courtyard. But . . ."

"But there's no way to complete the circuit."

"Not without leaving the building," Dawes said. She sighed. "I don't know. I don't know what comes next. Darlington would. But even if we figure it out . . . Four murderers, four pilgrims. We're running out of time to find them."

"You think the circle of protection won't hold?"

"I'm not sure, but I . . . I think our best chance is to perform the ritual on Halloween."

Alex rubbed her eyes. "So we're breaking all of the rules at once?" No rituals were allowed on Halloween, particularly anything involving blood magic. There were too many Grays drawn by the excitement of the night. It was just too risky. Not to mention Halloween was only two weeks away.

"I think we have to," said Dawes. "Rituals work better at times of portent, and Samhain is supposed to be the night the door opens to the underworld. There are theories that the first Gauntlet was built at Rathcroghan, in the Cave of Cats. That's where Samhain originated."

Alex didn't like any of it. She knew what Grays were capable of when drawn by blood or powerful emotion. "That barely gives us any time to find two more killers, Dawes. And the new Praetor will be installed by then."

"I'm not a killer."

"Okay, two more reluctant but efficient problem solvers."

Dawes pursed her lips but went on. "We'll need someone to watch over us too, to keep our bodies safe in case anything goes wrong."

Again Alex had the sense that this was all beyond them. They needed more people, more expertise, more time. "I doubt Michelle is going to volunteer."

Her phone rang and she swore when she saw the name. Once again she'd fucked up.

"I'm sorry," she said before Turner could lay into her. "I meant to get to the Bible quote, but—"

"We have another body."

Alex was tempted to ask if he was kidding, but Turner didn't kid. "Who?" she asked instead. "Where?"

"Meet me at Morse College."

"Just *Morse*, Turner. You don't say *Morse College*."

"Get your ass here, Stern."

"Turner thinks there's been a murder," Alex said as she hung up.

"Another one?"

No one had confirmed that Marjorie Stephen was a homicide, so Alex wasn't anxious to jump to any conclusions. And even if there had been two murders, that didn't mean they were connected. Except Turner wouldn't be calling her unless he thought they were and that the societies were involved.

"Go on," Dawes said. "I'll keep looking around here."

But there was something bothering Alex. "I don't get it," she said, turning in a slow circle, taking in the vastness of the place. She and Mercy usually studied in one of the reading rooms. She'd never been up to the stacks. Even the scope of a building this big was tough to get her head around. "*Johnny and Punter's friends built a Gauntlet. That's what our buddy Bunchy said. You really want me to believe it stayed a secret this long?*"

"I've been thinking about that too," Dawes said. "But what if . . . what if Bunchy got it wrong? What if Lethe built the Gauntlet into Sterling?"

"What?"

"Think about it. People from Bones and Keys working together? The societies don't share secrets. They hoard their power. The only time they worked together was to form Lethe and that was only to—"

"Save their own asses."

Dawes frowned. "Well, yes. To create a society that would reassure the administration and keep the other societies in line. An oversight body."

"You're saying the oversight body thought it would be a good idea to hide a secret door to hell in plain sight?"

There was color in Dawes's cheeks now. Her eyes were bright. "Harkness, Whitney, and Bingham are considered Lethe's founding fathers. Harkness was Wolf's Head, and he's the one who tapped James Gamble Rogers to build half of campus, including this library."

"But why would Lethe build it if they weren't going to use it?" It didn't make sense.

"Are we sure they didn't?" Dawes asked. "Maybe they knew they were messing with potentially catastrophic things and they didn't want people to know."

Maybe. But it didn't quite hold together.

"Isn't the whole goal to see the other side?" Alex asked. "To unravel the mysteries of the beyond? It's why I was tapped into Lethe. If they'd gone to the underworld, they would have left a record. They would have talked about it, debated it, dissected it."

Dawes looked uneasy, and that made Alex even more nervous. Something about all of this felt wrong. Why build a Gauntlet you didn't intend to use? Why wipe away any record of it? They weren't seeing the whole picture, and Alex couldn't help but think someone didn't want them to.

It was one thing to hurl yourself headfirst into the dark. It was another to feel like someone had deliberately turned off the lights. Alex had the same sensation she'd had the night she'd strolled through Eitan's door and been tricked into revealing her power. They were walking into a trap.

13

When Alex had seen Marjorie Stephen's body, she'd wondered if Turner had been imagining things, seeing murder because murder was his job. The professor had looked almost peaceful, the finality of her death barely a disruption. The building and the world around her undisturbed.

Not Dean Beekman. The intersection in front of Morse—the same spot where Tara Hutchins's body had been found last year—was crammed with police cars, their lights flashing in lazy circles. Barriers had been erected, and uniformed cops were checking student IDs before they allowed access to the courtyard. Turner was waiting for her when she arrived and shepherded her inside without a word.

"How are you going to explain having me here?" Alex asked as she slipped blue booties over her shoes.

"I'm telling everyone you're my CI."

"Great, now I'm a snitch."

"You've been worse. Get inside."

The front door to Dean Beekman's office was hanging at an angle and mud had been tracked through the entry. The heavy desk had been knocked askew and books lay scattered across the floor next to a spilled bottle of red wine. The professor was on his back, as if he'd been sitting in the chair and it had simply fallen backward. His legs were still hooked over the seat. One of his shoes had fallen off and the lamp beside him had been tipped over.

Had the dean dozed off reading by the fire and been surprised by his attacker? Or had he put up a fight and been shoved back into his chair? He looked silly, almost cartoonish with his feet up in the air that way, and Alex wished there weren't so many people around to see it. Stupid. What did Dean Beekman care now? Alex had never had a class with him, wasn't even sure what he taught, but he was one of those professors everyone knew. He wore a tweed bucket hat and a Morse scarf, and rode his bike everywhere on campus, the bell jingling merrily as he waved to students. He was called Beeky and his lectures were always packed, his seminars legendary. He also seemed to know everyone interesting who had ever gone to Yale, and he'd brought a slew of famous actors and authors to tea at Morse.

No one had said a word about Marjorie Stephen in the days since she'd been found dead. Alex doubted anyone but the professor's students and colleagues at the Department of Psychiatry knew she'd passed. But this was going to be something entirely different.

She didn't want to look closely at the body, but she made herself peer into the dean's face. His eyes were open, but they didn't have the same milky cast Alex remembered from the first crime scene. It was hard to tell if he looked older than he should. His mouth was open, his expression startled but still genial, as if greeting a friend who had appeared unexpectedly at his door.

"His neck is broken," said Turner. "The coroner will tell us if it happened when the chair went over or before."

"So no poison," she said. "But you think this is connected to Marjorie Stephen's death?"

"This was on his desk." Turner waved her over to where a typed piece of paper lay atop the blotter: *Bewray not him that wandereth.*

"Isaiah again?"

"That's right. It completes the line we found with Professor Stephen: *Hide the outcasts, bewray not him that wandereth.* Did you find anything at Lethe about it?"

She shook her head. "I haven't had a chance to go digging." *I've been too busy figuring out how to break into hell.* "I don't know anything about Isaiah."

"He was a prophet who predicted the coming of Christ, but I don't see what that has to do with two dead professors."

Alex studied the bookshelves, the messy desk, the rigid body. "Does this . . . It feels wrong. It's too showy. The Bible quotes. The body tipped over. There's something . . ."

"Theatrical?" Turner nodded. "Like someone thinks this is amusing."

Like someone was playing a game. And demons loved games and puzzles, but their only resident demon was currently trapped in a circle of protection. Was someone at the societies toying with them?

"Did Professor Stephen know Beekman?"

"If they were connected, we'll find out. But they weren't in the same department. They weren't even in the same field. Dean Beekman taught American Studies. He had nothing to do with the psych department."

"And the poison that killed Professor Stephen?"

"Still waiting on the tox report."

The societies didn't like eyes on them, but that didn't mean someone hadn't gone rogue. Even so, none of it really made sense.

"It's the clues," she said, chewing over the thought. "Those Bible quotes don't fit. If someone was using magic to . . . I don't know, get revenge on their professors, they wouldn't leave clues. That feels unhinged."

"Or like someone pretending to be unhinged."

That would mean a lot more trouble. As much as Alex didn't want these deaths to be her problem, she couldn't pretend the uncanny wasn't at work here. Magic was transgression, the blurring of the line between the impossible and the possible. There was something about crossing that boundary that seemed to shake loose all the morals and taboos people took for granted. When anything was within your grasp, it got harder and harder to remember why you shouldn't take it—money, power, your dream job, your dream fuck, a life.

"Tell me I'm jumping at shadows, Stern, and you can go back to lurking in that haunted house on Orange."

Il Bastone was one of the least haunted places in New Haven, but Alex didn't see the point of getting into that discussion.

"I can't," Alex admitted.

"Can't you . . . work your contacts on the other side?"

"I don't have ghost informants, Turner."

"Then maybe try making some friends."

Again, Alex had the sense that she was missing something, that if Darlington had been here he would know what to look for; he would be able to do this job. So maybe Darlington was exactly who they needed. Turner wanted answers, and he just might be able to offer them something in return. Four pilgrims. Four murderers. Alex wasn't sure if it was wise to trust Turner, but she did, and she wanted him on their side.

"Turner," Alex asked. "You ever kill someone?"

"What kind of question is that?"

"So yes."

"It's none of your goddamn business."

But it might be. "How long do you have to be here?"

Turner gave an exasperated snort. "Why?"

"Because I want to show you something."

Board game; cardboard, paper, bone
Provenance: Chicago, Illinois; c. 1919
Donor: Book and Snake, 1936

A version of the Landlord's Game that bears strong resemblance to its later incarnation, Monopoly. Place names taken from Chicago and surrounds. Dice are crafted from bone, most likely human. Some evidence suggests the handmade board was created at Princeton, but the dice were added and the game came into heavy use during Prohibition, when a brief flurry of occult activity centered around D. G. Nelson's bookshop resulted in an increased demonic presence on the north side of the city. The bright colors and constant bargaining required by the game make it instantly appealing, while two factors—impenetrable rules and interminable gameplay that can last hours, if not days—render it virtually unwinnable. It is, in short, a perfect trap for demons.

Unfortunately, one of the dice was lost at some point and efforts at replacement have proven unsuccessful.

—*from the Lethe Armory Catalogue as revised*
and edited by Pamela Dawes, Oculus

14

Turner couldn't just walk away from an active crime scene, but he agreed to pick her up the next morning after Modern Poets. Word of Dean Beekman's death had spread quickly, and an uneasy mood settled over campus. Life continued on, the rush of people and business to be done, but Alex saw groups of students standing with their arms around each other weeping. Some wore black or tweedy bucket hats. She saw flyers up for a vigil in the Morse courtyard. She couldn't help but think of the morning after Tara's body had been found, the false hysterics, the gossipy buzz that had moved through the university like a giddy swarm of hornets. Alex understood that Beeky had been beloved, a father figure, a character woven into the fabric of Yale. But she remembered the excitement that had followed Tara's death, the danger a step removed, a new flavor to be tried without any risk.

This was true grief, real fear. Alex's professor began her lecture by talking about how Dean Beekman and his wife had hosted her at their home one Thanksgiving and how anyone who knew Beeky never felt alone at Yale. The dean's office at Morse had been sealed off and safety officers posted at the door—Yale police, not NHPD. The university president was holding an emergency meeting for concerned students in Woolsey Hall that night. The *Yale Daily News* had written up a brief summary of the murder—a suspected robbery, police already pursuing a strong lead outside of the New Haven community. That smacked of spin: *Don't worry, parents, this isn't a Yale crime, it isn't even a New Haven crime. No need to pack your children off to Cambridge.* If Professor Stephen's death had barely caused a ripple, Dean Beekman's murder was like someone heaving a grand piano into a lake.

Turner picked up Alex in front of one of the new hotels on Chapel, far enough from the crime scene and campus that neither of them had to worry about being spotted. She tried to prepare him on the way to Black Elm, but he didn't say a word as she gave him the bare-bones account of her theory on Darlington and how against all odds she'd been proven right. Turner just let her talk, sitting in cold silence, as if he were a mannequin who'd been placed behind the steering wheel to demonstrate safe driving. Only yesterday she'd given Mercy a similar speech, but Mercy had soaked it all up and come back hungry for more. Turner looked like he might just drive them both off a cliff.

She had texted Dawes that they were on their way to Black Elm because it seemed like the right thing to do, but Alex regretted it as soon as she saw her standing at the front door in her shapeless sweats, her bright red hair in its usual lopsided bun, like a lumpy candle topped by an unexpected flame. Her lips were compressed in a disapproving line.

"She looks happy," Turner observed.

"Does anyone look happy when they see the cops coming?"

"Yes, Miss Stern, people having their shit stolen or trying to avoid being stabbed usually do seem happy to see us."

At least she knew Turner had been listening on the drive over. Only talk of magic and the occult could put him in this kind of mood.

"Centurion," Dawes greeted him, and Alex winced.

"My name is Detective Abel Turner and you damn well know it. You look exhausted, Dawes. They're not paying you enough."

Dawes looked surprised, then said, "Probably not."

"I left an open case file to be here. Can we get this going?"

Dawes led them inside, but once they were trailing Turner up the stairs, she whispered, "This is a bad idea."

Alex agreed, but she also didn't see what choice they had.

"He's going to tell Anselm," Dawes fretted as they followed Turner down the hall to the ballroom. "The new Praetor. The police!"

"No, he's not." At least Alex hoped he wouldn't. "We need his help and that means we need to show him what we're up against."

"Which is what exactly? Just admit you're making it up as you go along."

She was. But something in her gut was pulling her back to Black Elm and she had dragged Turner right along with her.

"If you have any other ideas, just say the word, Dawes. Do you know any murderers?"

"Other than you?"

"He can help us. And he needs our help too. Dean Beekman was murdered."

Dawes stopped dead. "What?"

"Did you know him?"

"Of course I knew him. Everyone knew him. I took one of his classes when I was an undergrad. He—"

"Christ on a bike."

Turner had frozen in the doorway to the ballroom and he did not look like he had any intention of going in. He took a step backward, one hand extended as if to ward off what he was seeing, his other hand resting on his gun.

"You can't shoot him," Alex said with all the calm she could muster. "At least I don't think you can."

Dawes ran to the doorway, placing herself between Turner and the golden circle like some kind of human shield. "I told you this was a terrible idea!"

"What is this?" demanded Turner. His jaw was set, his brow lowered, but there was fear in his eyes. "What am I even seeing?"

All Alex could offer was, "I told you he was different."

"Different is you lost a few pounds. You got a haircut. Not . . . this."

At that moment Darlington's eyes opened, bright and golden. "Where have you been?" Turner started at the sound of Darlington's voice, human but for that cold echo. "You reek of death."

Alex groaned. "You're not helping."

"Why did you bring me here?" Turner bit out. "I asked for help with a case. I thought I made it clear I don't want any part of this crazy cult shit."

"Let's go downstairs," said Dawes.

"Stay," said Darlington, and Alex couldn't tell if it was a plea or a command.

"I think Darlington can help you," she said. "I think he's the only one of us who can."

"That thing? Listen, Stern, I don't know how much of this is real and how much is . . . hocus-pocus bullshit, but I know a monster when I see one."

"Do you?" Alex felt her anger rising. "Did you know Dean Sandow was a killer? Did you know Blake Keely was a rapist? I showed you what's behind the door. You can't just shut it and pretend you never saw."

Turner rubbed a hand over his eyes. "I sure as hell wish I could."

"Come on."

Alex marched into the room and hoped he would follow. The air was lush with heat. That sweet scent was everywhere, that wildfire smell, the stink of disaster riding the wind, the kind that sends coyotes running from the hills and into suburban backyards to crouch and howl by swimming pools.

"Detective," said the creature behind the golden wall.

Turner hovered in the doorway. "That really you?"

Darlington paused, considered. "I'm not entirely sure."

"Goddamn it," Turner muttered, because despite the horns and the glowing symbols, Darlington seemed nothing but human. "What happened to him? What is all this? Why the fuck is he naked?"

"He's trapped," Alex said, as simply as she could, "and we need your help to get him out."

"You don't mean filing a missing persons report, do you?"

"Afraid not."

Turner gave himself a shake as if he still wondered, even hoped he might be dreaming. "No," he said at last. "No. I don't . . . This isn't my job and I don't want it to be. And don't tell me this has anything to do with our bosses at Lethe because I know that squirrelly look on Dawes's face. She's afraid I'm going to tattle on you."

"Your case—"

"Do not start with me, Stern. I like my job—no, I love my job—and whatever this is . . . It's not worth all the money in the devil's pocket. I'll solve the case on my own with good old detective work. *Hide the outcasts* and all that shit—"

"*Bewray not him that wandereth*," Darlington said, finishing the quote.

Alex almost expected thunder and lightning, some cosmic response to a half demon, or maybe more-than-half demon, reciting from the Bible.

"That's the one," Turner said uncomfortably.

"Told you," whispered Alex.

"You came from the crime scene," said Darlington. "It's why you wear death like a shroud."

Turner cast Alex a glance, and she wished Darlington would just talk like Darlington. But Turner was a detective and he couldn't help himself. "The quote is familiar to you?"

"Who was killed?"

"A professor and the dean of Morse College."

"Two bodies," mused Darlington; then a faint smile crossed his face, mischievous, almost hungry in its glee, nothing human about it. "There will be a third."

"The hell does that mean?"

"Exactly."

"Explain yourself," Turner demanded.

"I always admired virtue," Darlington murmured. "But I could never imitate it."

Turner threw up his hands. "Has he completely lost his mind?"

Somewhere far below the doorbell rang at the same time that Dawes's phone buzzed.

They all jumped, all but Darlington.

Dawes drew in a sharp breath. She was staring at her phone. "Oh God. Oh God."

"Who are they?" Alex asked, looking down at the screen, where a well-dressed couple was trying to peer through the windows by the front door.

"They look like real estate agents," said Turner.

But Dawes looked more terrified than when they'd opened a portal to hell. "Those are Darlington's parents."

15

Turner shook his head. "You're like kids who got caught raiding the liquor cabinet."

Alex's mind sped through possible strategies, excuses, elaborate lies. "Both of you stay out of sight until I take care of them."

"Alex—"

"Just let me handle them. I'm not going to punch anyone."

At least she hoped she wasn't. Translating Latin and tracking down Bible quotes weren't in her skill set, but she'd been lying to parents most of her life. The problem was she was short on information. Darlington had never talked about his mother and father, only his grandfather, as if he'd sprung from the moss that clung to the stones of the old house and been carefully tended to by an aging and cantankerous gardener.

She needed the old man. The one she occasionally saw lurking around the house in his bathrobe, a pack of crushed Chesterfields in his pocket.

Come on, Alex thought, trying not to panic as she hurried down the stairs. *Where are you?*

She could hear the Arlingtons pounding on the kitchen door now. She glanced at Dawes's phone and saw their frustrated expressions.

"The Mercedes is in the drive," his father muttered.

"He's making us wait on purpose."

"We should have called first."

"Why?" his mother complained. "He never answers."

Alex yanked on her sweater, though she was still covered in perspiration from the heat of the ballroom. She needed to cover her tattoos, look respectable, authoritative.

There. The old man was sitting in the sunroom with Cosmo at his feet.

"I need your help," Alex said.

"What the hell are you doing in my house?" he asked plaintively.

So Alex had been right. He wasn't some Gray who had wandered in and liked the atmosphere. Ghosts weren't drawn to empty places naturally. This had to be Darlington's grandfather.

C'mon. She held out her hand and tugged. The man's mouth made a startled *oh*, and then he was rushing into her with a rattle like an old cough. Alex tasted cigarettes and something tar-like. *Cancer.* She was tasting cancer. He'd been weak when he died, in terrible pain, and his rage had burned through him with such glowing heat she could taste it too. She didn't need his strength, she needed his memories, and they came on clear and fast, just like the Bridegroom's had when she'd let him into her mind.

She was looking at Black Elm, but it was beautiful, alive, full of light and people. Her father's friends, the old foreman from the boot shop. She was running through the halls, chasing a white cat out to the garden. It couldn't be Cosmo, this was too long ago, and yet . . . the cat turned to look at her with one scarred eye. *Bowie Cat.*

There had been no brothers and sisters, just a single son, always one boy to tend to the business, to Black Elm. He wasn't lonely. This was his palace, his fortress, the ship he captained in every game. He was smoking stolen cigarettes up in the tower room, looking out over the trees. He hid his treasures beneath the loose windowsill—comic books and slabs of taffy, then whiskey and smokes and copies of *Bachelor.* He was watching his father weep as the old man signed the papers that would close the factory. He was pulling Jeannie Bianchi down a dark hall, panting in her ear as he came in her hand.

He dressed in a black suit and grieved his mother. He wore the same black suit to put his father in the ground. He bought his wife a maroon Mercedes and they made love in the back seat, right there in the driveway. "Let's go to California," she whispered. "Let's drive there today." "Sure," he said, but he didn't mean it. Black Elm needed him, as it always had. He was watching her from the doorway to the den, feet curled under her, listening to music he didn't like or understand, drinking from great big glasses of vodka. She looked at him, stood on unsteady legs, turned the volume up. "It's going to kill you," he warned her. "It's already got your liver." She turned the music up louder. It did get her in the end. He had to buy a new black suit. But he couldn't blame her for not being able to stop. Things you love, things you need, they don't stop taking.

He was holding a child in his arms, his son . . . no, his grand-son, a second chance to get it right, to forge this boy from factory steel, a true Arlington, strong and capable, not like his fool of a son, weak-willed, flitting from one failure to the next, an embarrassment. If Daniel hadn't looked so much like an Arlington, he would have suspected that his wife had found some weak-chinned artist to spend her afternoons with. It was like looking into a fun house mirror and seeing yourself sapped of all spine. But he wouldn't make the same mistakes with Danny.

The house was different now, quiet and dark, no one but Berna-dette humming in the kitchen and Danny running through the halls as he once had. He hadn't expected to grow old. He hadn't really understood what old was, his body in gradual rebellion, loneliness crowding in as if it had just been waiting for him to slow down so it could catch him. He had been fearless once. He had been strong. Daniel and his wife canceled their visit. "Good," he said. But he didn't mean it as much as he wanted to.

When had death crept in? How had it known where to find him? Silly question. He'd been living in this tomb for years.

"Kill me, Danny. Do this for me."

Danny was crying, and for a moment, he saw the boy as he was, not the Arlington paragon, but a child really, lost in the caverns of Black Elm, endlessly tending to her needs. He should tell him to run and never look back, to be free of this place and this withering legacy.

Instead he seized the boy's wrist with his last bit of strength. "They'll take the house, Danny. They'll take everything. They'll keep me alive and drain it all away, saying it's for my care. Only you can stop them. You must be a knight, just take the morphine and inject it. See, it even looks like a lance.

"Now go," he said as the boy wept, "they mustn't find out you were here."

He regretted only that he would die alone.

But death hadn't been able to keep him from Black Elm. He found himself here again, free of pain and home once more, forever wandering up and down the stairs, in and out of rooms, always feeling like he'd forgotten something but unsure of what it was. He watched Danny eat scraps from the kitchen, sleep in his cold bed, buried beneath old coats. Why had he cursed this child to serve this place the way that he himself had? But Danny was a fighter, an Arlington, galvanized, resilient. He wished he could speak words of comfort, encouragement. He wished he could take it all back.

Danny was standing in the kitchen, mixing up some foul concoction. He could feel his grandson's desperation, the misery in him as he stood over a bubbling pot and whispered, "Show me something more." He'd set out a fancy wine goblet, but he paused before he poured that odd red mess into it. Danny set down Bernadette's old Dutch oven and jogged down the hall.

The old man could sense death in the pot, catastrophe. *Stop. Stop before it's too late.* He swiped at it, trying to knock it from the stove, willing himself back into the world, just for a moment, a second. *Just give me the strength to save him.* But he was weak, useless, no one and nothing. Danny returned, carrying that ugly keepsake box, *Arlington Rubber Boots* emblazoned on the porcelain lid. He'd kept it on his desk. He'd let Danny play with it as a kid. Sometimes he'd surprise him by putting a quarter in it, or a piece of gum, a blue pebble from the back garden, nothing at all. Danny had believed the box was magic. Now he poured the poison into it. *Stop,* he wanted to cry, *Oh, please, Danny, stop.* But the boy drank.

Alex stumbled forward, knocking into the dining room table and nearly toppling before she caught herself on the edge. It was too much, the images too clear. She crumpled to her knees and vomited on the inlaid floor, trying to get her head to stop spinning, trying to peel away all of the past Black Elms and only see the present.

The doorbell rang again, an accusation.

"Coming!" she called.

She made herself stand and lurch to the powder room by the kitchen. She rinsed her mouth, splashed water on her face, drew her hair back into a low, tight ponytail.

"For fuck's sake, Cosmo, get away from that." The cat was sniffing around the pool of vomit. "Help me out here."

And Cosmo, as if he'd understood, did something he'd never done before: He leapt into her arms. She tucked him carefully against her, hiding his singed fur.

"The barbarians are at the gate," she whispered. "Let's do this."

Again the bell rang.

Alex thought of who she wanted to be in this moment, and it was Salome, the president of Wolf's Head she'd had to frighten into giving up use of the temple room. Rich, beautiful, used to getting her way. The kind of girl Darlington would date if he had no taste.

She opened the door slowly, in no rush, and blinked at Darlington's parents as if they'd woken her from a nap. "Yeah?"

"Who are you?" The woman—Harper, the name came with Alex's doubled vision, her sight coupled with the old man's eyes—was tall, lean, and dressed in perfectly tailored wool trousers, a silk blouse, and pearls. The man—contempt, pure and seething, rose up at the sight of him. He looked so much like Danny, Daniel, Darlington. *So much like me.* And yet he looked nothing like any of them. Alex had met a lot of low-level cons in her life, people who were always looking for the shortcut, the easy fix. They were perfect marks.

"Alexandra," she said, her voice bored, her hand stroking Cosmo's fur. "I'm watching the house for Darlington while he's in Spain."

"We—"

"I know who you are." She tried to soak the words with equal parts disdain and disinterest. "He doesn't want you here."

Daniel Arlington sputtered. Harper's eyes narrowed, and she raised a perfect brow.

"Alexandra, I don't know who you are or why our son appointed you watchdog, but I want to speak to him. *Now.*"

"Out of money again?"

"Get out of my way," said Daniel.

Alex's impulse was to give him a good hard shove and watch his bony ass land on the gravel drive. She'd seen these people in the old man's memories, barely a word for Danny, barely a thought. Even if her mother was terrible at paying the bills or providing anything resembling stability, she at least gave a damn. But Alex had to stay in rich-girl mode.

"Or what?" she said with a laugh. "This isn't your house. I'm happy to call the police and let them sort it out."

Darlington's father cleared his throat. "I . . . I think there's been some kind of misunderstanding. We always hear from Danny on holidays and he always takes our calls."

"He's in Spain," Alex said. "And he's seeing a therapist now. Setting boundaries. You should think about that."

"Come on, Daniel," said Harper. "This little bitch is high on her own power. When we return, it will be with a letter from our attorney." She marched back to the Range Rover.

Daniel wagged his finger in her face, trying to get some of his own back. "That's exactly right. You really have no business—"

"Run home, you weakling." The words came out as a snarl, deep, grizzled. That wasn't Alex's voice, and she knew Darlington's father wasn't seeing her face anymore either. "You held me hostage in my own house, you sniveling shit."

Daniel Arlington IV gasped and stumbled backward, nearly went to his knees.

Alex willed the old man to recede but it wasn't easy. She could feel him in her head, the ferocity of his determination, a spirit forever at war with itself, with the world, with everything and everybody around him.

"Stop screwing around, Daniel!" Harper shouted from the car, gunning the engine.

"I . . . I . . ." His mouth gaped, but he was just seeing Alex's placid face now.

The old man was like a barely leashed dog inside her mind. *Pussy. Candy-ass. How did I ever raise a son like you? You didn't even have the balls to face me, just kept me drugged up and helpless, but I got you in the end, didn't I?*

Cosmo squirmed in Alex's arms. She raised a hand and waved. "Bye-bye," she singsonged.

Daniel Arlington made it into the car, and the Range Rover took off in a spray of gravel.

"Thanks, Cosmo," Alex murmured as the cat leapt from her arms and pranced toward the back of the house to hunt. "And you."

She shoved the old man out of her mind with all her might. He appeared in front of her, bathrobe flapping, his naked, emaciated body peppered with white hair.

"That was a one-time ride," she said. "Don't think about trying to hijack this particular train again."

"Where's Danny?" the old man growled.

Alex ignored him and marched back to Dawes and Turner.

16

When Dawes was upset, she drove even more slowly, and Alex thought it might take them two hours to get back to campus.

"They're going to get lawyers involved," Dawes complained.

"They're not."

"They're going to pull in the Yale administration."

"They won't."

"For Pete's sake, Alex!" Dawes yanked the steering wheel to the right, and the Mercedes veered to the side of the road, nearly jumping the curb. "Stop pretending everything is going to be okay."

"How else are we supposed to get through this?" Alex demanded. "It's all I know how to do." She made herself take a deep breath. "Darlington's parents aren't going to come back with lawyers or involve Yale."

"Why wouldn't they? They have money, power."

Alex shook her head slowly. She'd seen so much in the old man's memories, felt it all. The only time she'd been through anything like that was when she'd let the Bridegroom in and experienced the moments of his murder. She hadn't just known he'd loved Daisy. She'd loved Daisy too. But this time there had been so much more, a lifetime of small pleasures and endless disappointment, every day and every thought shaped by Black Elm, by bitterness, by the hunger for something that might outlive his brief, weightless life.

"They don't have either," Alex said. "Not the way you think they do. It's why they keep pressuring Darlington to sell Black Elm."

Dawes looked scandalized. "But he'd never sell."

"I know. But if they find out he's missing, they'll try to take it from him."

They sat in silence for a long minute, the engine idling. Through the window Alex saw a narrow stretch of park, the leaves of its trees not yet ready to turn, but she was back at Black Elm, feeling its pull, the way it demanded love, lost in the loneliness of the place.

"They won't get lawyers involved because they don't want anyone looking at them too closely. They . . . Darlington's grandfather basically bought them off. He wanted to raise . . ." She'd almost said *Danny*. "They just left him there, and I think they kept the old man prisoner when he got sick." Until Danny had set him free. That was why he'd survived in hell, not just because he was Darlington, steeped in knowledge and lore, but because he had killed his grandfather.

It didn't matter that his grandfather had asked him to do it any more than it mattered Dawes had smashed in Blake's skull to save Alex's life.

"But they'll be back," Dawes said.

Alex couldn't argue with that. She'd scared the hell out of Darlington's father, but monsters didn't just go away with a warning. Harper and Daniel Arlington would come sniffing around again, looking for their share.

"Then we bring back Darlington and he can send them packing himself." He'd been Black Elm's protector, and he was still the only one who could defend it. "Who's going to help us find another murderer? I'm running out of favors with the societies."

"No one," said Dawes, but her voice sounded strange. "We'll need to get into the basement of the Peabody. But it's under renovation and there are cameras everywhere."

"We can use the tempest you brewed up last year. The one that messes with all the electronics. And let's pull in Turner. If we need to look up someone's record, he can manage it."

"I don't . . . I don't think that's a good idea."

"We either trust him or we don't, Dawes."

Dawes flexed her fingers on the steering wheel, then nodded. "We keep going," she said.

"We keep going," Alex repeated.

To hell and back.

Alex found Mercy and Lauren having a late lunch in the JE dining hall. The chatter was subdued, even among the Grays, and the room seemed bigger and colder, as if the college had dressed itself in mourning for Dean Beekman. Alex filled her tray with a giant heap of pasta and a couple of sandwiches she would tuck into her bag for later. Her phone pinged while she was filling her glass with soda. Six hundred dollars had been deposited in her bank account.

So Oddman had paid up. If a hump got square, Eitan would drop 5 percent in her account for a job well done. She should probably feel shitty about it, but saying no to the money wasn't going to do anyone any good.

When she sat down, she could see Mercy's eyes were red from crying and Lauren wasn't looking great either. Neither of them had done more than pick at their food.

"You guys okay?" Alex asked, suddenly self-conscious about her tray full of food.

Mercy shook her head, and Lauren said, "I'm messed up."

"Same," Alex said because it seemed like she should be.

"I can't imagine what his family is going through," said Mercy. "His wife teaches here too, you know."

"I didn't," Alex said. "What does she teach?"

Mercy blew her nose. "French literature. That's how I got to know them."

Vaguely Alex remembered that Mercy had won some big award for an essay on Rabelais. But she hadn't realized Mercy really knew Dean Beekman.

"What was he like?" she asked.

Mercy's eyes overflowed again. "Just . . . really kind. I was scared about going to a school so far from home and he put me in touch with other first-gen students. He and Mariah—Professor LeClerc, his wife—they just made room for you. I can't explain it." She shrugged helplessly. "He was like Puck and Prospero all wrapped up together. He made scholarship seem fun. Why would anyone want to hurt him? And for what? He wasn't rich. He can't have had anything worth . . . worth . . ." Her voice wobbled and broke.

Alex handed her a napkin. "I never met him. Did he have kids?"

Mercy nodded. "Two daughters. One was a cellist. Really good. Like I think she landed a seat in . . . I think it was in Boston or the New York Phil."

"And the other?" Alex felt like a ghoul, but if she had a chance to suss out a little information on the victim, she wasn't going to pass it up.

"A doctor, I think? A psychiatrist. I can't remember if she was going into research or practicing."

A psychiatrist. She might be connected to Marjorie Stephen, but Turner would figure that out easily enough.

"He was so popular," Alex ventured carefully. "I don't think I've ever heard anyone say anything negative about the guy."

"Why would they?" Mercy asked.

"People get jealous," Lauren said, dragging her fork through a puddle of ketchup. "I had a lecture right before one of his classes and his students would always show up early. Pissed off my professor."

"But that's about his students," Alex said, "not him."

Mercy folded her arms. "It's just sour grapes. I had a professor warn me off choosing him as my faculty adviser."

"Who?"

"Does it matter?"

Alex had promised to try not to lie, but she was already skirting the truth. "Just curious. Like I said, I've never heard a bad word about him."

"It was a group of them. From the English department. I show up for office hours to talk about a paper and three professors ambush me to insist I stay in the English major, telling me that Dean Beekman isn't about serious scholarship. They called him a glad-hander." She put her nose in the air and adopted a tone of disdain. "'All sizzle, no steak.'"

Lauren shook her head in disbelief. "I'm barely passing econ, and you have faculty staging interventions to keep you in their departments."

"It's nice to be friends with a genius," Alex said.

Lauren scowled. "It's depressing."

"Not if some of it rubs off on us."

"There are different kinds of smart," Mercy said generously. "And it didn't matter anyway. I told them I planned to major in American Studies."

Was professional jealousy enough to get a man killed? And what could that possibly have to do with Marjorie Stephen?

"Who were these assholes, and how do I avoid them?" Alex asked, fishing for names.

"I don't remember," said Mercy. "I had Ruth Canejo in Directed Studies, but I didn't know the other two. That's part of why it annoyed me so much. Like I was just a point they wanted to score."

Lauren rose to clear her tray. "I'm the kind of smart that's going to get a nap in before practice. We need to talk Halloween."

"A man was killed on campus," Mercy said. "You can't seriously think we're going to throw a party."

"It will be good for us. And if I don't have something to look forward to I'm not going to make it."

When Lauren was gone, Mercy said, "Why all the questions?"

Alex stirred her coffee slowly. She'd told Mercy she wouldn't lie, but she had to tread carefully here. "Do you know a professor in the psych department? Marjorie Stephen?"

Mercy shook her head. "Should I?"

"She passed away on Saturday night. In her office. There's a chance her death is just some kind of sad accident. But it's also possible she was murdered."

"You think the deaths are connected?" Mercy drew in a sharp breath. "You think there's magic involved?"

"Maybe."

"Alex, if the societies . . . if some bastard did this to Dean Beekman . . ."

"We don't know that's the case. I'm just . . . exploring every avenue."

Mercy put her head in her hands. "How do they get away with this? Isn't Lethe supposed to stop this kind of thing from happening?"

"Yeah," Alex admitted.

Mercy shoved back from the table, her tray rattling as she snatched up her bag, fresh tears in her eyes. "Then you stop them, Alex. You make them pay for this."

The Peabody originally stood at the corner of Elm and High Street, stuffed to the rooftop with items both interesting and obscure. Plans were made for a new building and the basement was dug, but materials were challenging to come by, what with the war being on. The collections from the original museum were scattered all over campus, in basements and carriage houses. It took so long to build the museum, and the documentation was so haphazard, that parts of the museum's collection were still being discovered in old outbuildings as recently as the 1970s. Of course there are some items in its mighty rooms that will never be catalogued, and in some cases, it's best that provenance remain unknown.

—*from* The Life of Lethe: Procedures and
Protocols of the Ninth House

Table; amethyst
Provenance: Unknown
Donor: Unknown

Records first appear c. 1930 after construction of the new Peabody. Please see closed collection notes.

—*from the Lethe Armory Catalogue as revised
and edited by Pamela Dawes, Oculus*

17

The following night Turner met Alex and Dawes outside of the Peabody, by the statue of a triceratops that Wolf's Head had accidentally animated back in 1982. Once the cameras were down, slipping into the museum was a matter of timing the rounds of the security guards. She mentioned the potential psychiatry connection to Turner and the professors who had bad-mouthed Dean Beekman, but he didn't seem impressed.

"You get names?"

"Ruth Canejo, but not the others."

"You find out anything about aging poisons?"

"Yes and no," Alex said, trying to keep the edge from her voice. It had only been two days since Turner had demanded her presence at the second crime scene. "There's something called a Wizening Stick that makes you look older if you chew on it long enough, but the effects don't last more than a few hours. And there's a poison called Tempusladro, the thief of time. It ages you internally."

"That sounds promising."

"No, it only ages your organs, speeds up the clock. But the whole point is that the victim looks like he died of natural causes. Young and dewy on the outside, shriveled on the inside."

"Then keep searching," Turner said. "Find something I can use. I need you and your demon boyfriend for the work I can't do."

"Then help us bring him out of hell."

Turner's face shuttered. "We'll see."

Alex had badgered him into meeting them by promising him that, once they had two more murderers to walk the Gauntlet, she'd leave him alone. She was surprised he'd agreed to come.

They shuffled past the main entry and down the stairs. Turner looked up at the dead eyes of the security cameras uneasily. They were still recording, but the magical tea in Dawes's thermos would keep the cameras from capturing anything but static. "You have a real gift for turning everyone around you into criminals, Stern."

"It's some light trespassing. You can say you heard a noise."

"I'm going to say I caught you two breaking in and decided to pursue."

"Would you both be quiet?" Dawes whispered furiously. She gestured to the thermos. "The tempest won't last all night."

Alex shut her mouth, trying to bite back the anger she felt toward Turner. She wasn't being fair, but it was hard to care about what was rational or right when she and Dawes were stuck fighting what felt like a losing battle to free Darlington. They needed allies, but Lethe and Michelle Alameddine weren't interested, and she hated feeling like she was begging for Turner's help.

And the Peabody was one more place where Darlington's presence was too close—the real Darlington, who belonged to New Haven as much as he belonged to Lethe or Yale. Alex had been to the Peabody with him, a place that had rendered him surprisingly quiet. He'd shown her the mineral room, the stuffed dodo bird, the photos and letters from Hiram Bingham III's expedition to "discover" Machu Picchu, where he'd found the great golden crucible currently tucked away in Il Bastone's armory.

"This was my hiding place," he'd said as they walked past the *Age of Reptiles* mural, "when things got bad at home." At the time, Alex had wondered how bad it could have been, growing up in a mansion. But now that she'd been in Darlington's grandfather's head, seen his memories of a little boy lost in the dark, she understood why that boy would come here, to a place full of people and noise, where there was always something to read or to look at, where no one would think twice about a studious kid with a backpack who didn't want to leave.

The basement was dark and warm, full of plumbing that rattled and belched, noisier than the quiet upper floors, where the exhibits had been packed up and stored in preparation for the upcoming renovation. Their flashlight beams floated over exposed pipes and boxes stacked to the ceiling, odd bits and pieces of scaffolding leaning crookedly against them.

At last Dawes led them into a room with a strange, musty smell.

"What is all this?" Alex asked as Dawes ran her flashlight over shelves of jars full of cloudy liquid.

"Pond water, hundreds of jars of it, from all over Connecticut, all from different years."

"What is the point of this exactly?" asked Turner.

"I suppose . . . if you want to know exactly what was in the pond water in 1876, this is the place for you. The basements are full of stuff like this."

Dawes consulted a plan and then walked to a shelf on the left-hand side of the room. She counted up the rows from the bottom, then counted across the dusty jars themselves. She reached between them and rooted around in back.

"If you try to make me drink that, I'm leaving," Turner muttered.

There was a loud *clink*. The shelf swung out and there, behind the dirty rows of jars, was a huge room with nothing in it but a massive rectangular table covered in multiple dust cloths.

"It worked," Dawes said with pleased surprise. She flicked a switch on the wall, but nothing happened. "I don't think anyone's been down here in a while."

"How did you even know this place existed?" Turner asked.

"I'm responsible for maintaining the armory archive."

"And a room in the Peabody basement is part of the Lethe armory?"

"Not exactly," said Dawes, and even in the shadows, Alex could tell she was uncomfortable. "No one wants to claim this. We're not even sure which society made it or if it's the work of someone else entirely. There's just an entry in the book for when it arrived and . . . its purpose."

Alex felt a chill settle into her. What were they about to see? She sent her mind searching for Grays in case something awful was about to happen, and braced herself as Dawes grabbed hold of one of the cloths. She gave a sharp pull, releasing a cloud of dust.

"A model?" Turner asked, sounding almost disappointed.

A model of New Haven. Alex recognized the shape of the green with its bisecting lines of protection and three pretty churches immediately. The rest was less familiar. She could identify some of the buildings, the general plan of the streets, but so much was missing.

"It's made out of stone," Alex realized, running a finger over one of the street names, *Chapel*, engraved directly into the pavement.

"Amethyst," said Dawes, though it looked more white than purple to Alex's eye.

"That can't be," said Turner. "It's one big slab, no lines, no cracks. You're telling me this was carved from one piece of stone?" Dawes nodded, and Turner's frown deepened. "That's not possible. Let's say someone could find a piece of amethyst this big, then get it out of a mine, then somehow manage the carving, it would have to weigh over a ton. How did they even get it down here?"

"I don't know," said Dawes. "It's possible it was carved right here, and the building went up around it. I don't even know if it was carved by human hands. There's really . . . there's nothing natural about it." She uncorked a bottle from her bag and poured it into what looked like a Windex bottle. "I'm going to read from the incantation. You just need to repeat."

"What's going to happen?" asked Alex.

"It's just going to activate the model."

"Sure," said Turner.

Dawes took out a notebook where she'd transcribed the spell and began to read in Latin. Alex didn't understand a word of it.

"*Evigilato Urbs, aperito scelestos.*"

Dawes gestured for them to repeat and they did their best to follow. "*Crimen proquirito parricidii.*"

Again they tried to echo her.

Dawes picked up the spray bottle and squirted it aggressively over the model.

Alex and Turner took a step back, and Alex resisted the urge to cover her nose and mouth. The mist smelled faintly of roses, and Alex remembered what the high priest had said about preserving bodies at Book and Snake. Was that what this map was? A corpse that needed to be brought back to life?

The cloud of mist drifted down onto the model, and the table seemed to explode into activity. Lights flickered on; a miniature amethyst buggy sped down the streets drawn by gemstone horses; a breeze moved through the tiny stone trees. Red spots began to appear in the stone, as if they were seeping up through it, spreading bloodstains.

"There," said Dawes, expelling a relieved breath. "It will reveal the locations of anyone who has committed homicide."

Turner's brow furrowed in disbelief. "You're telling me you found a magical map that does exactly what you need it to?"

"Well, no, the spell is tailored to our needs."

"So I could have it look for hot fudge sundaes? Women who love microbrews and Patriots football?"

Dawes laughed nervously. "No, it has to be a specific crime. You're not calling on the map to reveal criminals in general, just people who broke a specific law."

"Wow," said Alex, "if only the NHPD knew. Oh, wait."

"Can I find my murder suspect this way?" Turner asked.

"Possibly?" Dawes said. "It shows locations, not names."

"Locations," Turner repeated, frowning. "Not names. When was this created?"

"There's no exact date—"

"Roughly." His voice was harsh.

Dawes tucked her chin into her sweatshirt. "Eighteen fifties."

"I know what this is," Turner said. "What the actual fuck."

Dawes winced, and now Alex understood why she had worried about having Turner here.

"This thing wasn't built to find criminals," said Turner. "It was made to find runaway slaves."

"We needed a way to find killers," she said. "I didn't know what else—"

"Do you understand how fucked up this is?" Turner jabbed his finger at a grand-looking building on the New Haven Green. "That's where the Trowbridge house used to be. It was a stop on the Underground Railroad. People thought they would be safe here. They should have been safe here, but some asshole from the societies used magic . . ." He stumbled over the word. "*This* is what your magic is for, isn't it? This is what it does. Props up the people in power, lets the people with everything take a little more?"

Alex and Dawes stood silent in the quiet of the basement. There was nothing to say. Alex had looked into the face of what magic could do. She'd seen it in Blake Keely, in Dean Sandow, in Marguerite Belbalm. Magic was no different from any other kind of power, even if it still thrilled some secret part of her. She remembered standing in the kitchen of Il Bastone, screaming at Darlington. "Where were you?" she'd demanded. "Where were you?" Where had Lethe and all of its mysteries been when she was a child in desperate need of saving? Darlington had heard her that night. He hadn't argued. He'd known she wanted to break things and he'd let her.

"We can go," Alex said. "We can smash this thing to dust." It was all she could offer.

"How many times has this abomination been used?" Turner demanded.

"I'm not sure," Dawes said. "I know they used to use it to find bootleggers and speakeasies during Prohibition, and the FBI may have tried to use it during the Black Panther trials."

Turner shook his head. "Finish," he bit out. "I don't want to be in this room a minute longer than I have to."

Hesitantly, they bent their heads, turning their flashlight beams back to the pale violet surface of the map.

A clump of red stains had spread in one corner of the Peabody, a blooming poppy, lush with blood. Alex, Turner, Dawes. A posy of violence.

There were a few blots near the Hill and even two dots in the dorms, or where Alex thought the dorms were now. She couldn't quite orient herself. The map didn't look like it had been updated since the late 1800s, and most of the structures she knew well simply hadn't been built yet.

But High Street's name hadn't changed and there was a place Alex had no trouble identifying. The spot where a young maid named Gladys had fled, where her life had been stolen and her soul consumed by Daisy Whitlock. That act had created a nexus of power, and years later, the first tomb of the first secret society had been built over it.

"Someone's at Skull and Bones," she said. The building on the map was small, the first version of the tomb, before it had been expanded.

They stood together, looking at that red stain.

"It's Monday," said Dawes. "No ritual tonight."

That was good. If they could get there in time, they wouldn't have as many possible suspects to sift through, just a few people studying or hanging out.

"Let's go," said Turner, the bite still in his voice.

"Are we just leaving it that way?" Alex asked as they scooted back through the secret passage, leaving the bloody table behind.

"Don't worry," said Turner. "I'll be back with a sledgehammer."

Alex heard Dawes suck in a breath, distressed at the thought of any artifact being destroyed, no matter how vile. But she didn't say a word.

They slipped back through the room full of jars and out the side exit, trying to move quietly. As soon as Turner pushed on the bar to let them out to the street, an alarm began to wail.

"Shit," he said, ducking his head as Alex yanked up her hood.

They burst through the door and ran to his car. The tempest's power had diminished as the tea had gone cold, and she could only hope the museum's security cameras hadn't captured any clear images of their faces.

They wriggled into the car and Turner gunned the engine, squealing out into the empty street.

"Faster," Alex urged as he navigated the Dodge toward High Street. They needed to get to Skull and Bones before their murderer left, or they'd have to start this whole process all over again.

"I am not looking to draw attention," he growled. "And have you even thought about how you're going to figure out who the murderer is and get a killer to join your little hell crew?"

She hadn't. The cannonball had found her momentum.

Turner swung the Dodge right up to the curb in front of the ruddy stone tomb.

Alex had never liked this particular crypt. The others seemed almost silly, a kind of Disneyland version of a particular style—Greek, Moorish, Tudor, mid-century. But this one felt too real, a temple to something dark and wrong that they'd built right out in the open, as if the people who had raised those red stones knew no one could touch them. It didn't help that she'd seen the Bonesmen cut human beings open and root around in their insides, searching for a glimpse at the future.

"Well," said Turner as they climbed out of the car. "You have a plan, Stern?"

"We have to tread lightly," Dawes urged, coming up behind them, still clutching her notebook. "Skull and Bones is very powerful, and if word gets back to—"

Alex pounded on the heavy black door. She didn't know much about the tomb, except that there was a debate over the original architect and that it had supposedly been built with opium money.

No one answered. Turner stood back, arms crossed.

"Did we miss them?" asked Dawes, sounding almost eager.

Alex slammed her fist against the door again and shouted. "I know you're in there. Stop fucking around."

"Alex!" Dawes cried.

"If they're not home, who's going to care?"

"And if they are?"

Alex wasn't entirely sure. She raised her hand to knock again when the door cracked open.

"Alex?" The voice was soft, nervous.

She peered into the gloom. "Tripp? Jesus, is that ice cream?"

Tripp Helmuth, third-generation legacy and son to one of the wealthiest families in New England, wiped his hand over his mouth, looking sheepish. He was wearing long athletic tear-aways and a dirty T-shirt, his blond hair tucked under a backward Yale baseball cap. He was a member of Bones—or he had been. He'd graduated the previous year.

"You alone?" Alex asked.

He nodded, and Alex recognized the look on his face instantly. Guilt. He wasn't supposed to be here.

"I—" He hesitated. He knew he couldn't ask them in, but he also knew they couldn't stand there.

"You're going to have to come with us," Alex said with all the weary authority she could summon. It was the voice of every teacher, principal, and social worker she'd ever disappointed.

"Shit," said Tripp. "Shit." He looked like he was going to cry. *This* was their murderer? "Let me just clean up."

Alex went with him. She didn't think Tripp had the balls to make a run for it, but she wasn't taking any chances. The tomb was like all of the society crypts, fairly ordinary except for the Roman temple room used for rituals. The rest looked like most of the nicer places at Yale: dark wood, a few fancy frescoes, one red velvet chamber that had seen better days, and an abundance of skeletons, some famous, some less so. The canopic jars full of important livers, spleens, hearts, and lungs were all kept behind the walls of the temple room.

The tomb was dark except for the kitchen, where Tripp had been having some kind of midnight snack. There were cold cuts and bread on the table, and a half-eaten ice cream sandwich. It was a big, drafty room with two stoves and a huge walk-in freezer, all better suited to preparing banquets than serving a dozen college students. But when the alumni came to town, the Bonesmen had to make sure they put on a proper spread.

"How did you know I was here?" Tripp asked as he hastily returned everything to the fridge.

"Hurry up."

"Okay, okay." Alex noted his very full-looking backpack and wondered if he'd squirreled away more food in there. Hard times for Tripp Helmuth.

"How'd you get in?" Alex asked as he locked the doors and they headed to Turner's Dodge.

"I never turned my key in."

"And they didn't ask about that?"

"I told them I lost it."

That had been enough. Tripp was so hapless it was easy to believe he'd lose his key and anything else that wasn't stapled to his pockets.

"Oh God," Tripp said as Alex joined him in the back seat of the Dodge. "Are you a cop?"

Turner glanced in the mirror and said sharply, "Police detective."

"Of course, yeah, I'm sorry. I—"

"You'd best stop talking and use this time to think."

Tripp hung his head.

Alex caught Turner's eye in the mirror, and he gave a small shrug. If they were going to get Tripp in on this, they needed him scared, and Turner was very good at being intimidating.

"Where are we going?" Tripp asked as they headed down Chapel.

"Lethe House," Alex replied.

Most of the members of the societies viewed Lethe as a tiresome necessity, a salve to the Yale administration, and most had never bothered to set foot inside Il Bastone.

"What are you doing on campus?" Alex asked.

Tripp hesitated, and Turner snapped, "Don't try to put some kind of spin on this."

Bless Turner for playing along.

Tripp took off his cap, ran a hand through his greasy hair. "I . . . I was allowed to walk with my class, but I didn't graduate. I didn't have enough credits. And my dad said he wouldn't bankroll another semester, so I'm just . . . I'm doing marketing stuff for those Markham real estate guys? I'm actually getting pretty good at Photoshop. I've been trying to save up so I can finish, get my degree and all that."

That explained the backpack full of food, but Alex wondered why Tripp hadn't just lied on his application to whatever investment bank or trading firm he wanted to work for in Manhattan. The Helmuth name would open every door, and no one was going to raise questions when a third-generation legacy wrote *B.A. in Economics, Yale University* on his CV. But she wasn't going to say that. Tripp was just dopey and sincere enough that he wouldn't consider an outright lie.

He wasn't a bad guy. Alex suspected he'd go through his life described that way: not a bad guy. Not too bright, not too handsome, not too anything. He went on nice vacations and burned through second chances. He liked to get high and listen to the Red Hot Chili Peppers, and if people didn't necessarily like him, they were happy to tolerate him. He was the living, breathing embodiment of "no worries." But apparently Tripp's father was done not worrying.

"What's going to happen to me?" he asked.

"Well," Alex said slowly. "We can let the Bonesmen and their board know you were trespassing."

"And committing larceny," Turner added.

"I didn't take anything!"

"You pay for that food?"

"Not . . . not exactly."

"Or," said Alex, "we can keep this quiet and you can do a job for us."

"What kind of a job?"

One that might result in death or dismemberment.

"It won't be easy," said Alex. "But I know you're up to it. There might even be some cash in it."

"Really?" Tripp's whole demeanor changed. There was no distrust in him, no wariness. His whole life, opportunities had been dropping in his lap so easily he didn't question another. "Man, Stern. I knew you were all right."

"You too, buddy."

Alex offered up her knuckles for a fist bump and Tripp beamed.

18

Alex sat through Modern Poets with Mercy the next day, letting the words of "Invitation to Miss Marianne Moore" roll over her. *With heaven knows how many angels all riding on the broad black brim of your hat, please come flying.* When she read words like that, heard them in her head, she felt the pull of another life; she could see herself living it as clearly as if she were absorbing a Gray's memories, listening to the horrible, beautiful lines of "The Sheep Child," or setting down her pen as the professor of her history class on the Peloponnesian War compared Demosthenes to Churchill. *The victors choose who should be lauded as a bulwark against tyrants and who may be sneered at as the enemy of inevitable change.* In those moments, she felt something deeper than the mere need to survive, a glimpse at what it might mean if she could simply learn and stop trying so hard all the time.

She found herself fantasizing about a life not only without fear but without ambition. She would read, and go to class, and live in an apartment with good light. She would feel curious instead of panicked when people mentioned artists she didn't know, authors she'd never read. She would have a stack of books by her bedside table. She would listen to *Morning Becomes Eclectic*. She would get the jokes, speak the language; she would become fluent in leisure.

But the illusion couldn't be maintained, not when there were two dead faculty members whose murders might be linked to the societies, when Darlington was trapped in a circle of protection that might give way at any time, when Halloween was less than two weeks away and they had a ritual to perform, when she might die if they failed and might lose everything if they succeeded. The terror rushed back in, that gnawing sense of failure. The beauty of poetry and the pattern of history receded until all that was left was the dull and worrisome now.

Dawes pinged her halfway through lecture, and Alex called her on the way to her next class.

"What's wrong?" Alex asked as soon as Dawes picked up.

"Nothing. Well, not nothing, of course. But you've been summoned by the new Praetor."

"Now?"

"You can't keep putting him off. Anselm never bothered to arrange a tea after . . . what happened at Scroll and Key, and the Praetor is getting antsy. He has office hours from 2 to 4 p.m. in LC."

Practically next door to her dorm. Alex didn't find the thought comforting.

"You spoke to him?" she asked. "What did he sound like?"

"I don't know. Like a professor."

"Angry? Happy? Help me out here."

"He didn't sound anything really." Dawes's voice was cool and Alex wondered why.

"What time do you want to do this?"

"He wants to meet you, not me." Was that the problem? The Praetor didn't want to include Dawes?

"Wait, he's a professor? How long has he been here?"

"He's been teaching at Yale for twenty years."

Alex couldn't help but laugh.

"What?" Dawes demanded.

"If he's been here that long and we're just hearing about him now, he has to have been Lethe's last choice."

"Not necessarily—"

"You think people were lining up for the job? The last guy ended up dead."

"From a heart attack."

"Under mysterious circumstances. No one wanted the gig. So they had to tap this guy."

"Professor Raymond Walsh-Whiteley."

"If I didn't know you better, I'd think you were kidding."

"He was something of a wunderkind. Graduated from Yale at sixteen, postgraduate work at Oxford. He's a tenured English professor and, based on the opinion pieces he writes for *The Federalist*, very old-school."

Alex thought about making an excuse, putting this off awhile longer. But what good would that do? And better to meet with the Praetor now, one-on-one, than wait for Anselm to get around to arranging a dinner where she'd have to worry about a Lethe board member scrutinizing her too.

"Okay," she said. "I can go after lecture."

"I'll meet you at JE when you're done. We can try to hammer out the rest of the Gauntlet."

"Fine."

"Be polite," Dawes insisted. "And dress nicely."

That was really something coming from Dawes, but Alex knew all about playing the part.

Alex tried to stay focused in Electrical Engineering 101, but that was a challenge on her best days. It was offered in a cavernous lecture hall and was probably the most democratic course at Yale since everyone was only there to fulfill a requirement—including Alex, Mercy, and Lauren. They spent most of the hour quietly debating what drink they'd serve at Liquor Treat, eventually arriving at tequila shots and gummy worms.

Alex wasn't really surprised that parties and classes and homework were continuing on in the wake of the murders. Right now, the campus believed that one man had died horribly. No one knew that Marjorie Stephen might have been killed too. There'd been no memorials or assemblies for her. Beekman's death was shocking, grim, something to talk about over dinner and worry about if you were walking home after dark. But none of the students nodding off in their chairs around Alex had been at that crime scene or looked down into that old, startled face. They hadn't felt the sudden rupture that came with death, and so they simply kept on living. What else was there to do? Dress up like ghosts and ghouls and dead celebrities, drown the terror of their own mortality in grain alcohol and Hawaiian Punch.

Liquor Treat was considered a kind of pregame before people headed out to the real parties, and Alex could slip out early to prepare for the ritual at Sterling. There would be no uncanny activity to worry about at the Manuscript Halloween party this year. They'd been penalized for the drugs they'd managed to lose track of the previous semester and that had been used to victimize Mercy and other girls unlucky enough to cross paths with Blake Keely. But she would still have to oversee something called a songbird ritual for them on Thursday.

Alex walked back to JE with Mercy and Lauren. She would have to skip lunch if she was going to make it to the new Praetor's office hours. She darted into her room to change into her most respectable outfit: black jeans, a black sweater, and a white collared shirt she borrowed from Lauren.

"You look like a Quaker," Mercy said with disapproval.

"I look responsible."

"You know what she needs?" Lauren asked. She popped into her room and returned with a dark red velvet headband.

"Better," said Mercy.

Alex examined her prim, humorless face in the mirror. "Perfect."

Professor Raymond Walsh-Whiteley's office was on the third floor of Linsly-Chittenden Hall, his hours taped to the heavy wooden door. She hesitated. What exactly was she in for? A lecture? A warning? An interrogation about the ritual at Scroll and Key?

She tapped lightly and heard a disinterested "Come."

The room was small, the walls lined from floor to ceiling with overflowing bookshelves. Walsh-Whiteley was seated in front of a row of leaded-glass windows. The panes were thick and watery, as if they'd been made from heated sugar, and the gray October light had to fight its way through. A brass lamp with a green shade craned its neck over his cluttered desk.

The professor looked up from his laptop and peered over his glasses. He had a long, melancholy face, and thick white hair combed back from his forehead in what was almost a pompadour.

"Sit." He waved at the single chair opposite him.

It was strange to know that a former Lethe deputy had been living on campus all of last year, cozied away in this cubbyhole. Why hadn't anyone mentioned him? Were there others?

"Galaxy Stern," he said, leaning back in his chair.

"I prefer to be called Alex, sir."

"Small favors. I would have felt a fool calling someone Galaxy. Quite the whimsical name." He said *whimsical* with the same disgusted spin other people reserved for *fascist*. "Is your mother prone to such flights?"

A little truth couldn't hurt.

"Yes," Alex said. "California." She shrugged.

"Mmm," he said with a nod, and Alex suspected that he'd long since written off the whole state, possibly the entire West Coast. "You're an artist?"

"A painter." Though she'd barely touched a brush or even a piece of charcoal since last semester.

"And how are you finding the start of the school year?"

Exhausting? Terrifying? Way too full of dead bodies? But people were only really talking about one subject on campus.

"This thing about Dean Beekman is pretty terrible," she said.

"A tremendous loss."

"Did you know him?"

"He was not a man who could stand to remain unknown. But I do feel deeply for his family." He steepled his fingers. "I'll be blunt, Miss Stern. I am what is fondly called a dinosaur and less fondly described as a reactionary. Yale was once dedicated to the life of the mind, and while there were diversions and distractions, nothing could be as diverting or distracting as the presence of the fairer sex."

It took Alex a long moment to process what Walsh-Whiteley was saying. "You don't think women should have been admitted to Yale?"

"No, I do not. By all means, let there be higher education for women, but blending the sexes does neither any good. Similarly, Lethe is no place for women, at least not in the role of Virgil or Dante."

"And Oculus?"

"Again, best not to create an atmosphere of temptation, but as the office is solely dedicated to research and caretaking, I can make an exception."

"A kind of exalted nanny."

"Precisely."

Now Alex knew why Dawes had sounded so grumpy.

Walsh-Whiteley plucked a speck of lint from his sleeve. "I have lived long enough to see the supposedly harmless bleating of the counterculture become the culture, to see venerable academic departments overtaken by prattling fools who would uproot hundreds of years of great literature and art for the appeasement of little minds."

Alex considered her options. "Couldn't agree more."

Walsh-Whiteley blinked. "Beg pardon?"

"We're watching the death of the Western canon," she said with what she hoped was the appropriate amount of distress. "Keats, Trollope, Shakespeare, Yeats. Did you know they have a class focusing on the lyrics of popular songs?" She had come around to loving Shakespeare and Yeats. Keats bored her. Trollope delighted her. Apparently he'd invented the postbox. But she doubted Professor Walsh-Whiteley cared much about enjoyment, and she'd also really liked a semester of studying the Velvet Underground and Tupac.

He considered her. "Elliot Sandow was one such prattler. A repellent combination of self-righteous and spineless. I want it understood that I will have no trouble beneath the Lethe roof, no hanky-panky, no nonsense."

It was hard not to get hung up on a grown man unironically using the term *hanky-panky*, but Alex simply said, "Yes, sir."

"You have been without a Virgil or any kind of real leadership for too long. I don't know what bad habits you've accrued in that time, but there will be no room for them under my watch."

"I understand."

He leaned forward. "Do you? During Dean Sandow's ignominious tenure, a student went missing and is most likely dead. The societies were allowed to descend into a miasma of deprivation and criminal behavior. I wrote numerous complaints to the board, and I am relieved they did not fall on deaf ears."

She folded her hands in her lap, attempting to look small and vulnerable. "All I can say is that I'm grateful we'll have a . . . uh . . . firm hand on the tiller." Whatever the hell that meant. "Losing my Virgil was frightening. Destabilizing."

Walsh-Whiteley made a low chortling noise. "I can imagine that a woman with your background would feel quite out of place here."

"Yes," said Alex. "It's been a challenge. But didn't Disraeli say, 'There is no education like adversity'?" Thank goodness for the wisdom of dining hall tea bags.

"Did he?" said Walsh-Whiteley, and Alex wondered if she'd gone too far. "I'm no fool, Miss Stern, and I won't be swayed by glib speech. There is no room in Lethe for glad-handers or charlatans. I will expect prompt reports on the rituals you oversee. I will also be assigning additional reading—" Her distress must have shown because he held up a hand. "I also don't like to be interrupted. You will comport yourself as a deputy of Lethe at all times. Should the barest whiff of controversy touch you, I will recommend your immediate expulsion from Lethe and Yale. That Michael Anselm and the board have let you stay on after your shameful performance at Scroll and Key is beyond me. I have let Mr. Anselm know this in no uncertain terms."

"And?" Alex asked, her anger getting the best of her.

The Praetor sputtered. "And what, Miss Stern?"

"What did Michael Anselm say?"

"I . . . haven't been able to get hold of him. We're both very busy."

Alex had to tamp down a smile. Anselm wasn't returning his calls. And Lethe had avoided tapping him for Praetor until all their other options were exhausted. No one wanted to listen to good old Professor Walsh-Whiteley. But maybe that meant there was an opportunity here.

Alex waited to make sure he'd finished, weighing possible strategies. She knew it was probably pointless to try to make Walsh-Whiteley an ally, but shouldn't he want Daniel Arlington—a deputy of Lethe with all the proper credentials—back?

"My Virgil—"

"A tremendous loss."

The same words he'd used to describe Dean Beekman's murder. Meaningless. A wave of the hand.

Alex tried again. "But if there's a way to reach him, to bring him back—"

The Praetor's brows rose in disbelief and Alex braced for another rant, but his voice was gentle. "Dear child, the end is the end. *Mors vincit omnia.*"

But he's not dead. He's sitting in the ballroom at Black Elm. Or some part of him was.

Again Alex wondered how much Walsh-Whiteley knew.

"At Scroll and Key—" she ventured.

"Do not look for sympathy from me," he said sternly. "I expect you to know your own limitations. Any inspection or ritual activity must be vetted by me first. I will not see the Lethe name further degraded because the board has seen fit to relax standards that exist for a reason."

Inspection. That was the cover story Alex had offered Scroll and Key, and that Anselm had backed with their alumni. Alex had assumed Anselm would share all of his suspicions with the Lethe board. But maybe the board had kept them from the Praetor. After all, why rile a dog you knew loved to bark? And if the Praetor didn't know she and Dawes were trying to break into hell, that would be one less thing to worry about.

"I understand," she said, trying to hide her relief.

Walsh-Whiteley shook his head. His look was pitying. "It's not your fault you were put in this position. You simply don't have the skills or background to cope with what's being thrown at you. You are not Daniel Arlington. You are ill-equipped to play the role of Dante, let alone Virgil. But with my supervision and some humility on your part, we'll get through this together."

Alex considered stabbing him with a pen. "Thank you, sir."

Walsh-Whiteley took off his glasses, withdrew a cloth from his desk drawer, and polished the lenses slowly. His eyes darted left and Alex tracked the movement to a yellowing photograph of two young men, perched on a sailboat.

He cleared his throat. "Is it true you can see the dead?"

Alex nodded.

"Without any elixir or potion?"

"I can."

Alex had read the room as soon as she'd entered. The driftwood on the shelf beside the photo, shells and pieces of sea glass, the quote framed in a paperweight: *Be secret and exult, because of all things known, that is most difficult.* But she hadn't read Walsh-Whiteley— not successfully. She'd been too nervous to see the desperation lurking behind all of that bluster.

"There's a Gray here now," she lied. The office was blessedly free of ghosts, probably because the Praetor was one step shy of a cadaver himself.

He started, then tried to remain composed. "Is there?"

"Yes, a man . . ." A gamble now. "An older man." A frown puckered the professor's brow. "No . . . he's hard to make out. Young. And very handsome."

"He . . ." Walsh-Whiteley looked around.

"To the left of your chair," said Alex.

Walsh-Whiteley stretched out his hand, as if he could reach through the Veil. The gesture was so hopeful, so vulnerable, Alex felt an acute pang of guilt. But she needed this man on her side.

"Has he said anything?" the Praetor asked. The longing in his voice had an edge, sharpened over years of loneliness. He'd loved this man. He'd lost him. Alex resisted the urge to take another look at that photo on the mantel, but she felt sure Walsh-Whiteley was one of those smiling faces, young and suntanned and sure that life would be long.

"I can see Grays, not hear them," Alex lied again. Then added primly, "I'm not a Ouija board."

"Of course not," he said. "I didn't mean that."

Where's your sneer now? But she knew she had to tread carefully. Her grandmother had read fortunes in the leavings of Turkish coffee, bitter, dark, and so thick it seemed to take its own slow time down your gullet.

"You're selling people lies," Alex's mother had complained. A funny irony from Mira, who lived on the hope she found in crystals, energy baths, bundles of sage that promised purity, prosperity, renewal.

"I don't sell them anything," Estrea had said to her daughter.

That was true. Estrea Stern never charged for the fortunes she told. But people would bring over loaves of bread, tinfoil skillets of Jiffy Pop, babka, chewy strawberry candies. They would leave kissing her hands, tears in their eyes.

"They love you," Alex had said, marveling, watching with wide eyes from the kitchen table.

"Mija, they love me until they hate me."

Alex hadn't understood until she'd seen the way those same people had turned from her grandmother in the street, treated her like a stranger in line at the store, the cashier's eyes darting away, a perfunctory smile on her lips.

"I've seen them at their lowest," Estrea had explained. "When someone shows you their longing, they don't want to see you out buying cherry tomatoes. Now don't tell your mother."

Alex hadn't said a word about the people who came and went at her grandmother's apartment, because whenever her mother did find out about Estrea telling fortunes, she would spend the whole car ride home ranting. "She laughs at me because I pay to have my tarot read, and then she does this," Mira would rage, pounding the heel of her hand against the steering wheel. "Hypocrite."

But Alex knew why Estrea laughed at the fakes her mother cycled through in an endless wave of hope and disillusionment. Because they were liars and Estrea only told the truth. She saw the present. She saw the future. If there was nothing in the cup, she told her visitors that too.

"Read me," Alex had begged.

"I don't need a cup of coffee to read you, presiada," Estrea had said. "You will endure so much. But the pain you feel?" She took Alex's chin in her bony fingers. "You will give it back tenfold."

Alex wasn't sure about the math on that, but Estrea Stern had never been wrong before.

Now she studied the Praetor. He had that same hopeful look she'd seen at her grandmother's kitchen table, the ache in him radiating like an aura. Estrea had said she could never look into a heart and lie. Alex didn't seem to have inherited that particular trait. For the first time in a while, she thought of her father, the mystery of him, little more than a handsome face and a smile. She looked like him—at least that was what her mother had told her. Maybe he'd been a liar too.

"The Gray seems comfortable," she said. "He likes being here, watching you work."

"That's good," Walsh-Whiteley said, his voice hoarse. "That's . . . that's good."

"It can take time for them to share what they need to share."

"Of course. Yes." He slid his glasses back on, cleared his throat. "I'll have Oculus prepare a schedule of rituals the societies are seeking approval for. We'll go over that tomorrow evening."

He opened his laptop and returned to whatever work he'd been doing. It was a dismissal.

Alex looked at the old man in front of her. He would cry when she left; she knew that. He would ask her about this young man again; she knew that too. He might be kinder or more just with her for a time. That had been the goal, to ingratiate herself. But as soon as he doubted her, he would turn on her. Fine. She just had to stay in his good graces until Darlington really came home. Then the golden boy of Lethe could make it right.

She was halfway back to the dorms before the Praetor's words returned to her: *There is no room in Lethe for glad-handers or charlatans.* Three professors had confronted Mercy to try to keep her in the English department, and one of them had called the beloved Dean Beekman a glad-hander. An uncommon term. *He was not a man who could stand to remain unknown.*

Becoming Praetor meant gaining full access to Lethe's archives and resources—including an armory full of potions and poisons. The professor had been instated as Praetor just last week, right before the murders began, and he certainly didn't like Dean Beekman.

Motive and means, Alex considered as she unlocked the gate to JE. As for opportunity, she knew better than anyone: You had to make it for yourself.

19

Alex found Dawes in the JE reading room, hunched over a blueprint of Sterling and *Kittscher's Daemonologie*.

"This is the book Michelle told me to read," Alex said, picking it up and paging through it. "Does it talk about the Gauntlet?"

"No, it's a series of debates about the nature of hell."

"So more like a travel guide."

Dawes rolled her eyes, then wrapped her hands around her headphones as if she were clinging to a buoy. "Are you really not scared?"

Alex wished she could say no. "Michelle told me we'd have to die to complete the ritual. I'm terrified. And I really don't want to do this."

"Neither do I," Dawes said. "I want to know how to be brave. Like you."

"I'm reckless. There's a difference."

What might have been a smile curled the corner of Dawes's mouth. "Maybe. Tell me about the Praetor."

Alex sat down. "He's a delight."

"Really?"

"Dawes."

Dawes's cheeks pinked. "I did a little dive on him, and he wasn't a popular figure at Lethe. His Virgil hated him and lobbied against his selection, but there's no denying he was an academic superstar."

"The bad news is he has not mellowed with age. The good news is it looks like Anselm and the board are keeping him in the dark about what really happened at Scroll and Key."

"Why would they do that?"

"Because this guy seems to be held together by righteous indignation. I think he's been complaining to Lethe for years about how we're all slouching toward Bethlehem. They just want him to shut up and leave them alone."

"So now he's our problem."

"Something like that. I think our best bet is to just let him believe we're dim and incompetent."

Dawes folded her arms. "Do you know how hard I've had to work to be taken seriously? To have my dissertation taken seriously? Playing dumb doesn't just hurt us, it hurts every woman he comes into contact with. It—"

"Dawes, I know. But it's also really good cover. So let's just dance for him until we figure this out, and then I will happily stand aside while you crush his ego with your dazzling intellect, okay?"

Dawes considered. "Okay."

"Not to sound like Turner, but do we have a plan?"

"Sort of?" Dawes spread out a series of neatly typed pages that she'd highlighted with different colors. "If we can figure out how to finish the Gauntlet, we begin the walk at midnight. Once we find the four doorways, each threshold will need to be marked with blood."

"On Halloween."

"I know," Dawes said. "But we don't have a choice. If we get it right . . . something will happen. I'm not sure what. But the door to hell will open and four graves will appear. Again, the language isn't totally clear."

"Four graves for four murderers."

"Assuming we have four murderers."

"We will," Alex said, though Turner still hadn't given them a yes. If they had to go back to that hideous map, they would. But they'd have to do it fast. And finding someone who'd agree to be buried alive to rescue someone they'd never met wasn't going to be easy. "Do we need to . . . I don't know, bring weapons or something?"

"We can try, though I don't know what we'll be fighting. I have no idea what might be waiting on the other side. All I can tell you is that our bodies don't make the descent, our souls do."

But Alex remembered what she'd witnessed in the basement of Rosenfeld Hall. "Darlington *vanished*, I saw it happen. Not just his soul, his body too." One moment he'd been there with her, a scream on his lips, and then he was gone, along with the sound of his cry. There'd been no echo, no fade, just sudden silence.

"Because he was eaten," Dawes said, as if it were obvious. "It's the only way he was able to become . . . well, whatever he is."

"So none of us are going to turn into demons?"

Dawes renewed her grip on her headphones. "I don't think so."

"For fuck's sake, Dawes."

"I can't be sure," she said brusquely, as if the idea of losing her humanity was less concerning than the prospect of losing her job at Lethe. "There haven't been enough well-documented attempts to say what will happen. But just sending our souls is a kind of protection. Bodies are permeable, changeable. It's why we need someone watching over us, to serve as a connection to the living world. I just wish we weren't doing this on Halloween. We're going to draw a lot of Grays."

Alex felt a headache coming on. They had a little over a week to put all of this together, and she had that same feeling she'd had before they'd thrown themselves into the ritual at Scroll and Key. They weren't ready. They weren't equipped. They sure as hell weren't the right team for this job. What had Walsh-Whiteley said? *I expect you to know your own limitations.* It made her think of Len. For all his greed and misplaced ambition, he had practiced a strange kind of caution. He'd been stupid enough to think he could earn Eitan's trust and move up in the ranks, but he'd never tried so much as a smash-and-grab when they were short on cash because he knew they'd get caught. He wasn't a thief. He definitely wasn't a planner. It was why he'd loved using Alex to deal on campuses when she still looked like a kid, before desperation and disappointment had hollowed her out. Low risk, high reward. At least for Len.

Now Dawes was talking about trusting someone to fight off a bunch of Grays while they lay there helpless in the ground. For the first time Alex felt unsure.

"I don't like it," she said. "I don't want to bring a stranger into this. And are you going to tell them they have to drink Hiram's elixir so they can see Grays? That can be fatal."

"Michelle—"

"Michelle Alameddine isn't going to help us."

"But she was his Virgil."

Alex stared at Dawes. Pamela Dawes, who had saved her life more than once and who was prepared to walk side by side with her straight through the gates of hell. Pamela Dawes, who came from a nice family with a nice house in Westport, who had a kind sister to come pick her up at the hospital and pay her to watch the kids. Pamela Dawes, who had no idea what it meant to hurt so much to live you might wake up one morning ready to die. And Alex was glad of that. People shouldn't have to march through the world fighting all the time. But there was no way Alex was going to pressure Michelle Alameddine to do a job like this, not after she'd seen that tattoo on her wrist.

"We'll find someone else," Alex said. But she didn't know who. They couldn't just grab somebody off the street and offer to pay them, and they couldn't ask someone from the societies without risking that person going straight to the Lethe board.

"We could use magic," Dawes said tentatively. She was making slow spirals with her pen in the margin of her notes. "Bring someone on and then compel them so they can't remember—"

"Don't do that."

Alex and Dawes nearly jumped out of their seats. Mercy was sitting on a couch just behind their table.

"How long have you been there?" Alex demanded.

"I followed you from the courtyard. If you need someone to help, I can do it, but not if you're going to mess with my mind."

"No way are you getting involved." Alex said. "Absolutely not."

Dawes looked horrified. "Wait, who . . . what does she know?"

"Most of it."

"You *told* her about—" Dawes's voice dropped to an angry whisper. "About Lethe?"

"Yes," Alex snapped. "And I'm not going to apologize for it. She's the one who fished me out of my own misery last year. She's the one who called my mom and made sure I was okay when you were holed up at your sister's house watching old sitcoms and hiding under the blankets."

Dawes ducked her chin into her sweatshirt and Alex felt instantly terrible.

"I can help," Mercy said, breaking the silence. "You said you need someone to watch over you. I can do that."

"No." Alex cut her hand through the air as if she were slicing the thought in half. "You have no idea what you're signing up for. No."

Mercy crossed her arms. She was wearing a bright blue granny sweater today, crocheted roses gathered around the neck. She looked like a disapproving kindergarten teacher.

"You can't just say *no*, Alex."

"You could be killed."

Mercy scoffed. "Do you really think that will happen?"

"No one knows what will happen!"

"Can you give me a weapon?"

Alex pinched the bridge of her nose. At least Mercy was asking the right questions.

"You kind of don't get to say no, right?" Mercy continued. "You don't have anyone else. And you owe me for all the magical stuff."

"I don't want you to get hurt."

"Because you'd feel guilty."

"Because I like you!" Alex shouted. She forced herself to lower her voice. "And yes, I'd feel guilty. I rescue you, you rescue me. That's what you said, remember?"

"So if something goes wrong, that's what you do."

Dawes cleared her throat. "We do need someone."

Mercy stuck her hand out. "Mercy Zhao, roommate and body-guard."

Dawes shook it. "I . . . Pamela Dawes. Doctoral candidate and . . ."

Alex sighed. "Just say it."

"Oculus."

"That's a really good code name," said Mercy.

"It's my office," Dawes said with as much dignity as she could muster. "We're not spies."

"No," said Alex. "Espionage would be too easy for Lethe."

"Actually," Mercy said, "there's speculation that the term *spooks* for CIA operatives originated from so many recruits coming from Skull and Bones."

Alex laid her head down on the table. "You're going to fit right in."

"Just tell me where to start."

"Don't get excited," Alex warned. "We haven't even figured out how the Gauntlet works or if we've got this whole thing wrong."

Dawes gestured to the blueprint of Sterling. "There's supposed to be a circuit, a circle for us to complete, but . . ."

Mercy studied the blueprint. "It looks like you're headed around the courtyard."

"That's right," said Dawes. "But there's no way to complete the circuit. The path dead-ends at Manuscripts and Archives."

"No, it doesn't," said Mercy. "Just go through the University Librarian's office."

"I've been in that office." Dawes gave the blueprints a firm tap. "There's a door to Manuscripts and Archives and a door out to the courtyard. The sundial door. That's it."

"No," Mercy insisted. Alex felt like she was watching a boxing match where the fighters threw citations instead of punches. "I don't know why it isn't on the plan, but there's a door behind the librarian's desk, right beside the fireplace, the one with that funny quote in Latin."

"Funny quote?" Alex asked.

Mercy tugged on one of the rosettes at her neckline. "I can't remember what it's from, but it basically amounts to 'Shut up and go away, I'm busy.' The door is easy to miss because of the paneling, but my friend Camila showed it to me. We walked right through. It takes you to the Linonia and Brothers reading room."

Dawes looked like she was going to jump out of her chair. "To Linonia. Directly around the courtyard."

Alex hadn't followed much of their debate, but that she understood. A hidden door. A way to circle the courtyard that wasn't on the blueprints. "We can complete the circuit. We can finish the Gauntlet."

"See?" said Mercy with a grin. "I'm helpful."

Dawes leaned back in her chair and met Alex's gaze. "You're Virgil now. It's your call."

Alex threw up her hands. "Fuck it. Mercy Zhao, welcome to Lethe."

What must be understood is that demons are creatures of appetite. So though their powers are virtually without limit, their understanding is decidedly more constrained. This is why they are so easily distracted by puzzles and games: They are most engaged by what is immediately before them. This is also why the creation of material objects out of nothing proves so difficult. Gold out of thin air? Costly in terms of blood sacrifice, but easy enough. An alloy? Slightly more difficult. A complex item like a ship or an alarm clock? Well, you had best have a rigorous understanding of their workings because I can guarantee the demon will not. An organism more complex than an amoeba? Nearly impossible. The devil, my friends, is in the details.

—Kittscher's Daemonologie, *1933*

Knuckles of Shimshon, believed to be one of a set; gold, lead, and tungsten
Provenance: Unknown; date of origin unknown
Donor: Wolf's Head, 1998

These "brass knuckles" endow the wearer with the strength of twenty men. They were acquired during one of the many Middle Eastern digs sponsored by Wolf's Head and its foundation. But whether they were discovered at an architectural site or in a shop in some tourist quarter is unknown. Whether the hair forever trapped in gold belonged to the legendary hero or was simply a part of the enchantment placed upon the object is also unknown. But while the knuckles' provenance is shaky, the magic is not, and this most useful gift was added to the armory in 1998, in celebration of Lethe's centennial.

—from the Lethe Armory Catalogue as revised
and edited by Pamela Dawes, Oculus

20

D oes it ever feel like none of this is real?" Mercy whispered. They were sitting in the common room with Lauren and another member of the field hockey team, making construction-paper flowers for Liquor Treat. They'd set the room up as a gloomy garden with chocolate soil pots they'd fill with gummy worms. "All I can think about is Friday night."

They had a lot to accomplish before Halloween and only a few days to get it done. Alex had brought home recommended reading that Dawes had curated for her and Mercy, and they studied it in their room between classes and meals, then stashed it under their beds. She still didn't know how to feel about Mercy putting herself in danger, but she was also grateful to not feel so alone, and Mercy's excitement was a tonic to Dawes's constant worrying.

"*This* is real life," Alex reminded her, holding up a glue stick. "The stuff with Lethe . . . that's the distraction."

She was reminding herself as much as Mercy. The cool weather had shifted the feel of campus. There was something impermanent in the first months of the new semester, a warm softness that left it malleable in the waning days of what was no longer summer, but didn't yet feel like fall. Now hats and scarves emerged, boots replaced sandals, a kind of seriousness took hold. Alex and Mercy still cracked their windows or sometimes opened them wide—the dorm heaters had embraced the new season with too much zeal. But tucked away in the JE reading room or meeting with her philosophy TA at Bass, Alex felt a strange

sensation creep over her, a dangerous comfort in routine. She wasn't
sailing through her classes, but she was passing, a steady stream of Cs
and Bs, a cascade of hard-won mediocrity. *All of this can be lost*, she
told herself as she bent her lips to another cup of tea, feeling the steam
on her skin. This ease, this quiet. It was precious. It was impossible.

She was sticking googly eyes on a sunflower when her phone
pinged. Alex had almost forgotten about Eitan, or maybe hoped he'd
forgotten about her now that Oddman had paid his nut, and the
novelty of her as muscle had worn off. The text was an address Alex
didn't recognize, and when she looked it up, she saw it was in Old
Greenwich. How the hell was she supposed to get there?

"Do you want to take a theater class next semester?" Mercy asked.

"Sure."

"What's wrong?"

"Just my mom." In a way it was true.

"My parents won't like it," Mercy went on. "But I can tell them
it will help with public speaking. Shakespeare Acted is the only one
open to non–theater majors."

"Shakespeare again?" Lauren asked, repulsed. She was an econ
major and constantly complaining about anything that involved
more reading.

Mercy laughed. "Yeah."

I'll beat thee, but I should infect my hands. Alex couldn't remember
what it was from, but she was tempted to text it to Eitan. Instead she
texted Dawes and asked if the Mercedes was at Il Bastone.

Why? came the reply.

But Alex wasn't in the mood for the mother hen protecting her
boy's precious car. She was putting everything on the line for dear
Darlington and she needed transportation. She waited Dawes out
and eventually her phone pinged again.

Yes. Don't leave the tank empty.

Alex liked driving the Mercedes. She felt like a different person
in it, more beautiful, more interesting, the kind of woman people

wondered about, who wore ladylike little flats and spoke in a soft, bored drawl. Of course she'd bought the car for herself. It had just called to her from the lot—a sweet old thing. It wasn't practical, but neither was she.

Alex put on the radio. There wasn't much traffic on 95, and she thought about skirting the main roads to drive along the coast for a while, or looping up to get a peek at the Thimble Islands. Darlington had told her that some held famous mansions, while others were too small for much more than a hammock, and that Captain Kidd had supposedly buried his treasure on one of them. But she didn't have time to indulge her rich-girl road trip fantasies. She needed to finish this errand with Eitan and get back to prepare for the Manuscript ritual tomorrow. Alex wanted to reassure the Praetor that she was ready and did not require additional supervision.

By the time she reached Old Greenwich, dusk was falling, the sky softening to a deep, undiluted blue. Most towns didn't look nice right off the highway, but this place didn't seem to have a wrong side of the tracks. It was all pretty shop windows and rambling stone walls, lacy trees spreading black branches against the gathering dark. She followed the navigation down a gently curved road, past rolling lawns and sprawling old homes. Now Eitan's messages made more sense.

She'd had to look twice when he'd given her the name and the vig: *Linus Reiter, 50.*

50 large? she'd asked.

Eitan hadn't bothered to reply.

The name sounded like it could be a tech guy, and she knew Eitan had high-profile clients in Los Angeles, women who snorted Adderall to stay thin, TV execs who liked to party with poppers. None of that felt right for a place like this—tasteful, monied—but at least she understood how Eitan had let this guy get so far in. He must have known the dupe was good for it, and he was happy to gobble up the interest.

She slowed the car and then just sat, letting it idle as she stared at the address emblazoned on one of two big river-rock columns, each topped by a stone eagle.

"Fuck."

She was looking at a huge wrought iron gate set into a high wall covered in ivy. She couldn't see much beyond it except for the slope of a hill dense with trees and a gravel driveway disappearing into the evening gloom.

She scanned the wall and the gate for cameras. Nothing obvious, but that didn't mean much. Maybe people in Old Greenwich didn't think they needed protection. Or maybe they were just more discreet about it. If Alex got caught here, she was definitely getting arrested, and then Anselm and the board wouldn't bother with talk of second chances. They'd just toss her out of Lethe. Professor Walsh-Whiteley would probably throw a party. Or at least host a wine-and-cheese hour. But what choice did she have? She couldn't just say, *Oops! I rang the bell, but no one was home.*

Alex sat, undecided behind the wheel. She didn't see any Grays lurking around, and she wasn't sure she wanted to head up the hill without knowing she had backup. This guy could have a whole staff of goons on call like Eitan. But she also wasn't sure she was ready to let another Gray in, not after what had happened with the old man at Black Elm and that kid she'd used for the Oddman job. The connections were too powerful, too intimate. And there was always the chance one of them would get inside her and refuse to leave.

She reached into her coat pockets and felt the comforting weight of the brass knuckles she'd stolen from the Lethe House armory. "It's not really stealing," she murmured. "I'm Dante after all." *Virgil.*

Except she wasn't either right now. She was just Alex Stern and she had a job to do. She parked the Mercedes a few blocks away and looked up the satellite view of the property while she waited for full dark. The house was enormous, and it had to be at least a quarter of a mile up the long driveway. Behind it, she saw the blue lozenge of a swimming pool and some kind of guesthouse or pavilion.

At least beating up a rich guy would be a novelty.

She locked the car and gave it a pat for luck, then strolled to the eastern corner of the wall, grateful for the widely placed streetlamps. She'd seen no one on the road yet, except a slender woman jogging behind a double stroller. Alex slipped the brass knuckles over her fingers. They were actually solid gold and rough where the strands of Samson's hair had supposedly been woven through. She didn't know if that was myth or reality, but as long as they let her punch through walls, she didn't much care. *"My heels are fetter'd, but my fist is free,"* she whispered to no one. Or to Darlington, she supposed. *Samson Agonistes.* But he wasn't there to be impressed by her Milton.

The metal on her knuckles made her grip awkward, but the extra surge of strength in her hands let her pull herself over the wall with ease. Even so, she hesitated before dropping down onto the other side. She was in her black Converse, and all she needed was to break an ankle and freeze to death waiting for Dawes to come get her.

She counted to three and made herself jump. Thankfully the trees had already started to lose their leaves and the ground was soft with them. She jogged toward the house, paralleling the driveway, wondering if she was about to see flashlights or hear the shouts of security guards. Or maybe Linus Reiter had a hungry bunch of Dobermans to sic on her. But there was no sound except her footsteps in the mulch, the wind shaking the pines, and her own labored breathing. Darlington would have been laughing. *Twenty minutes a day on the treadmill, Stern. Sound body, sound mind.*

"Yeah, well, you're the one stuck doing naked yoga." She paused to catch her breath. She could see the hulking shadow of the house through the trees up ahead, but no lights on. Maybe Reiter really wasn't home. God, the thought was beautiful. Even so . . . 5 percent of $50,000. That would be more money than she'd ever had in her life. Eitan had suckered her into this work by threatening her mother, and she'd been too stupid to botch the first job, too used to falling in line. But maybe she'd gotten comfortable. Violence was easy. It was her first language, natural to slip back into, ready on her tongue. And she couldn't pretend that the little nest egg she'd started to build wasn't a kind of hedge, something to fall back on if Yale and Lethe and all of their promises fell apart.

When she finally arrived at the top of the hill, she paused at the tree line. The house was nothing like she'd expected. She'd imagined it would be all old brick and ivy like Black Elm, but it was an expansive, airy white thing, a pile of architectural meringue formed into a steeply tilted roof, striped awnings over the countless windows, a grand terrace perfect for lawn parties. She had no idea how she was going to get in. Maybe she should have glamoured herself, but she hadn't had time to plan.

Alex figured she was already guilty of breaking and entering, but the thought of smashing a window made her jittery—and that made her mad. So much for the cannonball. She wouldn't have hesitated if she'd been back in Oddman's neighborhood. It was Linus Reiter's wealth that frightened her. And for very good reason. This wasn't some bottom-of-the-pecking-order New Haven drug dealer, and Eitan wasn't going to pay her bail if this all went sideways.

"Fuck me," she muttered.

"Maybe a drink first."

Alex choked back a scream and whirled, her feet tangling. A man stood behind her in a spotless white suit. She checked herself, nearly toppling. She couldn't make out his face in the darkness.

"Did you come up here on a dare?" he asked pleasantly. "You're older than the kids who usually ring my doorbell and knock over my flowerpots."

"I . . ." Alex searched for a lie, but what was there to lie about? Instead she sent her mind seeking through the town. There were no Grays around the house or its grounds, and it wasn't until she reached a sprawling middle school building that she found that blur, that crinkle in her consciousness that signaled the presence of a Gray. Just knowing she could call on one was a comfort. "Eitan sent me."

"Eitan Harel?" he asked, his surprise clear.

"You owe fifty large," she said, feeling ridiculous. The estate looked impeccably kept, and from what she could see, Linus Reiter did too.

"So he sends a little girl to collect the debt?" Reiter's voice was bemused. "Interesting. Would you like to come in?"

"No." She had no reason to, and if she'd learned anything in her short and thorny life, you didn't walk into a stranger's house unless you had an escape plan ready. That went double for rich strangers.

"Suit yourself," he said. "It's getting chilly."

He strolled right past her and up the steps to the terrace.

"I need to collect tonight."

"That won't be possible," he called back.

Of course it couldn't be easy. Alex gave a tug on the schoolteacher, drawing her closer to the mansion, along the streets of Old Greenwich. But the Gray would be a last resort.

She followed Linus Reiter up the steps.

"So what's with the Gatsby act?" she asked as she followed him into a vast living room decorated with cream-colored couches and blue chinoiserie. White candles glowed on the mantel, the big glass coffee table, and the bar in the corner, illuminating shelves of expensive bottles that gleamed like buried treasure, amber, green, and ruby red. Billowing clouds of white hydrangeas were arranged in heavy vases. It was all very glamorous and grandmotherly at the same time.

"I was aiming for Tom Wolfe," said her host, heading behind the bar. "But I'll take what I can get. What can I offer you . . . ?"

He was searching for a name, but all she said was, "I'm on a schedule." If you were stupid enough to break rule number one and follow a stranger into his house, then rule number two was do not drink anything from a rich stranger who was on the precipice of being upgraded to rich weirdo.

Reiter sighed. "The modern world keeps such an unrelenting pace."

"Tell me about it. Listen, you seem . . ." She was unsure how to continue. *Pleasant? Genteel? A little eccentric but harmless?* He was surprisingly young, maybe thirty, and handsome in a delicate way. Tall, slender, fine-boned, his skin pale, his golden hair long enough to brush his shoulders, the rock god style at odds with that impeccable white suit. "Well, I don't know what you seem, but you're extremely polite. I don't want to be here and I don't want to threaten you, but that's my job."

"How long have you worked for Eitan?" he asked, assembling glasses, ice, bourbon.

"Not long."

He was watching her closely, his eyes a pale grayish blue. "You're an addict?"

"No."

"Then it's for money?"

Alex couldn't help the bitter laugh that escaped her. "Yes and no. Eitan has me in a bind. Just like you."

Now he smiled, his teeth even whiter than his skin, and Alex had to resist the urge to take a step back. There was something unnatural in that grin, the waxen face, the princely hair. She jammed her hands in her pockets, slipping her fingers back into Samson's knuckles.

"Darling girl," Reiter said. "Eitan Harel has never and will never have me in a *bind*. But I'm still trying to solve the puzzle of you. Fascinating."

Alex couldn't tell if he was hitting on her, and it didn't really matter. "You're not short on cash, so why not transfer the fifty to Eitan, and I'll leave you to whatever wealthy men get up to in their mansions on a quiet Wednesday night. You can move around the furniture or fire a butler or something."

Reiter took his drink and settled himself on one of the white couches. "I'm not giving that oily bastard a dime. Why don't you tell Eitan that?"

"I'd love to, but . . ." Alex shrugged.

Reiter made an eager humming sound. "Now things get interesting. Just what are you supposed to do when I don't hand over the money?"

"He told me to hurt you."

"Oh, very good," said Reiter, genuinely pleased. He leaned back and crossed his legs, spread his arms, as if welcoming an unseen crowd to enjoy his largesse. "I invite you to try."

Alex had never felt more tired. She wasn't going to hit a man who wasn't interested in defending himself. Maybe he got off on that shit or maybe he was desperate for entertainment. Or maybe he'd just never had reason to be afraid of someone like her and his imagination wasn't up to the task. But she could tell he loved his gracious home, his beautiful objects. That might be all the leverage she required.

"I'm short on time and I have a hot date with Chaucer." She tipped a vase off the mantel.

But the crash never came.

Reiter was standing in front of her, the vase cradled in his long white fingers. He'd moved fast. Too fast.

"Now, now," he tsked. "I brought that back from China myself."

"That so," said Alex, backing away.

"In 1936."

She didn't hesitate. She clenched the brass knuckles in her fist and swung.

21

Too slow. She struck nothing but air. Reiter was already behind her, one arm clamped around her chest, the fingers of his other hand gripping her skull.

"There is no debt, you stupid child," he purred. "I'm the competition. Harel and his nasty little compatriots want my territory. But why that rat sent you here, I cannot tell. A gift? An enticement? The question will be whether I can drink you dry without ruining my suit. It's a little challenge I like to set for myself."

His teeth—his *fangs*—sank into her neck. Alex screamed. The pain was acute, the needle prick, the abrupt agony that followed. Now she knew why there were no ghosts on the estate. This was where death lived.

Alex cried out to the Gray lurking reluctantly outside the gates. The schoolteacher rushed into her—the stale smell of a coatroom full of brown-bag lunches, a dusty cloud of chalk, and her relentless will. *Hands go up, mouths go shut.*

The vampire hissed and broke his hold, spitting blood from his mouth. Alex watched it spatter the couch, the carpet.

"So much for your suit."

His eyes glittered now, bright dimes in his too-pale face, fangs extended, wet with her blood. "You taste like the grave."

"Good."

She launched herself at him, flush with the Gray's strength, brass knuckles in place. She got in two good hits, heard his jaw crunch, felt his stomach crumple. Then he seemed to shake off the shock, regain his speed. He darted away, putting distance between them, and he rose, levitating, *flying*, weightless before her in his bloodstained whites.

Her mind screamed at the wrongness of him. How could she have mistaken this creature for human?

"A real puzzle," the vampire said. The two strikes with the brass knuckles would have killed an ordinary man, but he looked unfazed. "Now I understand why Eitan Harel sent an emaciated child after me. But what exactly are you, honey lamb?"

Fucking terrified. All she had was ghost strength and a scrap of magic borrowed—stolen—from Lethe. And clearly that wasn't going to be enough.

Had Eitan sent her here to die? She could worry about that later. If she lived. *Think.* What rattled this particular monster? The only time she'd seen him shaken was when she'd threatened his beautiful things, his glorious stuff.

Okay, you toothy motherfucker. Let's play.

She snatched a porcelain figurine off a side table, hurled it through the French doors, and lunged for the bar. She didn't wait to find out if he'd taken the bait, just let herself crash into the bottles, smashing whatever she could and knocking the candles into the mess of liquor. She saw one gutter out, and she released a helpless sob. But then the fire caught and bloomed, a graceful flame, a spreading vine. It gained strength, licking up the alcohol, sliding along the bar.

The vampire howled. Alex dove behind the flames, using them for cover, feeling the heat grow and trying to cover her mouth as smoke billowed up. She stripped off her hoodie and wound it into a make-shift torch, soaking it in liquor, fire gathering around it like a ball of cotton candy. She bolted for the French doors, and tossed the torch behind her, heard a *whoosh* as the curtains caught.

Alex threw herself through the window with a loud crash and felt the prickle of glass slicing her skin. Then she was running.

She had the Gray's strength within her, and she took long strides, ignoring the branches that stung her face, the throb at her neck where Reiter had bitten into her. She didn't bother with scaling the wall. She put her arms out in front of her and slammed through the gates. They gave way with a clang and she was sprinting down the street, fumbling for the keys to the Mercedes. But her pockets were empty. The hoodie. The keys had been in the hoodie. Dawes was going to kill her.

Alex ran, her sneakers smacking against the blacktop of the empty streets. She saw lights on in the houses. Could she veer off, beg for help, try to find sanctuary? She seized on the ghost's strength, felt it rush deeper into her as her legs pumped. It barely felt like she was touching the ground. She ran through the dark, through pockets of streetlight, into the town where the traffic was thicker, past the train station, until she was running the frontage road parallel to the highway. She dodged a car, heard the shriek of a horn, and then she was moving over water. A river? The sea? She could see the lights from the bridge, big houses with their own docks reflected on the surface. She was running past chain-link fences, dogs barking and yowling in her wake. She was afraid to stop.

Could he track her? Smell her blood? He hadn't liked the taste of her, that much was clear, at least not once she'd summoned the Gray. She didn't know where she was anymore. She wasn't even sure if she was running toward New Haven or away from it. She didn't feel human. She was a coyote, a fox, some feral thing that crept into yards at night. She was a ghost herself, an apparition glimpsed through windows.

But fatigue was seeping in. She could feel the Gray begging her to stop.

Ahead she saw a highway exit, and a gas station sitting in an island of light. She slowed her steps but didn't stop until she'd entered that bright dome of fluorescence. There were cars parked at the pump, a couple of semis pulled up in the big parking lot, travelers shopping in the mini-mart. Alex stopped in front of the sliding glass doors and bent double, hands on her knees, breath coming in gasps, afraid she might vomit as the adrenaline ebbed out of her body. The minutes ticked by, and she watched the road, the sky. Could Reiter actually fly? Turn into a bat? Did he have vampire buddies to send after her?

Had he already put out the fire at his splendid mansion? She hoped not. She hoped that fire would eat everything he loved.

At last she relinquished the schoolteacher, feeling the dregs of her strength drain away. She felt nauseous and so tired. She sat down on the curb, rested her head against her knees, and wept hot, frightened tears.

"It's all right."

Alex jumped at the soft voice, half-expecting to see Linus Reiter next to her.

But it was the schoolteacher. Her smile was gentle. She had died in her sixties, and there were deep creases around her eyes. She was wearing slacks, and a sweater, and a pin with a smiling rainbow on it that said *Very good! Muy bien!* Her hair was cut short.

There were no wounds that Alex could see, and she wondered how this woman had died. She knew she should turn away, pretend she couldn't hear her; any bond with a Gray could be dangerous. But she couldn't make herself do it.

"Thank you," she whispered, feeling fresh tears slide down her cheeks.

"We don't go to that house," said the teacher. "He buries them in the gardens."

"Who?" Alex asked, feeling herself begin to shake. "How many?"

"Hundreds. Maybe more. He's been there a very long time."

Alex pressed her palms against her eyes. "I'm going to get something to drink."

"Your neck," the teacher murmured, as if mentioning that Alex had a speck of food on her face.

Alex put her hand to her neck. She couldn't tell how bad the wound was. She released her ponytail, hoping her hair would hide the worst of it.

"Can I come with you?" the teacher asked as Alex rose on wobbly legs.

Alex nodded. She knew how much the Bridegroom had wanted to remember what it was like to be in a body, and even if every moment she spent with this Gray was perilous, she didn't want to be alone.

She let the teacher drift into her this time, at her own pace. Alex saw a classroom of bored faces, a few raised hands, a sunny apartment and a woman with long graying hair, dancing as she set the table. Love flooded through her.

Alex let it carry her into the mini-mart. She bought rubbing alcohol, cotton balls, and a box of big bandages, along with a liter of Coke and a bag of Doritos. She kept her head down and paid in cash, glancing out at the parking lot, still afraid she'd see a dark shape descending.

She went to the bathroom to clean herself up. But as soon as she shut the door and looked in the mirror, she had to stop again.

Maybe she'd expected two clean little puncture wounds like in the movies, but the marks in her neck were jagged and ugly, crusted with blood. He hadn't pierced her jugular or she'd be dead, but there was plenty of mess. She looked like she'd been mauled by an animal, and she supposed she had. Alex wiped away the blood, ignoring the sting of the alcohol, grateful for it. She was cleaning him away, scrubbing out any trace of him.

Her neck looked better when she was done, but Alex was still afraid. What if that thing had infected her with something? And why the fuck hadn't anyone told her vampires were real?

Alex slapped a bandage on her neck and walked out to the curb. She sat down in the same spot and took a big swig of soda.

Eventually the teacher reemerged looking almost delirious with pleasure from the sugar. It would be polite to ask her name, but Alex had to set some limits.

"Do you have someone to call?" the woman asked.

She sounded like so many of the school counselors and social workers Alex had breezed through in her childhood. The good ones at least.

"I have to call Dawes," she said, ignoring the confused look from the burly guy in plaid flannel pumping diesel into his truck and watching her talk to no one. "I just don't want to." Alex felt sick with grief for the Mercedes, abandoned back in Old Greenwich. It was possible the vampire wouldn't find it, or not for a while. She didn't know anything about vampires. Did they have some preternatural sense of smell or an ability to track their victims? She shuddered.

"You seem like a good kid," said the teacher. "What were you doing there?"

Alex took another swig. "You were a counselor, weren't you?"

"Is it that obvious?"

"It's nice," Alex admitted. But this Gray couldn't save her any more than the other kind people who had tried.

She pulled her cell from her jeans pocket, grateful that it hadn't gotten lost in the chase. There was no point to calling Dawes, not yet. She needed someone with a car.

Alex nearly burst into tears when Turner actually picked up.

"Stern," he said, his voice flat.

"Turner, I need your help."

"What else is new?"

"Can you come get me?"

"Where are you?" he asked.

"I'm not sure." She craned her neck, looking for a sign. "Darien."

"Why can't you call a car?"

She didn't want to call a car. She didn't want to be near another stranger.

"I . . . Something happened to me. I need a ride."

There was a long pause, then sudden silence, as if he'd turned off a television. "Text me your address."

"Thanks."

Alex hung up, found the location of the service station, and sent it to Turner. Then she stared at her phone. The fear was leaving her, replaced by fury, and it felt good, like that rubbing alcohol, cleaning her wounds, waking her up.

She dialed.

For once Eitan picked up immediately. He'd been watching, waiting to see if she survived.

She didn't bother with a greeting. "You set me up."

"Alex," he chided. "I thought you will win."

"How many did you send before me? How many didn't come back?"

There was a slight pause. "Seven."

She brushed fresh tears from her eyes. She wasn't sure when she'd started crying again, but she needed to keep her voice steady. She could do that. The anger was with her, simple, familiar. She didn't want to seem weak.

"Was there really a debt?" she asked.

"Not exactly. He is taking customers from me and my associates. Foxwoods, Mohegan Sun, all good markets."

Reiter was a rival dealer. Alex supposed even vampires had to make a living.

"Fuck you and your associates."

"I thought you could fix. You are special."

Alex wanted to scream. "You painted a target on my back."

"Reiter will not bother with you."

"How the fuck do you know?"

"I have guests, Alex. You want I should send you some money?"

She'd known for a long time that she might have to kill Eitan. She'd thought about doing it back in Los Angeles, but he was always surrounded by guards like Tzvi, men with guns who wouldn't think twice about putting her down. And the deal Eitan had proposed had seemed so simple, like something she could handle, just one job. *Do this and you're done. Good girl.* But of course that hadn't been the end of it. She'd gotten Eitan's money and she'd made it look easy, so it was always going to be one more favor, one more job, one more hump who owed, one more sob story. And what about her mother? What about Mira going for power walks to the farmers' market? Going to work every morning thinking her daughter was safe at last, and that she was safe too?

Alex hung up and stared out at the harsh lights near the pumps, the gleaming sign ablaze with gas prices, the shine of flannel guy's truck. It felt like the service station was some kind of beacon. But what were they calling out to with all of this bright light?

Killing Eitan would free her, but she'd have to be smart about it, find a way to get him alone, make him vulnerable the way she was. And she had to take her mom out of the equation, to make sure that if she screwed up, Mira wouldn't pay and that she couldn't be used as leverage again. To do that she needed money. A lot of it.

"Do you want me to stay with you?" the teacher asked.

"Would you? Until my ride gets here?"

"You're going to be okay."

Alex managed a smile. "Because I seem like a good kid?"

The teacher looked surprised. "No, kiddo. Because you're a killer."

When Turner's Dodge arrived, Alex waved goodbye to the teacher and gratefully slid into the passenger seat. He had the heater on and the radio was tuned to some local NPR station describing the day in the markets.

They drove in silence for a while and Alex was actually nodding off when he said, "What did you get yourself into, Stern?"

There was blood on her clothes and a bandage on her neck. Her shoes were covered in mud, and she still smelled of smoke and the booze she'd splattered all over Linus Reiter's living room.

"Nothing good."

"That all you're going to say about it?"

For now it was. "How's your case going?" She hadn't told him about her suspicions regarding the Praetor and his rivalry with Beekman yet.

Turner sighed. "Not well. We thought we'd found a connection between Dean Beekman and Professor Stephen."

"Oh yeah?" Alex was eager to talk about anything that wasn't Linus Reiter.

"Stephen blew the whistle on data coming out of one of the labs in the psych department. She had concerns that it was massaged by at least one of the fellows and that there'd been shoddy oversight from the professor who published the findings."

"And the dean?"

"He headed up the committee that disciplined the professor in question. Ed Lambton."

"Judges," Alex murmured, remembering Professor Stephen's finger resting between the Bible pages. "It makes a kind of sense."

"Only if you're being literal," Turner replied. "Judges isn't about judges the way we think of them. It was just another word for leaders in biblical times."

"Maybe the killer didn't go to Sunday school. Did Lambton lose his job?"

Turner shot her an amused glance. "Of course not. He's got tenure. But he's on paid leave and had to retract the paper. His reputation is in ruins. The psych study was on honesty so he's become a bit of a punch line. Unfortunately, I can't find any holes in his alibi. There's absolutely no way he could have gone after Dean Beekman or Professor Stephen."

"So now what do you do?"

"Follow the other leads. Marjorie Stephen had a volatile ex-husband. Beekman had an old harassment charge on the books. We're not short on enemies."

I know the feeling.

"Beekman was connected to the societies too."

"Was he?" Alex asked. Had Turner scooped the Professor Walsh-Whiteley lead?

"He was in Berzelius."

Alex snorted. "Berzelius is barely a society. They don't have any magic."

"Still a society. Do you know Michelle Alameddine?"

He knew she did. He'd seen them together at Elliot Sandow's funeral. Was Turner interrogating her?

"Of course," she said. "She was Darlington's Virgil."

"She also spent time in the psych ward at Yale New Haven. She was part of a study led by Marjorie Stephen, and she was in the city the night Dean Beekman was killed."

"I saw her," Alex admitted. "She said she had to catch a train back to New York, that she was having dinner with her boyfriend."

"We have her on camera at the train station. Monday morning."

Not Sunday night. Michelle had lied to her. But there could be countless reasons for that.

"How did you know about the psych ward?" Alex asked. "That should be confidential, right?"

"It's my job to find out who murdered two faculty members. That kind of concern opens a lot of doors."

Silence stretched between them. Alex thought of all the supposedly sealed records, the court cases, the write-ups by therapists and doctors in her past. The things she thought no one would ever know about her. She felt fear crowding in and she had to push it away. There was no point waltzing with old partners when her dance card was already full.

She shifted in her seat to face him. "I don't want to ask you to go back to that map with me. But Halloween is two days away and we need to find our fourth."

"Your fourth. Like you're playing doubles tennis." Turner shook his head. He kept his eyes on the road when he said, "I'll do it."

Alex knew she shouldn't look a gift cop in the mouth, but she couldn't quite believe what she was hearing. Turner had no love for Darlington, no sense of obligation. He hated everything that Lethe stood for, especially after that trip to the Peabody basement. "Why?"

"Does it matter?"

"We're about to go to hell together. So yeah. It matters."

Turner stared ahead. "Do you believe in God?"

"No."

"Wow, not even a beat to think about it?"

"I've thought about it. A lot. Do *you* believe in God?"

"I do," he said with a firm nod. "I think I do. But I definitely believe in the devil, and if he gets hold of a soul and doesn't want to let it go, I think you have to try to pry it away from him. Especially if that soul has the makings of a soldier."

"Or a knight."

"Sure."

"Turner, this isn't some kind of holy war. It's not good versus evil."

"You sure?"

Alex laughed. "Well, if it is, are you sure we're the good guys?"

"You killed those people in Los Angeles, didn't you?"

The question hung between them in the car, another passenger, a ghost along for the ride. Alex considered just telling him. What would it feel like to be free of the secret of that night? What would it mean to have an ally against Eitan?

She watched the light from the highway splashing bright, then dark across Turner's profile. She liked him. He was brave, and he was willing to stroll into the underworld to rescue someone he hadn't particularly liked just because he believed it was right. But a cop was a cop.

"What happened to those people back in Los Angeles?" he pushed. "Helen Watson. Your boyfriend Leonard Beacon. Mitchell Betts. Cameron Aust. Dave Corcoran. Ariel Harel."

The same thing that happens to anyone who gets close to me.

Alex studied the road slipping by, caught a glimpse of someone studying the screen of his phone against the steering wheel, a billboard for some band playing at Foxwoods in November, another for an accident attorney. She didn't like the way Turner had rattled off those names. Like he knew her file inside out.

"It's funny," she said at last. "People talk about life and death as if there's some kind of ticking clock."

"There isn't?"

Alex shook her head slowly. "That *tick tick tick* isn't a clock. It's a bomb. There's no countdown. It just goes off and everything changes." She rubbed her thumb over a spot of blood on her jeans. "But I don't think hell is a pit full of sinners and a guy with horns playing bouncer."

"You believe what you need to, Stern. But I know what I saw when I walked into that room back at Black Elm."

"What?" Alex asked, though some part of her desperately didn't want to know.

"The devil," said Turner. "The devil trying to make his way out."

22

Alex was glad Dawes wasn't at Il Bastone.

She let herself in, grateful for the house, its wards, its quiet. It was nearly 8 p.m. Only a few hours had passed since she'd set out for Old Greenwich. The lights flickered and soft music floated through the halls, as if Il Bastone knew she'd been through something terrible.

She washed Reiter's blood off the brass knuckles in the kitchen sink, returned them to their drawer in the armory, then dug through the cabinets to find the balm Dawes had used on her feet the night she'd sleepwalked to Black Elm. The schoolteacher had lent her enough strength to escape, but it was Alex's body that had taken the punishment. She was cut up and bruised, her lungs hurt, and her whole body throbbed from her run across county lines.

In the Dante bedroom, she set out the first aid supplies she'd purchased on the pretty writing desk and then headed to the bathroom to peel back her bandage.

The wound on her neck was already closing, and there was no fresh blood. It shouldn't have healed up so fast. Did that mean he actually had pierced her jugular and it had just started healing right away? She didn't know. She didn't want to know. She wanted to forget Linus Reiter and his angelic face and all of that pain and fear. She could feel his teeth sliding into her, his grip on her skull, the knowledge that she was nothing but food, a cup he held to his lips, a vessel to be emptied.

She hadn't been afraid, truly afraid, in a long time. If she was honest, she had enjoyed facing off against Darlington's parents, Odd-man, the new Praetor. When Dawes had summoned a herd of fire-breathing horses from hell, she'd been scared but okay. She liked forgetting about everything except the fight in front of her.

But those had been fights she could win. She wasn't strong enough to beat Linus Reiter any more than she was clever enough to get out from under Eitan Harel's thumb. They were the same man. Linus would have happily drunk her dry and planted her in his backyard to feed the roses. Eitan would just keep using her, sending her on jobs until she didn't come back.

She rubbed balm into the wound, replaced the bandage, and looked for a clean pair of Lethe sweats. She'd forgotten to bring back the last couple of pairs to be laundered, so she had to go up to the Virgil bedroom to pillage Darlington's closet. They were too long and too baggy, but they were clean.

Her next stop was the Lethe library. She drew the Albemarle Book from the shelf outside, ignoring the faint screams and the puff of brimstone that emerged from its pages. The book held the memory of whatever had been researched last, and Dawes had clearly been studying some version of the underworld.

Alex drew a pen from the wicker table beside the shelf, then hesitated. She knew she needed to be very specific in her request. Vampires were all over folklore and fiction, and she didn't want to have to sort through what was myth and what might actually be useful. Also, if you were too vague with the library, the walls started shaking, and there was a good chance it might cave in entirely. Maybe she should start smaller.

She scrawled, *Linus Reiter*, and returned the book to its place. The shelf rattled gently, and when it had settled, Alex let it swing open to the library.

There were more than a dozen books on the shelves, but as Alex sorted through them, she realized most were focused on the Reiter family and their grand home in Old Greenwich, Sweetwell. The Reiters were German immigrants and had made their money manufacturing boilers and water heaters. Sweetwell and its surrounding land had always passed from one Reiter heir to the next, but Alex suspected they were all the same man.

She was surprised to see one of Arnold Guyot Dana's scrapbooks on the library shelf, a fat volume bound in navy blue, *Yale: Old and New* emblazoned in gold on its spine. Darlington had been obsessed with the scrapbooks dedicated to New Haven and Yale, and had cherished volumes sixteen through eighteen, which, along with Hiram Bingham III's diary, had been pilfered from the Sterling Library years ago to hide vital information on Lethe and the flow of magical artifacts through the city.

Alex flipped through the thick pages of newspaper clippings, old photographs, and maps, until her eyes landed on a photo of a group of young men at Mory's, all stern-faced, all suited. And there was Linus, in the back row, his face solemn, his pale blue eyes nearly white in the old picture. He looked softer somehow, more mobile in this photo than he had been sitting in his own living room. Had he been human then? Or already turned and having a laugh? And how was she supposed to best a drug-dealing blue blood Connecticut vampire?

Kittscher's Daemonologie was also on the shelf, the same book Michelle Alameddine had recommended and that Dawes had been using for research. Alex flipped through, still hoping for a catalogue of monsters and ideally how to best them. But the book was as Dawes had described: a series of debates on hell between Ellison Nownes, a divinity student and devout Christian, and Rudolph Kittscher, an atheist and member of Lethe.

Nownes seemed to be arguing for Turner's version of hell—a place of eternal punishment for sinners: *Whether there be nine circles or twelve, whether pits of fire or lakes of ice, though the architecture of hell be indeterminate, its existence and purpose are not.*

But Kittscher disagreed: *Superstition and bunk! We know there are other worlds and planes and that their existence enables the use of portals—why, ask any Locksmith if he thinks he's simply disappearing from one place and reappearing in another. No! We know better. There are other realms. And why should we not understand "hell" as one of these realms?* Here, the transcript noted "loud applause."

Some of what they were saying went right over Alex's head, but she was pretty sure Kittscher was suggesting the existence of hell—and heaven—was a bargain between demons and men: *Just as we may be nourished by meat or fowl, or survive upon a diet of simple roots and berries, so demons are nourished by our base emotions. Some feed on fear or greed or lust or rage, and yes, some hunger after joy. Heaven and hell are a compromise, nothing more, a treaty binding demons to remain in their realm and feed only upon the dead.*

This was where the crowd turned on Kittscher and the notes described Nownes as "red-faced." *Nownes: This is what comes of a vision of a world without God—not only a life but an afterlife devoid of any higher morality. You suggest that we, creatures born of God and made in His image, are the lowliest of beasts, timid rabbits trapped in a snare, made not for great study or high achievement, but to be consumed? This is the purpose and fate of humanity?*

Kittscher had laughed. *Our bodies are food for worms. Why should our souls not be made meals too?*

At that point both parties had nearly come to blows and a recess had been taken.

Alex rubbed her eyes. She'd been straight with Turner: She didn't believe in his Sunday school version of the underworld. But she wasn't sure she bought into Kittscher's theory either. And why had this turned up in her search regarding Linus Reiter?

She combed through the index for any mention of him, then slid her finger down to *V*, for vampire. A single page was listed.

Kittscher: Think on the vampire.
(Jeering from the assembly.)
Herman Moseby: What's next, leprechauns and kelpies?
(A call to order from the moderator.)
Kittscher: Have you never wondered why in our stories some seduce and some terrify? Why some are beautiful and others grotesque? These disparate stories are proof that demons remain in our world, some who feed on misery or terror, others who feed on desire, all of whom take the forms most likely to elicit those emotions.

(Terrence Gleebe is recognized by the moderator.)
Gleebe: In this scenario, is blood a vehicle or incidental to the process?
(Laughter from the assembly.)

Alex touched her fingers to the bandage on her neck. "Incidental, my ass."

She thought of handsome Linus Reiter in his white suit. Why would a vampire become a drug dealer? There had to be a thousand ways to make money when you had that kind of power and that much time. But what if you fed on desperation? What if the money meant nothing but you required an endless buffet of fear and need? Alex remembered the hangers-on at Eitan's house, the losers at Ground Zero, her own aching sadness, the desolation that had been her life, the scraps of hope she'd wrung from the moments of peace that a little weed, a little alcohol, a pop of Valium could provide.

So if Kittscher was right and vampires were demons, at least she knew what she was dealing with. But how to keep the monster at bay?

She left the library and took out the Albemarle Book, wrote: *how to avoid vampires, nonfiction.* Then she hesitated. Why had the library provided her with information on a vampire when she had specifically asked for books mentioning Linus Reiter? She kept the Albemarle Book open and returned to the round table where she'd left *Kittscher's Daemonologie.* Reiter hadn't been listed in the index. She flipped to the back of the book.

Minutes taken by Phillip Walter Merriman, Oculus, 1933.
In attendance:

The participants were listed by society, and there, under Skull and Bones: *Lionel Reiter.*

He'd been there. Under a different name, but he'd been in this house, under Lethe's roof. Maybe he'd been mortal then. But maybe there had been a demon in one of the societies, inside Il Bastone, and no one had been the wiser. And what about the date? 1933. A year after Sterling had been built. Did that mean there really had been a first pilgrimage to hell? Was that the subtext here? Who had known about the Gauntlet, and was this less a heated argument about philosophic hypotheticals than a very real debate about the possibility of traveling to the underworld?

And if demons fed on humans, on their happiness or their pain, even their blood, was there another variable she had to consider? She remembered Marjorie Stephen, old before her time, eyes milky and gray. What if there hadn't been any poison? Could Reiter be involved? Or some other demon having his fun? Taunting them with scripture? Turner would have told her if they'd found neck wounds on Professor Stephen or Dean Beekman, but before tonight, Alex hadn't known vampires were real. What else might be lurking out there in the dark?

Alex felt panic rising up to choke her. She thought of all those studious young men from well-to-do families debating morality and immortality, arguing semantics, while a monster enjoyed their hospitality. *Because we're all a bunch of amateurs.* Lethe pretended they knew the score when they didn't even know the game. But this house, this library, could still protect her.

After three more searches, she had regained some small sense of calm, and she had a list of recommendations culled from the few books she could find in English that covered repelling demons and vampires, most of them involving weapons made of salt. According to the books she skimmed, stakes, beheading, and fire all worked because they killed just about anything. Crosses and holy water were dependent on the faith of the user, since they lent courage, not real protection. Garlic was only effective as a repellent toward a particular type of succubus. And the wards worked. That was what mattered. In the armory, she located a wide lacy collar made of tiny salt pearls that dated back to colonial times and that she could tuck neatly under her shirt. She lay down in the Dante bedroom, beneath the velvet blue canopy, and dreamed she was playing croquet on Linus Reiter's lawn. She was barefoot and the grass was wet. She could see blood seeping up between her toes.

"Intriguing," he whispered, but in the dream, he was Darlington, in a white suit with glowing golden horns. He smiled at her. "Hello, honey lamb. Have you come to be devoured?"

The house behind him was no longer Sweetwell but Black Elm, covered in ivy, somehow lonelier than even a vampire's castle on a hill.

Alex drifted inside; she knew the way, that same strange sense of compulsion drawing her on. The rooms seemed bigger, their shadows deeper. She climbed the stairs to the ballroom, and Darlington was there, in the circle, but he was her Darlington, just as she remembered him the night he'd disappeared from Rosenfeld Hall, handsome, human, dressed in his long dark coat, his weathered jeans.

Through the windows she could see the demon with his curling horns, standing amid the discarded croquet set on the lawn, gazing up at her with golden eyes.

"There are two of you," Alex said.

"There have to be," Darlington replied. "The boy and the monster. I am the hermit in the cave."

"I saw everything. In your grandfather's memories. I saw you try to survive this place."

"It wasn't all bad."

Alex felt her lips twist. "Of course it wasn't. If it was all bad, you could just let go."

"When did you get so wise, Stern?"

"When you went on sabbatical to purgatory."

"I could hear them," he said, eyes distant. They were dark brown, tea left to brew too long. "My parents. When they were yelling at the front door."

"Should I have let them in?"

His gaze snapped to hers, and in his rage she could see the echo of the demon. "No. Never. They turned the power off, after I inherited this place. They thought they could freeze me out." His shoulders lifted, dropped. His anger fell away from him like an ill-fitting garment. He looked so tired. "I don't know how to not love them."

How many times had Alex wished she could feel only resentment toward Mira? Or nothing at all? That was the problem with love. It was hard to unlearn, no matter how harsh the lesson.

"Is this real?" she asked.

But Darlington only smiled. "This isn't the time for philosophy."

"Tell me how to reach you."

"Come closer, Stern. I'll tell you everything you want to know."

Was she afraid? Was this the real Darlington, or was he the monster waiting in the garden? Some part of her didn't care. She stepped forward.

"Was it you that night?" She could see the circle of protection was fraying, dissolving into sparks. *He is dangerous. He is not what you think.* "At Book and Snake? Did you use the corpse to spell my name?"

"Galaxy Stern," Darlington said, his eyes flashing gold, "I have been crying out to you from the start."

When Alex woke, the sheets were soaked with sweat, and the wound at her neck was leaking pale pink rivulets of blood.

It is interesting to contemplate which of Aesop's fables were chosen for illustration in Bonawit's very fine glasswork. Is there a lesson in the choices? That may depend on how each fable is read. Take "The Wolf and the Crane": In the course of eating too quickly, a greedy wolf gets a bone stuck in his throat. To the crane he says, "Use your slender beak to pull it out and I will give you a fine reward." The crane obliges, placing his head inside the wolf's jaws and extracting the bone, but when the work is done, the wolf grants the crane no prize. Isn't it enough that he has let such a fool escape his bite? Traditionally, we are told the moral is "There is no reward for serving the wicked." But we might just as well understand the story to posit this question: "Isn't it a merry thing to cheat death?"

Less famous but also found in these same windows is the tale of "The Kid and the Wolf." Separated from his herd, a young goat encounters a wolf. "As I must be eaten," he says, "will you not play me a tune that I may die dancing?" Happy to have music with his meal, the wolf obliges, but from across the pasture, the huntsman's hounds hear his playing. Chased through the woods, the wolf marvels at his own foolishness, for he was born a butcher, not a piper. The moral offered in most readings is strange indeed: "Let nothing keep you from your purpose." Then are we to understand ourselves as the wolf? Why is the clever goat not our model? Take then this lesson: "When faced with death, better to dance than to lie down for it."

—*A Reconsideration of the Decoration of*
Sterling Memorial Library,
Rudolph Kittscher (Jonathan Edwards '33)

23

Alex waited until daylight to walk home to the dorms and change her clothes. She borrowed a soft gray cashmere sweater from Lauren, and put on her least-shabby-looking pair of jeans. She wanted to seem responsible, like a good investment, but there was nothing she could do about her scuffed-up boots.

When she'd called Anselm to ask for a meeting, she had expected him to tell her to meet with the new Praetor instead. But he was coming up on the Metro-North that afternoon and agreed to squeeze her in.

"You'll have to forgive the name of the place," he'd said. "I have a meeting there before I head back to the city, but I can meet you for a late lunch."

Shell and Bones. It was an oyster bar right on the water. Alex checked to make sure her salt collar wasn't visible beneath her borrowed sweater, then nudged her bike out onto the street. She forgot sometimes that New Haven was so close to the sea, that it was truly a port town.

The ride down Howard was surprisingly pretty, past leaves turning colors and homes that got grander as they neared the waterfront. They were nothing like the mansions of Old Greenwich. There was something public about their big porches, their windows facing the road, as if they were meant to be seen and enjoyed instead of being hidden behind a wall.

Dawes hadn't taken the news of the missing Mercedes well, because of course the car was not just a car.

"What do you mean you lost it?" she'd cried.

"I didn't lose it. I know where it is."

"Then tell me so I can go get it. I have a spare set of keys. We—"

"We can't."

"Why not?"

Because I'm afraid. Because it's too dangerous. But Alex couldn't explain it all. Linus Reiter. What she'd been doing in Old Greenwich. The dream of Darlington restored to himself in the circle. *I have been crying out to you from the start.* It was too much.

"You lost him," Dawes seethed. "And now this."

"I didn't lose Darlington," Alex said, striving for patience. "He isn't a shiny penny I dropped somewhere. Elliot Sandow sent a hellbeast to eat him, so go to the cemetery and bitch at his tombstone if you want to."

"You should have—"

"What? I should have what? Known the right spell to speak, the right incantation? I should have grabbed him so we could go to hell together?"

"Yes," Dawes said on a hiss. "Yes. You're his Dante."

"Is that what you'd have done?"

Dawes didn't answer, and Alex knew she should let it lie, but she was too tired and bruised to be kind. "I'll tell you what you would have done, Dawes. You would have pissed yourself. You would have frozen just like I did, and Darlington would be just as gone."

Silence on the other end of the phone and then, as if she'd never spoken the words and didn't quite know how to make the syllables match, Dawes shouted, "Fuck you! Fuck you! Fuck you!"

Something about that stuttered bit of profanity pierced Alex's miserable mood. The anger gusted out of her and she felt the sudden urge to laugh—which she knew would be a huge mistake.

She took a deep breath. "I'm sorry, Dawes. You don't know how sorry I am. But the car doesn't matter. I matter. You matter. And I promise we'll get it back. I just . . . I just need a little grace right now."

After a long moment, Dawes said, "Okay."

"Okay?"

"Yes. For the time being. I'm sorry I was rude."

Then Alex did laugh. "You're forgiven. And you should swear more, Dawes."

Alex knew the restaurant was at a yacht club, but it wasn't what she'd anticipated. She'd thought there would be a valet, men in blue blazers, women in pearls. Instead it was an ordinary-looking building on the waterfront, with a flag out front and a big parking lot. Alex locked her bike to the railing by the steps. She would have liked to wear her hair up, look a bit more conservative, but the marks on her neck were still red and swollen, as if her body was staving off an infection, and if she just slapped another bandage on her neck, she'd look like she was trying to hide a hickey.

Anselm was waiting at a four-top on a covered deck that faced the ocean, the harbor crowded with boats, their masts tilting one way or the other, some of them christened after women, others with names like *The Hull Truth*, *Knotty Girl*, *Reel Easy*. He'd slung his arm over the chair beside him, and he looked like an ad for an expensive watch. The other tables were crowded with Yalies and their parents, businessmen taking long lunches, a few older women in quilted coats lingering over glasses of rosé.

"Alex!" he said when he caught sight of her, his voice warm and vaguely surprised, as if he hadn't invited her there. "Have a seat." He waved over a server who placed a menu in front of her. "I've already eaten, but please, get whatever you like."

Alex wasn't going to say no to a free meal. She thought she should probably order something like mussels or grilled fish, but years of eating her mother's all-grain, sprouted carob experiments had left her with a lifelong craving for junk food. She ordered the sliders and a Coke for the caffeine.

"I wish I could eat like you," Anselm said, patting what looked like a flat stomach. "Youth is wasted on the young. If I'd known what middle age would look like, I would have spent more time eating fried chicken and less time at the gym."

"You're middle-aged?"

"Well, I will be . . . What?"

Alex realized she was staring. "Sorry, you just seem different, more relaxed."

"Is that surprising? Believe it or not, I don't relish chastising undergraduates."

"Dawes is a Ph.D. candidate."

He cast her a glance. "I think you know what I mean."

Now that the new Praetor had been appointed, Anselm seemed like a different person, unburdened by the worries and obligations of Lethe.

"I'm surprised you're back in Connecticut," she said. "I thought I'd have to come to New York."

"I'm usually in Connecticut once or twice a month for meetings. It's why the board asked me to step in and oversee things at Lethe. And given what happened to Dean Beekman, I thought it couldn't hurt to check in. He was a legend. I think everyone who knew him is pretty shaken."

"Did you know him?"

He cocked his head to one side. "Is this why you wanted to have lunch? Does Centurion have you checking alibis?"

"No," Alex said, which was true. And there was no reason for her to suspect Anselm had anything to do with Marjorie Stephen or Dean Beekman. "I'm sorry. After everything that happened last year." She shrugged. "Old habits."

"I get it. The people who were supposed to protect you didn't really do the job, did they?"

And they never had. But Alex didn't want to think too much on that, not at this table with this stranger on a sunny afternoon. "I guess not."

"Lethe asks a lot of us, doesn't it?"

Alex nodded. She felt nervous and her palms were damp. Between her miserable nightmares, she'd lain awake last night, trying to think of the best approach for this. But Anselm had offered her an opening so she was going to take it. "It does," she said. "You've seen my file."

"And now you're rolling in clover."

"Something like that."

"Tell me about California."

"It's like this, but the water is warmer and the people are better-looking."

Anselm laughed and Alex felt herself unwind a little. She'd been prepared for Anselm in authority mode, but this guy wasn't all bad. He'd clearly had a couple of glasses of wine with lunch and he was enjoying being out of the office. She could work with this.

"Who were you meeting?" she asked.

"A few friends working out of Stamford. You know where the old AIG offices are?"

"Not really."

"You're not missing much. Anyway, they're kind of black sheep in our business, but I like underdogs and they needed some advice."

"*Hide the outcasts,*" she murmured.

Anselm laughed again. "That's a pull."

So Anselm knew the Isaiah quote. But if he was somehow involved in the murders, he probably wouldn't have volunteered that knowledge. "You don't strike me as the religious type."

"Not at all, but that's an essential bit of New Haven lore. God," he said, shaking his head. Not a single carefully styled hair moved. "I'm even boring myself."

"Go on," she said. "I like this kind of stuff." Especially if it could help her catch a murderer and put her in Turner's good graces.

Anselm looked skeptical, but said, "It's from the sermon John Davenport gave in support of the three judges."

Judges. Interesting. "That clears up everything."

Again his brows rose, and Alex realized why she liked this version of Anselm. He reminded her just a little of Darlington. Not the Darlington she'd known but who he might have been if he hadn't grown up in Black Elm and fallen in love with Lethe, a slicker, less hungry Darlington. A Darlington less like her.

"You've never been to Judges Cave?" Anselm asked. "Okay, so the year is 1649, and Cromwell orders the execution of Charles I. Fifty-nine judges sign the death warrant. All well and good. Off with his head. But just a decade later, the monarchy is restored, and his son Charles II—"

"Junior."

"Exactly. Junior isn't pleased with what happened to his father or the precedent of killing off kings. So, ruthless he must be. He sentences all of the judges to death."

"That's a lot of dead judges." And it lined up with Turner's initial theory of the crime, that the disgraced Professor Lambton had gone after the people who had sat in judgment on him.

"Some of them were executed, others fled to the colonies. But there are British soldiers everywhere and no one is particularly excited about harboring fugitives and bringing down Junior's wrath. Except for the good citizens of New Haven."

"Why?"

Anselm gestured to the boats in the harbor as if they might have an answer. "It's always been a contrary town. The good Reverend John Davenport steps up to the pulpit and preaches, '*Hide the outcasts. Bewray not him that wandereth.*' And hide the outcasts they do. When the British come snooping around, the townspeople keep their secrets and the judges hide out near West Rock."

"At Judges Cave?"

"It's technically just a cluster of big rocks, but yes. Their names were Whalley, Goffe, and Dixwell."

Alex hadn't lived in New Haven long, but she knew those names. They were streets that branched off of Broadway. Follow Whalley long enough and you'd end up in West Rock. Three streets. Three judges. Three murders.

There will be a third. That was what Darlington had meant. He'd been trying to make the connection for them even as his demon half had been toying with them, enjoying the riddle the killer had set.

"What happened to the judges?" Alex asked. "Did they get caught?"

"Lived to a ripe old age. Two of them ended up somewhere in Massachusetts, but Dixwell changed his name and lived out his days in New Haven. His ashes are interred beneath the New Haven Green. British troops used to travel here just to piss on his gravestone, one hundred years after he died. That's how big a deal these guys were. Martyrs to liberty and all that. And now they're a footnote, a bit of trivia for me to try to impress you with over lunch."

Alex wasn't sure whether to be uncomfortable or flattered at the idea of Anselm trying to impress her.

"Have you ever wondered why the death words work?" He leaned forward. "Because we all amount to nothing in the end and there is nothing more terrifying than nothing."

Alex hadn't really cared why they worked so long as they did. "You know a lot about this place."

"I like history. But there isn't any money in it."

"Not like the law?"

Anselm lifted a shoulder. "Lethe makes a lot of promises, so does Yale, but none of them come true in New Haven. This is a place that will never repay your loyalty."

Maybe not much like Darlington after all. "And Lethe?"

"Lethe was an extracurricular. It's silly to think of it as anything else. Dangerous even."

"You're warning me." Just as Michelle Alameddine had.

"I'm just talking. But I don't think you came here to listen to me pontificate about Cromwell and the perils of growing old in Connecticut."

So this was it. "You said you read my file. My mom . . . my mom isn't doing great."

"She's ill?"

Was chasing after any whiff of a miracle diagnosable? Was there a name for someone doomed to seek invisible patterns in gemstones and horoscopes? Who thought life's mysteries might be revealed by eliminating dairy from your diet? Or gluten or trans fats? Could Los Angeles be called an illness?

"She's fine," Alex said. "She's just not a realist and she's not good with money." That was putting it mildly.

"Does she embarrass you?"

The question startled her, and Alex wasn't ready for the rush of emotion that came with it. She didn't want to feel small and naked, a child without protection, a girl alone. The semester had only just begun and she was already exhausted, worn down to nothing, the same girl who had arrived at Yale over a year ago, swinging at anyone and anything that might try to hurt her. She wanted a mother to keep her safe and give her good advice. She wanted a father who was something more than a ghost story her mother refused to tell. She wanted Darlington, who was here but who wasn't, whom she needed to navigate all this madness. It all crashed in on her at once, and she felt the unwelcome ache of tears at the back of her throat.

Alex took a sip of water, got herself under control. "I need to find a way to help her."

"I can get you a paid summer intern—"

"No. Now. I need money." That came out harsher than she'd meant it to, the real Alex jutting her chin out, tired of small talk and diplomacy.

Anselm folded his hands as if bracing himself. "How much?"

"Twenty thousand dollars." Enough to get Mira out of her lease and settled somewhere new, enough to keep her going until she landed a new job. All of that was assuming Alex could convince her mother to leave Los Angeles. But Alex thought she could. She'd use compulsion if she had to, if it would save her mother's life and hers.

"That's quite a loan."

"A gift," she corrected. "I can't pay something like that back."

"Alex, what you're asking—"

But it was time to be very clear. "You read my file. You know what I can do. I can see the dead. I can even speak to them. You want information? You want access to the Veil? I can get it for you. And I don't need some stupid ritual at Book and Snake to do it."

Now Anselm was staring. "You can hear them?"

She nodded.

"That's . . . that's incredibly risky."

"Believe me, I know."

"But the possibilities . . ." Anselm's expression was unreadable. His easy laughter and charm had evaporated into the salt sea air. He might want to be done with Lethe and all of its strange magic, but he also knew how much the Ninth House valued that kind of access, how much power it might yield. Sandow had once called Lethe "beggars at the table," authorities without authority, hands out for any crumb of magic the other societies might be willing to part with. Alex's gift could change that, and power was a language they all understood.

"Alex," he said, "I'm going to ask you something and I need you to be honest with me."

"Okay."

"You told me you were willing to put aside your attempts to reach Darlington, that you were ready to let that go." Alex waited. "You don't seem like the kind of person who lets things go."

Alex had known he might push and this part was easy. Because she knew exactly what he wanted to hear.

"You've seen my file," she repeated. "You know what Lethe offered me. I'm not here because I want to wear a cloak and play wizard. You all think the world beyond the Veil is something special, but that's just because you haven't had to look into that particular abyss your whole life. I didn't come to Yale for magic, Mr. Anselm."

"Michael."

She ignored him. "I didn't come here for magic or for fun or because I wanted to make friends and learn to talk about poetry at cocktail parties. I came here because this is my one and only chance at a future that doesn't look like that file. I'm not going to throw it away for a rich kid who was nice enough to talk down to me a few times."

It was all true. All but the last part.

Anselm studied her, weighing what she'd said. "You said Lethe owed him."

"I'm not Lethe."

"And you have nothing planned?"

"Nothing," Alex said without hesitation.

"I want your word. I want you to swear on your mother's life, because if you're fucking with me, there will be no money, no rescue plan. I'm not in the business of charity."

"You have my word."

"You've been quite the surprise, Alex Stern." Anselm rose. He tossed a few bills on the table. Then stretched and turned his face to the light. "A good lunch. A little sun and sea, a chat with a beautiful woman. I feel almost human. We'll see if it lasts all the way to New York." He stuck out his hand. His palm was warm and dry, his blue eyes clear. "Keep your nose clean and make sure things stay quiet. I'll get you that money."

Anselm was nothing like Darlington now. He was a tan in a suit. He was a wealthy grifter looking for an edge and willing to use her to get it. He was one more thief rummaging through artifacts in a country not his own. He was the Lethe Alex understood, not the Lethe Darlington had loved.

Alex shook his hand. "Sold."

24

The night before Halloween, they met in the dining room at Il Bastone. It felt more formal than the parlor, and Dawes had argued that they needed the space. Alex hadn't really understood until she saw the oversized blueprints of Sterling spread across the table. Dawes brought out her beloved whiteboard and prepared a pot of hot cider that filled Il Bastone with the smell of fermenting apples.

Mercy had changed clothes three times before they left their dorm room, finally arriving on a snug tweed jacket and velvet skirt.

"You know you're doing us the favor, right?" Alex had asked.

"Dress for the job you want."

"What job do you want?"

"I don't know," Mercy said. "But if magic is real, I want to make a good impression."

Do we all hunger for this? Alex wondered as she shepherded Mercy into Il Bastone, watching her eyes grow wide at the sight of the sunflower staircase, the stained glass, the painted tiles that framed the fireplace. Why raise children on the promise of magic? Why create a want in them that can never be satisfied—for revelation, for transformation—and then set them adrift in a bleak, pragmatic world? In Darlington she'd seen what grief over that loss could do to someone, but maybe the same mourning lived inside her too. The terrible knowledge that there would be no secret destiny, no kindly mentor to see some hidden talent inside her, no deadly nemesis to best.

Maybe that grief, that longing fostered by stories of more beautiful worlds and their infinite possibility, was what made them all such easy prey for Lethe. Maybe it made Mercy dress in velvet and tweed and put fake emeralds in her ears, driven by the dream of finding her way through the back of the wardrobe. Alex just hoped there wouldn't be something awful waiting behind the coats.

Earlier that night, she'd had to watch the members of Manuscript tie a chart-topping pop singer to a chair, crane her neck back, and place a nightingale in her mouth, securing it with a tiny rope bridle. Then they'd waited for the bird to shit down her throat. It was supposed to bring back her legendary voice. *That* was the truth of magic—blood and guts and semen and spit, organs kept in jars, maps for hunting humans, the skulls of unborn infants. The problem wasn't books and fairy tales, just that they told half the story, offering up the illusion of a world where only the villains paid in blood, the ogre stepmothers, the wicked stepsisters, where magic was just and without sacrifice.

They found Turner sitting at the dining room table, poring over the notes Dawes had prepared. Alex suspected he was mostly trying to ignore Tripp, who was stuffing himself in front of the elaborate spread of charcuterie, fondue, and geometric bits of puff pastry laid out in the kitchen.

"Alex!" he cried when he saw her, his mouth half full of cheese. "Your buddy Dawes is a sick cook. Like insane."

Dawes, ladling hot cider into a cup, looked caught between acute delight and stern disapproval, and the result was a kind of constipated half smile. She was in jeans instead of her usual sweats, her hair combed into a French braid. Even Tripp had worn a blue blazer and a polo instead of his usual T-shirt and sweats. Alex felt suddenly underdressed.

"Let's get started," Turner said. "Some of us have work in the morning."

And some of us have papers due, thought Alex. Not to mention a stack of reading that grew ever higher: *To the Lighthouse*, which had bored her; *Novel on Yellow Paper*, which had surprised her; page after page of Herodotus, which had quickly made her rethink her new-found passion for Greek history; long, opaque poems by Wallace Stevens, which sometimes put her in a kind of dream state and other times lulled her straight to sleep. If she could have chosen something other than the English major, she would have, but she wasn't equipped for anything else. Which meant she might come into even closer contact with their new Praetor.

They'd met in the parlor that afternoon to discuss Alex's preparations for the songbird ritual at Manuscript. Professor Walsh-Whiteley had sipped sherry and nibbled biscotti while he perused Alex's index cards, then given a brief sniff and said, "Passable."

Alex had struggled to retain a victory whoop, though it had been difficult to maintain that triumphant mood once she actually understood what the ritual entailed. She'd wanted to go home and never think about it again, but she was determined to get her report typed up and sent to the Praetor before they attempted the Gauntlet. *No reason to worry, sir. No need to pay close attention.*

"Turner," Alex murmured as they took their seats at the table, "does Professor Lambton have kids?"

"A son. Lives out in Arizona. And yes, he has an alibi." He answered instantly, and Alex realized he might be sitting at this table, but his mind was elsewhere, constantly turning over the details of the faculty murders.

"You might want to check that alibi again."

"Why? What do you know?"

"The quotes we've been chasing all lead back to the execution of Charles I. But it was his son who went looking for revenge."

"And how did you suddenly figure this out?"

"I'm a sleuth," Alex said, tapping her head and enjoying his eye roll way too much. "I did some digging. Pieced it together." She wasn't about to mention her lunch with Michael Anselm, or start talking about demons and vampires and the possibility that someone had bled the life from Marjorie Stephen. Not until she knew there was something more to it than her own paranoia.

Dawes clinked her knife against her water glass, the sound

surprisingly clear and resonant. She flushed pink beneath her freckles when everyone turned to look at her and said, "We . . . should start?"

Tripp joined them at the table, his plate heaped high, a bottle of beer in his other hand. "Do we have to take an oath or something?"

"Don't die. Try not to be an asshole," Turner said. "That's the oath. Let's get on with it."

Dawes wiped her hands on her jeans and took up her position beside the whiteboard, where she'd drawn a rough plan of Sterling. She pointed to the entrance, to the first station of the Gauntlet.

"We'll arrive at eleven sharp to get settled. Stay in the Linonia Room. We'll be using a very basic shrouding glamour to keep ourselves hidden when the library closes."

"What are we going to tell Lauren?" Mercy whispered as Dawes described where in Linonia they should hide and which part of the room would be glamoured. "She's going to be furious if we leave the party early."

Alex wasn't sure. It would have to be something so dull Lauren wouldn't want to come along.

"There is very little guidance to work from," Dawes continued. "But it would be wise to fast for at least six hours before. Do *not* consume any meat or dairy."

"Only vegans go to hell?" Tripp said with a laugh.

Dawes looked at him with her stern, studious eyes. "You're going to want empty bowels."

That shut him up fast.

Dawes gestured to Mercy. "Our sentinel will be stationed in the courtyard. The four pilgrims will walk the Gauntlet together starting at one o'clock exactly."

"How are we protecting Mercy?" Alex asked.

Mercy held up a small red notebook. "I've got my death words."

"You'll want to commit them to memory," said Dawes.

Mercy grinned. "*Quid tibi, mors, faciam quae nulli parcere nosti?*"

"You speak Latin?" Tripp asked disbelievingly.

Mercy's smile faded, and she cast Tripp a look of pure contempt.

"When I have to. Death words work better in dead languages, okay?"

Alex was surprised at the edge in Mercy's voice, but Tripp just shrugged. "If you say so."

"What does it mean?" asked Turner.

"*What am I going to do with you, Death, who spares no one?*" quoted Mercy. "It's funny, right? Like Death is a bad party guest."

"I'm all for Latin," said Alex, "but death words aren't going to help against a demon."

"I have something in mind for that," said Dawes.

"Salt armor," Mercy said.

Dawes beamed at her. "Exactly."

Alex was embarrassed to feel a pang of jealousy at that proud look, another unpleasant reminder that she was the interloper here.

"What happens when the library closes?" asked Turner.

"We walk the stations of the Gauntlet together." Dawes gestured to the sideboard. "Mercy will set the metronome ticking. The rhythm has to remain uninterrupted until the ritual is complete."

That didn't make much sense to Alex. "I don't think they had metronomes in Thonis."

"No," agreed Dawes. "In times past, a whole group of people would have stood sentinel and kept the beat with drums or other instruments. But we don't have a group and we don't know how long we'll be. We can't risk Mercy getting fatigued or interrupted."

Tick tick tick. The bomb waiting to go off.

"We'll begin outside at the scribe," Dawes continued, "and mark the entrance with our mingled blood."

Turner shook his head. "This is some satanic shit."

"It's not," said Dawes defensively. "The blood binds us and should wake the Gauntlet."

"So we'll know we're on the right path?" Alex asked.

Dawes gnawed on her lower lip. "That's the idea. Each pilgrim has a designation that determines the order we use to walk the Gauntlet. Soldier first, then scholar, then priest, then prince." She cleared her throat. "I believe I should take the role of scholar. Given Turner's religious leanings, he can take the office of priest."

"I can be the soldier," Tripp offered.

"You're the prince," said Alex. "I'm the soldier. I'll walk first."

"That means you'll also be the one to close the circuit," warned Dawes. "You'll walk that final stretch alone."

Alex nodded. That was the way it should be. She was the one who had let the hellbeast consume Darlington in that basement. She'd be the one to close the circle.

"By then," Dawes said, "we'll all have taken our positions in the courtyard. Each of the four doorways will be marked with blood. We'll need a signal so we can all begin the walk to the center of the courtyard at the same time." She set down a metal disc.

"A pitch pipe?" asked Mercy.

Dawes nodded. "It was enchanted sometime in the fifties to ensure perfect harmony. I'm hoping it will help us stay in sync if things get . . . difficult."

Alex didn't want to dwell too long on what that might mean. "We're sure the courtyard is the spot?"

Dawes pointed to a series of Post-its she'd laid out on a plan of the Selin Courtyard. "Four doorways. Four pilgrims. Four compass points. And the inscriptions can't be a coincidence. Remember the Tree of Knowledge? This is engraved above the stone sundial on the librarian's door. *Ignorance is the curse of God. Knowledge the wing wherewith we fly to heaven.*"

"*Henry VI,*" said Mercy and glanced at Alex with a grin.

Alex smiled back. "More Shakespeare."

"There's also this." Dawes held up a photo of a stone grid of numbers.

"Sudoku?" asked Tripp.

Dawes looked at him as if she wasn't sure whether to put him to bed with a hot water bottle or hit him with a shovel. "It's the magic square from Albrecht Dürer's *Melencolia*. Every direction you add the numbers, the sum is always the same. I think it's a gesture toward containment."

"A perfect puzzle for a demon to get caught up in," Alex said.

"Exactly. And of all the details from Dürer's works, it has no real reason to be in this courtyard."

"What's at the center?" Turner asked. "What are we all marching toward?"

Mercy wrinkled her nose. "There's a fountain, but it's not much to look at. More of a big square basin with some cherubs stuck on the corners."

"It was added later," Dawes said. "After the library was built. Because something was seeping up through the stones."

Silence settled over the room.

Turner scrubbed a hand over his head. "Fine. We get to the middle. Then what happens?"

Now Dawes hesitated. "We descend. I don't know what that entails. Some people describe hallucinations and an actual sensation of falling, others describe a complete disconnect from the body and a feeling of flight."

"Sweet," said Tripp.

"But that could be because of the datura."

"That's a poison," said Turner. "Had a case where a woman was growing it in her backyard, putting it in lotions and ointments."

"It does have medicinal uses," said Dawes. "It just needs a steady hand."

"Sure," said Turner. "Are you going to tell them its other name?"

Dawes looked down at her notes and mumbled, "Devil's trumpet. The pilgrims are anointed with it before they begin. It loosens the soul's tether to this world. We can't cross over without it."

"And then we die," said Alex.

Tripp gave a nervous laugh. "Metaphorically, right?"

Slowly, Dawes shook her head. "From what I can tell, we'll be buried alive."

"Shit," said Turner.

"The verb is unclear," Dawes offered. "It might mean buried or submerged."

Tripp pushed back from the table. "Are we sure . . . Is this a good idea?"

"We're out of good ideas," said Alex. "This is what we have left."

But Turner wasn't interested in Tripp's nerves. "So we die," he said as if he were asking for directions to the bank. "Then what?"

Dawes had bit so deeply into her lip a thin line of blood had appeared. "At some point, we should encounter Darlington—or the part of him still stuck in hell. We secure his soul in a vessel, then we return to this plane and take it to Black Elm. That's when we'll be at our most vulnerable."

"Vulnerable how?" Alex asked.

Turner tapped the open book in front of him. "If we don't close off the Gauntlet, something can follow us."

"Something?" Mercy finally sounded scared, and Alex was almost grateful for that. She needed to take this seriously.

"What we're doing is considered theft," said Dawes. "We have no reason to think hell will give up a soul easily."

Tripp gave another nervous laugh. "Like a hell heist."

"Well . . ." Dawes mused. "Yes, that's accurate."

"If it's a heist, we should all have jobs," said Tripp. "The thief, the hacker, the spy."

"Your job is to survive," Turner bit out. "And to make sure you don't do anything stupid that gets the rest of us killed."

Tripp held up his hands, agreeable as always. "No doubt."

"We do need to move fast and stay on our guard," said Dawes. "Until the two parts of Darlington's soul are brought together, we'll be targets."

For any demons that pursued them. For creatures like Linus Rei-ter. What if he was watching? What if he knew what they meant to do? Again Alex felt that crawling paranoia, that sense of their ene-mies multiplying.

"Are you so sure we're going to find his soul?" Turner asked.

Dawes dabbed at her lip with her sleeve. "His soul *should* want to find union with its other half, but that's all about the vessel we choose. It needs to be something that will call to him. Like the deed to Black Elm or the Armagnac Michelle Alameddine left him."

Except the deed had burned to ash months ago and the Armagnac had been blown to bits at Scroll and Key.

"Like a grail," said Tripp. "That would be good."

"Maybe a book?" suggested Mercy. "A first edition?"

"I know what it should be," said Alex. "If I can find it."

Dawes had somehow reopened the cut on her lip. "It has to be precious. It has to have power over him."

Alex's memory was not her own—it belonged to the dead Daniel Tabor Arlington III watching his grandson mix an elixir over the sink in Black Elm, knowing the poison could kill him, unable to make him stop. She remembered what Danny—Darlington—had chosen to use as his cup in that moment of reckless desire: the little keepsake box from some long-ago, better time, the box he had once believed was magic and was determined to make magic again.

"It's precious," Alex said.

The dream of a world beyond ours, of magic made real. The way through the wardrobe, and maybe back again.

25

Halloween on campus was mild during the day, almost as if the students were embarrassed by their desire to play—a few people in capes or silly hats, a professor in a jack-o'-lantern sweater, an a cappella group singing "Time Warp" on the steps of Dwight Hall. Celebrations were even more subdued in the wake of Dean Beekman's murder. But even that quiet excitement was enough to rile up the Grays. They sensed the anticipation, the feeling of a holiday that buzzed through classrooms and libraries and dorm rooms. Alex tried not to let it get to her, but the noise of the dead—their sighs and exclamations and chatter—was difficult to ignore. Only Morse was quiet, the place where Beeky had been killed. There the living didn't feel free to celebrate, and the dead wanted to stay far from the killing ground.

Alex and Mercy went all out decorating the common room as a kind of penance for abandoning Lauren, hanging chains of paper flowers over the ceiling and walls so that it looked like a goth garden. When they'd told her they were helping to work a candy exchange for parents at Mercy's church, Lauren just said, "You guys are the worst," and continued taping up skeins of crepe paper. She had a group of her field hockey friends to go out with later that night.

Liquor Treat got going around eight. Alex poured tequila shots and Mercy filled cups with chocolate soil and gummy worms while Lauren put on records in her sexy-gardener short-shorts. But Alex and Mercy didn't touch the alcohol, and Alex made herself avoid the candy too. She was taking Dawes's instructions seriously, and that meant she was dizzy with hunger and grumpy about it.

Early that morning, Alex had gone to Black Elm. She'd picked up the mail, put out fresh food and water for Cosmo, and then walked the length of the first floor to the office that looked out over the back garden. She knew Darlington had worked in there sometimes; she had even gone through the drawers of the mahogany desk when she was searching for his notes on the Bridegroom's murder case.

But the office felt different than the rest of the house. Because it had belonged to the old man. It was a big, gloomy room, heavily paneled in dark wood, a long-dormant fireplace taking up the bulk of one wall. The only photos were black-and-white shots of the Arlington Rubber Boots factory, a man in a dark suit holding the hand of an unsmiling child in front of an old-fashioned motorcar, and a framed wedding picture that, judging by the bride's dress, had to be from the turn of the century. The Arlingtons before the curse had come upon them and their shining prosperity had gone to rot.

The box was on the desk, a palm-sized porcelain thing with a scene of children playing in the snow printed on the top. On the inside of the hinged lid, *Merry Christmas from Your Arlington Rubber Boots Family!* had been inscribed in blue script framed by snowflakes. But the well of the box was stained reddish brown. From the elixir. Darlington's attempt to see to the other side, the dream that had almost killed him, and that had led him to Lethe.

"That thing upstairs isn't Danny."

The old man was standing next to Alex. She could feel him inching closer, hoping to climb inside her, eager to be in a body again. Alex had been shaken by her run-in with Linus Reiter, the dream of Darlington in the circle, the unpleasant task of kissing Michael Anselm's ass, the constant fear of another command coming down from Eitan before she found a way to clear the books. But she wasn't about to become a carnival ride for some bitter old bastard who had cared more about his legacy than the little boy he'd trapped in this castle.

"That so?" She turned on Daniel Tabor Arlington III in his blue bathrobe. "Darlington deserved better than you or your crap son, and this isn't your house anymore. *Death is the mother of beauty*," she snarled. All that Wallace Stevens ought to be good for something.

The old man vanished, his expression indignant.

Alex glanced up at the ceiling, and the next thing she knew she was climbing the stairs, moving down the hall. She hadn't meant to go to the second floor. She was just supposed to retrieve the box and get out of Black Elm fast. Or was she lying to herself? Had she wanted to see Darlington before they attempted the Gauntlet? She didn't try to fight whatever force took hold of her this time. She let herself be carried into the heat and golden light of the ballroom.

He was standing close to the circle's edge, gaze locked on her. He was the demon she remembered, naked, monstrous, beautiful. Not the young man she'd spoken to her in her dream. Heat seemed to eddy around them, something stranger than a mere change in temperature, a crackle of power that she could feel against her skin. The circle of protection flickered. Was it growing fainter? Dissolving as it had in her dream?

"We're coming to get you," she said. "You need to be ready."

"I can't hold on much longer."

"You have to. If . . . if it doesn't work, we'll come back to strengthen the protections."

"You can certainly try."

Alex was unpleasantly reminded of Linus Reiter, sprawled on his cream-colored couch, daring her to hurt him.

"Tonight," she repeated.

"Why wait?"

"It isn't easy to figure out a Gauntlet and assemble a search party of killers willing to go to hell. And Dawes says our chances are better on a night of portent."

"As you like, Wheelwalker. You choose the steps in this dance."

Alex wished that were true. She had the powerful urge to draw closer, but the fear inside her was just as strong.

"Was it you in the dream? Was it real? Is this?"

His smile was the same as it had been in the dream when he said, "This isn't the time for philosophy, Stern."

The hair rose on her arms. But was that confirmation or just another riddle for the demon to taunt her with?

"Why are you doing this?" he asked. The demon's cool voice wavered, and he was only Darlington now, scared, desperate to find his way home. "Why risk your life and your soul?"

Alex didn't know how to answer. She was putting her future at stake, her mother's safety, her own. She was asking other people to put their lives on the line. Turner thought this was a holy war. Mercy wanted to wield the weapon that had been used against her. Tripp needed spending cash. And Dawes loved Darlington. He'd been her friend, one of the few who had bothered to take the time to know her and too dear to lose because of that. But what was Darlington to Alex? A mentor? A protector? An ally? None of those words seemed sufficient. Had some soft-boiled part of her fallen for the golden boy of Lethe? Or was this something less easily named than love or desire?

"Do you remember when you walked me through the ingredients for Hiram's elixir?" she asked.

She could still see him standing over the golden crucible in the armory, his graceful hands moving in clean precision. He'd been lecturing her on the duties of Lethe, but she'd barely been listening. His sleeves were rolled up, and she'd been uncomfortably distracted by the shift of muscles in his forearms. She'd done her best to inoculate herself against Darlington's beauty, but sometimes she still got caught off guard.

"We stand between the living and the dead, Stern. We wield the sword no one else dares lift. And this is the reward."

"A chance at a painful death?" she'd asked.

"Heathen," he'd said with a shake of his head. "It's our duty to fight, but more than that, it's our duty to see what others won't and never avert our eyes."

Now, standing in the ballroom, she said, "You didn't turn away. Even when you didn't like what you saw in me. You kept looking."

Darlington's gaze shifted and flickered like firelight. Gold and then amber. Bright and then shadowed. "Maybe I know a fellow monster when I see one."

It felt like a cold hand shoving her away. Like a warning. She wasn't stupid enough to ignore it.

"Maybe," Alex whispered.

She made herself turn, leave the ballroom, walk down that dark hall. She forced herself not to run.

Maybe they were just two killers, cursed to endure each other's company, two doomed spirits trying to find their way home. Maybe they were monsters who liked the feeling of another monster looking back at them. But enough people had abandoned them both. She wasn't going to be the next.

Matching luminaries
Provenance: Aquitaine, France; 11th century
Donor: Manuscript, 1959

Believed to have been invented by heretical monks to hide forbidden texts. The glamour will remain strong for as long as the
lanterns are lit. Those outside of the light's reach will find their fear
increasing as they draw closer. Ordinary candles may be used and
refreshed accordingly. Donation made after storage above the Manuscript nexus created some kind of disturbance in the enchantment
and two members of the 1957 delegation were lost for over a week
in shadow.

—from the Lethe Armory Catalogue as revised
and edited by Pamela Dawes, Oculus

Halloween is an evangelical holiday. If you don't celebrate, you're
forced to hide from those who do lest they slap a mask on your face
and demand you caper about in the name of fun.

—Lethe Days Diary of Raymond Walsh-Whiteley
(Silliman College '78)

26

They met at the library at eleven o'clock and holed up in one of the niches in the Linonia and Brothers reading room. Dawes had somehow chosen the exact spot where Alex loved to sit and read and fall asleep with her boots on the grate of the heater. How many times had she looked out at the courtyard through the wavy glass of the windows without knowing she was looking at the gateway to hell?

They set the pair of luminaries they'd procured from the armory at opposing corners of the entry to the reading nook. What they created when lit wasn't precisely a glamour, but a swarm of thick shadow that repelled any curious gaze.

Fifteen minutes before midnight, a voice came over the loudspeaker reminding students that the library was closing. People laden with backpacks and satchels trudged out to make the walk home to dorms or apartments in a forced march past Halloween partiers. Security guards came through next, passing their flashlights over the shelves and reading tables.

Alex and the others waited, watching the flicker of the luminaries in the corners, pressed against the walls for no good reason, trying to be as quiet as possible. Tripp had worn the same polo, blazer, and backward cap he'd had on at their planning dinner. Turner was in what looked like expensive gym clothes and a puffer jacket. Dawes was in her sweats. Mercy had chosen fatigues paired with a black sweater and looked like the chicest member of a special forces unit. Alex was in Lethe sweats. She didn't know what this night would bring, but she was tired of losing perfectly good clothing to the arcane.

Shortly after midnight and without warning, the lights clicked off. All that remained were dim security lights along the floors. The library had gone silent. Dawes took out a thermos. To disrupt the alarm systems, she had brewed the same tempest in a teapot they'd used to break into the Peabody, but she'd steeped the tea longer and acquired a better-insulated container.

"Hurry," she said. "I don't know how long it will last."

They got Mercy settled in the courtyard, and Alex and Dawes helped her into the salt armor—gauntlets, bracers, a helm that was far too big for her head. She even had a salt sword. It was all very impressive, but Alex had to wonder if it would stop a monster like Linus Reiter. When Mercy pulled a vial of Hiram's elixir from her pocket, Alex wanted to swat it out of her hand. But the time for warnings and worry had past. Mercy had made her choice and they needed her here, their sentinel. Alex watched her pop the cork and down the contents, her eyes squeezed shut as if she were swallowing medicine. She shuddered and coughed, then blinked and laughed.

At least the first dose hadn't killed her.

When Mercy was positioned by the basin with the ticking metronome set on the ground beside her, they crowded around the security desk at the front of the library, checked the Rose Walk for students passing by, then slipped outside.

"Quick," said Dawes as one by one they made incisions on their arms.

"We should have done it across our palms," said Tripp. "The way they do in movies."

"No one gets infections in movies," Turner shot back. "And I actually need the use of my hands."

Alex hadn't realized he had a holster and gun beneath his jacket. "I don't think that's going to do you much good in hell."

"Couldn't hurt," he replied.

Dawes took a small bottle from her pocket and dribbled oil onto her thumb. She smeared it across each of their foreheads. This had to be the datura.

"Are we ready?" Dawes asked.

"Hell yeah!" said Tripp.

"Keep your voice down," snapped Turner. But Alex appreciated Tripp's enthusiasm.

Dawes took a deep breath. "Let's begin."

They each touched their fingers to the blood welling from their arms.

"Soldier first," Dawes said. Alex daubed her blood onto each of the four columns marking the entrance. Dawes followed, placing her blood over Alex's, then Turner, and finally Tripp.

He looked at the smudge of their mingled blood and stood back. "How will we know if—"

Tripp was interrupted by a sound like a sigh, a whoosh of air as if a window had been thrown open.

The heavy wooden door beneath the Egyptian scribe had vanished, leaving nothing but darkness. No glimpse of the library nave beyond, no sign of life or light. It was like looking into nothing. A cold wind blew through on a moan.

"Oh," said Dawes.

They stood in stunned silence, and Alex realized that, for all of their talk and preparation, none of them had really believed it would work. Despite every miracle and horror she had witnessed in her time at Yale, she hadn't been able to buy into a pathway to the underworld hidden right beneath their noses. Had some other group of fools once stood at this doorway awakened by their blood, on this same precipice, trembling and afraid? Dawes claimed the Gauntlet had never been used. But again Alex had to wonder, if that was the case, why build it at all?

"Alex is first, right?" Tripp asked, a quaver in his voice.

Her courage had shriveled at the sight of all of that empty. But there was no time to second-guess. She could hear people approaching down the street. *Come get me, Stern,* he'd said. *Please.*

Alex touched her hand to the porcelain box in her pocket and stepped through the door.

Nothing happened. She was standing in Sterling's cavernous nave. It looked no different than it had before.

Dawes bumped into her, and they both stumbled out of the way as Turner and then Tripp came through.

"I don't get it," said Tripp.

"We have to walk the path," Dawes said. "That was only the start."

Single file, they made their way down the nave toward the *Alma Mater* mural: soldier, scholar, priest, and prince, shrouded in gloom. A strange, shuffling parade. They turned right at the mural and marked the arches beneath the Tree of Knowledge with their blood. Again, the corridor beyond seemed to dissolve, as if their reality had dropped away and left a gaping void. Again, Alex took a deep breath, the diver preparing to sink beneath the surface, and stepped through.

On their right, they passed the glass door through which Alex would enter, but it wasn't her time yet. The soldier would close the circle. They moved down the corridor, past Death peering over the student's shoulder, and into the vestibule full of Jost Amman's woodcuts. Above them Alex could just make out the black iron silhouettes of the mermen with their split tails, monster and man, man and monster.

The cut on Alex's arm had begun to close, so she had to squeeze it to get the blood to well up again. One by one they anointed the doorway beside the stone spider, beneath the inscription of Yale's motto. Light and Truth. It felt like a joke when the door disappeared into flat black darkness.

"This is your station," Dawes whispered, the first words any of them had spoken since they'd stepped back into Sterling.

Tripp's jaw was set. His fists were clenched. Alex could see he was shaking slightly. She almost expected him to just turn on his heel and march right out of the library. Instead he gave a single, firm nod of his head.

Alex gave him a quick squeeze on the shoulder. It was easy not to take Tripp seriously, but he was here facing the same shapeless dread as the rest of them, and he hadn't complained once. "See you on the other side."

They moved on, passing into another narrow hallway that would take them to the University Librarian's office. It was even darker here, the walls crowding in on them. The office felt less empty than suddenly abandoned, the desk chair askew, papers in messy piles.

There was nothing remarkable about this door, but emblazoned on the other side of it was a large stone sundial and two stained glass knights standing guard.

They made fresh cuts and daubed the door jamb with their blood, ready this time for the gap of darkness that opened and the icy wind that blew through.

"Keep your head straight," Turner said as he took up his post.

The secret door was right behind them, beside the big stone fireplace with its grumpy Latin, barely visible unless you knew where to look for the outline hidden in the paneling. Alex and Dawes passed through it and into another dark, tiny vestibule that had no real purpose—unless you were trying to circumnavigate the courtyard.

They emerged in Linonia and Brothers, on the opposite end of the room from the niche where they'd hidden. Here again, it felt as if the place had been abandoned, as if the absence of the human could be felt.

At last they stood at the original entrance to the courtyard, Selin's name emblazoned across the stone lintel in golden letters.

Alex didn't want to leave Dawes there. She didn't want to be alone in this dark cathedral of a building.

"The niches are all empty," Dawes said.

"They are?" Alex asked, completely lost.

Dawes had the silver pitch pipe in her hands and her voice was quiet but steady. "All over the library, you can see these spaces, these stone frames where a sculpture of a saint should be, like in a cathedral. But they're all empty."

"Why?"

"No one really knows. Some people think they ran out of money. Some people say the architect wanted the building to look like it had been sacked. All of its treasures stolen."

"What do you think?" Alex asked. She could feel they were in uncertain territory, that this story, these words were what Dawes needed to keep going.

"I don't know," Dawes said at last. "We all have hollow places."

"We're going to bring him home, Dawes. We're going to make it out of this."

"I believe you. At least the first part." She took a deep breath, set her shoulders. "I'll be watching."

Alex smeared her blood onto the entry. Dawes followed. This time the big double doors looked like they collapsed in on themselves, folding like paper as the wind howled through. It was louder now, moaning, as if whatever was on the other side of the darkness knew they were coming.

"Look," Dawes said.

The script above the door had shifted into a different language.

"What does it say?" Alex asked.

"I don't know," Dawes said. She sounded breathless. "I don't even recognize the alphabet."

Alex had to force her feet to move. But she knew it wouldn't get any easier. It never did.

"Be ready," she told Dawes, and then she was rounding back past the entrance and down the nave once more. The soldier. The one to walk alone. Alma Mater gazed benevolently down at her, surrounded by artists and scholars, flanked by Truth, naked in her allegory.

It wasn't until Alex was right in front of the mural that she realized what had changed. They were all staring at her now. The sculptor, the monk, Truth with her mirror, Light with her torch. They were watching her, and whatever human features the artist had granted them did not seem quite natural anymore. Their faces looked like masks, and the eyes peering through them were too bright, alive and keen with hunger.

She made herself keep walking, resisting the urge to look back, to see if somehow one of them had pried itself free of the frame and crept after her. She passed beneath the Tree of Knowledge, noting the sculptural niche at its center. Empty. How had she never noticed that before?

Finally, she arrived at the glass door that would lead her to the courtyard. A panel of yellow and blue stained glass marked the entrance. She had looked it up. Daniel in the lions' den.

"We're coming for you, Darlington," she whispered. She could hear the soft ticking of the metronome.

Once more she touched the porcelain box in her pocket. *I have been crying out to you from the start.* She dipped her thumb into her blood and dragged it across the door.

It vanished. Alex stared into the starless void, felt the cold of it, heard the rising wind, and then, floating above it, the soft sweet hum of middle C. *Come on along. Come on along.* She stepped into the courtyard.

As soon as her boot hit the stone path, the ground seemed to shake.

"Shit," Tripp squeaked from somewhere to her left.

She could see now: ordinary night, Mercy at the courtyard's center, Dawes, Tripp, and Turner at the other corners.

She kept walking, kept marching toward the basin, keeping time with the metronome. With every step came another little earthquake. *Boom. Boom. Boom.* Alex could barely keep her footing.

Ahead she saw Mercy, her face panicked, trying not to tip over.

They were all stumbling now, the stones of the courtyard buckling beneath them, but still the metronome ticked away.

Maybe the ground would just open up and swallow them. Maybe that was what Dawes had meant by *submerged.*

"Is this supposed to happen?" Tripp shouted.

"Keep going," Alex yelled, lurching forward.

"The basin!" cried Mercy.

The square basin was overflowing, water gushing past the cherubs, pooling at its base, and coursing through the crevices between the stones, creeping toward them. Alex felt a weird relief that it wasn't blood.

The water struck her boots. It was hot.

"It stinks," muttered Tripp.

"Sulfur," said Turner.

It's just a river, Alex told herself. Though she didn't know which one. All borderlands were marked by rivers, places where the mortal world became permeable and you could cross into the afterlife.

They splashed through, the water level rising, still marching, still in unison. When they reached the fountain, they stood staring at each other as the water boiled and bubbled over the sides. The cherubs sat at each of the basin's corners, gazing into its center, eyes trained on nothing. But maybe they'd simply been keeping a watch, waiting for the door to open.

Dawes's teeth were dug into her lower lip; her chest rose and fell in short, shallow pants. Tripp was nodding as if he heard secret music, a psych-up song from some collection of Jock Jams. Turner's face was stern, his mouth set in a determined line. He was the only one of them with experience in anything close to this. He'd probably kicked a few doors down in his time, without knowing what trouble might be waiting on the other side. But this wasn't really like that, was it?

They were pilgrims. They were cosmonauts. They were as good as dead.

"On three," Dawes said, her voice cracking.

They counted together, their voices barely audible over the rush of the water.

One.

A wind rose suddenly, that cold wind they'd all felt rushing through the darkness. Now it shook the courtyard trees and rattled the windows in their casements.

Two.

Light seemed to bloom from the stones at their feet and Dawes gasped. When Alex looked down, there was no paving, no grass. She was looking into the water, and it just went down and down.

Dawes cast a desperate glance at Mercy and handed her the silver pitch pipe. "Watch over us," she pleaded.

"Run if you have to," Alex said.

Three.

Their eyes met and they clasped the sides of the basin.

The Descent

Alex didn't remember falling, but suddenly she was on her back in the water, sinking fast, the river closing over her. She tried to push toward the surface, but something grabbed her wrist, an arm wrapped around her waist. She screamed, felt the water rush in. Fingers pushed into her mouth, trying to dig into her eye sockets, clawing into the skin of her arms and legs, their grip cold and unrelenting.

Buried alive. This wasn't supposed to be what it was like. It was supposed to feel like falling, like flying. She tried to shout for Dawes, for Mercy, for Turner, but there were fingers shoving into her throat, making her gag. They were in her ears, pushing between her legs.

What if Dawes and the others were still up there? The thought sent a fresh bolt of terror through her. She'd thrown herself into hell, but what if they were still in the courtyard? Or they were soaring into some better realm while she alone was torn apart? Because she was the problem. She had always been the problem. The only real sinner in the bunch. Turner had, what? Brought down a bad guy in the line of duty and it still tormented his Eagle Scout conscience? Dawes had killed Blake to save Alex's life. Muddleheaded Tripp had no doubt bumbled into something he couldn't handle.

But Alex was the real thing. She'd taken a bat to Len, to Ariel, to all the rest, and she'd never lost a minute of sleep over the things she'd done. Something on the other side was waiting to claim her. It had been waiting a long time, and now that it had hold of her, it wasn't going to let go. Those hands were hungry. She'd felt the pull of that appetite drawing her across the city to Black Elm. She'd told herself it was because she was special, the Wheelwalker, but maybe the real reason she'd been able to pierce the circle of protection was because she didn't belong among the mortal, law-abiding citizens of this world. She'd never been punished for her crimes, never felt remorse, and now she'd plunged right into a reckoning.

The fingers seemed to press straight through her, hooks lodging in her skin and bones. She struggled for a gulp of air, hot and stinking of sulfur. She didn't care. She could breathe again. The water was gone. The fingers weren't clogging her throat. It ached to open her eyes, but when she did, she saw black night, shooting stars, a rain of fire. Was she falling? Flying? Shooting toward something or drowning in darkness? She didn't know. Sweat dribbled down her neck, the heat coming from everywhere, like she was being cooked in her own skin.

She hit the ground hard, the impact sudden, driving a short, broken sob from her chest.

She tried to sit up. Slowly, she began to see shapes emerge in the dark . . . a staircase, a high ceiling. She put her hand on the floor to try to push to her feet and felt something warm and squirming. She recoiled, but when she looked down, there was nothing there, just the rug, a familiar pattern, the polished boards, the coffered ceiling overhead. Where was she? She couldn't remember. Her head hurt. She'd gone to open the door and Alex had screamed at her, told her to stop. No, that wasn't right.

Pam tried to make her legs work. She touched her fingers to the back of her head, to the aching spot on her scalp where she could feel her pulse, then snatched her fingers back, gasping at the pain. Why couldn't she think?

She was supposed to order pizza. Maybe she should cook instead. Alex had been heading upstairs to shower. They were grieving. To-gether. She remembered Dean Sandow speaking those horrible, final words. *No one will be made welcome.* Tears filled her eyes. She didn't want to cry. She didn't want Alex to find her weeping—it was only then that she really grasped where she was: at the base of the stairs at Il Bastone, shards of stained glass scattered around her. She touched the back of her head again, ready for the pain this time.

Someone had knocked her into the wall when she'd opened the door. An accident. She was clumsy. She'd gotten in the way. Wrong place, wrong time. But hadn't she locked the door? And why was it still open? Where was Alex?

Music was playing. A song she knew by the Smiths. She heard voices somewhere in the house, footfalls, someone running. She made herself stand, ignoring the wave of nausea that flooded her mouth with saliva.

Pam heard something howl outside and then a flood of hairy bodies crowded through the front door. *The jackals.* She'd seen them only once before, when Darlington called them. She cringed against the wall, but they rushed right past her, a pack of fur and snapping teeth, the wild animal scent of dust and dung and oily fur rising from them in a cloud.

"Alex?" she ventured. Someone had broken in, pushed past her. Alex was okay, wasn't she? She was the kind of girl who was always okay. "A survivor," Darlington had once said, admiration in his voice. "Rough around the edges, but we'll see if we've mined a diamond, won't we, Pammie?"

Pam had done her best to smile. She'd never liked that phrase, *diamond in the rough.* All that meant was they had to cut you again and again to let the light in.

She hadn't been sure if she wanted Alex to fail. She'd felt a certain consolation when their new Dante arrived and she got her first look at this scrawny girl with her bowstring arms and hollow eyes. She was nothing like the cultured, poised girls who had come before. Pam's first impulse had been to feed her. But the way you'd feed a stray, carefully, coaxingly, never from your hand. Darlington hadn't seemed to understand that Alex was dangerous. Although she never asked anything of Dawes. She never gave her orders or made demands. She cleaned up her own messes and skulked around like a rat who was afraid of being noticed by the barn cats. There was no *Could you do me a huge favor and whip up something so I can surprise my roommates?* No *Can I throw a few extra things in the wash?*

Pam had felt restless, useless, and grateful all at once. Darlington had muttered his complaints about the girl, but then that night when they'd gone to Beinecke, everything had changed. They'd come back and smashed half the glassware and gotten roaring drunk, and Pam had fastened her headphones over her ears, put on Fleetwood Mac, and done her very best to ignore them. She'd found them passed out in the parlor the next morning, but to Alex's credit she'd stayed and tidied up right alongside Darlington.

And then he'd disappeared, and Dawes hadn't been able to forgive this girl who charged through the world like an unintended consequence, a calamity for everyone and everything around her.

I have to move, she told herself. *Something is happening, something bad.* She had the sickly feeling she'd had when her parents argued. The house didn't feel right. *It's okay, bunny,* her mother would say, tucking her in at night. *We're all okay.*

For a second Pam thought she might be hallucinating or about to black out, but no, the lights really were flickering. She heard dishes crash from the kitchen, then a cry from above.

Alex.

Pam grabbed hold of the banister and dragged herself up the stairs. Dread made her feet heavy. She spent every day afraid, of saying the wrong thing, asking the wrong question, humiliating herself. Standing in line, scrambling for change, she felt her face flush, her heart race, thinking of all the people behind her, waiting. That was all it took to flood her body with terror. She should be used to fear. But God, she did not want to climb these stairs. She heard men's voices, then Alex. She sounded furious, and so scared. Alex never sounded scared.

Suddenly the jackals were rushing past her again, whimpering and yelping, nearly knocking her from her feet. Why were they going? Why had they come at all? Why did she feel like a stranger in this house she'd spent years in?

At last she reached the landing, but she couldn't make sense of any of what she saw. There was blood everywhere. The musky stink of animals hung thick in the air. The dean was slumped against the wall, his femur jutting from his leg, a sudden white exclamation point in search of a sentence. Dawes gagged. What was this? What had happened here? Things like this didn't happen at Il Bastone. They weren't allowed.

Alex was on her back on the floor and there was a boy on top of her. He was beautiful, an angel with golden curls and the loveliest face she'd ever seen. He was weeping, trembling. They looked like lovers. He had his hands in Alex's hair, as if he meant to kiss her.

And there was something in Pam's hands too, warm and softly furred and squirming, a living thing. She could feel its heartbeat against her palms. No. It was just a piece of sculpture, cold and lifeless, the bust of Hiram Bingham III. They kept it on a cane stand by the front door. She couldn't remember picking it up, but she knew what she was supposed to do with it.

Hit him.

But she couldn't.

She could call the police. She could run away. But the stone was too heavy in her hands. She didn't know how to hurt someone, even someone awful like Blake Keely, even after he'd hurt her. Blake had shoved his way into the house and let her lie bleeding on the floor. He'd hurt the dean. He was going to kill Alex.

Hit him.

She was a little girl on the playground, too tall, heavy-breasted, built all wrong. Her clothes didn't fit. She got tangled in her own feet. She was huddled at the bus stop trying not to react as boys from the high school drove by shouting *Show us your tits*. She was choosing the back row of every classroom, hunched up in the corner. Afraid. Afraid. She'd spent her whole life afraid.

I can't.

She wasn't made like Alex or Darlington. She was a scholar. She was a rabbit, timid and defenseless, no claws or teeth. Her only choice was to run. But where would she run with Darlington gone, the dean, Alex? Who would she be if she did nothing?

She was standing over them, looking down on the boy and Alex. She saw them from a great height, and she was the angel now, maybe a harpy, descending with sword in hand. She raised the bust and brought it down on the beautiful boy's head. His skull gave way, the sound wet and soft, as if he'd been made of papier-mâché. She hadn't meant to hit him so hard. Or had she? *Little bunny, what did you do?* She watched as he slumped to the side. Her own legs gave way and now she wept. She couldn't help it. She wasn't sure if she was crying for Blake or Darlington or Alex or herself. She bent and vomited. Why wouldn't the room stop moving?

Pam lifted her head, felt cool air on her cheeks, salt spray. The floor tilted back and forth, a ship adrift on the waves. She clung to the ropes.

"Try to keep up, Tripp."

The storm shouldn't have been a big deal. They'd checked the weather. They always did. Temperature. Pressure. Predicted wind speed.

But every time he was out on the boat, Tripp felt a twitching sense of panic. He was okay when it was just him and his dad or his other cousins, but when Spenser joined them, he got weird. It was like his brain just stopped doing what it was told.

His feet and hands felt bigger. He got slower. Suddenly he had to think, really think, about his left and his right, port and starboard, which was fucking ridiculous. He'd been sailing since he was a kid.

Spenser was just so good at everything. He rode horses and ATVs. He raced bikes and cars. He knew how to shoot, and he *worked* for a living, made his own money, and he always had some beautiful girl on his arm. Some beautiful *woman*. They were all accomplished and silky and Tripp felt like a kid around them, even though he was the one at Yale, and Spenser was only a few years older.

Tripp didn't even understand why Spenser got to take the helm. They'd both sailed competitively, so had his father, but Spenser just slid into the role with a big white smile. Part of it was the way he looked. Sharp, lean. He didn't have that Helmuth baby face. He had a real jaw, the look of someone you didn't want to fuck with.

Spenser always addressed Tripp's father as *sir*. "A pleasure to be aboard, sir, she handles like a dream." Then he'd sling an arm around Tripp's neck and crow, "Tripp, my man!" before he leaned in and whispered, "How's it going, shitstain?"

When Tripp stiffened up, Spenser would just laugh and say, "Try to keep up."

And that was how the day went. *Grab that line! Get it on the winch! Is that kite ready? Come on, Tripp, try to keep up!*

The storm that came in wasn't a big one. It wasn't scary. At least no one else seemed to think it was. Tripp had pulled on a life vest, slinging the thin snake of fabric around his neck, strapping it at his waist as he stood in the companionway. You barely knew it was on—it wouldn't inflate unless it hit the water—so what was the big deal?

But as soon as Spenser saw him, he burst out laughing. "The fuck is wrong with you? It's *rain*, dumbass."

Tripp's father just turned his face to the sky and laughed, the wind lifting his hair. "Now this is some weather!"

Tripp hated it. The gray swells like the humped shoulders of some big animal, nudging the ship, playing with it. You could really feel the sea beneath you, just how big it was, just how little it cared, the way it could smash a mast, crack a hull, drown them all with a single shrug. All he could do was hold on tight—*one hand for yourself, one for the ship*, that was the rule, same as the life vest—make himself keep smiling, and pray he wouldn't vomit, because he'd never hear the end of it.

Spenser hadn't been fooled.

"Shit your pants yet, pussy?" he said with a grin. "Try to keep up."

Tripp wanted to scream at him to fuck off and leave him alone. But that would only make things worse. *Can't you take a joke, Tripp? Jesus.*

His only hope was to keep pretending that he was in on it, that he loved Spenser the way everyone else did, that it was all good fun. It was pathetic to be scared of a little storm, or his stupid, cocky cousin. Except he had every reason to be terrified of them both. The storm, at least, was just being a storm. It wasn't out to hurt him. Spenser was something different.

When Tripp was eight, the whole family had gathered at his family's house for his birthday. Spenser was a jerk even back then, but Tripp hadn't cared about Spenser that day. It was *his* birthday and that meant *his* friends, and a new PlayStation, and the ice cream *he* liked even though Spenser had shoved his bowl of cookies and cream away and snapped, "I hate this shit."

Tripp had eaten cake and opened his presents and played in the pool until his friends had gone home and it was just family. He had a sunburn. They were going to cook out that night. He felt lazy and happy, and when he thought about the fact that he didn't have school tomorrow, that he still had the rest of the weekend to do nothing, it was like he was taking in big gulps of sunshine with every breath.

He'd been swimming around in the shallow end with his new snorkel when he'd emerged to see Spenser standing at the edge of the pool in his long board shorts, his blond hair hanging in a sun-streaked sheaf over his eyes so that Tripp couldn't quite make out his expression. Tripp had scanned the yard. He'd learned Spenser doled out fewer pinches and punches when someone else was around. But Tripp's dad and his younger brother were setting up a volleyball net on the other side of the grass. His mother and the other cousins must have already gone inside.

"What's up?" he'd squeaked, already moving for the steps.

But Spenser was faster. He was always faster. He dropped into the water with barely a splash and slapped his hand against Tripp's chest, shoving him backward.

"You have a good day?" Spenser asked.

"Sure," Tripp had said, unsure of why he was suddenly so frightened, struggling not to cry. There was no reason to cry.

"You need your birthday dunking. Twenty seconds underwater. That's nothing. Even for a little bitch like you."

"I'm ready to go in."

"Are you serious?" Spenser said in disbelief. "Dude, just when I thought you were being cool. You're telling me you can't handle a few seconds underwater?"

Tripp knew it was a trap, but . . . what if it wasn't? What if he just did this thing and then he and Spenser would be okay, they'd be friends, like Spenser was friends with everyone. *I thought you were being cool.* He could be cool.

"Just put my head under water for twenty seconds?"

"Yeah, but if you're too much of a bitch . . ."

He's not going to drown me, Tripp thought. *He's an asshole and he'll hold me under for a while, but he's not actually going to try to kill me. He's going to try to scare me and I'm not going to let him.* Tripp liked that idea a lot.

"Fine," Tripp said. "Twenty whole seconds. Time me."

And he dunked his head under.

He felt Spenser's hands on his shoulders right away. He knew Spenser wanted him to struggle, but he wasn't going to do it. He was going to be still, hold his breath, stay calm. He counted the seconds in his head, slow. He knew Spenser would hold him under longer and he was ready for that too.

Spenser shoved him lower, got his foot on Tripp's chest. *Don't panic, stay still.* His other foot pushed down on Tripp's belly, trying to drive the air out, and Tripp had to give up a little, the bubbles escaping to the surface. Spenser's right foot traveled and Tripp understood what he was doing seconds before he felt Spenser's heel grind down into his crotch, his toes digging into Tripp's balls.

Now Tripp was wriggling, pinned to the bottom of the pool, trying to push Spenser off. He knew Spenser was enjoying it, and he hated himself for reacting, hated the way his flesh crawled at the feeling of that foot with its seeking toes. His mind wasn't cooperating anymore. His chest hurt. He was scared. Why had he thought he could handle this? *He'll let me go. He has to let me go.* Spenser was mean, not a psychopath. He wasn't a killer. He was just a jerk.

But what did Tripp really know about how far Spenser would go? Spenser liked to mess around. He'd put chili powder in their dog's food and laughed until his eyes watered when she whimpered and cried. Once, when Tripp was really small, Spenser had kept him from getting to the bathroom, knocking him into the wall again and again, shouting "Pinball! Pinball!" until Tripp had wet himself. So maybe Spenser really was bad, the kind of bad in books and movies.

He'd be laughing now, enjoying the way Tripp tried to buck him off.

What a dumb way to die, Tripp thought as he gave in, as he opened his mouth and water flooded down his throat, the chlorine sharp in his nose, the terror complete as he tore at Spenser's calves, and the world went black.

The next thing he knew he was looking up at his father's sun-tanned face. Tripp was coughing and he couldn't stop, the pain in his lungs hot and tight, as if his whole chest had caught fire and the burn had hollowed him out.

"He's breathing!" his father cried.

Tripp was on his back in the grass, blue sky above, the clouds small and perfectly contained like a cartoon. His mother's hands were balled into fists she'd pressed against her mouth, tears on her cheeks. He saw his cousins above him, his uncle, Spenser's father, and Spenser too, his eyes narrowed.

Tripp tried to point to him, to speak the words as his father sat him up. *Spenser did it on purpose.* But he was coughing too hard.

"That's it, buddy," his father said. "You're all right. Just breathe. Take it slow."

He tried to kill me.

But Spenser's cold eyes were on him and Tripp felt like he was still pinned to the bottom of the pool. Spenser wasn't like him, wasn't like any of them. What wouldn't he do?

As if in answer, Spenser burst into tears. "I thought he was just joking around," he said, swallowing back sobs. "I didn't realize he was in trouble."

"Hey," Tripp's father said, clapping a hand on Spenser's shoulder. "This was an accident. I'm just grateful you got to him when you did."

Someone must have looked over to the pool, must have shown too much interest. Spenser would have acted quickly, pretended he was trying to save Tripp. And who would think otherwise? Who could imagine?

"Should we take him to the hospital?" Tripp's mother asked.

Spenser gave the faintest shake of his head.

Everyone was staring at Tripp, worried about him. Only Spenser's mother was standing away from the circle; only she was watching her son. There was worry in her eyes. Or maybe it was fear. *She knows what he is.*

"I'm fine," Tripp said hoarsely, and Spenser's lips twitched in a smile that he covered with another sob.

Nothing changed after that. But Tripp was careful never to be alone with Spenser again.

Even at eight years old, Tripp knew he wasn't smart or charming or handsome like Spenser. He knew that if he'd pointed his finger that day, told the truth, no one would have believed him. They'd say he'd misunderstood, maybe even that there was something wrong with him to think such a thing. *He* would be the monster. So maybe something had changed after all, something inside Tripp, because now he saw that Spenser would always win, and worse, he knew why. Spenser would win because everyone liked him better. Even Tripp's own parents. It was that simple. That understanding sat in his chest, lodged against his heart, a heaviness that stayed with him, long after his lungs had stopped hurting and the cough had gone. It made him fearful, awkward, and it was why, ten years later on a sailboat caught in a minor storm, Tripp was the only one who saw it when Spenser went into the sea.

It happened quickly. Spenser liked to sneak up on Tripp, startle him, try to get him to drop something or just give him a sharp jab in the side. So Tripp tried to always stay aware of where Spenser was, and he was watching when Spenser strode across the deck and ducked under the boom. His body was hidden behind the mainsail, only his legs visible, and for a second Tripp couldn't figure out what he was doing. Everyone else was focused on their own jobs, on getting through the storm. Tripp glanced back at his father, who was taking his turn at the helm now, his gaze fixed on the horizon.

Tripp saw Spenser reach down, bending over the railing to grab for a line that had slipped off the deck and was trailing in the water. That wasn't good—a trailing line could get sucked under the ship, mess with the tiller or the keep—but Spenser should have called for help. Instead he was hanging over the rail, both hands outstretched. Tripp had time to think, *One hand for yourself, one hand for the ship,* before the wave struck, a gray wash of water, a cat's paw batting at a toy, and Spenser was gone.

Tripp stood frozen for the briefest second. He even opened his mouth to cry out. And then he just . . . didn't. He looked around, realized everyone was still absorbed in their own tasks, shouting at each other, tense but enjoying the wind and the wild rain.

Without running, without haste, Tripp followed the path Spenser had taken, ducked under the boom, then straightened up, hidden from the others as Spenser had been. He saw Spenser in the gray waves, his red windbreaker like a warning flag, his head appearing and disappearing. And Spenser saw him too. Tripp felt sure of that. He raised his arm, desperately waving, shouted, the sound snatched away by the wind. Tripp was close enough to see his mouth open, but he couldn't tell if the sound he heard was Spenser's cry or his own imagination.

He knew that each second mattered, that the distance between the ship and Spenser was growing with every moment. The railing beneath his palm squirmed like a warm body, soft with fur. Tripp recoiled, drew his hand to his chest, but there was nothing to see, only cold metal.

There was still time to do the right thing. He knew that. He knew the man-overboard drill. His job was to keep his eyes on Spenser and shout for help, hold on to the railing with one hand, and use the other to point out his location. It was just too easy to lose sight of someone among the peaks and valleys of the waves. The crew would bring the boat about. They'd throw out a line and drag Spenser from the water, and Spenser would shove him and demand to know why he hadn't moved faster, what the fuck was wrong with him. Tripp's father would wonder too. Spenser wouldn't be afraid, just angry. Because Spenser always won.

He was barely visible now. A life vest would have kept him afloat. If he'd put one on. Tripp had to squint to see the red windbreaker in the water.

He took hold of the railing with one hand and lowered himself down to sit so he was secure—the way he'd been taught. Then he reached down to take hold of the line that was trailing over the edge, the one Spenser had tried to bring in.

Tripp spared a last glance over his shoulder at the slate-colored sea, crowded with eager waves, looking for their chance.

"Try to keep up," he whispered and set to work hauling in the line. He coiled it neatly, felt the rope move easily in his hands, his body confident with new grace, the knots like a song he'd always known.

He felt the weight against his heart ease at last. Rain spattered his cheeks, but he wasn't afraid.

It was only weather. The sea settled. He was on solid ground.

"It's just rain," Carmichael said. "You afraid you're gonna melt, sugar?"

Turner made himself laugh because Carmichael thought he was funny, and hell, sometimes he was.

The day was cold, the streets slick and black, wet eel skin bordered by heaps of dirty snow sagging in the rain. It wasn't even proper rain, just a pattering damp that made Turner desperate for a hot shower. If there had been a market for shitty East Coast mornings, New Haven could have made a killing.

Carmichael slumped beside him in one of his rumpled Men's Wearhouse suits, tapping his fingers in the "We Will Rock You" rhythmic jabs he always used when he was craving a cigarette. His wife, Andrea, had demanded he quit, and Car was doing his best. "She won't even kiss me until I've gone a month smoke-free," Car complained, shoving a stick of gum into his mouth. "Says it's a filthy habit."

Turner agreed, and he wanted to send Andrea a bouquet for pushing Carmichael to quit. He wasn't sure he'd ever get the smoke stink out of his seat cushions. Turner could have said no that first day when he'd picked up Carmichael in front of his tidy yellow house with the turf lawn. He just hadn't had the balls.

Chris Carmichael was practically a living legend. He'd been on the force for twenty-five years, made detective at age thirty, and his close rate was so high, uniforms called him the Sandman because he'd put so many cases to bed. Carmichael did not fuck around. Having him as your rabbi meant prime cases, promotions, maybe even commendations. Car and his buddies had taken Turner out drinking after he'd earned his spot on the squad, and somewhere during the bleary night of whiskey and the bleating of a bad Journey cover band, Carmichael had clamped his hand on Turner's shoulder and leaned in to demand, "You one of the good ones?"

Turner hadn't asked him to explain, hadn't told him to take his bullshit elsewhere. He'd just smiled and said, "Damn right, sir."

Carmichael—Big Car—had laughed and cupped the back of Turner's head with his meaty hand and said, "That's what I thought. Stick with me, kid."

It was a friendly gesture, Carmichael letting everyone know Turner had his approval and his protection. It was a good thing, and Turner told himself to be glad. But he'd had the uneasy sense of the world doubling, of some other timeline where Big Car put his hand atop Turner's head and shoved him into the back of a police car.

On this morning, he'd picked up Carmichael and they'd gone to get coffee at a Dunkin'. Or Turner had gone. He was the junior detective and that meant doing shit work in shit weather. He always kept an umbrella with him, and it always made Car chuckle.

"It's just rain, Turner."

"It's a silk suit, Car."

"Remind me to introduce you to my tailor so we can get to lowering your standards."

Turner smiled and hurried into the donut shop, nabbed two black coffees and a couple of breakfast sandwiches.

"Where we headed?" he asked when he slid back into the car and handed over the coffee.

Carmichael shifted in his seat, trying to get comfortable. He'd been a boxer in his youth, and you still wouldn't want to be on the wrong side of his right hook, but his big shoulders sloped a little now and his gut hung over his belt. "Got a tip King Tut might be holing up in a duplex on Orchard."

"You shitting me?" Turner asked, his heart starting to race.

That explained why Car had been so twitchy this morning. They'd been looking into a series of B&Es in the Wooster Square area and they'd come up empty again and again. It had been like beating their heads against a wall until one of Carmichael's CIs had pointed them toward Delan Tuttle, a small-time crook who'd gotten out of Osborn just weeks before the break-ins had started. He looked good for the robberies, but he wasn't at the address he'd registered with his parole officer, and every lead they'd had on him had gone cold.

Turner could at least relax a bit now. Carmichael had set off all his alarm bells that morning, too bright-eyed, too excited. Turner's first thought was that Car was high. It did happen—never with Carmichael, and rarely with detectives, but when you were working back-to-back shifts as a beat cop, it wasn't unheard of to snort a little Adderall—or coke if you could get it—to keep you from sleepwalking through hour twelve.

Turner kept clean, of course. He had enough hoops to jump through without worrying about a urine test. And he'd never had trouble staying awake on the job. His father had said it best: *You get the habit of looking out, you don't ever lose it.* Eamon Turner ran an appliance repair shop, and eventually he would die in front of a row of used stereos and DVD players—not at the hands of one of the kids who occasionally rolled up on the shop hoping to find a flat-screen or some hidden treasure, but from a heart attack that felled him silently. Business had been bad for a long time, and his father's body wasn't found until late afternoon when Naomi Laschen had come to pick up her ancient panini press. Turner had told himself it wasn't a bad way to go, but he'd been tormented by the thought of his father dying alone in a room full of obsolete machines, running down the way they all did in the end.

Now Turner squealed out of the parking lot and headed toward Kensington. "How do you want to handle this?"

Car took a big bite of his sandwich. "Let's come down on Elm, past that auto repair place. Get our bearings." He cut Turner a glance and grinned, grease on his chin. "Your little storm cloud go home for the day?"

"Yeah, yeah," Turner said with a laugh.

Turner was moody. Always had been. He had to watch for it. If people picked up on that mood too often, suddenly they started steering clear, invitations to grab a beer dried up, no one pulled you in when they needed an extra man. It could be enough to kill a career. So Turner tried to smile, keep his shoulders loose, make things easy for everyone around him. But today he'd woken up feeling that weight bearing down on him, that prickle in the back of his skull, the sense that something bad was brewing. The shit weather and weak coffee hadn't helped.

From the time he was a kid, Turner had an ear for trouble coming. He could spot an undercover without even trying, always knew when a black-and-white was about to round a corner. His friends thought it was spooky, but his father told him it just meant he was a natural detective. Turner liked that thought. He wasn't particularly good at sports or art or school, but he did have a sense for people and what they might do. He knew when someone was sick, like he could smell it on them. He knew when someone was lying even if he wasn't sure how he knew. He'd just get that prickle at the back of his skull that told him to pay attention. He learned to listen to that feeling, and that if he kept smiling, kept the dark part of his heart hidden, people really liked talking to him. He could get his mom or his brother or his friends or even his teachers to tell him a little more than they'd set out to tell.

Turner also learned to expect the look of shame that came over their faces when they realized how much they'd said. So he practiced not showing too much sympathy or too much interest at all. That way they could convince themselves they hadn't said anything worth being embarrassed about. They didn't feel weak or small, and they had no reason to avoid him. And they never suspected that Turner remembered every single word.

On the force, they called him Prince Charming, chalked up his way with witnesses and informants to his looks. But they never understood that the charm that got some perp talking about his mom, his dog, the pull he'd done as a favor to a friend just out of the joint, was the same charm that got Turner's fellow officers yapping about their lives and their troubles over shots at Geronimo.

The prickle usually came before the phone rang with bad news, or before the wrong knock at the door. But ever since he'd joined the force, he'd been on high alert, like he was *always* sure something bad was about to happen. He didn't know how to sort that kind of paranoia from actual alarm.

"Of all the things," his mother had said when he told her he was enrolling at the academy. "Why ask worry to stay awhile?"

She'd wanted him to be a lawyer, a doctor—hell, a mortician. Anything but police. His friends had laughed at him. But he'd always been the outlier, the good boy, the hall monitor.

"The overseer," his brother had said to him once. "Say what you want, but you like that badge and gun."

Turner didn't think that was true. Most of the time. He'd done a lot of talking about changing the system from the inside, about being a force for good, and he'd meant it all. He loved his family, loved his people. He could be their sword and their protector. He needed to believe he could. At the academy, the brass had wanted him there, boosting their stats. There'd been enough black and brown faces and everyone on their best behavior. Not so much when he'd been in uniform. Then it was all us-versus-them, a sense of dread every time he passed the invisible line between work and his own neighborhood. After he made detective, it was even worse, a constant sense of premonition—never proven, never disproven.

And plenty of bad things did happen, but Turner was determined not to let them get to him. *It's the long game,* he told himself when the hazing got rough. Survive the bad job to get to the great career, to get to the top of the mountain, where he could actually see what needed to be done, where he would have the power to do it. He knew he could be a legend like Big Car, better than Big Car. He just had to endure. They put shit in his shoes, he stepped right in it, stomped around the locker room pretending he didn't notice, making them laugh. They got a hooker to hike up her dress and fuck a nightstick on the hood of his car, he laughed and cheered and pretended to enjoy it. He would play until they got tired of playing. That was the deal he made with himself.

It all paid off when Carmichael's partner retired and Turner got his slot. That was Big Car's doing. Turner wanted to believe that it was because he'd been a good sport about paying his dues, or because he was a genuinely great detective, or because Car respected his ambition. And that all might be true, but he also knew Car wanted to be seen buddying up to a Black man. Carmichael was getting older, closer to retirement, and he didn't have a spotless record. He had a questionable shoot in his file—the kid had been armed, but he was still a kid—and a couple of complaints lodged by suspects who said he'd gone rough on them. All in the past, but all the kind of thing that could come back to bite you on the ass if you weren't careful. Turner was cover. And that was fine. If partnering with Carmichael would move him up the ladder, he was happy to play brown shield for him.

As they pulled up a few blocks from the duplex, Turner scowled.

"We sure this is an actual lead?" he asked.

"You think my CI is fucking with me?"

Turner bobbed his head toward the rundown building, the garbage cans lying on their side in the muddy front yard, the snow covering the driveway, the heaps of junk mail on the front porch. "Looks like a roust."

"Fuck," said Carmichael. Sometimes CIs called the cops in when they needed to get squatters out of a building. And it definitely looked like no one was living in that duplex. At least no one paying rent.

The rain had faded to mist and they sat with the engine idling, enjoying the heat of the car.

"Come on," said Carmichael. "Let's see what we see. Take the car around back."

Once they were parked on the street behind Orchard, Car heaved his big body out of the passenger side. "I'll knock. You stay on the back in case he runs."

Turner almost laughed. Maybe King Tut was up there sitting on a stash of laptops and jewelry from the Wooster Square jobs, or maybe a few teenagers were camping on a mattress smoking weed and reading comic books. But once Big Car pounded on that door, they were bound to bolt, and it would be up to Turner to corral whoever came down those back stairs. Car wasn't going to embarrass himself trying to sprint through the streets of New Haven.

Turner watched Carmichael slip into the alley beside the house and took up his position by the back stairs. He peered through the dirty window to the first floor—an empty hallway, no furniture except a rug that had seen better days, more mail piled by the slot.

A minute later, he saw Car's shadow appear in the front window and heard the loud *thud thud thud* of his fist pounding on the door. A pause. No sounds from the house. Then again, *thud thud thud*. "New Haven PD!" Car bellowed.

Nothing. No scramble of feet, no window sliding open above.

Then Car kicked the door in. "New Haven PD!" he shouted again.

Turner stared at Car through the window. The hell was he doing? They hadn't actually been summoned here by a landlord. There was no reason for them to smash their way in.

Car gestured for Turner to follow.

"Fuck it," said Turner. What else were they going to do this morning? King Tut was their only lead, and no way Big Car was getting jammed up on an illegal search. Turner drew his weapon, took a few steps back, then slammed his shoulder into the door, feeling it give way.

Before he could even ask Car what they were doing, Car had a finger to his lips and was pointing up the stairs. "There's someone up there. I heard it."

"Heard what?" Turner whispered.

"Could have been a cat. Could have been a girl. Could have been nothing."

The prickle spread from the back of Turner's neck. Not nothing.

"Clear the ground floor," said Car. "I'm going up."

Turner did as he was told, but there wasn't much territory to cover. A living room with a stained mattress and dirty clothes heaped on top, a bare kitchen where nearly every cupboard was open, as if someone had searched it. Two empty bedrooms, a bathroom with a rotting floor where it looked like a pipe had burst.

"Clear," he shouted. "I'm coming up!"

He had one foot on the bottom step when he heard Car shout. A shot rang out, then another.

Turner sprinted up the steps, weapon drawn. He felt it squirm in his hand, looked down, and saw nothing but the hard black shadow of his sidearm.

Fear was messing with his head. Not fear for himself. Fear for what he might do, who he might hurt, his brother's voice in his head: *You like that badge and gun.* Turner always said the same prayer. *Please, God. Don't let it be a kid. Don't let it be one of us.*

"Carmichael?" he called out.

No answer came. No sound. The layout of the second floor was almost identical to the floor below.

Turner spoke into his radio. "Detective Abel Turner. I am at 372 Orchard. Shots fired, request backup and medical."

He didn't wait for the response, sweeping through the first bedroom, the bathroom. As he entered the second, he saw a body on the floor.

Not Carmichael. His mind took a minute to understand. The man on the ground, a boy really, couldn't be older than twenty, a hole in his chest, a hole in the floorboards beside him. Carmichael standing over him.

Turner recognized Delan Tuttle from his file. King Tut. Bleeding out on the ground.

"Shit," said Turner kneeling beside the body. "You hit?" he asked Car, because that's what he was supposed to say. But he knew Car wasn't hit, the same way he knew this kid wasn't strapped. His eyes scanned the room, hoping a weapon might materialize.

"I called a bus," Carmichael said.

That was something at least. But an ambulance wasn't going to do Tuttle any good. The boy didn't have a pulse. No heartbeat. No weapon.

"What happened?" Turner asked.

"He took me by surprise. He had something in his hand."

"Okay," Turner said. But he wasn't okay. His heart was hammering away in his chest. The body was still warm. Tuttle had been hit almost directly in the center of his chest, as if he'd stood still for it. He was wearing a T-shirt, jeans. He had to be cold, Turner thought. The heat wasn't on in here. There was no furniture. It had snowed just two days before. And the room was barren—no old cigarettes or food wrappers, not even a blanket. There were no signs he or anyone else had been squatting here.

He'd come here to meet someone. Maybe Carmichael.

"We don't have much time," Car said. He was calm, but Car was always calm. "Let's get our stories straight."

What story was there to get straight? And where was the mysterious object Tuttle was supposed to have had in his hand?

"Here," said Car. He had a white rabbit by the neck. It was wriggling in his fist, its soft feet treading the air, its eyes wide, the whites showing. Turner could see its heart thumping against its furry chest.

Then he blinked and Car was holding a gun out to him. "Wipe it," he said.

Turner had meant to be stern, but he found a nervous smile spreading across his face. "You can't be serious."

"Ambulance is gonna be here soon. Rat squad and the rest. Don't screw around, Turner."

Turner looked at the gun in Carmichael's hand. "Where did you get it?"

"Found it at a scene a while back. Call it an insurance policy."

Insurance. A gun they could plant on Tuttle. "We don't have to—"

"Turner," Carmichael said. "You know I'm good police and you know how close I am to punching out. I need you to back me here.

The kid drew on me. I discharged my sidearm. That's all there is to it. A good clean shoot."

Good. Clean.

But everything about this felt wrong. Not just the shoot. Not just the body cooling on the floor behind him.

"What was he doing here, Car?"

"The fuck do I know? I got a tip, I followed it."

But none of that added up. Why had they been chasing their tails for weeks on what should have been a routine investigation into a series of robberies? Where were the goods Tuttle had supposedly taken? Why hadn't Tuttle run when he heard Carmichael pounding at the door? Because he'd been expecting him. Because Carmichael had set him up.

"You were meeting him here. He knew you."

"Don't start getting smart, Turner."

Turner thought of the new deck Carmichael had put on his house last summer. They'd sat out there, barbecuing, drinking longnecks, talking about Turner's career. Car had said his brother-in-law was a contractor, got him a deal. Turner had known he was lying, but it hadn't bothered him. Most police who had been around long enough were a little bent, but that didn't make them crooked. And he'd already seen Car's wife wore better clothes than any detective's wife should. Turner knew his labels, he liked a nice suit, and the women he dated appreciated that he could speak that language. He could tell a genuine Chanel bag from a knockoff, and Car's wife always had the real thing slung over her arm.

Bent, not crooked. But maybe Turner had been wrong about that.

In the distance, a siren began to wail. They couldn't be more than a minute or two away.

"Turner," Carmichael said. His eyes were steady. "You know what the choice is here. I go down, you go down with me. There are questions about me, there are going to be questions about you too." He held the gun out. "This fixes all of it for us. You're too good to be brought down by my fuckup."

He was right about that. Turner felt himself reaching for the gun, saw the weapon in his hands.

"And what if I say no?" Turner asked, now that the gun was out of Car's reach. "What if I say there was nothing in Tuttle's record to indicate he was slick enough to get away with multiple B&Es without help?"

"You're reaching, Turner."

He was. He didn't know how involved Car had been in the robberies. Maybe he'd just taken a little cash or a spare laptop to look the other way. But the prickle was telling him that this was no mistake. It wasn't a fuckup. It was a setup. And King Tut was only part of it.

Carmichael shrugged. "Your prints on that piece, kid. Your word against mine. You've got a bright future. I knew that first time I met you. But you can't do the job alone. You need friends, people you can trust. Can I trust you, Turner?"

The prickle racing over Turner's skull turned to the crackle of wildfire. If he was involved with Tuttle and the robberies, why not get rid of him quietly? Why bring Turner here to witness the shoot?

Turner saw it all then. Car hadn't just chosen him as cover because he was Black. He'd chosen him because Turner was ambitious—so hungry to get ahead, he could be nudged. He could be used. Tuttle's dead body was Carmichael's chance to bring Turner into the fold. Two birds with one stone. Once Turner wiped the gun and wrapped Tuttle's finger around that trigger, once he repeated Carmichael's lies, he would belong to Big Car.

"You set this up. You set *me* up."

Carmichael looked almost impressed. "I'm watching over you, kid. I always have. There's no big decision to make here. Do the smart thing and you're on the fast track, my heir apparent. There will be nothing in your way. Or try to play hero and see how far it gets you. I have a lot of friends, Turner. And it won't just be you who feels the heat from this particular burn. Think about your mama, your granddad, how proud they are of you."

Turner tried to understand how he'd walked into a pile of shit this big. Why hadn't he seen trouble coming this time? Or had he just gotten complacent? He'd been waiting for disaster so long, he'd gotten too used to fear. His alarms had tripped so often, he'd started ignoring them. And now he was crouching by a dead body, being threatened by a man who could destroy his career with a whispered word, who wouldn't think twice about hurting the people he loved if he wronged him. He was about to cross a line into a country he didn't want to know. He would never find his way home.

"I don't want to do this," Turner said. "I'm . . . I'm not a criminal."

"Neither am I. I'm a man doing his best in a tough situation, just like you. Doing wrong doesn't make you wrong."

But it might. Turner wasn't stupid enough to believe this would be the last favor, the last lie. This was only the beginning. Car would always have more friends and better connections. He'd always be a threat to Turner's family, his career. Do the wrong thing and he'd keep rising, so long as he kept Car's secrets, followed his commands. Do the right thing and he'd tank his career and put his family in Carmichael's crosshairs. Those were his choices.

"That kid you killed," said Turner. "That was a bad shoot, wasn't it?"

"He wasn't a kid. He was a criminal."

"So you know your way around. You're not going to let us get jammed up with some amateur-hour bullshit."

"I've got you."

There was Turner's answer, loud and clear. He'd been on one side of the law and now he was firmly planted on the other. How long had it taken? Thirty seconds? A minute?

"You're one of the good ones," Car said, his eyes kind. "You'll come back from this."

"You're right," said Turner, taking his first steps away from the rules he'd always understood and abided by. He didn't know if he'd come back from this. But Car wouldn't.

Turner rose and shot Chris Carmichael twice in the chest.

Big Car didn't even look surprised. It was like he'd always known, like he'd been waiting just the same way Turner had for something bad to happen. He didn't so much fall as sit down and then slump to the side.

Turner wiped the piece clean just as Car had told him to. He tucked it into Tuttle's hand, fired another shot so the gunshot residue would at least seem plausible, though there was so much flying around this crime scene, the forensics would be shit anyway.

He heard sirens shrieking, tires squealing, officers shouting to each other as they surrounded the building.

"I'm sorry," he whispered to Delan Tuttle. "He'll be a hero."

He couldn't fight the tears that came. That was okay; the officers arriving would think he was crying for Big Car, his partner, his mentor. Chris Carmichael, the legend.

I'll play until they get tired of playing—that was the promise he'd made himself. He was a good detective and no one was going to tell him differently. No matter how much shit they made him walk through, no matter how much blood he got on his hands.

Only then did he realize that sense of foreboding was gone. No prickle. No fear. They'd done all they could to him.

He closed his eyes, counted to ten, listened for the sound of boots on the stairs. The sirens faded until all he could hear was the sound of his own breathing, in and out. The rain had stopped.

She stopped breathing. That was how she knew it had all gone wrong.

Hellie wanted to stay there, lying on her side, watching Alex sleep. When men slept, it was as if all the violence drained out of them, the ambition, the trying. Their faces went soft and gentle. But not Alex. Even in sleep there was a furrow between her brows. Her jaw was set.

No rest for the wicked, Hellie wanted to say. But the words died even before they could form on her tongue. She knew she'd been about to laugh, but it was as if the laugh had no place to take root in her. No belly to brew in, no lungs to gather breath with.

Hellie could feel herself breaking apart now that she had no body to hold on to. She wasn't sure when it had happened.

Not soon enough. Not fast enough to spare her all the pain that went before. Last night was a bad night in a string of bad nights.

She somehow knew the memories would start to fade as soon she let go of the world. She wouldn't have to think of Ariel or Len or any of it. The shame would go, the sorrow. All she had to do was leave. She would empty like an overturned cup. The pull of that glorious nothing was almost irresistible, the promise of forgetting. She would shed her skin. She would become light.

But she couldn't go. Not yet. She needed to see her girl one more time.

Alex's eyes opened. Fast, no stutter of the eyelids, no easy road out of sleep.

She looked at Hellie and smiled. It was like watching a flower bloom, the wariness gone, leaving nothing but gladness behind. And Hellie knew she'd made a terrible mistake in staying, in holding on to say a last goodbye, because God, this was bad. So much worse than knowing she was dead. She wanted to believe she wouldn't miss any part of her sad, wasted life, but she would miss this; she'd miss Alex. The longing for her, for one more moment of warmth, for one more breath, hurt worse than anything in life had.

Alex's nose wrinkled. Hellie loved the sweetness in her, that it hadn't shriveled in the relentless hailstorm of shit that was life with Len. "Good morning, Smelly Hellie."

Dimly Hellie realized that she had vomited in the night. Maybe she had choked on it. She couldn't be sure. There had been so much fentanyl in her system. She'd needed it. She had wanted to obliterate herself. She'd thought she'd feel clean, but now that it was done, she was still stuck with this weight of sadness.

"Let's get the fuck out of here," Alex said. "For good. We're done with this place."

Hellie nodded, and the ache was a wave that just keep growing, threatening to crest. Because Alex meant it. Alex still believed something good was bound to happen, had to happen to them. And maybe Hellie had believed too, not in the loopy dreams of college classes and part-time jobs that Alex liked to get lost in. But . . . had Hellie believed that none of this shit would stick to her? At least not permanently. None of this tragedy belonged to her. It was trouble she had picked up, but she would set it down again, get back to the real business of being human, of the life she was meant to have. This apartment, these people, Len and Betcha and Eitan and Ariel and even Alex—they were a pause, a way station.

But it hadn't worked out like that, had it?

Alex reached for her, reached through her. She was weeping now, crying out for her, and Hellie was crying too, but it didn't feel the way it had when she was alive. No heat in her face, no hitching breaths, it was like dissolving into rain. Every time Alex tried to hold her, she glimpsed flashes of her life. The desk in Alex's little-girl bedroom, carefully arranged with dried flowers and dragonfly barrettes. Sitting in a parking lot with the older kids, passing a bong around. The crumpled wing of a butterfly lying on damp tile. Each time, it was like stepping out of the sun into a cool, dark room, like sliding underwater.

Len slammed into their bedroom, Betcha close behind. She felt a pang of fondness for them, now that she could see them at a distance. Betcha's belly stretching his T-shirt. The smattering of acne on Len's forehead. But then Len had his hands on Alex, his palm shoved over her mouth.

Everything was going the way it always did, from bad to worse. They were talking about what to do with her body, and then Len backhanded Alex, and Hellie thought, *Okay, that's enough.* Enough of this life. There was nothing more to see here. No happy memory to leave on. She felt herself drifting and it didn't feel good, but it did feel better than what had come before.

She slipped through the wall and down the hall to the living room. She saw Ariel on the couch in his undershorts. But she didn't want to think about him or the things he'd done to her. The shame felt distant, like it belonged to someone else. That was okay. She liked that.

What was she waiting for? No one was going to speak for her; nothing was going to change. There would be no real goodbye, no sign she had ever been in the world. Her parents. God. Her parents would wake up to a call from the police or the morgue telling them that she'd been found in an alley. She was so sorry, so terribly sorry, but soon the guilt would be gone too, as if all that was left of her was a shrug.

Len and Betcha were fumbling with the apartment door while Alex cried, and Ariel said something. He laughed, a high-pitched giggle, and it was like being thrown back into her body, hearing him laugh as he pushed his way into her. This wasn't supposed to be the end of it all.

Alex was staring at her. She could still see Hellie when no one else could. Hadn't that always been the way with them?

But had Hellie ever really seen Alex?

Because now that she was looking, really looking at her, she could see Alex wasn't just a girl with warm skin and a clever tongue and hair shiny as a mirror. A ring of blue fire glowed around her. Alex was a doorway, and through her, Hellie could see the stars.

Let me in. The thought comes from nowhere, a natural thing: She sees a door, and so she wishes to walk through it.

Alex *hears* her. Hellie knows this because Alex says, "Stay."

Let me in. Is it a demand?

Alex extends her hand.

Hellie is ready. She is pouring into Alex. She is baptized in blue flame. The sorrow is gone and all she knows is how good the bat feels in her hand.

She is stepping out onto the field, and her teammates are chanting, "Give 'em hell, Hellie!" Her parents are in the stands, and they are beautiful, copper bright, and kind. This is the last moment she remembers before everything started going wrong and kept going wrong, when she still knew who she was.

She is standing at the plate in the sunshine. She knows how strong she is. There is no confusion in her, no pain. She flexes her gloved fingers over the handle of the bat, testing its weight. The pitcher is trying to give her eyes, psyche her out, and she laughs, because she's that good, because no one and nothing can stop her.

"Do you get nervous?" her little sister asked once.

"Never," Hellie said. "What is there to be nervous about?"

She doesn't want to die. Not really. She just doesn't want to feel anything anymore because everything feels bad. She wants to find her way back to this moment, to the sun, and the crowd, and the dream of her own potential. There is no worry about college or grades or the future. It will all come easy as it always has.

She shuffles her feet against the plate, tests her swing, the weight of the bat, watches the pitcher, sees the sweat on her brow, knows the girl is afraid.

Hellie sees the windup, the throw. She swings. The crack the bat makes when it connects with Len's skull is perfect. She pictures his head sailing over the fence. *Going. Going. Gone.*

She could swing that bat all day. There is no regret, no sadness.

They swing the bat. They swing again. This is the way they say their goodbyes, and only when every last word has been spoken does she notice there's a rabbit in the middle of the room, sitting on the blood-soaked carpet.

"Babbit Rabbit," Hellie whispers. She picks him up, seeing the red smears her hands leave on his soft white sides. "I thought you were dead."

"We're all dead."

For a second Hellie is sure the rabbit is speaking to her, but when she looks up, she sees Alex. The old living room at Ground Zero is gone, the blood, the bits of brain, the broken bat. Alex is standing in an orchard full of black trees. Hellie wants to warn her not to eat the fruit that grows on them, but she is already floating, fading away. Not even a shrug now. Going. Going.

27

Alex wasn't sure what had happened. There was something warm and soft in her arms and she knew it was Babbit Rabbit. Hellie had— *She* had picked him up. Where was she? It was too dark to see and she couldn't quite make sense of her thoughts. She went to her knees and heaved once, twice. Nothing came up but a mouthful of bile. A dim memory surfaced of Dawes telling her to fast.

"It's okay," she whispered to Babbit Rabbit.

But her arms were empty. He was gone.

He was never there, she told herself. *Get your shit together.*

But she'd felt him in her arms, warm and alive, his little body whole and safe as he was meant to be, as if she'd done her job and protected him from the start.

The ground felt soft beneath her hands, covered in damp, fallen leaves. She looked up and realized she was staring through the branches of a tree, many trees. She was in some kind of forest . . . no, an orchard, the branches black and glittering and heavily laden with fruit, its skin darkest purple. Where the peel had split, she saw red seeds that gleamed like jewels. Above, the sky was the plum of a bad bruise. She heard a soft humming and realized the trees were thick with golden bees tending to black hives high in the branches. *I was Hellie.* Hellie in death. Hellie at the plate. The misery of that night at Ground Zero clung to her like the smell of smoke. She'd never get free of it.

Alex glimpsed something moving through the rows of trees. She stumbled to her feet.

"Turner!" She regretted calling his name immediately. What if whatever was in the orchard only looked like Turner?

But a moment later, he, and then Dawes, and then Tripp emerged from the trees. No one looked quite like they should. Dawes wore parchment-colored robes, the cuffs stained with ink, and her red hair had been elaborately arranged in thick braids. Turner wore a cloak of gleaming black feathers that shimmered like the back of a beetle. Tripp was in armor, but the kind that looked like it had never seen battle, enamel white, an ermine cape fastened over his left shoulder with an emerald brooch the size of a peach pit. The scholar, the priest, and the prince. Alex held out her arms. She was wearing armor too, but it was forged steel, made for warfare. The armor of a soldier. It should have felt heavy, but she might as well have been wearing a T-shirt for all she felt the weight of it.

"Are we dead?" Tripp asked, his eyes so wide she could see a perfect white ring around his irises. "We have to be, right?"

He wasn't quite looking at her; in fact, no one was. None of them were making eye contact. They'd fallen through each other's lives, seen the crimes they'd committed, big and small.

No one should know another person that way, Alex thought. *It's too much.*

"Where are we?" Turner asked. "What is this place?"

Dawes's eyes were red, her mouth swollen from crying. She reached up to touch one of the branches, then thought better of it. "I don't know. Some people think the fruit from the Tree of Knowledge was a pomegranate."

Turner raised a brow. "That doesn't look like any pomegranate I ever saw."

"It looks pretty good," said Tripp.

"Do not eat anything," Dawes snapped.

Tripp scowled. "I'm not stupid." Then his expression changed. He looked caught between wonder and fear. "Holy shit, Alex, you're . . ."

Dawes bit deep into her lip and Turner's grim mouth flattened even more.

"Alex," whispered Dawes. "You're . . . you're on fire."

Alex looked down. Blue flame had ignited over her body, a low, shifting blaze, like the forest floor in a controlled burn. She touched her fingers to it, saw it move as if caught up by her touch. She remembered this flame. She'd seen it when she faced Belbalm. *All worlds are open to us. If we are bold enough to enter.*

She reached beneath her breastplate, felt the cold shell of the Arlington Rubber Boots box tucked against her ribs. All she wanted was to lie down and grieve for Hellie, for Babbit Rabbit. She was crouched over a stranger's body as the rain fell outside. She was perched at the rail of a ship, the sea rising and falling beneath her. She was standing at the top of the stairs at Il Bastone, feeling the weight of stone in her hands, the terrible power of decision.

Alex gripped the box tighter. She hadn't come this far to cry for past mistakes or tend to old wounds. She forced herself to meet their gazes—Turner, Tripp, Dawes.

"Okay," she said. "Let's go find Darlington."

Again the world shifted and Alex braced to be thrown into someone else's head, into some other awful memory, like the world's worst playlist. She hadn't been a passenger or an observer. She had *been* Dawes, Tripp, Turner, and Hellie. Her Hellie. Who should have been the one to survive. But this time it was just the world around Alex moving and she could suddenly see a path through the trees.

They emerged from the orchard into what looked like a sprawling outdoor mall that had been abandoned, or maybe never finished. The buildings were massive, some with arched windows, others square. Everything was spotlessly clean and a color somewhere between gray and beige.

Alex looked behind them and the orchard was there, the black trees rustling in a wind she couldn't feel. Her ears were still full of the bees' humming.

She heard someone singing and realized it was coming from a mirror set into a large elliptical basin of smooth gray rock. No—not a mirror, a pool of water so still and flat it looked like a mirror—and in it, she could see Mercy standing guard over their bodies—all of them lying on their backs in ankle-deep water in the library court-yard, floating like corpses.

"Is that really her?" Tripp asked. All his bravado was gone, wrung out of him by the descent. And they were only at the beginning.

"I think so," said Alex. "Water is the element of translation. It's the mediary between worlds." She was quoting the Bridegroom, words he'd spoken to her as they stood up to their waists in a river, in the borderlands.

Mercy was singing to herself. *"And if I die today I'll be a happy phantom . . ."*

Good choice. The whole song was death words. Alex could hear the metronome ticking steadily away behind Mercy's tune.

"Where do we start?" asked Turner.

His expression was stony, as if in the wake of all that misery there was nothing to do but lock down. He had his answer now, about what Alex had done in Los Angeles. And she had her answers to questions she'd never thought to ask Turner. The Eagle Scout. The killer.

Alex squinted out at the flat gray day. Could it even be day if there was no sun visible? The bruised sky stretched on and on, and wherever they were . . . No pits of fire. No obsidian walls. It felt like a suburb, a new one, for a city that didn't exist. The streets were spotless, the buildings nearly identical. They had the shape of the strip malls that lived on every corner of the valley, full of nail salons and dry cleaners and head shops. But there were no signs over the doors here and no customers. The storefronts were empty.

Alex turned in a slow circle, trying to stifle the wave of dizziness that overtook her. Everything was the same sandy, washed-out beige, not just the buildings but the grass and the sidewalks as well.

She felt an unpleasant shiver move over her. "I know where we are."

Dawes was nodding slowly. She'd put it together too.

They were standing in front of Sterling. Except Sterling was the orchard now, the basin full of water was the Women's Table in their world. And that meant that all the rest . . .

"We're in New Haven," said Tripp. "We're at Yale."

Or something like it. Yale stripped of all its grandeur and beauty.

"Good," she said with a confidence she didn't feel. "Then we at least know the layout. Let's go."

"Where exactly?" asked Turner.

Alex met Dawes's gaze.

"Where else?" she said. "Black Elm."

It should have taken them an hour on foot to reach Black Elm from campus. But time felt slippery here. There was no weather, no movement of the sun overhead.

They crossed through a concrete courtyard and then down to what she thought was Elm Street, but it was lined with big apartment buildings. When Alex looked behind, it was as if the street had shifted. There was an intersection where there hadn't been one before, a right turn where there'd been a left.

"I don't like this," said Tripp. He was shaking. Alex remembered the slide of the wet rope, the sea heaving beneath her.

"We're okay," she said. "Let's keep moving."

"We should . . . leave bread crumbs or something." He sounded almost angry, and Alex supposed he had good reason. This wasn't an adventure. It was a nightmare. "In case we get lost."

"Ariadne's thread," Dawes said, her voice unsteady.

The silence was too complete. The world too still. It felt like they were traveling through a corpse.

Alex kept her hand wrapped around the porcelain box. *I'm coming to get you, Darlington.* But she couldn't stop thinking of Hellie. She could still feel Babbit Rabbit in her arms. He'd been alive. For a moment, they'd all been together again.

Alex didn't know how long they'd been walking, but the next thing she knew they were standing outside of a chain-link fence. A huge sign read, *Future Home of The Westville: Luxury Living.* The render was of a sleek glass building towering over a landscaped slice of lawn, a Starbucks at the base, happy people waving to each other, someone walking her dog. But Alex knew this path, the lumps of stone that had once been columns, the birch trees now cut down to stumps.

"Black Elm," Dawes whispered.

It seemed wise to keep their voices low. The houses along the street looked empty, their windows shuttered, their lawns gray and bare. But Alex caught movement from the corner of her eye. A curtain pushed aside from an upstairs window? Or nothing at all.

"We're being watched," said Turner.

Alex tried to ignore the fear that moved through her. "We need bolt cutters if we're going to get past that fence."

"You sure?" Turner asked.

Alex looked down. The flame surrounding the Arlington Rubber Boots box was brighter, nearly white. She walked toward the fence, and then she was walking through it, the metal melting away to nothing.

"Cool," said Tripp. But he sounded like he wanted to cry.

The driveway to Black Elm seemed longer, the road stretching like a gallows walk between the stumps of trees. But the house itself wasn't visible.

"Oh no," moaned Dawes.

Of course. The house wasn't visible because it wasn't a house anymore, just a forlorn pile of rubble. Alex caught a glimpse of something moving between the heaps of rock.

"I don't like this," Tripp said again. He had his arms crossed over his body as if to protect himself. Alex felt a softness toward him she hadn't before. She could still taste the sharp tang of chlorine at the back of her throat, feel Spenser's foot digging into her crotch and the weight of Tripp's shame, forever pinning him beneath the water.

"Alex," Turner said quietly. "Look back. Slowly."

Alex glanced over her shoulder and had to fight to keep her walk steady.

They were being followed. A big black wolf was stalking them from about one hundred yards away. When she glanced back again, there were two, and she saw a third slinking through the trees to join them.

They didn't look right. Their legs were too long, their spines humped, the long curve of their snouts too crowded with teeth. Their muzzles were wet with drool and crusted with something brown that might have been dirt or blood.

Alex and the others passed a big puddle that had formed in front of what had once been the front door, and in the murky water, Alex saw Mercy pacing around the library courtyard. *She's okay. That has to count for something.*

"There!" Dawes cried.

She was pointing at the ruins of Black Elm and there was Darlington—Darlington as she remembered him, as he'd been in her dream, handsome and human in his long, dark coat. No horns. No glowing tattoos. He had a rock in his hands, and as they watched, he lugged it over to what might have been the beginning or end of a wall, and laid it carefully atop the other stones.

"Darlington!" Dawes shouted.

He didn't stop moving, didn't alter his gaze.

"Can he hear us?" Tripp asked.

"Daniel Arlington," Turner boomed as if he was about to read Darlington his rights.

Darlington didn't break his stride, but Alex could see his chest rising and falling as if he were fighting for air. "Please," he gritted out. "Can't . . . stop."

Alex drew in a sharp breath. When Darlington spoke, she'd seen the whole scene waver—the ruin of Black Elm, the bruised sky, Darlington himself. She saw dark night and a well of yellow flame, heard people crying out and saw a great golden demon with curling horns towering over all of it. She heard it speak. *Alagnoth grorroneth.* Nothing but a growl but she could sense the words in it: None go free.

"How do we help him?" Dawes asked.

Alex stared at her. Dawes hadn't seen it. None of them had. Tripp looked scared. Turner had one eye on the wolves. Neither of them had reacted to what Alex had seen when Darlington spoke. Had she imagined it?

"Keep an eye on the wolves," she murmured to Turner and stepped into the rubble.

Darlington didn't look up, but he spoke that word again: "Please."

The world wavered, and she saw the demon, felt the heat from that well of flame. Darlington wanted to break free, just as he'd wanted to point them to the Gauntlet, but he didn't have control.

She drew the Arlington Rubber Boots box from her pocket and opened the lid. Some part of her had hoped that would be enough, but still Darlington trudged back and forth, hefting rock after rock, placing them with infinite care. Was this object not precious enough? Had she gotten it wrong?

Alex gripped the lid and remembered all she'd seen in the old man's memories. Darlington when he'd still just been Danny, alone in the cold shelter of Black Elm, trying to stay warm beneath coats he'd found in the attic, eating canned beans from the pantry. Danny, who had dreamed of other worlds, of magic made real and monsters to be bested. She remembered him with his cobbled-together recipe for the elixir, standing at the kitchen counter, ready to tempt death for a chance to see the world beyond.

"Danny," she said, and it was not just her voice that emerged, but the old man's as well, a gruff harmony. "Danny, come home."

Darlington's shoulders slumped. His head bowed. The rock slid from his hands. When he looked up, his eyes met hers, and in them she saw the anguish of ten thousand hours, of a year lost to suffering. She saw guilt in them too, and shame, and she understood: That golden demon was Darlington too. He was both prisoner and guard here in hell, tortured and torturer.

"I knew you'd come," he said.

Darlington burst into blue flame. Alex gasped, heard Tripp shout and Dawes cry out. The flame licked over the rubble like a river flowing through the shattered ruin of Black Elm, and leapt into the box.

Alex slammed the lid down. The box rattled in her hands. She could *feel* him in there, feel the vibration in her palms. His soul.

She was holding his soul in her hands, and the power of it coursed through her, too bright to contain. It had a sound, the ring of steel on steel.

"I've got you," she whispered.

"Your armor!" Dawes cried. Alex looked down. She was back in her street clothes. So were the others.

"Why did it disappear?" Tripp asked. "What's happening?"

Dawes shook her head as if she was trying to drive the fear out of it. "I don't know."

Alex tucked the box against her chest. "We have to get back to Sterling. To the orchard."

But when she turned to the road, nothing was where it should be. The driveway was gone, the stumps of trees, the fence, the houses beyond. She was looking at a long stretch of blacktop highway, a motel in the distance, a horizon of low foothills studded with Joshua trees. None of it made sense.

The wolves were still there and they were drawing closer.

"There's someone with Mercy," said Tripp.

Alex whirled. Tripp was gazing into the puddle. She could see a man's silhouette in the doorway of the library courtyard. He was arguing with Mercy.

"There's something wrong with the ritual," Dawes said, "with the Gauntlet. I don't hear the metronome anymore."

"Alex," Turner said, his voice low.

"We have to—" She had meant to say something about Sterling, about completing the ritual. But she was staring into the yellow eyes of four wolves.

They were blocking the path between Black Elm and the highway.

"What do they want?" Dawes quavered.

Turner squared his shoulders. "What do wolves ever want?" He drew his gun, then yelped. He held a bloody rabbit in his hand.

The wolves lunged.

Alex screamed as jaws closed around her forearm, the wolf's teeth sinking deep. She heard the bone snap, felt bile rise in her throat. She fell backward, the creature on top of her. She could see its filthy muzzle, the blood and drool matted around its teeth, the crust of yellow pus around its wild golden eyes. But she still had hold of the box. The wolf shook her as the flames on her body caught on its oily coat. She could smell its fur burning. It growled low in its throat. It wasn't letting go. She could see black spots in her vision. She couldn't pass out. She had to get free. She had to get to Sterling. She had to get to Mercy.

"I'm not letting go either," she snarled.

She turned her head to the side and saw the others wrestling with the rest of the pack, and the rabbit, white fur spotted with blood, nibbling at a beige blade of grass, bloody handprints on its sides, ignored by the wolves.

She gripped the box harder, but she could feel herself starting to fade out of consciousness. Could she outlast this monster? The wolf was on fire now, its flesh roasting. It was whimpering, but its jaws remained clamped on her broken arm. The pain was overwhelming.

What did it mean if they died in hell? Would their bodies rest easy above, unbattered and whole? What would happen to Mercy?

She didn't know what to do. She didn't know who to save or how. She couldn't even save herself. She'd promised Darlington she would get him out. She'd believed she could keep them all alive, that this was one more thing she could bluff and bare-knuckle her way through.

"I'm not letting go." But her voice sounded distant. And she thought she heard someone, maybe some*thing*, laughing. It wanted her here. It wanted her broken. What would hell look like for her? She knew damn well. She'd wake up back in their old apartment, back with Len, as if none of this had ever happened, as if it had all been some wild dream. There would be no Yale, no Lethe, no Darlington, no Dawes. There would be no secret stories, no libraries full of books, no poetry. Alex would be alone all over again, staring into the deep black crater of her future.

Suddenly the wolf's jaws released and Alex screamed louder as the blood rushed back to her arm. It took her a moment to understand what she was seeing. Darlington was fighting the wolves, and he was neither demon nor man but both. His horns blazed golden as he wrenched one of the beasts off Turner and hurled it into the rubble. It yelped and fell in a heap, its back broken.

The box. It was still in her hands, but it was empty now, that bright, victorious vibration gone. He'd slipped free. To save them.

He tore another monster off Dawes and his eyes met Alex's as he snapped the wolf's neck. "Go," he said, voice deep and commanding. "I'll keep them at bay."

"I won't leave you."

He tossed the wolf that had been tormenting Tripp into the desert sand, and it ran, whimpering, tail between its legs. But there were more coming, shadows slinking between the crooked silhouettes of the Joshua trees.

"Go," Darlington insisted.

But Alex couldn't. Not when they were this close, not when she'd held his soul in her hands. "Please," she begged. "Come with us. We can—"

Darlington's smile was small. "You found me once, Stern. You'll find me again. Now go." He turned to face the wolves.

Alex made herself follow the others, but all the fight had gone out of her. This wasn't how it was meant to be. She wasn't supposed to fail again.

"Come on!" Turner demanded, dragging Tripp and Dawes down the desert highway.

There were more wolves waiting, blocking the road.

"How do we get past them?" Tripp cried.

"This isn't how this works," Dawes said, her voice raw with fear. She had blood on her forearm and she was limping. "They shouldn't be trying to stop us from leaving."

Turner stepped forward, hands held up as if hoping the wolves would part like the Red Sea. "*Yea, though I walk through the valley of the shadow of death, I will fear no evil . . .*"

One of the wolves cocked its head, like a dog that didn't understand a command. Another whimpered, but it wasn't a sound of distress. It sounded almost like a laugh. The largest of the wolves padded toward them, head lowered.

"*For thou art with me,*" Turner proclaimed. "*Thy rod and thy staff they comfort me. Thou preparest a table before me in the presence of mine enemies—*"

The big wolf opened its mouth, its tongue lolled out. The word that emerged from its jaws was low and growling, but unmistakable: "Thief."

Without thinking Alex took a step backward, terror rising like a scream in her head at the wrongness of it. Tripp's mouth hung open, and Dawes groaned, panic overtaking them both. Only Turner stood fast, but she could see he was trembling as he shouted, "*Thou anointest my head with oil; my cup runneth over. Surely goodness and mercy shall follow me—*"

The wolf's lips split, showing its jagged teeth, its black gums. It was smiling. "*If a thief is found breaking in,*" it said, the words rolling like growls, "*and is struck so that he dies, there shall be no bloodguilt for him.*"

Turner dropped his hands. He shook his head. "Exodus. That fucking wolf is quoting scripture at me."

Now another wolf was creeping forward, head low. "*All who came before me are thieves and robbers.*" Alex caught movement from the left and right. They were being surrounded. "*But the sheep did not listen to them.*" The last word was little more than a snarl.

"It's because we tried to take Darlington," said Dawes. "We tried to take him home."

"Back-to-back!" Alex cried. "Everyone with me!" She had no idea what she was doing, but she had to try something. Tripp was crying now and Dawes had squeezed her eyes shut. Turner was still shaking his head. She'd warned him this wasn't some grand battle between good and evil.

Alex slapped her hands together, rubbing her palms against each other as if she were trying to keep warm, and sure enough the flames leapt. "Come on," she muttered to them, to herself, still unsure of what she was asking for or who she was pleading with. The unwanted magic that had plagued her from her birth. Her grandmother's spirit. Her mother's crystals. Her absent father's blood. "Come on."

The big wolf lunged forward. Alex swept her hand out and the blue flame went with it, unfurling with a crack like a whip. The wolves leapt back.

Again she lashed out, letting the flame course through her, an extension of her arm, her fear and anger flooding through her and finding form in blue fire. *Crack. Crack. Crack.*

"What is this?" Turner demanded. "What are you doing?"

Alex wasn't sure. The blazing arcs of flame weren't dissipating. As Alex released them, they hung in the air, writhing, seeking direction, finally finding one another—and when they did they began to churn, forming a circle around her and the others, brilliant white and gleaming.

"What is it?" Tripp shouted.

Dawes met Alex's eyes and now her fear was gone. Alex saw the determined face of the scholar shining back at her. "It's the Wheel."

The ground beneath their feet shook. The wolves were lunging at them, snapping at the blue and white sparks rising from Alex's fire.

A crack opened beneath Alex's feet and she stumbled.

"Stop," shouted Tripp. "You have to stop."

"Don't!" cried Dawes. "Something's happening!"

And Alex didn't think she *could* stop. The fire was sparking through her now, and she knew if she didn't release it, it would burn her up from the inside. There would be nothing left but ash.

Alex looked back at Black Elm. The wolves had abandoned their attack on Darlington to launch themselves at the burning wheel. His horns had vanished, and he had a stone in his hand. She watched him carefully set it atop the wall.

I'll come back for you, she vowed. *I'll find a way.*

The earth beneath them split with a deafening boom. They fell, surrounded by a cascade of blue flame. Alex saw the wolves falling too. They blazed white as the fire caught hold of them, brilliant as comets, and then Alex saw nothing at all.

It is not just our right to make this journey, but our duty. If Hiram Bingham had never scaled the peaks of Peru, would we have his Crucible and our ability to see behind the Veil? The knowledge we have gained cannot remain academic. I could well point to the money and time spent, the generosity of Sterling, the labor and ingenuity of JGR, Lawrie, Bonawit, the many hands that toiled to construct a ritual of this size and complexity. They had the will to commit themselves to the project and the means to attempt it. It is now our duty to show the courage of their convictions, to prove we are men of Yale, rightful heirs to the men of action who built these institutions, instead of pampered children who balk at the thought of getting our hands dirty.

—Lethe Days Diary of Rudolph Kittscher
(Jonathan Edwards College '33)

I am without energy or will to record what has happened. I know only despair. There is but one word I need write that may encompass our sins: *hubris.*

—Lethe Days Diary of Rudolph Kittscher
(Jonathan Edwards College '33)

28

Alex was on her back. At some point it had started to rain. She wiped the water from her eyes and spat the taste of sulfur from her mouth.

"Mercy!" she shouted, shoving to her feet and coughing. Her arm was whole and unbroken, but the world was spinning. Everything looked too rich, too saturated with color, the lights too yellow, the night lush as fresh ink.

"Are you okay?" Mercy was beside her, drenched from the rain, her salt armor somehow keeping its form.

"I'm fine," Alex lied. "Is everyone here?"

"Here," said Dawes, her face a white blur in the downpour.

"Yeah," said Turner.

Tripp was sitting in the mud, arms cradled over his head, sobbing.

Alex looked around, trying to get her bearings. "I saw someone up here."

"Did you stop the metronome?" Dawes asked.

"I'm sorry," Mercy said. "He told me to stop it. I didn't know what to do."

"It's certainly not your fault, Miss Zhao."

"Shit," Alex muttered.

She didn't know what she'd expected—a vampire, a Gray, some other new and exciting ghoul. All of those seemed easier to manage than Michael Anselm. They'd taught Mercy how to deal with undead intruders, not a living bureaucrat.

He stood in the doorway beneath the stone carving of Dürer's magic square, arms crossed, protected from the rain. Amber light from the hallway cast him in shadow.

"Everybody up," he said, his voice thrumming with anger. "And out."

They got to their feet, shivering, and shuffled out of the muddy courtyard.

Alex was struggling to make her mind work. The wolves. The blue fire. Had she saved them? Or had Anselm inadvertently come to their rescue by interrupting the ritual and pulling them out? And where had the wolves come from? Dawes had said there shouldn't be obstacles like that. Could Alex blame Anselm for those too?

"I feel like someone dropped a house on me," said Turner.

"Hell hangover," said Tripp. He'd wiped his tears away and color was returning to his cheeks.

"Take off your shoes," Anselm snapped. "You will not track mud over these floors."

They wriggled out of their shoes and socks, then walked barefoot into the library behind Anselm, the stone floor like a slab of ice.

In the dim light from the generators, Anselm shepherded them to a back entrance that led to York Street, where he allowed them to sit on the low benches and pull their wet shoes back on.

"Detective Turner," said Anselm, "I'll ask you to remain." He pointed at Mercy and Tripp. "You and you. I've called cabs."

"I don't have any cash," Tripp said.

Anselm looked like he was going to throw a punch. He drew out his wallet and slapped a twenty into Tripp's wet palm. "Go home."

"I'm fine," said Mercy. "JE is right next door."

"The armor," said Anselm, "does not belong to you."

Mercy removed the breastplate, gauntlets, and greaves and stood there awkwardly.

"Miss Stern," said Anselm, and Alex took the pile of armor.

"Go get warm," she whispered. "I'll be home as soon as I can."

She hoped. Maybe she was about to be driven past the New Haven city limits and dumped in a ditch.

Alex shoved the armor into the soaked canvas tote they'd brought with them. She saw the luminaries were in there too. Anselm must have retrieved them.

Tripp waved as he headed out the door. Mercy backed slowly away, as if waiting for some sign from Alex to stay, but all Alex could do was shrug. This was it. This was what she and Dawes had feared so much. But the knowledge of what they might lose hadn't been enough to stop them. And now they'd literally gone through hell and returned with nothing to show for it.

At least she hadn't lost the Arlington Rubber Boots box. She touched her fingers to it in her damp pocket. She had held Darlington's soul in her hands. She had felt the force of his life, new-leaf green, morning bright. And she had failed.

She expected Anselm to escort them to the Hutch or maybe the Praetor's office, for some kind of formal reprimand. But apparently he wasn't interested in letting them get dry.

"I truly don't know where to begin," Anselm said, shaking his head like a disappointed dad on a sitcom. "You brought a stranger into Lethe's dealings, multiple strangers."

"Tripp Helmuth is a Bonesman," said Turner, leaning against the wall. "He knows about Lethe."

Anselm turned cold eyes on him. "I'm well aware of who Tripp Helmuth is, and who his father is, and his grandfather, for that matter. I'm also aware of just what would have happened if he'd been hurt tonight. Are you?"

Turner said nothing.

Alex tried to focus on what Anselm was saying, but she couldn't think straight. One moment she was ravenous, as if she hadn't eaten in days, and in the next breath, the world tilted and she wanted to vomit. She was still fighting the wolves. She was still in Hellie's head, swinging that bat. She was feeling the terrible loss of leaving a world she hadn't been sure she wanted to stay in. The sorrow was unbearable. It wasn't supposed to go that way. It should have been Alex who never woke up, who died on that old mattress, lost to the tide, washed up on that apartment floor. It should be Alex buried beneath the rubble of Black Elm in hell.

Dawes had her fists balled at her sides. She looked like a melted candle. Her dark red hair plastered against her pale skin like a failed flame. Turner's face was impassive. He could have been waiting in line for coffee.

"You somehow found a Gauntlet," Anselm continued in that measured, barely leashed voice, "*on the Yale campus*, and thought it was appropriate to keep it to yourself. You performed an unsanctioned ritual that put countless people and the very existence of Lethe at risk."

"But we found him." Dawes said the words softly, her eyes on the floor.

"I beg your pardon?"

She looked up, chin jutting forward. "We found Darlington."

"We would have gotten him back here," Turner said. "If you hadn't interrupted us."

"Detective Turner, you are hereby relieved of your duties as Centurion."

"Oh no," said Turner flatly. "Anything but that."

Anselm's face flushed. "If you—"

Turner held up a hand. "Save your breath. I'm going to miss the extra cash and that's about it." He paused at the door and turned back to them. "This is the first real thing I've seen Lethe or any of you wand-waving, cloak-wearing hacks try to do. Say what you want, but these two don't back down from a fight."

Alex watched him go. His parting words made her stand up straighter, but pride wasn't going to do her any good now. For that matter, she'd never seen anyone in the societies wave a wand, though she suspected there were a few in the Lethe armory. Which she might never see again. Somehow that was the worst of it—not just to be exiled from Yale and all the possibilities that went with it, but to be barred from Il Bastone, a place she'd dared to think of as home.

She remembered Darlington, stone in his hand, forever trying to save something that couldn't be saved. Was that why she couldn't turn her back on the golden boy of Lethe? Because he couldn't let go of a lost cause? Because he'd thought she was worth saving? But what good had she done either of them? What was going to happen to him if no one remained in Lethe to fight for his rescue? And what was going to happen to her mother now that she'd blown her chance at securing a sliver of Lethe's money from Anselm?

A jolt of fury shook her helplessness loose. "Let's get on with it."

"Are you so eager to be cast out of Eden?" Anselm asked.

"I'm not sorry for what I did. I'm just sorry we failed. How did you find us anyway?"

"I went to Il Bastone. Your notes were everywhere." Anselm brushed the rain from his brow, clearly fighting for calm. "How close were you?"

She could still feel the vibration of Darlington's soul in her palms, the power of it moving through her. She could still hear that ringing, the sound of steel on steel. "Close."

"I told you both there would be consequences. I didn't want to be put in this position."

"No?" Alex asked. Men like Anselm somehow always found themselves in *this position*. The keeper of the keys. The man with the gavel. "Then you should have listened to us."

"You are both hereby barred from the use of Lethe's properties and assets," said Anselm. "After tonight, if you set foot inside any of our safe houses, it will be considered an act of criminal trespass. If you attempt to use any of the accounts, artifacts, or resources associated with Lethe, you will be charged with theft. Do you understand?"

That was why he hadn't brought them to the Hutch, the place where Alex had once taken refuge, where she had bandaged herself up on more than one occasion, where Dawes had once defended her against Sandow. She could hear cars passing in the rain outside, the whoop of revelers headed home from some Halloween party.

"I need a verbal confirmation," said Anselm.

"I understand," whispered Dawes, tears spilling onto her cheeks.

"You should put her on probation," said Alex. "Go ahead and banish me. We all know I'm the bad apple here. Dawes is an asset Lethe can't afford to lose."

"Unfortunately, Miss Stern, I don't think Lethe can afford to keep either of you. The decision is made. *Do you understand?*"

There was an edge to his voice now, his red-tape, follow-the-rules calm fraying against his anger.

Alex met his gaze. "Yes, sir. I understand."

"I don't deserve your contempt, Alex. I offered to help you, and you looked me in the eye and lied to me."

A bitter laugh escaped her. "You didn't offer to help me until you knew I had something you wanted. You were using me and I was happy to whore for you for the right price, so let's not pretend there was something noble in that transaction."

Anselm's lip curled. "You don't belong here. You never have. Crass. Uncouth. Uneducated. You are a blight on Lethe."

"She fought for him," Dawes rasped.

"Excuse me?"

Dawes wiped her sleeve across her runny nose. Her shoulders were still slumped, but her tears were gone. Her eyes were clear. "When you and the board wanted to pretend Darlington couldn't be saved, we found a way. Alex fought for him, *we* fought for him, when no one else would."

"You put this organization and the lives of everyone on this campus at risk. You tampered with forces far beyond your understanding or control. Do not think to paint yourselves the heroes when you broke every rule intended to protect—"

Dawes gave a long sniffle. "Your rules are shit. Let's go, Alex."

Alex thought of the Hutch in all of its shabby glory, the old window seat, the painted scenes of shepherds and fox hunts on the walls. She thought of Il Bastone, its warm lamplight, the front parlor where she'd whiled away the summer, snoozing on the couch, reading paperbacks, feeling safe and easy for the first time in her life.

She saluted Anselm with both middle fingers, and followed Dawes out of Eden.

29

When Alex woke the next morning, her body ached and she couldn't stop her teeth from chattering, despite the covers piled on top of her. Her defiance and anger were gone, drained away by nightmares of Darlington crushed beneath Black Elm, Hellie fading before her eyes, Babbit Rabbit's bloodied little body.

After Anselm had banished them, Alex had invited Dawes to stay with her and Mercy at the dorm. It was closer to the Hutch than her apartment. But Dawes had wanted to be alone.

"I just need some time to myself. I—" Her voice broke.

Alex had hesitated, then said, "Someone needs to go to Black Elm."

"The cameras are all clear," said Dawes. "But I'll check in on him tomorrow."

Whatever I am will be unleashed upon the world. Alex had seen the circle of protection flicker herself. "You shouldn't go alone."

"I'll ask Turner."

Alex knew she should volunteer, but she wasn't sure she could face Darlington—in any form. Did he know how close they'd come? He'd been there. He'd saved her yet again, and sacrificed his chance at freedom. She wasn't ready to look him in the eye.

"You went to see him," said Dawes. "The night before the ritual."

Alex must have been spotted on the camera. "I had to get the vessel."

"He won't talk to me. Just sits there meditating or whatever."

"He's trying to keep us safe, Dawes. The way he always did."

Except this time he was the threat. Dawes nodded, but she didn't look convinced.

"Be careful," Alex said. "Anselm—"

"Black Elm isn't Lethe property. And someone has to take care of Cosmo. Of both of them."

Alex watched Dawes disappear into the rain. She wasn't made to take care of anyone or anything. Hellie was proof of that. Babbit Rabbit. Darlington.

She had trudged home in the wet, changed into dry pajamas, eaten four Pop-Tarts, and fallen into bed. Now she rolled over, shaking with chills and famished.

Mercy was sitting up in bed, a copy of *Orlando* open in her lap, a cup of tea steaming atop the upended vintage suitcase she used as a bedside table.

"Why can't we just try again?" Mercy asked. "What's stopping us?"

"Good morning to you too. How long have you been up?"

"A couple of hours."

"Shit." Alex sat up too fast, the head rush immediate. "What time is it?"

"Almost noon. On Monday."

"*Monday?*" Alex squeaked. She'd lost all of Sunday. She'd slept nearly thirty-six hours.

"Yup. You missed Spanish."

What did it matter? Without her Lethe scholarship there would be no way for her to stay at Yale. She'd lost her chance to get away from Eitan. She'd lost her chance at a new life for her mother. Would they let her finish out the year? The semester?

But all of that was too miserable to contemplate.

"I'm starving," she said. "And why is it so cold in here?"

Mercy dug in her bag. "I brought you two bacon sandwiches from breakfast. And it's not that cold. It's because you brushed up against hellfire."

"You're a beautiful angel," Alex said, snatching the sandwiches from Mercy and unwrapping one. "Now what the fuck are you talking about?"

"You never study."

"Not never," Alex mumbled, mouth full.

"I read Dawes's notes, not the actual source material, but contact with hellfire can leave you feeling cold and even result in hypothermia."

"Was that the blue flame?"

"The what?"

Alex had to remember that Mercy had no idea what had happened in the underworld. "What does hellfire look like?"

"Not sure," said Mercy. "But it's considered the fabric of the demon world."

"What's the treatment?"

Mercy closed her book. "That's less clear. Soup made from scratch and Bible verses were both suggested."

"Yes, please, and no, thank you."

Alex dragged herself out of bed and fumbled around in her dresser. She pulled a hoodie over her sweats. Was she even allowed to wear Lethe sweats anymore? Was she supposed to return them? She had no idea. She had a lot of questions she should have asked Anselm instead of flipping him off, but it had still been very satisfying.

She found the tiny bottle of basso belladonna wedged against the back of the drawer and squeezed drops into both of her eyes. There was no way she was getting through this day without a little help.

What's stopping us? Mercy had asked. The answer was nothing. Alex didn't want to go through hell again. But if they'd done it once, then they'd know what to expect the second time around. Dawes would have to choose a night of portent—assuming she and the others were willing to make a second run at the Gauntlet—and they wouldn't have armor for Mercy, but they could load her up with other protections, figure out a way around the alarms if they couldn't brew another tempest. Why not try again? What was there to lose? They'd come close enough that they had to take another shot.

She checked her phone. There was a text from Dawes from the day before.

All clear at Black Elm.

No changes? she texted back.

A long pause followed and then finally: *He's right where we left him. The circle doesn't look right.*

Because it was getting weaker.

They might not be able to wait for a night of portent. That was the other problem. Anselm had scolded them for putting Lethe and the campus in danger. But he didn't really understand the game they were playing. He didn't know Darlington was caught between worlds, that the creature sitting in the ballroom at Black Elm was both demon and man. And Alex wasn't going to tell him. As soon as Anselm understood what they'd done, he'd find some spell to banish Darlington to hell forever rather than risk another use of the Gauntlet.

"I'm sorry last night was such a shit show," Alex said.

"Are you kidding?" said Mercy. "It was great. I'm pretty sure I saw William Chester Minor. Honestly, I thought it would be a lot tougher."

You should have been fighting wolves with us.

"I think I'm going to get kicked out of school," Alex blurted.

"Is that . . . a prediction or a plan?"

Alex almost laughed. "A prediction."

"Then we have to get Darlington back. He can plead your case to Lethe. And maybe scare them with a lawsuit or something."

Maybe he could. Maybe he'd have more on his mind after a prolonged stay in hell. They wouldn't know until they walked the Gauntlet again. But God, Alex was tired. The descent had been a beating and it wasn't just her body that hurt.

She texted their group chat: *Everyone okay?*

Tripp's reply rolled in first. *I feel like shit. I think I have a cold.*

All Turner said was *Check.*

If someone has a kitchen, I can make soup. That should help, Dawes replied and Alex felt a fresh wave of guilt. Dawes had a microwave and a hot plate at her cramped apartment, but no real kitchen. They should be gathering at Il Bastone, healing up for the next fight, making a plan. She thought of the house waiting for them. Did it know what they had attempted? Was it wondering why they hadn't returned?

Alex rubbed her hands over her face. She felt tired and lost. She missed her mom. She loved Mercy, but for the first time in a while, she really wanted to be by herself. She wanted to eat that second bacon sandwich, then curl up and have a good long cry. She wanted to go to Black Elm and run straight up those stairs, tell Darlington or the demon or whatever he was all about fighting Linus Reiter, her troubles with Eitan. She wanted to tell him every last terrible thing and see if he flinched.

"You okay?" Mercy asked.

Alex sighed. "No."

"Should we skip class?"

Alex shook her head. She needed to hold on to this world as long as she could. And she didn't want to think about Darlington or Lethe or hell for a few hours. If Lethe didn't let her finish out the semester, then what would she do? Locate the exits. Make a plan. She wasn't the girl she'd been. She wasn't helpless. She knew how to handle Grays. She had power. She could get a job. Go to community college. Hell, do some ghost-listening and hire herself out to some rich Malibu douchebags. Galaxy Stern, psychic to the stars.

She took a long hot shower, then changed into jeans and boots and the heaviest sweater she had. Their Shakespeare and the Metaphysical class was in LC, and Alex wondered what would happen if she ran into the Praetor. Would Professor Walsh-Whiteley look at her with pity? Give her the cut direct? But if the professor was somewhere in the rush of students, she didn't see him.

They were filing into class when Alex heard her name being called. She glimpsed a familiar head of dark hair in the crowd.

"Be right back," she told Mercy, slipping into the flow of people. "Michelle?"

Had the Praetor already sent for Michelle Alameddine to replace her?

"Hey," Michelle said. "How are you holding up?"

Better than *I told you so.* "I don't really know yet. Are you meeting with Walsh-Whiteley?"

There was the faintest pause before Michelle said, "I had an errand to run for the Butler."

"Here?" Michelle did look put together for a work meeting—dark skirt, gray turtleneck, suede boots, and a matching bag. But she worked in gifts and acquisitions at the Butler Library. An errand should bring her to Beinecke or Sterling, not the English department.

"It was the easiest place to meet."

Alex didn't have Turner's sense for truth, that prickle she'd felt when she'd been in his head, but she still knew Michelle was lying. Was she trying to spare Alex's feelings? Or was she supposed to keep any Lethe business confidential now that Alex had been excommunicated?

"Michelle, I'm fine. You don't have to tiptoe around me."

Michelle smiled. "Okay, you got me. No meeting in LC. I had to be in New Haven and I wanted to see how you were."

No one is looking out for us but us. That was what Michelle had said when she'd tried to warn Alex not to use the Gauntlet. Even so . . .

"All this back-and-forth must be wiping you out. How was dinner with your boyfriend's parents?"

"Oh, fine," she said with a small laugh. "I've met them before. As long as we avoid talking politics, they're great."

Alex considered her options. She didn't want to spook Michelle, but she didn't want to keep dancing either. "I know you didn't go back to the city that night."

"What are you talking about?"

"You told me you were going back to New York. You said you had a train to catch, but you didn't leave until the next morning."

Color flooded Michelle's cheeks. "How is that any of your business?"

"Two murders on campus means I get to be skeptical."

But Michelle had regained her composure. "Not that it's your concern, but I'm seeing someone here and I try to come to town a few times a month. My boyfriend is fine with it, and even if he weren't, I don't deserve to be interrogated. I was worried about you."

Alex knew she was supposed to apologize, to make nice. But she was too tired to play diplomat. She had held Darlington's soul in her hands, and in it she'd felt the heavy, slumberous tuning of a cello, the sudden, exultant flutter of birds taking flight. If Michelle had stuck her neck out, even a little bit, they might have been better prepared. They might have succeeded.

"Worried enough to show up with a smile," Alex said, "but not enough to help Darlington."

"I explained to you—"

"You didn't have to make the descent with us. We needed your knowledge. Your experience."

Michelle licked her lips. "You made the descent?"

So she hadn't talked to Anselm or the board, hadn't met with the Praetor. Was she really just worried about Alex? Was Alex so unused to the idea of kindness that she instantly distrusted it? Or was Michelle Alameddine a champion liar?

"What are you doing here, Michelle? What were you really doing in New Haven the night Dean Beekman died?"

"You're not a detective," Michelle clipped out. "You're barely a student. Go to class and stay out of my personal life. I won't waste my time on you again."

She turned on her heel and disappeared into the crowd. Alex was tempted to follow her.

Instead she slipped into her Shakespeare lecture. Mercy had saved her a seat, and as soon as Alex was settled, she checked her phone. Dawes was headed to Tripp's loft to cook.

Alex pinged Turner privately.

Michelle Alameddine is on campus and I think she just lied about why.

Turner's reply came quickly. *What did she tell you?*

Said she was running an errand for the Butler Library.

She waited, watching the screen. *Doubt it. She doesn't work at the Butler.*

Since when?

She never did.

What was this? Why had Michelle lied to her—and to Lethe—about her job at Columbia? Why was she really on campus, and why had she tracked Alex down? And what about the fact that, when Alex had referred to two murders, Michelle hadn't blinked? As far as anyone on campus knew, there had been only one murder. Marjorie Stephen, a woman Michelle actually knew, had supposedly died of natural causes. But Michelle had no reason to hurt either professor. At least not one Alex knew about.

She couldn't concentrate on the lecture, though she'd actually done the reading. Part of the reason she'd let Mercy talk her into this class was because she'd covered two semesters of Shakespeare's plays already. There was plenty more to read, because there always was, but at least she hadn't had to bluff her way through every lecture.

Maybe there was an upside to all this disaster. No more struggling through classes. No more watching divas swallow bird shit for the sake of a hit album. Alex tried to imagine what life might look like on the other side of all this, and it was too easy to picture. She didn't want to go back to the hot, seasonless glare of Los Angeles. She didn't want to work a shit job and make shit pay and get by on scraps of hope, days off, a beer and a fuck to make the month more bearable. She didn't want to forget Il Bastone, with its tinny stereo and its velvet couches, the library that had to be cajoled into giving up its books, the pantry that was always full. She wanted late mornings and overheated classrooms, lectures on poetry, too-narrow wooden desks. She wanted to stay here.

Here. Where their professor was comparing *The Tempest* to *Doctor Faustus*, tracing lines of influence, the words singing through the room. *Why, this is hell, nor am I out of it.* Here beneath the soaring ceiling, the brass chandeliers floating weightless above, surrounded by panels of tawny wood and that Tiffany window that had no business in a classroom, alight with deep blue and green, rich purple and gold, groupings of angels who weren't quite angels despite their wings, pretty girls in glass gowns with halos that read *Science*, *Intuition*, *Harmony*, while *Form*, *Color*, and *Imagination* clustered around *Art*. The faces always looked strange to Alex, too solid and specific, like photographs that had been pasted into the scene, *Rhythm* the only figure who looked out of the frame, her gaze direct, and Alex always wondered why.

The Tiffany window had been commissioned in honor of a dead woman. Her name, Mary, was inscribed on the book that one of the kneeling angels-not-angels was holding. The panels had been packed away during the Black Panther trials, in case of riots. They'd been mislabeled and left to molder in boxes, until someone stumbled over them decades later, as if the campus was so sated with beauty and wealth, it was easy to forget something extraordinary, or simply mourn it as lost.

What's the point of it? Alex wondered. And did it need a point? The windows were beauty for its own sake, for the pleasure of it, smooth limbs, flowing hair, boughs heavy with flowers, all of it hiding in a lesson on virtue, meant as a memorial. But she liked this life full of pointless beauty. It could all disappear as easily as a dream, only the memory of it wouldn't fade the way dreams did. It would haunt her the rest of her long, mediocre life.

A girl was leaning against the wall beneath the Tiffany window, and Alex had to ignore the twinge she felt at the gleam of her golden hair and honey skin. She looked like Hellie. And no one had a tan like that before winter break.

In fact, she looked exactly like Hellie.

The girl was staring at her, blue eyes sad. She was wearing a black T-shirt and jeans. Alex's heart was suddenly racing. She had to be hallucinating, another symptom of her literal hangover from hell. She knew better, but a wild hope entered her head before she could stop it. What if Hellie had somehow found her through the Veil? What if she had felt Alex's presence in the underworld and crossed over to find her at last? But Grays always looked the way they had in death, and Alex would never forget Hellie's pallid skin, the drying vomit on her shirt.

"Mercy," Alex whispered, "do you see that girl under the Tiffany window?"

Mercy craned her neck. "Why is she staring at you? Do we know her?"

No, because Alex had erased every bit of her old life, the good right along with the bad. She hadn't propped a photo of Hellie on top of her dresser. She'd never even spoken her name to Mercy. And the girl standing there beneath all those angels-not-angels couldn't be Hellie because Hellie was dead.

The blond girl drifted toward the back door of the lecture hall. This felt like a test, and Alex knew damn well she should stay right where she was, pick up her pen, pay attention, take notes. But she couldn't not follow.

"I'll be right back," she whispered to Mercy, and grabbed her coat, leaving her bag and books behind.

It's not her. She knew that. Of course she knew that. She pushed the door open onto High Street. Dusk was falling, the November night coming on early. Alex hesitated, standing on the curb, watching the girl cross the street. The blacktop looked like a river and she didn't want to wade in. The High Street bridge seemed to float over it, its winged stone women reclining gently against the arch. The architect had been a Bonesman. He'd designed and built their tomb as well. She couldn't remember his name.

"Hellie?" she called, halting, uncertain, afraid. But of what? That the girl would turn or that she wouldn't?

The girl didn't stop, just crossed into the alley beside Skull and Bones.

Let her go.

Alex stepped into the street and jogged after her, following the polished gold of her hair up the steps, into the sculpture garden where she'd talked to Michelle only a week ago.

Hellie stood beneath the elms, a yellow flame in the blue light of dusk. "I missed you," she said.

Alex felt something tear loose inside of her. This wasn't possible. Mercy had seen this girl. She wasn't a Gray.

"I missed you too," Alex said. Her voice sounded wrong, hoarse. "What is this? What are you?"

"I don't know." Hellie gave the smallest shrug.

It had to be an illusion. A trap. What had they done in hell that could make this possible? There was danger here. There had to be. Wishes didn't just get granted. Death was final, even if your soul continued on—to the Veil or heaven or hell or purgatory or some demon realm. *Mors vincit omnia.*

Alex took a step, then another. She moved slowly, half-expecting the girl—*Hellie*—to bolt.

Her eyes caught a movement in the branches above. The curly-haired Gray, the little dead boy, was crouched there, whispering something to himself, the sound soft, like the rustle of leaves.

Another step. Hellie was California sunshine, clear blue eyes, a girl out of a magazine. It couldn't be. They'd said their goodbyes in blood and vengeance, in the shallow, murky waters of the Los Angeles River. She'd been carried by Hellie's strength back to the apartment where her cold body remained. She had begged Hellie to stay, and then she had lain down, halfway hoping she wouldn't wake up. When she had, the cops had been shining a light in her eyes, and Hellie, the only sunshine in her life, was gone.

"Shit, Alex," Hellie said. "What are you waiting for?"

Alex didn't know. A laugh bubbled up, or maybe a sob. She broke into a run, and then her arms were around Hellie, her face buried in her hair. She smelled like coconut shampoo, and her skin was warm as if she'd been lying in the sun. Not a Gray, not some undead thing, warm and human and alive.

What if this wasn't a punishment or a trial? What if, for once, luck was running in her direction instead of away? What if this was her prize for so much hurt? What if, this time, magic had worked the way it was supposed to, the way it did in stories?

"I don't understand," she said as they sank onto a bench beneath the tree. She smoothed the silky blond hair back from Hellie's suntanned face, marveling at her freckles, her nearly white lashes, the chip in her front tooth from when she'd careened off her skateboard in Balboa Park. "How?"

"I don't know," whispered Hellie. "I was . . . I don't know where I was. And now I'm . . ." She looked around in confusion. "Here."

"Yale."

"What?"

Alex laughed. "Yale University. I go here. I'm a student."

"Bullshit."

"I know, I know."

"You holding?"

Alex shook her head. "I don't . . . I'm not really into that anymore."

"Right," Hellie said with a laugh. "College girl. But I need something. Just to take the edge off."

Alex wasn't going to say no. Not when Hellie was here in front of her. Alive. Golden and perfect. "I'll figure something out."

"Okay."

"You don't have to whisper," Alex said, rubbing Hellie's arms. "We're safe here."

Hellie glanced over her shoulder, then past Alex, as if she was expecting something to come lurching out of the dusk. "Alex," she said, still whispering, "I don't think we are."

"I've got you. I promise. I'm stronger now, Hellie. I can do things."

"Len—"

"Don't worry about him."

"He misses you."

Alex felt something cold slide through her. "I don't want to talk about him."

"You should give him another chance."

"He's *dead*. I killed him. *We* killed him together."

"I was dead too, wasn't I?"

"Yeah," Alex said, and now she was whispering too. "You were. And I missed you every day."

"You should have come for me," Hellie said, her eyes dark in the gloom, gleaming with tears. "You should have helped me."

"I didn't know I could." Alex didn't want to cry, but it was pointless to fight the tears. "It's okay. I promise. I can protect you."

Hellie's look of disbelief stung. "You couldn't protect me before."

It was true. Only Alex had survived Ground Zero, Len, Ariel.

"Things are different now."

"Len can help us."

Alex brushed Hellie's tears away. "Stop talking about him. He's dead. He can't hurt us."

"He can watch out for us. We can't do this alone."

Alex wanted to scream, but she forced calm into her voice. She didn't know what Hellie had been through since she'd died. She didn't know what it had taken to get back to the mortal world.

"I'm telling you, it's not like that anymore. You can stay with me. I can help you get a job, go to school, whatever you want. It'll be just like we always said. We don't need him."

"That's just pretend, Alex." Hellie's scorn was so firm, so familiar, that Alex felt a flickering doubt. What if none of this was real? The courtyard. The towers of Jonathan Edwards and Bones. Yale. What if it was all some stupid fantasy she'd spun for them?

Alex shook her head. "It's real, Hellie. Come on." She stood, tugging at her hand. "I'll show you."

"No. We have to stay here. We have to wait for Len."

"Fuck Len. Fuck all of them."

Something rustled in the bushes. Alex whirled, but there was nothing there. She looked up to the branches of the tree. The little boy ghost was whimpering softly, crouched on the branch. Not playing, not hide-and-go-seek. He was terrified. Of what?

Alex pulled on Hellie's hands, drawing her to her feet.

"We have to go, okay? We can talk about Len or whatever else, but let's just get out of here. I'll get you something to eat . . . or anything you need. Please."

"You said you could protect us."

"I can," Alex said. But she felt a little less certain. Against Grays?

Sure. Against bad boyfriends? She could damn well do her best. But she also knew that night was falling, and there were creatures like Linus Reiter somewhere out there. "I need you to trust me."

Hellie's eyes were sad. "I did."

If Hellie had come back angry or vengeful or hungry for blood, Alex could have handled it, maybe even welcomed it. They would have set fire to the world together. But this ache of guilt and shame was too much. She was going to drown in it.

"Tell me what to do to make it right," Alex said. "Tell me what to say."

Hellie cupped her cheek. Her thumb brushed Alex's lower lip. "You know that mouth is only good for one thing, Alex. And talking isn't it."

Alex recoiled. Hellie didn't talk that way. Len did.

But Hellie's fingers dug into her skull, pulling her closer.

"Hellie—"

"He was good to us," Hellie hissed. "He took care of us."

"Let go of me."

"He was all we had and you killed him."

"He wanted to throw you out like a bag of trash!"

"You let me die."

Hellie threw her to the ground and Alex went to her knees in the dirt. She felt the kick to her side, and then her face was shoved into the ground, the stink of rotting leaves and rainwater filling her nose.

"*You* let me die, Alex. Not Len."

Hellie was right. If she'd just woken up when Hellie came in that night, if she'd made it home sooner, if she hadn't fallen asleep in the theater in the first place, if she'd told Len no, they were done. If she'd kept them in Vegas, they could be there right now, staring at all the pretty glass at that big hotel, smelling the perfume and the old-cigarette smell beneath it.

Hellie pushed at the back of Alex's head, but Alex wasn't fighting, she was crying, because she'd failed Hellie again and again and again.

"That's right." Hellie flipped her over and shoved a handful of rotting leaves into Alex's mouth. "I choked on my own vomit lying next to you. But you blamed Len for that? I let Ariel fuck me. He put some kind of electric prod inside me. He thought it was funny the way I jumped when he fucked my ass. I did it for us. I made the sacrifices, but here you are with your new friends and your new clothes, pretending you loved me."

"I did love you," Alex tried to say. *I love you still.*

"You should have died, not me. I was the one who finished school. I was the one with a real family. You let me die and you stole the life that should have been mine."

"I'm sorry. Hellie, please. I can fix it—"

Hellie hit her, a glancing blow, not enough to really hurt, just enough to shut her up.

Her body sitting atop Alex was warm. Too warm. Her hands had been warm when Alex held them. Her cheeks had been hot when Alex touched her face.

Even though she was just wearing a T-shirt.

Even though it was night in November in New Haven.

Alex reached beneath her collar for the string of salt pearls. Gone, they'd fallen off somewhere . . . No, the broken wire was still there, two pearls hanging on. She seized one and crushed it in her hand, hurling the dust into the moist air.

The thing on top of her shrank back, a sharp, high mewl escaping its lips. Its eyes were black, not that Ocean Pacific blue Alex loved so much. Because this monster wasn't Hellie at all. Because magic never did the kind thing. There would be no prize at the end of all your suffering. There was no reward but survival. And dead was dead.

"That's what I thought," Alex said, spitting leaves and dirt from her mouth, staggering as she tried to push to her feet. How many times before she didn't get back up?

"You left me," Hellie said, and her voice was broken.

It didn't matter that Alex knew it wasn't really Hellie. Nothing could stop the hurt inside her, the regret. Those were real. But this time Alex could see something else in Hellie's eyes, not just pain but something eager. Appetite.

Demons are nourished by our base emotions. Fed by lust or love or joy. Or misery. Or shame.

"You're hungry, aren't you?" Alex said. "And I'm just standing here filling you up."

Hellie grinned, sweet and familiar. "You always taste good to me, Alex."

"You're not Hellie," Alex snarled. Her arm shot out, and the little Gray entered her with a high, wailing scream on his lips. She tasted camphor, heard the clip-clop of horse hooves, smelled rose water—his mother wore it. She shoved the demon with both hands, but it didn't stumble backward. It leapt onto the low wall that bordered the garden, body poised.

Alex's mind was screaming. Angel-not-angel. Hellie-not-Hellie. But it looked like her, moved with her grace.

"You can't just leave us," the demon said with Hellie's voice. "We're your family."

And they had been. Not just Hellie, but Len too. Betcha. They were all she had for such a long time. She'd wanted to scrape it all clean, leave nothing but a hollow, just like that bomb-blast hole at the old apartment. She'd built something new and shiny right over that empty place.

"Why do you get the second chance?" Hellie demanded, stalking toward her. "The new life?"

Alex knew she should run, but she found herself trying to form an answer, some reason it had been her and not Hellie. *It's a puzzle. It's a trap.* But it was also true. Hellie should have been the one to survive.

Hellie's hand slid around her throat, squeezing. It was almost a caress.

"It should have been me," she said. "I was the one who was meant to bounce back. I was supposed to leave you behind."

"You're right," Alex gasped out, feeling fresh tears on her cheeks, the will to fight slipping away from her. "It should have been you." Alex had never belonged in this life, every day a struggle, a new opportunity for failure, a war she couldn't win. Hellie would have breezed through it all, beautiful and brave. "It should have been you," she repeated, the words breaking on her sobs as her fingers closed over the last of her salt pearls. *But it wasn't.* "Life is cruel. Magic is real. And I'm not ready to die."

She slammed the pearl into the demon's forehead, feeling it explode beneath her palm. It was as if the thing's skull gave way, crumpling in like wet sand, dissolving into a bloody crater. The demon shrieked, its skin hissing and bubbling.

Alex ran—down the stairs, into the street. The Hutch was closer, but she bolted for Il Bastone, letting the little Gray's strength carry her. She needed the library. She needed to feel safe again.

She fumbled with her phone and called Mercy without breaking her stride. "Where are you?"

"Home. I have your bag. You—"

"Stay there. Don't open the door to anyone who . . . I don't know . . . anyone who shouldn't be alive."

She hung up and sprinted across Elm. Even with the Gray's strength, her legs were already shaking, her muscles exhausted from the ordeals of the last week.

Alex risked a glance back, trying to scan the crowds of students in their hats and coats. She paused to punch another number into her phone. She was running again before Dawes picked up.

"Are you still with Tripp?" Alex asked. Her voice was thready and breathless. "Get to Il Bastone."

"We're not allowed at Il Bastone."

"Dawes, just get there. And get Turner and Tripp there too."

"Alex—"

"Just fucking do it! I brought something back with me. Something bad."

Alex looked over her shoulder again, but she wasn't sure what she expected to see. Hellie? Len? Some other monster?

There was nothing to do but keep running.

30

As she raced down Orange Street, Alex could feel the little Gray clamoring to be released, rattling around her head like someone had given him too much sugar. But she wasn't letting him go until she knew she could get inside Il Bastone.

Alex took the steps in a single, awkward leap. What would it mean if this door remained closed to her now? If the Lethe board had already banished her from this place of protection? From quiet and safety and plenty?

But the door flew open. Alex lurched inside, falling forward. She felt the little Gray's ghost yanked free, the wards preventing him from entering, even hidden inside her body. He left in a sulky rush, taking his strength with him. The door slammed behind her, hard enough that the windows shook.

Alex felt her thighs wobbling with fatigue. She used the banister to pull herself up, felt the cool wood beneath her palm, pressed her forehead against the finial, the ridges of the sunflower pattern hard against her skin. This was home. Not her dorm room. Not the wreckage she'd left behind in Los Angeles.

She drew a few long breaths and made herself peer through the window in the front parlor. Hellie—or the demon pretending to be Hellie—stood on the sidewalk across the street. How had Alex mistaken a monster for the real thing? Hellie had the confident grace of an athlete, easy in her beauty, even when their lives were fraying at the edges. But the thing across the street held itself taut, wary, its hunger barely leashed.

I was the one who was meant to bounce back. I was supposed to leave you behind.

"Shut up," Alex muttered. But she couldn't pretend those words were a demon lie. The wrong girl had died at Ground Zero.

Alex picked up her phone and texted the group. *There's a blonde outside of Il Bastone. Looks like a girl. IS NOT A GIRL. Use salt.*

But her eye caught movement on the sidewalk. Dawes and Tripp. Had they seen her message?

Alex hesitated. She didn't have time to raid the armory for salt and weapons. She had no salt pearls left. Fine. She couldn't stand there and do nothing.

You stole my life. You stole my chance.

Alex shuddered and threw open the door. "Dawes!"

The demon leapt across the street, straight for Alex on the porch of Il Bastone, its gait wild, and loping, and inhuman. Alex braced for impact.

The demon lunged over the low black fence and then shrieked, falling to the ground in a heap, its flesh bubbling as Dawes and Tripp hurled fistfuls of salt at it.

She should have known Pamela Dawes would come prepared.

"Get inside!" Dawes shouted.

Alex didn't need to be told twice. She stumbled up the stairs and back into the entry hall. Once Dawes and Tripp were inside, they locked the door, then nearly jumped when the bell at the back of the house rang.

Mercy and Turner were outside.

"We're safe in here?" Turner asked, eyes scanning the hallway as they entered.

An unnerving thought entered Alex's mind. "What did you see?"

Turner was moving from room to room closing curtains as if expecting sniper fire. "A dead man."

"Oh God," Mercy gasped. She was standing at the front window in the parlor staring out at the street.

Hellie was there, but she wasn't alone now. Blake Keely was with her, his head whole and perfect and wedding cake handsome. A middle-aged man in a cheap-looking suit was there too—arms crossed, rocked back on his heels, as if he'd seen it all and wasn't impressed—along with a tall, rangy guy who couldn't have been more than twenty-five.

"Spenser," Tripp said. "You . . . you guys see him? I thought I was imagining things."

Alex recognized them all. She'd seen them in hell. All of their victims. All of their demons.

"We didn't close the door," Dawes said, her voice rough, frightened. "We didn't complete the ritual. We—"

"Don't say it," said Tripp. "Do not say it."

Dawes shrugged, her face pale. "We have to go back."

It was half a question, a plea for someone to correct her.

"Come on," Alex said. "Let's go to the library."

Dawes tucked her hands inside her sweatshirt. "If Anselm—"

But Alex cut her hand through the air. "If Anselm could have locked us out, he would have. This is our house."

Dawes hesitated, then she gave a firm nod. "First, we cook."

Dawes got a pot of chicken soup and dumplings going and sent them upstairs with a list of search terms to write in the Albemarle Book. When the shelf swung open on the library, Alex was surprised to find the room seemed bigger, as if the house knew a larger group required more space.

They sat down to read, each with a tidy pile of index cards provided by Dawes from what Alex suspected was a limitless supply. It was too soon for them to be together again, after what they'd seen and all they'd been through. They needed time to shake off each other's memories, to push all that grief and sadness back into the past before they contemplated another descent. But they didn't have that luxury.

Everyone other than Mercy was still suffering from the aftereffects of the first journey. Alex saw the signs. They were all shivering with the cold. Tripp had dark smudges beneath his eyes, his usually ruddy cheeks gone sallow. She had never seen Turner anything less than immaculate, but now his suit was rumpled and there was stubble on his chin. They looked haunted.

If they were really going to attempt a second trip to the underworld, it couldn't just be a rescue mission. They needed to know how to fight off the wolves or whatever hell sent after them. Plus, they had to lure their demons back to hell and make sure nothing followed them home when they made their return. But right now they had to figure out how to keep those demons at bay before they all lost their minds.

Alex had been over some of this ground when she was trying to find a defense against Linus Reiter, and she knew they were in trouble. Unlike Grays, demons weren't deterred by memento mori or death words; they had no pasts they wished to cling to, no memories of being human, no unfinished business. Darlington or Michelle Alameddine should have been with them in this library. Someone who actually knew how to name these enemies and best them.

"What have you found?" Dawes asked when she emerged through the library door an hour later.

"No soup?" Tripp looked like he'd just learned there was no Santa Claus.

"It needs to reduce," Dawes said. "And we don't eat in the library."

"Are they still outside?" Mercy asked.

Dawes nodded. "They . . . they look very solid."

Turner tapped the book he was reading. "You thought Darlington got eaten, right? By Mammon?"

"Maybe," Dawes said cautiously. "There are a lot of demons associated with greed. Devils. Gods."

Greed is a sin in every language. That was what Darlington had said. Sandow's hunger for money. Darlington's desire for knowledge.

"But these demons aren't trying to make us feel greed, are they?" asked Turner.

Ambition, drive, desire. What was the opposite of that?

"Hopelessness," said Alex. That was what she'd felt as Hellie—*not Hellie*—screamed at her, a sense of inevitability, that this was her due, that she was only getting what she deserved. She was a criminal who had stolen the chance at this gilded life, and of course there would be a price to pay. It was why the demon tormenting her wore Hellie's face instead of Len's or Ariel's. Because Alex had never shed a tear for them. It was Hellie's loss she had wept over. "They want us to feel hopeless."

"I thought Hellie was a blonde," Dawes said.

"She is," said Alex. "Was."

Mercy nodded. "I saw her too. In our Shakespeare lecture."

Dawes's face was troubled. Without a word they followed her out of the library and down the hall to the Dante bedroom, to the windows overlooking Orange Street.

The demons were still there, a pack of them in the shadows between the streetlamps.

Hellie's golden hair looked black, her eyes dark. Her clothes . . . all black.

"She looks like you, Alex," Dawes said. And she was right.

Alex took in the warm hue of Blake Keely's hair, something like the bright red of Dawes's bun. Detective Carmichael had been wearing a cheap suit when she'd first glimpsed him, but now that suit looked sharp, the lines more elegant, the tie a deep lilac, something Turner might wear. And did Spenser look a bit more hapless, a bit less tough and rugged?

What had Alex thought when she'd gazed at Not Hellie across the street from Il Bastone? That she didn't have Hellie's easy, athletic grace. That she looked wary, taut. Because she was looking at herself. That live-wire anger was Alex's own.

Alex pulled the heavy blue curtains closed. She'd learned to love this room, the patterns the stained glass made in the late afternoon, the claw-foot tub she still hadn't worked up the courage to use. "I think I know what happened to Linus Reiter."

"Who?" asked Tripp.

"He's a vampire I tangled with out in Old Greenwich. It's . . . it's how I lost the Mercedes."

Dawes drew in a sharp breath.

"A vampire?" Mercy sounded terrified and thrilled all at once.

"For fuck's sake," said Turner.

"Linus Reiter was a student here at Yale," Alex continued. "But he had a different name then. He was a Bonesman. And I think he's one of the people who used that Gauntlet back in the thirties. I think Linus—or really Lionel Reiter—went to hell."

"We can't be sure of—"

"Come on, Dawes. Why build it if they didn't intend to use it? Why kill off an architect—"

"They killed an architect?" Mercy squeaked.

"No one killed Bertram Goodhue!" Dawes snapped. Then she bit her lip. "At least . . . I don't think anyone killed Bertram Goodhue."

Alex found herself pacing. She couldn't stop seeing the creature on the sidewalk. Hellie-not-Hellie. Alex-not-Alex.

"They offed the original architect," Alex said. "They built this insane puzzle into a giant cathedral. Why? Just to see if they could? As some kind of grand gesture?"

"They've done crazier shit," said Turner.

He wasn't wrong. And she could imagine these careless, daring, terrible boys making just this kind of trouble. *On a lark*, Bunchy might say. But she didn't think that was what had happened this time.

"They built the Gauntlet," she said, "and then they went to hell. Lionel Reiter, member of Skull and Bones, was one of the pilgrims."

Tripp took off his cap, ran a hand through his sandy hair. "And he brought a demon back?"

"I think he did. And I think it got the best of him. Literally. I think it drained away his hope and stole his life."

"But you said Reiter was, uh . . . a vampire." Tripp whispered the word, as if he knew how unlikely it sounded.

"Vampires are demons," Dawes said quietly. "At least that's one theory."

It made damn good sense to Alex. Reiter fed on misery; blood was just the vehicle. And of course he wasn't Reiter at all. He was a demon who had fed on the real Reiter until he walked like him, spoke like him, looked like him. Just like the demons down on the sidewalk.

Lionel Reiter had been the son of a wealthy Connecticut family. They made boilers. They built a gracious home. They sent their son and heir off to New Haven to practice his Latin and Greek and make business connections. And Lionel had done well for himself, even made it into the school's most prestigious society. He'd made friends with young men whom he brought home for horseshoes and tennis on the lawn in the summer, sledding and carols in the winter. Young men with names like Bunchy and Harold.

He'd been ushered into a world of the arcane and he'd felt safe, even as he'd watched men cut open and their insides jostled by the hands of a haruspex. He'd stood in his robe and made his recitations, and he'd felt the thrill of all that power and known he was protected by his wealth, by his name, by the mere fact of not being the man on the table. He'd joined the members of Bones, and Scroll and Key, and maybe Lethe one fateful night. He'd walked the Gauntlet and seen . . . what? Unless Alex was very wrong about these merry wanderers of the night, they weren't murderers. So where had they gone in hell? What corner of the underworld had they visited and what had they seen there? And what had they brought back with them when they returned?

"There's no record, is there?" Turner asked. "Of their little sojourn in hell? They scrubbed the books."

"They tried," said Alex. But the library had known what Reiter was, probably because there had once been documentation of their attempt to use the Gauntlet. "We should look up the Lethe Days Diary of whoever was serving as Virgil when Reiter was a senior."

Turner leaned against the wall, keeping one eye on the demons below. "I want to make sure I understand you. If we don't put these . . . things back where they came from, they're going to become vampires?"

"I think so," Alex said. Vampires wearing their faces, fed on their souls.

"They're going to eat the heart out of us," Tripp rasped. "Spenser was . . . He said . . ."

"Hey," Alex said. "He's not Spenser."

Tripp's head snapped up. "He *is*. Spenser was just like that. He knew . . . he always knew the meanest thing to say."

Alex didn't need convincing. She remembered feeling frightened and helpless, knowing no one would believe that Spenser was a monster. It had been like being a little girl all over again, surrounded by Grays, alone without magic words or handsome knights or anyone at all to protect her.

Alex sat down next to Tripp on the bed. She had pushed him into something he wasn't equipped for, and he was feeling it worse than all of them.

"Okay, so Spenser was pretty fucking bad. But you have to try to remember what those things down there feed off of. They're trying to make you feel defeated before you even try. They want to make you feel hopeless and small."

"Yeah, well," Tripp said, eyes on the carpet. "It worked."

"I know." She looked around the room at the others, all of them tired and frightened. "Who else tangled with one of them?"

"Carmichael showed up," said Turner. "But he didn't say much. Just scared the shit out of me in the squad room."

Dawes tucked her hands inside her sweatshirt. "I saw Blake."

"Did he talk?"

Her chin dropped. Dawes doing her disappearing act. Her voice was low and thready. "He said plenty."

Alex wasn't going to push on the details, not if Dawes didn't want to give them up. "But all they did was talk?"

"What else would they do?" Turner asked.

Alex wasn't sure how to reply to that. Why had Hellie attacked her when the other demons had stuck to words? Was it because Alex had chased her down? Or did Alex just have a gift for the worst possible outcome?

"Hellie got physical with me."

"They can . . . they can hurt us?" Tripp was digging his fingers into his thighs.

"Maybe it's just me," said Alex. "I don't know."

"We need to plan for the worst," said Turner. "I'm not going into what might be a knife fight thinking I'm in for a lively debate."

Mercy had been silent through all of it, but now she stepped forward looking like she was about to perform a solo in an a cappella group. "I . . . I think I found something. In the library. Something to help."

"Let's eat first," Alex said. Tripp needed that soup. And maybe a shot of whiskey.

31

Alex was surprised at just how much the soup helped. She felt warm for the first time since she'd burst out of the underworld and into the cold New Haven rain. Nothing felt quite as dire. Not with dumplings in her belly and the taste of dill on her tongue.

"Shit, Dawes," said Tripp, grinning as if Spenser and every other bad thing had been forgotten, "can you please just come stay in my loft and make me fat?"

Dawes rolled her eyes, but Alex could tell she was pleased.

None of them looked toward the windows, where the curtains remained drawn.

They'd gone seeking the Lethe Days Diary from Lionel Reiter's time at Yale. Rudolph Kittscher had served as Virgil then, but while his *Daemonologie* had been allowed to remain, his diaries were gone. All part of the cleanup job.

Even so, Dawes was thrilled with the protection spell Mercy had found. It needed only ingredients from Lethe's stores, and she thought they could manage it in Hiram's Crucible. She gave them each a list of supplies to gather, and they spent the next hour in the dim light of the armory, searching the small drawers and glass cabinets, disturbed by nothing except Tripp humming frat rock and occasionally yelping when he touched something he wasn't supposed to.

"Why do you even have this stuff?" Tripp complained, sucking on his finger after a locket that had belonged to Jennie Churchill bit him.

"Because someone has to keep it safe," Dawes said primly. "Please focus on your list and try not to blow anything up."

Tripp's lower lip jutted out, but he went back to work, and a minute later he was singing "Under the Bridge" in a passable falsetto. Alex didn't have the heart to tell him she'd gladly spend the next two semesters in hell if it meant never hearing the Red Hot Chili Peppers again.

The recipe was seemingly banal—a slew of herbs of protection, including sage, vervain, and mint, along with heaps of ground amethyst and black tourmaline, crow feathers bound with rosemary, and dried jackdaw eyes that struck the base of the crucible with a clatter like pebbles. With Turner's help, Dawes removed several of the baseboards beneath the crucible, revealing a heap of coals. Dawes whispered a few words in Greek, and they glowed red, gently heating the bottom of the big golden bowl.

"This is the greatest moment of my life," Mercy said in a giddy whisper.

"All of it comes with a price tag," Alex warned. Those coals never cooled completely, never extinguished, never needed replenishing. They'd been used by Union Pacific to take dominance over the rails, and the creation of each briquette had required a human sacrifice. No one knew whose blood had been shed to create them, but the suspicion was working men, immigrants from Ireland, China, Finland. Men whom no one would come looking for. The coals had arrived at Yale through William Averell Harriman, Bonesman. Most of the coals had been lost or stolen, but these remained, another cursed gift to Lethe, another bloody map hidden in a basement.

"We have enough supplies to do this once," Dawes said as Alex and Mercy hefted sacks of salt from Prahova and the secret chamber at Zipaquirá and tipped them into the crucible. "Can someone get me an ash paddle?"

Tripp snorted, then blurted a hasty sorry when Dawes glared at him.

Alex found the glass cabinet hung with everything from a Model 1873 Winchester that carried the doom Sarah Winchester was so certain had followed her out to California; a broomstick that dated back to a Scottish witch-burning in the 1600s, charred black but unharmed by the pyre; what might have been a solid gold scepter; and a slender stick of ash, carved and sanded to smooth perfection. It looked a bit like a wizard's staff if the wizard had planned on making brick-oven pizza.

"We have to stir continuously," Dawes said as she began to combine the ingredients, moving the paddle in steady time. "Now, spit."

"Pardon?" said Turner.

"We need enough saliva to dissolve the salt."

"My moment to shine," said Tripp and let fly.

"This is disgusting," Mercy said as she daintily spat into the cauldron.

She wasn't wrong, but Alex would take this over another trip to the Manuscript aviary any day.

"Okay, who wants to try the paddle?" Dawes asked without breaking the rhythm. "Keep to the beat."

"How long do we do this?" Turner asked, taking the paddle from her smoothly.

"Until the mixture quickens," Dawes said as if that explained everything.

One by one they took their turns stirring with the ash paddle until their arms reached fatigue. It didn't seem magical, and Alex felt a twitchy self-consciousness. Magic was supposed to be mystical, perilous, not a mess in the bottom of a giant mixing bowl. Maybe some part of her wanted the others to be impressed with what Lethe could do, with the power in their arsenal. But Dawes didn't seem concerned at all. She was entirely focused on the task, and when the crucible began to hum, she grasped the paddle in Alex's hands and said, "Give it to me."

Alex stepped back and felt the heat building in the floor, radiating from the crucible.

The mixture sparked and hissed, the glow lighting Dawes's determined face. Her hair had come down from her bun and spread over her shoulders in damp red coils. Sweat gleamed on her pale brow.

Fuck me, Alex thought, *Dawes is a witch.* She worked magic with her potions and brews and healing ointments, with her soups made from scratch, her plastic containers of broth in the fridge, just waiting to be needed. How many times had she healed Alex and Darlington with cups of tea and tiny sandwiches, with bowls of soup and jars of preserves?

"Keep the rhythm!" Dawes commanded, and they beat their hands against the side of the crucible, the sound louder than it should have been, filling the room and making the walls shake as heat rose from Dawes's cauldron in shimmering waves.

Alex heard a loud *pop*, like a cork bursting from a champagne bottle, and a cloud of amber smoke burst from the crucible, flooding Alex's nose and mouth, making her eyes sting. They all bent double, coughing, the rhythm lost.

When the dust cleared, the only thing left in the crucible was a heap of powdery white ash.

Mercy cocked her head to the side. "I don't think it worked."

"I . . . I thought I got the proportions right," Dawes said, her confidence dissipating with the smoke.

"Hold on," Alex said. There was something down there. She bent over the edge of the crucible, reaching. It was deep enough that the lip dug into her belly and she had to tip forward off her toes. But her fingertips brushed something solid in the ash. She dragged it out and dusted it off. A salt sculpture of a snake nestled in the palm of her hand, sleeping in a circle, its flat head resting against its body.

"A talisman," said Dawes, her cheeks glowing with pride. "It worked!"

"But what does it—" Alex choked back a gasp as the snake uncoiled in her hand. It spiraled around her forearm, all the way up to her elbow, then vanished into her skin.

"Look!" Mercy cried.

There were gleaming scales all over Alex's bare arms. They glowed brightly and then dimmed, leaving nothing behind.

"Was that supposed to happen?" she asked.

"I'm not sure," said Dawes. "The spell Mercy found—"

"It was just a guardian spell," Mercy finished. "Do you feel any different?"

Alex shook her head. "Battered, bruised, and full of quality soup. No change."

Tripp reached into the crucible, nearly toppling into it. Turner grabbed him by the waistband of his shorts and hauled him back. There was some kind of bird in Tripp's hand.

"Is it a gull?" he asked.

"It's an albatross," Dawes corrected, her voice troubled.

As they watched, its white salt wings unfurled. It took flight, circled once around Tripp, then landed on his shoulder, folding into his body as if it had found the perfect place to roost. A pattern of silvery feathers cascaded over Tripp and disappeared into his skin.

"They're amazing birds," said Mercy, her hands flapping as if she too were about to take flight. "They can lock their wings in place and sleep while they fly."

Tripp grinned, arms outstretched. "No shit?"

"No shit," said Mercy. It was the most civil exchange they'd had.

Hesitantly, Dawes reached into the ash. "I . . . What is that?"

The tiny salt creature in Dawes's hand had enormous eyes and strange hands and feet that looked almost human. It sat as if it were hiding its face.

"It's a slow loris," said Mercy.

"It's adorable is what it is," said Alex.

The salt loris peeked out from behind its hands, then climbed up Dawes's arm, its movements graceful and deliberate. It nuzzled her ear and then curled into the crook of her neck, dissolving. For a moment, Dawes's eyes seemed to glow like moons.

Turner didn't look impressed. "Is it going to kill those demons with cuteness?"

"They can be deadly," Mercy said defensively. "They're the only primates with a poisonous bite, and they move nearly silently."

"How do you know all of this?" Alex asked.

"I was a really lonely kid. The advantage to being unpopular is you get a lot more reading done."

Alex shook her head. "Boy, did you come to the right place."

"I've read about the loris," said Dawes. "I'd just never seen one. They're nocturnal. And they make terrible pets."

Alex laughed. "Sounds about right."

Turner sighed and peered into the heap of ash. "There better be a fucking lion in there." He drew a sculpture out of the crucible. "A tree?" he asked incredulously.

Tripp burst out laughing.

"I think it's an oak," said Dawes.

"A mighty oak?" offered Mercy.

"Why did everyone else get something good and I got a damn plant?"

"The spell indicated the guardians would come from the living world," Dawes said. "Beyond that—"

"An oak is alive!" Tripp giggled, doubling over. "You can acorn your enemies into submission."

Turner scowled. "This is some—"

The oak sprang alive in his palm, shooting toward the ceiling, spreading in a vast canopy of white salt branches, its roots exploding over the floor and knocking Tripp to the ground. They wrapped around Turner and sank into his skin. For a moment it was impossible to tell the tree from the man. Then the glimmering branches evaporated.

Mercy was the last. Alex helped her balance as she tipped into the cauldron. She drew out a prancing horse, its mane flowing like water behind it.

As soon as Mercy set her feet back on the floor, the horse sprouted wings and reared back on its hind legs. It circled the room, seeming to grow larger and larger, its hooves shaking the ground. It leapt directly at Mercy, who screamed and threw up her hands in defense. The horse vanished into her chest, and for a moment, two massive wings seemed to extend from Mercy's back.

She murmured a word Alex didn't understand. She was beaming.

"We need to cleanse the ash," said Dawes.

"Wait," said Tripp. "There's something else in there."

He tipped over the edge of the crucible again and plucked a sixth salt figure from the leavings.

"A cat?" Turner asked, peering at the sculpture in his palm.

Dawes released a sob and pressed her hand over her mouth.

"Not just any cat," Alex said, feeling an unwelcome ache in the back of her throat.

There was a scar across one of the cat's eyes, and there was no mistaking that indignant face. The ritual had chosen Cosmo as Darlington's guardian, although she doubted that was the cat's true name. She remembered the white cat she'd seen in the old man's memories. Just how long had this creature been around?

"Will they really protect us?" Tripp asked.

"They should," said Dawes. "If you're under threat, lick your wrist or your hand or . . . I guess anywhere you can reach."

"Gross," said Mercy.

Dawes pursed her lips. "The alternate spell requires that I remove someone's tibia to stir the pot."

"No, thank you," said Turner.

"I can make it fairly painless."

"*No, thank you.*"

Alex remembered the address moths Darlington had used to remove her tattoos, a gift he'd given her, an attempt to show her that the uncanny might be good for something other than causing her misery. This was the cozy magic of childhood imagining. Friendly spirits offering protection. Cats and snakes and winged beasts to stand guard over their hearts. She tucked the salt Cosmo into her pocket, beside the Arlington Rubber Boots box she carried with her everywhere now. She needed magic to work for them for once. If they could bring Darlington home, if they could drag those demons back where they belonged . . . well, who knew what might be possible? Maybe she wouldn't have to be haunted by Hellie or Darlington or anything else anymore. Maybe the Lethe board would take pity on her. She could make them the same offer she'd made Anselm. She'd happily barter her gifts if it meant she got to keep the keys to this kingdom.

"How soon can we try to go back?" Alex asked.

Dawes clicked her tongue against her teeth, calculating. "The full moon is in three days. We should wait until then. The door will open for us. It just won't be easy this time."

"Easy?" Turner asked in disbelief. "I don't want to go through every damn minute of the worst moment of your lives again. Thank you very much."

"I mean the portal will be harder to open," said Dawes. "Because we won't have the advantage of Halloween."

"I don't think so," said Alex. "That thing is going to swing open wide for us."

"Why?"

"Because something on the other side is going to be pushing on it, trying to get through. The tough part is going to be closing it up again."

"We should . . ." Dawes chewed the inside of her cheek as if she'd stored words there for winter. "We should be prepared for . . . something worse."

Tripp dragged his Yale sailing cap off his head, leaving his hair rumpled. Alex noticed his hairline was starting to recede. "Worse?"

"Demons love puzzles. They love tricks. They won't just let us walk back into their realm and play the same script twice."

Tripp looked like he wanted to crawl into the crucible and never come out. "I don't know if I can do it all over again."

"You don't have a choice," Mercy said. Her voice was harsh, and Tripp looked like he'd been slapped. But Alex finally understood why Mercy disliked Tripp so intensely. He was too much like Blake. He wasn't a predator—his only cruelty was the casual kind, the blade of having more than everyone else and not quite knowing that was a weapon in his hands—but on the surface, he was cut from the same smug cloth.

"We *all* have a choice," said Turner.

Alex opened her mouth to argue—that they didn't if they wanted to live without torment, that they still had debts to pay—when she smelled smoke.

"Something's burning," she said.

They charged down the stairs.

"The kitchen!" Turner shouted.

But Alex knew Dawes hadn't left the stove on.

The ground floor was filling with smoke, and as they reached the base of the staircase, Alex saw the stained glass windows glowing with the light of flames. The demons had set fire to the entrance of Il Bastone.

"They're trying to smoke us out!" said Turner. He already had his phone in his hand, dialing for the fire department. "Where's your extinguisher?"

"The kitchen," Dawes said on a cough and ran to retrieve it.

Alex turned to Mercy and Tripp. "Go out the back. And *stay together*. Wait for me outside, okay?"

"Okay," said Mercy with a firm nod. "*Move*," she told Tripp.

Il Bastone's smoke alarm began to beep, a plaintive, wounded bleat. Alex waited only long enough to see Mercy and Tripp start down the hall; then she was racing toward the kitchen. She intercepted Dawes and grabbed the extinguisher. She'd had to use one when Len had started a grease fire in their apartment kitchen when he was cooking bacon, but she still fumbled with it.

Turner seized it from her hands.

"Come on," she said.

She threw open the front door. Flames had consumed the grass and hedges. They were roaring up the front columns. Alex felt as if she were burning too, as if she could hear the house screaming.

The demons stood in the firelight, and behind them, their shadows seemed to caper and dance. She heard the whoosh of the fire extinguisher as Turner fought to damp the flames. But Alex didn't stop. She strode toward the demons.

"Alex!" Turner shouted. "What the fuck are you doing? This is what they want!"

The thing pretending to be Hellie grinned. She looked leaner now, hungrier. More like Alex. But not quite. Her hands curled into claws. Her eyes were dark and wild, her mouth crowded with teeth.

"You want me, you bargain knockoff?" Alex demanded. She dragged her tongue across her wrist. "Come and get me."

The thing ran at her and then shrieked, darting backward, its grotesque smile fading. Alex saw her own shadow had shifted, as if she'd grown a hundred arms—not arms, snakes. They hissed and snapped around her, lunging at the demons, which cowered away from her.

"Alex," said the thing called Hellie—and she was Hellie again, her eyes that stormy watercolor blue and filled with tears. "You promised you would protect me."

Alex's heart twisted in her chest, the grief too powerful, too familiar. *I'm sorry. I'm sorry.*

The serpents wavered, as if they sensed her hesitancy. Then Alex breathed in and coughed, tasting the smoke on the air, the cinders of her home burning. She heard the crackle of rattlers, their tales shaking with her rage, a warning.

"Last call," she snarled at Not Hellie. "You're going back where you came from."

Hellie's eyes narrowed. "This is *my* life. *You're* the impostor."

Fine. Maybe Alex was nothing more than a thief who had stolen someone else's second chance. But she was alive and Hellie was dead and she was going to protect what was hers—even if she didn't deserve it, even if it might not be hers for much longer.

"This isn't your life," she said to the thing that wasn't Hellie. "And you are trespassing."

One of the snakes lunged forward, its bite so fast Alex didn't see more than a blur, and then the demon recoiled, clutching its smoking cheek.

"You can't banish us that easily," Hellie whined. She looked almost like Len now, hair straggly, forehead pocked by acne. "We know you. We know your smell. You are nothing but a stepping stone."

"Maybe," Alex said. "But right now I'm the bouncer and you better run."

Alex knew they hadn't gone far. Their demons needed freshly harvested misery to survive in this world. They'd be back and better prepared.

She heard sirens wailing down the street, and as she turned, she saw the flames were no longer lapping at Il Bastone. The front of the house was charred and spattered with foam, the stone around the doorway blackened and smoking, as if the building had exhaled a deep sooty breath. The fire on the hedges and grass had been extinguished—flattened by Turner's roots. The mighty oak. As she watched, they seemed to retract. Her snakes had vanished too.

She couldn't untangle the mess of fear and triumph she felt. The magic had worked, but what were its limits? They wouldn't be safe until those demons were back in their jar with the lid screwed on tight, and just how were they going to manage that? And how were they going to explain this to the Praetor and the board? She'd been bold enough claiming Il Bastone was her house, but she wasn't even a member of Lethe anymore.

"Find the others," said Turner. "I'll talk to the hose haulers. I called it in and I'm still police even if you're both . . ."

"Banished?" offered Alex. It was possible the Praetor wouldn't even realize they'd been at Il Bastone since the fire had started outside. But if he took more than a cursory glance inside, he was going to see the leftovers of their dinner and anything else they'd left behind. She wasn't sure how serious Anselm had been about *criminal trespassing* and she didn't want to find out.

Mercy, Tripp, and Dawes were waiting in the alley, stamping their feet in the cold.

"You're all right?" she asked as she approached.

"Alex," said Tripp, bracing his hands on her shoulders. "That was *sick*. They actually ran from you! Spenser looked like he was going to shit himself."

Alex pried his hands free. "Okay, okay. But they aren't done with us. We all need to stay alert. And you need to remember that's not Spenser."

"Absolutely," said Tripp with a somber nod. "Still fucking cool."

Mercy rolled her eyes. "How bad does the house look?"

"It isn't terrible," Dawes said hoarsely. "Hopefully the firefighters will tell Turner the extent of the damage."

"You sound like shit," said Tripp.

Mercy blew out an exasperated breath. "I think what he means is that it sounds like you inhaled a lot of smoke."

"There's an ambulance," said Alex. "You should get checked out."

"I don't want anyone knowing we were here," objected Dawes.

Alex didn't like the relief she felt at that, but she was glad Turner was willing to cover for them and that Dawes was willing to go along.

The firefighters and paramedics had been joined by two black-and-whites, and Alex saw Professor Walsh-Whiteley, bundled up in a long overcoat and a dapper little cap, approaching Turner, who was talking to two uniformed cops.

"The Praetor's here," Alex said.

Dawes sighed. "Should we talk to him? Try to explain?"

Alex made eye contact with Turner, but he gave the faintest shake of his head. The old Alex wondered if he was covering his own ass, laying a trail of trouble that would lead away from him and directly to her and Dawes. They'd make easy scapegoats. And it was Alex who had brought them back to Il Bastone, who had claimed it as hers.

"We should get out of here," Alex said, herding them toward the parking lot. They could slip out on Lincoln Street, wait for Turner there.

"I didn't see Anselm," said Dawes.

Tripp didn't seem to care. "Maybe he went back to New York?"

"Probably."

He had a family. He had a life. But Alex felt uneasy. It had been two days since he'd shut down their trip to hell, and they hadn't heard a word from him. No formal dismissal or follow-up, and Il Bastone hadn't been barred to them. Anselm had interrupted the ritual at Sterling. Alex didn't know what rules governed demons, but what if they'd set their sights on him too?

She glanced back at Il Bastone, watching the smoke rise off the building in soft clouds, a warning flame, a ritual fire.

She trailed behind the others and laid a hand on the wall, as if she were placing her palm against the flank of an animal to soothe it. She thought of her mother's apartment, scarves thrown over the lamps, crystals and faeries in every corner. She thought of Ground Zero, its walls spattered in blood, of Black Elm rotting around Darlington like a tomb. Alex felt the stones hum.

Turner would fight in his own way, with law and force and all the power his badge afforded him. Dawes would use her books, her brains, her infinite capacity for order. And what tools did Alex have? A little magic. A talent for misfortune. The ability to take a beating. It would have to be enough.

This is my home, she vowed, *and nothing will take it from me.*

The Salt Pearls of Emilia Benatti; salt and silver wire
Provenance: Mantua, Italy; early 17th century
Donor: Unknown, possibly gifted from the secret collection at the
New Haven Museum

The mechanism by which salt protects against demons is still largely a mystery. We know that salt is understood as a spiritual purifier and is used to ward against evil in many cultures. Its more pedestrian uses also spark the imagination—as a scouring agent, a catalyst for vinegar used in cleansing, a natural preservative that wards off decay, a restorative for failing flowers and fruit. Soldiers were paid in it. Gifts of it were once offered between friends. But what is the significance of Elisha pouring salt into Jericho's waters to restore them at God's command? After a funeral, why do some Japanese households scatter salt over their floors? And why do all of our records indicate that salt, above all other substances, is most effective in the dispatching of demonic bodies—both immaterial and corporeal?

Whether Emilia Benatti enchanted the pearls herself or simply acquired them, we also do not know. But she and her family were some of the few to survive the demon plague that struck Mantua in 1629. Her descendants immigrated to America around 1880 and settled in New Haven, where they became prominent members of the Italian community and can be seen at the St. Andrew Society Feast photographed in 1936. The pearls may have been discarded along with other superstitions of the Old World, but how they came to be documented and preserved in the New Haven Historical Society's secret collection is unknown.

—*from the Lethe Armory Catalogue as revised*
and edited by Pamela Dawes, Oculus

32

They all squeezed into Turner's Dodge like a gloomy, soot-covered carpool—Dawes up front; Tripp, Alex, and Mercy jammed into the back. No one was walking home alone tonight.

They dropped Dawes at her div school apartment first. Turner and Alex escorted her to the door, and they warded the whole building with salt knots.

"We'll meet up tomorrow," Alex said before Dawes shut the door on them. "Check in on the chat every hour."

Tripp was next, and he leaned forward through the gap in the front seats to give Turner directions to a big block of apartments not far from the green.

The building was nice. Exposed brick, warm faux-industrial lighting. Tripp's dad might have cut him off, but Tripp had to be drawing on some kind of trust fund. Hard times looked different to a Helmuth.

They warded the exterior and then drew a salt knot atop Tripp's welcome mat for good measure.

"You, uh, want to come in?" Tripp asked. All of his excitement had ebbed away, the fear creeping back in.

"You can crash with us," Alex offered. "We have a couch in the common room."

"No, I'm cool. I've got my seabird, right?"

"Check in on the chat," said Turner. "And don't go out if you don't have to."

Tripp nodded and offered up his knuckles for a fist bump. Even Turner obliged.

On the way down the stairs, Turner said, "I'm going to Black Elm when we're done. I want to know Darlington is still corralled in his pen."

Alex nearly stumbled. "Why?"

"Don't act the fool with me. You saw Marjorie Stephen. She had the life drained right out of her. Nothing natural about it."

"That doesn't mean Darlington had something to do with it."

"No, but he might know if one of his kind did. If there's something running around out there wearing Marjorie Stephen's face."

"He's not a demon," Alex said angrily. "Not like they are."

"Then call it a wellness check. I just want to know he's contained."

They rode back to campus in silence, and Alex and Mercy said their goodbyes to the detective on York Street.

"You sure you don't want help with the salt and all that?" he asked.

"No," said Alex. "Our room is warded. We'll do our entryway too, but I'm leaving the courtyard open. I need access to Grays. You know the knot pattern?"

"Yeah." Turner had said he could handle warding his place himself. Alex had the feeling he didn't want her at his house or apartment or wherever he lived. He didn't want Lethe and the uncanny bleeding into his real life. As if he could close the cover on this particular book when this ugly chapter was finished.

"If Carmichael shows up, don't listen to him. Don't let him get in your head."

"Don't coach me, Stern."

"Don't get that fancy suit rumpled, Turner."

He gunned his engine. "See you tomorrow night."

They didn't wait to watch his taillights disappear. They didn't want to be outside longer than they had to be.

The dorm felt strangely normal, every bedroom lit gold, music and talk filtering down to the courtyard.

"How is life still just rolling along?" Mercy asked as they passed people bundled up in their scarves, cups of hot tea or coffee in their gloved hands. The trees seemed to have lost their summer green overnight, the yellow leaves curling like bright scraps of rind from a peeled moon.

Usually Alex liked the feeling of the normal world, the sense that there was something to return to, that there was more than Lethe and magic and ghosts, that she might have a life waiting for her when this strange work was done. But tonight all she could think was that these people were easy prey. There was danger everywhere and they couldn't see it. They didn't have any idea what might be stalking them as they laughed, and argued, and made plans for a world they barely understood.

Lauren was in the common room, tucked into the recliner with a problem set, Joy Division on the record player.

"Where the fuck have you guys been?" she asked. "And why do you smell like a forest fire?"

Alex's tired brain searched for a lie, but it was Mercy who answered. "We had to help finish up the candy exchange and some house caught fire on Orange."

"The church again? Are you guys going all Jesusy on me?"

"I do like the free wine," said Alex. "Are we out of Pop-Tarts?"

"There's Tastykakes on top of the fridge. My mom sent them. You guys really scared me, okay? You need to tell me if you're just going to disappear. There was a murder on campus, and you're just walking around in the middle of the night like nothing happened."

"Sorry," said Mercy. "We lost track of time and we were together so we didn't think about it."

Lauren sipped from the big bottle of water she took everywhere. "We should start thinking about where we want to live next year."

"Now?" asked Alex, stuffing a Krimpet into her mouth. She wasn't ready to stare down the barrel of her lack of a future just yet. Even so, she didn't have many friends, and knowing Lauren actually wanted to spend another year with her felt good, like maybe she didn't have to wear her damage like a warning sign.

"Do we want to live on campus or off campus?" Lauren asked.

"We can butter up some seniors, find out which apartments look good."

"I might do a semester abroad," said Mercy.

Since when? Alex wondered. Or was Mercy just looking for an excuse to get away from her and Lethe?

"Where?" Lauren demanded.

"France?" Mercy said unconvincingly.

"Oh my God, fuck France. Everyone there has an STD."

"No, they do not, Lauren."

Alex took another Krimpet and sat next to Mercy on the couch. "You're telling me you wouldn't choose Paris over New Haven?"

"Nope," Lauren said. "And that is called loyalty."

It wasn't until they were settling in for the night that Alex had the chance to ask Mercy about France. "Are you really going abroad?"

"Now that I know magic is real?" Mercy had put on a vintage pajama set and slathered her face with cream. "No way. But wouldn't it be easier to come and go with all of this Lethe stuff if we didn't have to worry about Lauren asking questions?"

"I'm not in Lethe anymore," Alex reminded her. "Neither are you. And we're being hunted by demons."

"I know, but . . . I can't just go back to not knowing."

It isn't up to us anymore. Alex didn't say it, but she lay awake for a long time, staring into the dark. She'd lived with magic her whole life, even if she'd never called it that. She hadn't had a say in the matter. The one choice she'd gotten to make was agreeing to take Dean Sandow up on his offer when he'd appeared beside her hospital bed, when she'd been invited into Lethe. And now that choice was being taken away too. How long could she keep running from men like Eitan? From demons like Linus Reiter? From the monsters in her past who had become so very present?

She didn't remember falling asleep, but she must have because she bolted awake to the sound of her phone ringing.

Dawes.

"You okay?" Alex asked, trying to get her bearings. She'd overslept again. It was after 9 a.m.

"The Praetor just called. He wants to meet with you today."

Was this it? The official dismissal? The formal fuck-you?

"What did he say?" Alex pressed.

"Just that in light of last night's events, the Praetor requires Virgil's presence at his office hours."

Not at Il Bastone or the Hutch. "He still called me Virgil?"

"He did," Dawes said on a tired sigh. "And he called me Oculus. Maybe there's some kind of process we have to go through before we're . . . I don't know. Stripped of our offices."

Alex looked out the window into the courtyard. The morning sky was dark, the pavement damp. Slate-colored clouds promised more rain. It was too cold to be sitting outside, but there was a girl slouched on a bench below in just a T-shirt and jeans. Not Hellie looked up at Alex and grinned, her smile crooked, her teeth too long. Like the wolves they'd fought in hell. As if the longer she went hungry, the harder it was for her to pretend to be human. But it was the man beside her that sent a bolt of fear through Alex. His hair was long and blond, his suit white, his fine-boned face made nearly gentle by the gray autumn light. Linus Reiter gazed up at her, his expression bemused, as if someone had told a joke he didn't really find funny.

Alex yanked the curtains closed. Fuck having access to Grays. She needed to ward the courtyard. Maybe the whole campus.

"Alex?"

Dawes was still on the phone.

"He's here," Alex managed, the words emerging in a strangled whisper. "He's . . ."

"Who is?"

Alex slumped down next to the bed, knees drawn up, her heart pounding. She couldn't quite take a full breath. "Linus Reiter," she gasped. "The vampire. In the courtyard. I don't . . . I can't . . ." She could hear the blood rushing in her ears. "I think I'm going to pass out."

"Alex, tell me five things you see in your room."

"What?"

"Just do it."

"I . . . My desk. A chair. The blue tulle on Mercy's bed. My *Flaming June* poster. Those sticky stars someone put up on the ceiling."

"Okay, now four things you can touch."

"Dawes—"

"Do it."

"We have to warn the others—"

"Just do it, Virgil."

Dawes had never called her that. Alex managed a shaking breath.

"Okay . . . the bed frame. It's smooth. Cold wood. The rug—kind of soft and nubbly. There's glitter in it. Maybe from Halloween."

"What else?"

"My tank top—cotton, I think." She reached up and touched the dried roses on Mercy's bedside table. "Dry flowers, like tissue paper."

"Now three things you hear."

"I know what you're doing."

"Then do it."

Alex drew another long breath in through her nose. "The flowers rustle when I touch them. Someone's singing down the hall. My own fucking heart pounding in my chest." She rubbed a hand over her face, feeling some of her terror recede. "Thanks, Dawes."

"I'm going to text the group to warn them about Reiter. Remember, your salt spirit should work against him too."

"How can you sound so calm?"

"I wasn't attacked by a vampire."

"It's daytime. How—"

"I'm assuming he's not in direct sunlight. He'll keep to the shadows, and he certainly won't be able to hunt until dusk falls."

That wasn't reassuring.

"Alex," Dawes insisted, "you have to stay calm. He's just another demon and he can't change shape or get in your head."

"He's fast, Dawes. And so strong." She'd been no match for him, even with the strength of a Gray inside her. She'd barely escaped him once, and she wasn't sure she'd be that lucky again.

"Okay, but all of the reading I've done says he won't stay away from his nest for long. He can't."

His precious nest full of priceless objects and white flowers. That Alex had set fire to.

Alex made herself get up and pull back the curtain. Not Hellie was gone. She saw Reiter moving across the courtyard toward the gates that would take him out of JE and hopefully away from campus. Someone in dark clothes and a hooded jacket walked beside him, keeping a white umbrella above Reiter's head.

"What if Reiter gets peckish on the way home?" Alex said. "I brought him here. I put all these people in his sights."

"Stop it. Reiter knew about Yale long before you. I think . . . I think he's here to frighten you. And maybe because we used the Gauntlet."

Now Dawes's voice wavered. If Alex's theory—really Rudolph Kittscher's theory—was correct, then Reiter was actually a demon who had followed the real Lionel Reiter out of hell and taken on his form and identity. He'd fed on Reiter's soul and now he sustained himself with blood. Had the demons that followed them through the portal to hell called to him somehow? Did he care that the Gauntlet had been awakened, or did he just want payback for Alex wrecking his fancy things?

It didn't matter. There was only one way to deal with him.

"Add him to the list, Dawes. We get rid of the demons and we get rid of Reiter too."

"It's not going to be easy," Dawes said. Now that the task of taking care of Alex was done, she seemed less sure. "The things they know . . ."

Alex looked down at the empty bench. "Do you want to tell me what Blake said?"

There was a long pause. "He was outside of my window this morning. In the snow. Whispering."

Alex waited.

"He said he was innocent. That he never hurt anyone. That his mother cried herself to sleep every night. He said . . ." Dawes's voice wobbled.

Alex knew Dawes didn't want to go on. But demons ate shame, fruit grown from seeds cultivated in the dark.

"Hellie told me I stole her life," Alex said. "That I should have been the one to die, not her."

"That isn't true!"

"Does it matter?"

"Maybe not. Not if it feels true. He said . . . Blake said I killed him because I'm the kind of girl he would never bother to fuck. He said . . . he said he could tell what my . . . what I looked like down there. That I was ugly."

"God, that really does sound like Blake."

What were these demons made of? Hellie's sadness. Blake's cruelty. Alex's shame. Dawes's guilt. But what else? What was the difference between ambition and appetite? These creatures wanted to survive. They wanted to be fed. Alex understood hunger and what it could drive you to do.

"It isn't true, Dawes. We have to keep saying it until we believe it."

It was just too easy to let those words take hold.

"Is he there now?" Alex asked.

"The loris bit him." Dawes giggled. "It climbed right through the window and bit him on the cheek. He just started screaming, 'My face! My face!'"

Alex laughed, but she remembered the snakes lunging for Hellie's cheek. As if the salt spirits didn't like the lie of the demons, the pretense of the human masks they wore.

Her phone pinged. A *Call me* text from Turner. Why didn't he ever just call *her*?

When she hung up with Dawes, she checked the group chat: Everyone had checked in, and Dawes issued her warnings regarding Reiter. They were all armed with salt and they would meet at Il Bastone before dark. They'd be safer when they were behind the wards together.

Alex called Turner, expecting to hear he'd sighted Big Car lurking at the station.

"You okay?" she asked.

"What? Fine." Of course Turner was fine. He was the mighty oak. "We picked up Ed Lambton's son."

It took Alex a beat to remember who Lambton was. The professor at the center of the double murder. "I thought he was in Arizona."

"Andy Lambton is in New Haven. We apprehended him outside the apartment of one of his father's fellows."

"One of the people who falsified data?"

"Exactly. We'd put a protective detail on the other faculty involved with his censure and on the fellows who worked in the lab."

So the Charles II lead had been right, the son avenging the father. But it all seemed so theatrical, so bizarre. "He really killed two people because he thought his dad got the short end?"

"It looks like it. I want you to meet him."

"Worst blind date ever."

"Stern."

"Why, Turner?" The detective had been willing to involve her on the periphery of the case, a look at the crime scene, a chat about theories, but meeting a suspect was a very different thing. And now that Alex might be out of Lethe and Yale forever, she wasn't sure she had the heart or the will to dig into a murder mystery. "You've never wanted me in your business before."

"There's something wrong here and no one else seems to agree."

"He's got an alibi?"

"His alibi didn't hold up. And he confessed."

"Then what's the problem?"

"Do you want to meet this guy or not?"

She did. She liked that even after she'd fallen out of favor with Lethe, Turner still gave a damn what she thought. Besides, if Turner believed something was off, there was. She'd been in his head, looked through his eyes. She'd seen the world as he did, the details of it, the signs and signals everyone else missed or ignored. She'd felt the prickle at the base of her skull.

"I have to meet with the Praetor this afternoon," she said. "I can go after that. But you'll have to give me a ride over to the jail."

"He's not at the jail," said Turner. "He's at Yale New Haven."

"The hospital?"

"The psych ward."

Alex wasn't sure how to respond. She'd spent enough time in and out of rehabs, scared-straight programs, and twenty-four-hour observation holds that she didn't ever want to set foot on one of those wards again. But she also wasn't going to tell Turner any of that. Maybe she didn't have to. He'd seen her life through Hellie's eyes.

"I need to know what you told the cops and the Praetor about the fire," she said.

"Vandalism," said Turner. "No way to pass it off as an accident. They didn't find accelerant and the fire didn't build, it just went up. That's a mystery they aren't going to unravel."

Hellfire? Something else? Which weapons did the demons have at their disposal? Maybe Turner could just arrest Linus Reiter and save them all a lot of trouble.

As she dressed, she tried to think of anything but the Praetor and what might come next. She wanted to go back to Il Bastone. She wanted Turner to post uniforms outside the house to keep it safe. She wanted some promise of protection for her mother, her friends, herself. She'd thought of Il Bastone as a kind of fortress, buttressed by magic and history and tradition. She wondered if Not Hellie knew just how much the fire had shaken her.

She touched her wrist where the salt snake had wound around her skin. She wasn't helpless anymore. At least next time she tussled with the thing that wasn't Hellie or the monster that wasn't truly Lionel or Linus Reiter, it might be closer to a fair fight.

Alex muddled through her morning classes, trying to shake the dread that sat heavy in her gut. Was this the last lecture? The last hasty breakfast between classes? The last time she would sit in WLH and try to think of something clever to say in section?

Professor Walsh-Whiteley held office hours from two o'clock to four o'clock in the afternoon, and Alex thought about waiting until the last possible moment to show up, but the worry was too much for her. Better to get it over with, to know how far she'd fallen so she could start dragging herself back to high ground.

She popped into Blue State to get a coffee and a bagel to fortify herself. There was always a young Gray outside the empty building next door, dressed in a plaid flannel, sometimes hovering behind the window near where there had once been a jukebox when it was a pizza place. Occasionally, she thought she heard him humming the singsong strains of "Hotel California." But today, he was sitting on the steps, as if he was waiting for the door to open so he could buy a slice. Alex let her eyes pass over him, then stumbled when someone gave her a shove from behind.

She barely caught herself and spilled hot coffee down her coat.

"The fuck?" she said, whirling around.

For a long second, she didn't recognize Tzvi, couldn't reconcile the presence of Eitan's bodyguard here, in New Haven, but there was no mistaking his wiry body, the tidy beard, the stony expression.

"Hello, Alex." Eitan stood just behind Tzvi in an ugly leather coat, hair cut close and smelling of expensive aftershave. A golden Chai glinted at his neck.

Her first thought was *run*. Her second was *kill them both*. Neither was a reasonable option. If she ran, they'd find her. And murdering two people in broad daylight on the streets of New Haven did not seem like a strategic move.

They stood staring at each other on the crowded sidewalk, people navigating past them on the way to classes or meetings.

"Come on," she said. She didn't want to be seen with either of them. They stood out—the coats, the hair. It wasn't so much that they were criminals but that they were Los Angeles criminals. Too slick and glossy for New Haven. She led them to the driveway that ran between the music school and the Elizabethan Club.

"Here is good," said Eitan, and with a combination of frustration and pride she realized he didn't want to be out of sight of the busy street. She didn't know if Eitan and Tzvi were afraid of her, but they were being cautious. That was the problem with Eitan. He was very good at staying alive.

"You've been to Elizabethan Club?"

Alex shook her head.

"You have to be member. They have Shakespeare's First . . ."

"Folio," Alex said without thinking. And a first edition of *Paradise Lost*. All kinds of literary treasures squirreled away in a vault. And more importantly they served a plush afternoon tea. Darlington was a member, but he'd never taken her there.

"Yes! Folios," said Eitan. "You're on your way to class?"

Alex thought about lying. It would be easy enough to claim she worked in the dining halls. She'd told Eitan she was moving east with her imaginary boyfriend. He'd even offered to get her a gig at one of the casinos. She had hoped he would leave her alone, but instead the jobs on the East Coast had picked up right where the West left off. Eitan had business everywhere and friends who he was happy to grant favors.

Even so, if Eitan was here, that meant he knew more than he should. He would have already had someone dig up everything he could on her, and if he'd been able to find her in the middle of a campus packed with students, he must have been watching her for a while.

"No," she said. "I'm done for the day. I was going back to the dorms."

"We'll go with you."

That was one step too far. No way was she bringing these assholes anywhere close to Mercy and Lauren.

"What do you want, Eitan?"

"Let's be nice, Alex. Be polite."

"You almost got me killed. That does something to my manners."

"I'm sorry. You know this. I like you. You do good work for me. Reiter has been difficult."

He did sound genuinely sorry. The way someone would be sorry for eating the last slice of cake or being late to a dinner party.

"Do you have any idea what he really is?" Alex asked.

"I don't need to know," said Eitan. "He is problem. You are solution."

"You want me to go back there?" Not a chance. It had been bad enough seeing Reiter lurking in the courtyard, but if Dawes was right, he was weaker when he had to hide from daylight and when he was away from his nest. In his lair, he had the advantage. Even the thought of that big white house made her lungs tighten, caught her breath, wound it fast on a spool. What had the Gray teacher said? He'd killed hundreds, maybe more.

"You're happy here," Eitan said.

Alex wasn't sure what happy looked like. She was pretty confident it didn't involve being hounded by demons or losing her scholarship. "Happy enough."

"Fix Reiter for me, we can be done. You can have new life. You don't have to worry about Tzvi showing up at your door."

"That's why you came here? To send me to die?"

"I had business in the city. And this is a good market. Lots of young people. Lots of pressure. Everyone trying to have fun."

That felt like a threat. Was Eitan going to push her to deal on campus? There had to be a line somewhere. There had to be an end to this. Alex felt too aware of the people around her, their vulnerability, their weakness. Easy prey—for demons and for men like Eitan. He didn't belong here and neither did she. They were serpents in the garden.

Alex weighed her choices. "I take care of Reiter, we're done. That's the deal. No more jobs. No more bargains."

Eitan smiled and patted her shoulder. "Yes."

"And if I don't come back . . ." Alex dug her nails into her palm, remembering the feeling of Reiter's fangs entering her body. "If I don't come back, you throw some money my mom's way. Make sure she's okay."

"Don't talk like this, Alex. You will be fine. I see what you can do."

Alex held his gaze. "You have no idea what I can do."

He didn't flinch. Eitan wasn't going to let her get him alone, but he wasn't scared of her. She might have sway with the dead, but he ruled the living.

Again he patted her shoulder, as if he was offering encouragement to a child. "Finish this job and we say goodbye, yes?"

"Yes," said Alex.

"This is fair. You make amends. Everyone is happy."

She doubted he was right about that, but all she said was, "Sure."

"Good girl," said Eitan.

He wasn't right about that either.

33

Alex waited for Eitan and Tzvi to disappear into the big black Suburban idling by the curb. She should have noticed it, but she'd been focused on the wrong threats.

She pressed her back against the wall in the alley and slid down, rested her head in her hands. She needed to get back to the dorms, to someplace with cover, where she could be alone to think, but her legs were shaking.

Eitan had been *here* at Yale. He knew where to find her. And she wasn't stupid enough to believe that if she somehow survived another encounter with Linus Reiter, Eitan was going to be done with her. He wasn't going to give up a weapon in his arsenal, not when he was so sure he had her under his thumb. How much did he know about her? What other leverage could he find? He couldn't have discovered the secrets of Lethe, but had he followed her to Il Bastone? Black Elm?

A shadow fell over her and she looked up to see a girl with dark hair.

"It's all over," she said. "It's all slipping away. How long did you think you could keep pretending?"

Alex had the eerie sense that she was looking into a mirror. Not Hellie's hair was black and parted in the middle, her eyes black as oil. *She's feeding on me.* Alex's hopelessness had called to her like a dinner bell.

Alex knew it, but the sadness in her made it hard to think. She felt like she was at the bottom of a well. She was supposed to fight. She was supposed to protect herself. But when she thought about moving, about taking any kind of action, it was like she was scrabbling at the well's stone walls, wet with moss. It was impossible to find a grip. She was just too tired to try.

Not Hellie's tattoos had begun to emerge. Peonies and skeletons. The Wheel. Two snakes meeting at her collarbones.

Rattlers.

Got a little viper in you. Ready to strike.

That was what the real Hellie had told her. The Hellie who had loved her, who had protected her to the very end and beyond. And this fucking impostor was wearing her face.

"Those don't belong to you," Alex growled. She forced herself to drag her arm to her mouth, push her tongue over her knuckles.

Her salt spirit lunged, the snakes snapping at Not Hellie. The demon backed away, but slower than the last time.

"Leave her alone!"

Alex looked up to see Tripp striding down the alley. She wanted to shout at him to keep his voice down, but she was so damn glad to see him bustling to her rescue she couldn't be bothered to worry about a scene.

She was thankful for the shadows of the alley when she saw him lick his arm and his albatross screeched forward, slamming into Not Hellie.

The demon cringed away with a high-pitched whimper, but she was smiling as she scuttled back to the crowded street. And why not? Her belly was full.

Alex wasn't sure what anyone walking past had seen. Maybe they simply hadn't noticed the snakes, the seabird, a girl scurrying off in a way that was not quite human. Or maybe their minds skipped right over it, filling in an explanation that would allow them to keep on with their daily lives, the memory of anything odd or uncanny gratefully forgotten. She could have died in the shadows of that alley, and they would have walked on by.

"You okay?" Tripp asked. He was jumpy, crackling with energy and nerves.

"No." She didn't actually feel like she could stand.

"You look awful."

"Not helpful, Tripp."

"But the albatross worked."

It had. Alex wanted to believe that her snakes would have come through, but it seemed like they were tied to her own state of mind.

"Thanks," she said, dragging herself to her feet. She was shaky and weak, and when Tripp offered her his arm, she was embarrassed to have to take it.

"It feels so bad," he said as they walked back to Blue State and took refuge at one of the tables.

"Spenser been after you?"

"As soon as I left my apartment. I had to go to work. My trusty seabird helped."

Maybe so, but Tripp didn't look great. He was pale and his cheeks had a sunken look, as if he hadn't been eating, even though she'd seen him only a day before.

Alex bobbed her head toward the chalk menu behind the counter. "Any chance that chili is made from scratch?"

"Yeah, but I think it's vegan."

"Beggars can't be choosers."

When Tripp went up to the counter, Alex called Dawes. "We need to check the cameras at Black Elm."

"What am I looking for?"

"A black Suburban in the driveway."

"I would have gotten an alert if anyone was there."

"Okay. Just keep an eye out."

"Who are you expecting?"

Alex hesitated. The full moon was only two nights away, but that felt like a distance she didn't know how to cross. "I'm just being careful," she said.

"Since you mentioned Black Elm," Dawes began, "I need—"

"Late for the Praetor," Alex said hurriedly and hung up.

She didn't feel good about it, but Dawes was going to ask if she could go to Black Elm to check on Darlington, feed Cosmo, pick up the mail. She should. It was her turn and Dawes had done plenty. But right now she couldn't think about that. She needed to meet with the Praetor, to deal with Eitan. She needed to find her escape hatch. Her failures were stacking up too high, and the thought of facing Darlington behind that golden circle, still trapped between worlds, still not whole, made her feel hopeless all over again.

She texted the group chat with a warning: *Keep your mood up. They know when we're low.*

"You think that's true?" Tripp asked when he returned with two bowls of chili and a chocolate chip muffin.

"I do."

Tripp took a bite of chili and wiped his mouth with the sleeve of his sweatshirt. "I don't know if I can take much more of this. Spenser—"

"It's not Spenser."

"You keep saying that, but what difference does it make?"

"We have to remember what they are. They're not the people we loved or hated. They're just . . . hungry."

Tripp took another bite, then pushed the bowl away. "It's Spenser. I can't explain it. I know what you're saying, but it's not just the shit he says. It's that he's enjoying it."

Alex thought of what she'd read in *Kittscher's Daemonologie*. If Rudolph Kittscher was right, then demons had been getting by on the emotions of the dead for a very long time, and that was nothing compared to feasting on the pain and pleasure of the living. Why wouldn't they be enjoying themselves now that they were in the mortal realm? The buffet was open.

"Listen, Tripp . . . I'm sorry I got you into this."

"I totally get it. You were just doing your job."

Alex hesitated. "You . . . you know this wasn't sanctioned by Lethe, right? We were never going to make trouble for you with Skull and Bones."

"Oh, I know."

"And you helped us anyway?"

"Well, yeah. I needed the cash and . . . I don't really know where I am, y'know? My friends are all working in the city. I still don't have my degree. I don't even know if I want it anymore. I like Darlington and . . . I don't know. I like being one of the good guys."

Is that who we are? There was no greater good here, no fight for a better world. But what had Mercy said? *You rescue me. I rescue you. That's how this works.* To pay your debts, you had to know who you owed. You had to decide who you were willing to go to war for and who you trusted to jump into the fray for you. That was all there was in this world. No heroes or villains, just the people you'd brave the waves for, and the ones you'd let drown.

Alex and Tripp said their goodbyes at the green. She felt better than she had an hour before, but the double nightmare of Eitan and Not Hellie had left her roughed up. She wasn't in any condition to meet with the Praetor, but there was no way around it.

"My God," he said when she tapped on his office door. "You look terrible."

"It's been a rough few days."

"Come in. Sit down. Can I offer you tea?"

Alex shook her head. She wanted to get this over with, but she felt so rotten she let herself slouch in the chair as he set an electric kettle to boil. She just didn't have it in her to put on a performance, and there was no reason to anymore.

"Well," said the Praetor as he sorted through a selection of teas. "Where shall we start?"

"The fire last night . . ."

He gave a dismissive wave. "New Haven."

So Walsh-Whiteley had believed Turner's claims of vandalism. Maybe he hadn't gone inside. Maybe after being summoned from his warm bed, he'd been only too happy to go home.

"It was far worse in the eighties," the Praetor continued. "New Haven was quite the punch line. Biscuit?"

He held out a blue tin to her.

Alex was baffled, but she didn't say no to food. She took two.

"There was an upside, of course. We threw some marvelous parties at the old clock factory and there was simply no one around to care. The murals are still there, you know. Some of the students from the architecture school painted them. Beautiful, really, in a crumbling-into-the-tarn kind of way."

Why was the Praetor reminiscing about his graduate party days instead of lecturing her about the Gauntlet, or her crimes against Lethe and the university, or the process for ousting her and Dawes—or better yet some plan to rehabilitate them? If Alex didn't know better, she'd think he was trying to build some kind of camaraderie with her. Was he just savoring the lead-up to a grand send-off?

"Now," said Walsh-Whiteley, settling himself behind his desk with a mug of tea. "Let's begin."

"I . . . Is there something I'm supposed to sign?"

"For the wolf run? No, they all know the risks they're taking. It's why they'll do the mass transformation on land. I believe they've chosen"—he consulted his notes—"condors for the air run next semester."

Alex tried to make sense of what the Praetor was saying. She knew he was referring to the Wolf's Head ritual scheduled for tomorrow night. They would transform as a pack and have the full run of Sleeping Giant State Park. They weren't allowed to attempt flight this early in the school year because there had been so many injuries and accidents in the past. But Alex had assumed the ritual would be put on hold until . . . well, she hadn't thought about what Lethe would do with no Dante and no Virgil. She assumed Michelle Alameddine would be asked to come back.

So why was the Praetor looking at her like he expected her to bust out a bunch of index cards and start talking about spiritual safety procedures?

"I'm sorry," she said. "Do you still want me overseeing the wolf run?"

Walsh-Whiteley raised a brow. "I certainly hope you don't expect me to drag my old bones out to Sleeping Giant in the dead of night. Come now, Miss Stern. Your report on Manuscript was very solid. I expect you to maintain that standard."

What the hell was going on? Was the board waiting to make a decision on expelling her and Dawes?

Alex felt a skittering sense of worry. There was another possibility. She hadn't seen or heard from Anselm since he'd interrupted their trip to hell. What if Anselm had never made it back to New York? What if he'd never had the chance to speak to Walsh-Whiteley or the board?

"Sir, I apologize," she said, trying to get her bearings. "I haven't had time to prepare."

The corners of Walsh-Whiteley's mouth turned down. "I recognize you have a gift, Miss Stern, and perhaps I should not have asked you to . . . demonstrate it on my behalf. But you should understand that I will not be making allowances for shoddy work just because you were born with an unusual talent."

"Again, I apologize. I've . . . been under the weather."

"You certainly don't look well," the Praetor conceded. He settled the cover on the tin of biscuits. Apparently cookies were for closers. "But we have an obligation to the societies and there's a full moon on Thursday. Focus, Miss Stern. There will be consequences if—"

"I'll be there," Alex said. She could start the evening with a mass transformation of sixteen undergrads and finish up with a quick trip to the underworld. "And I'll be ready."

Walsh-Whiteley didn't look convinced. "Email me your notes and we can arrange to meet at the Hutch until the repairs are done at Il Bastone. I've petitioned the board for funds."

"You've been in touch with the board?"

"Of course I have. And you can be certain that should you not live up to your obligations—"

"Right, yes. Understood."

Alex got to her feet and was backing out of the door before Walsh-Whiteley could settle into his rant. She knew she should try to stay and appease the Praetor, but she needed to talk to Dawes. They had somehow managed to dodge a bullet, and that meant they still had access to all of Lethe's resources. Maybe they'd gotten lucky. Or maybe Michael Anselm's luck had run out.

34

"Something's wrong," she told Dawes as she hurried across campus to meet Turner. "The Praetor didn't say anything about the Gauntlet or disciplinary action."

"Maybe Anselm changed his mind?"

"He was furious, Dawes. There's no way he decided to give us another chance."

"You think something . . . one of the demons . . ."

"See if you can find out if he's been home."

"How am I supposed to do that?"

"Call his house, pretend you work with him."

"Alex!"

"Goddamn it, Dawes, do I have to do all of this myself?"

"If 'this' is unethical, then yes!"

Alex hung up. She felt frantic, exposed, like Not Hellie could be around any corner. Or Eitan. Or Linus Reiter. *Demons aren't smart,* Dawes had once told her, *they're cunning.* Alex had to wonder how many people had said the same thing about her.

"Okay, so what would I do?" she muttered to herself, watching her breath plume in the cold air as she hurried toward Chapel Street.

Hang back and watch. Look for an opportunity. Find a way to shift the odds in her favor.

If something had happened to Anselm . . . well, that would take care of one of their problems. But Lethe wasn't just going to shrug off his disappearance, not when two faculty members were dead too.

Alex stopped in front of the University Art Gallery. Marjorie Stephen. Dean Beekman. Could Anselm be a victim as well? Not if Turner had the right suspect in custody. Ed Lambton's son had no reason to go after someone barely associated with Yale anymore. Unless they'd been making the wrong connections from the start.

A few minutes later, Turner pulled up in his Dodge and Alex slid into the passenger's seat, grateful for the heat.

"Jesus," she said. "Did you sleep at all?"

He shook his head, a muscle ticking in his jaw. He was sharply dressed as always, navy wool suit with the subtlest pinstripe, slate-colored tie, Burberry overcoat laid neatly over the back seat. But he had dark smudges under his eyes and his skin looked ashen. Turner was a handsome man, but a few more nights playing tag with his personal demons and he might not be.

"What line did it use?" Alex asked.

Turner navigated the Dodge back into traffic. "It didn't show up as Carmichael this time. Thought it would be cute to wait for me in the parking lot dressed up like my grandfather."

"Bad?"

He gave a single, terse nod. "For a second I thought . . . I don't know."

"You believed it was him."

"The dead stay dead, right? But he . . . It looked like him, sounded like him. I felt *happy* when I saw him, like it was some kind of miracle."

A gift. A reward for all the pain. Exactly the way Alex had felt when she'd held Hellie. Losing that again had almost broken her.

That was why Turner looked terrible. Not because he hadn't slept, but because the demon had fed on him.

"I don't know how much longer I can handle this," Turner said.

"How did you get free?"

"He told me we were both in danger, that I had to go with him, and I was halfway down the block when I realized how fast he was moving, how light on his feet. My grandfather had arthritis. He couldn't take a step without hurting. I said . . . Maybe some part of me knew he wasn't right. I said, '*Heal me, Lord, and I will be healed.*'"

"Did he burst into flames?"

Turner barked a laugh. "No, but he looked at me with this soft little smile, like I'd said something about the weather. My grandfather loved scripture. He had a pocket Bible, carried it everywhere with him, kept it over his heart. If I quoted God's word to him, his face should have lit up like a sunrise."

Cunning, but not smart.

"Then things got ugly," said Turner. "Even though I knew it wasn't him, I didn't want to use the oak on him, to push him away. He seemed . . ." Turner's voice tightened, and Alex realized he was fighting back tears. She'd seen him angry, frustrated, but never grieving, never lost. "He was so old and frail. When I turned on him, he looked scared and confused. He . . ."

"It wasn't him," Alex said. "That thing was feeding on you."

They pulled into a parking lot.

"I know, but—"

"It still feels like shit."

"It really does." He stared straight ahead, at the chain-link fence and the big brick building beyond. "You know they call the devil the Father of Lies? I don't think I ever really understood what that could mean until now."

Alex tried not to squirm in her seat. Every time Turner got biblical, she felt uneasy, as if he was telling her about some grand hallucination and it was her job to nod sagely and pretend she saw miracles too. Then again, she'd spent her whole life seeing things no one else did; maybe she could extend him the benefit of the doubt.

For a moment she felt that pull to tell him everything, what Eitan had asked of her, the jobs she'd done for him, the fact that he had been here, in New Haven. Turner knew what it was like to be backed into a corner, to do the wrong thing because all the right things just got you in deeper.

Instead she got out of the car. "I think something may have happened to Michael Anselm."

"Because he didn't show up at Il Bastone?"

"I figured he went back to New York, but I met with the new Praetor just now and he didn't say a word about the Gauntlet or all of us getting kicked out of Lethe."

"Could be Anselm wanted to talk to the board in person."

"Could be," Alex said. They hustled across the street to the entrance, and passed through a revolving door into a big, anonymous lobby. It didn't really look like a hospital. They might have been anywhere. "Or maybe something got to him before he made it back to the city."

Turner flashed his badge and ID at the desk, and they headed for a bank of elevators.

"I thought the demons were tied to us. Why would they seek out Anselm?" He sounded worried, and Alex understood why. None of them wanted these things going after their friends and family.

"Who says something else didn't get loose? Anselm stopped the ritual. Maybe there was blowback."

"You're guessing," Turner said. "Or, as we call it in the business, pontificating out of your ass. For all you know, Anselm had a fight with his wife and he just hasn't gotten around to screwing us."

"It's all guessing, Turner. But it doesn't have to be."

Turner sighed. "Fine. I'll see if I can look into it without raising any alarms. Now would you focus?"

Focus, Miss Stern. But Alex didn't want to focus. All of it was too familiar. The white walls, the inoffensive art on them, the reception carpet giving way to cold tile. These were the places where she'd learned to lie, to pretend she was an ordinary kid who'd fallen in with a bad crowd, to tell kind social workers and curious shrinks that she liked to make up crazy stories, that she enjoyed the attention.

There had been truth mixed in too. She didn't want to hurt her mom. She knew she was a source of headache, heartache, financial trouble, maternal woe. She wanted to make friends, but she didn't know how. Tears had come easily. The hardest thing had been hiding how desperate she was to get better, how much she wanted to be free of the things she saw. The single upside to psych wards was that Grays hated them even more than the living.

Only once had she given in and told the truth. She'd been fourteen years old, already hanging with Len's crowd. She'd already let him fuck her in his narrow bed with the dirty sheets. They'd smoked before, after. She'd been disappointed by the mess of it, but tried to go along, made the noises that seemed to excite him. She'd stroked his narrow back and felt something that might have been love or just a desire to feel love.

Her mother had dragged her in for evaluation, and she'd gone along because Len had told her if she played her cards right, they'd prescribe her something good, and also because it was better than getting sent somewhere to be scared straight again. Guys in fatigues could shout at her and make her do push-ups and clean bathrooms, but she'd been scared her whole fucking life and she just kept getting more crooked.

Alex had actually liked the doctor she'd met with that day at Wellways. Marcy Golder. She'd been younger than the others, funny. She had a pretty tattoo of a rose vine around her wrist. She'd offered Alex a cigarette, and they'd sat together, looking out at the distant ocean. Marcy had said, "I can't pretend I understand everything in this world. It would be arrogant to say that. We think we understand and then boom! Galileo. Bam! Einstein. We have to stay open."

So Alex had told her the things she saw, just a little about the Quiet Ones who were always with her, who only disappeared in a cloud of kush. Not everything, just a little, a test.

But it had still been too much. And she'd known it right away. She'd seen the understanding in Marcy's eyes, the studied warmth, and, beneath it, the excitement that she couldn't hide.

Alex had shut up quick, but the damage was done. Marcy Golder wanted to keep her at Wellways for a six-week program of electroshock treatment combined with talk therapy and hydrotherapy. Thankfully it had been out of Mira's budget, and her mother had been too much of a hippie to say yes to clapping electrodes on her daughter's skull.

Now Alex knew none of it would have worked for her because the Grays were real. No amount of medication or electricity could erase the dead. But at the time, she'd wondered.

Yale New Haven was at least trying to keep itself human. Plants in the corners. A big skylight above and pops of blue on the walls.

"You okay?" Turner asked as the elevator rose.

Alex nodded. "What's bothering you about this guy?"

"I'm not sure. He confessed. He has details of the crimes, and the forensics all line up. But . . ."

"But?"

"Something's off."

"The prickle," she said and Turner startled, then rubbed his jaw.

"Yeah," he said. "That's it."

The prickle had never led Turner astray. He trusted his gut, and maybe he trusted her now too.

A doctor came out to meet them, middle-aged, with highlighted blond hair cut into fashionable bangs.

"Dr. Tarkenian is going to observe," said Turner. "Alex knows Andy's father."

"You were one of his students?" the shrink asked.

Alex nodded and wished Turner had prepped her better.

"Andy and Ed were very close," the doctor said. "Ed Lambton's wife passed a little over two years ago. Andy came out for the funeral and encouraged his father to move out to Arizona with him."

"Lambton wasn't interested?" Turner asked.

"His lab is here," said Dr. Tarkenian. "I can understand that choice."

"He should have taken his son up on the offer. By all accounts, his doctoral candidates had almost no oversight. His head just wasn't in it."

Alex saw the way that assessment troubled Tarkenian.

"You knew him," Alex said.

Tarkenian nodded. "I did my doctoral work with him years ago.

I'm afraid you didn't see him at his best." Her expression hardened. "And I knew Dean Beekman too. He didn't deserve that."

She led them down the hall to a sunroom where a man in his thirties was seated, handcuffed to a wheelchair, his back to a spectacular view of New Haven. His lips were chapped, and his fingers flexed and unflexed on the armrests as if they knew a secret rhythm, but otherwise he looked fine. Healthy. Normal. He had dark hair and a close-cropped beard streaked with gray. He looked like he worked at a microbrewery.

That could be me, she thought. *That* was *me*. She'd met Dean Sandow in a hospital. She'd been handcuffed to the bed, no one yet sure if she was a victim or a suspect. Some people were probably still trying to figure that out.

Behind Andy Lambton, gray clouds hung low over the city. She could see the gap of the New Haven Green, East Rock in the distance, the big Gothic spike of Harkness Tower, though she doubted anyone could hear the bells from here.

"That's quite a view," Alex said, and Andy shuddered.

They sat down across from him.

"How are you, Andy?" Turner asked.

"Tired."

"Has he been sleeping?" Turner asked the doctor.

Alex cut him off. "Don't talk like he's not right here. You sleeping okay?"

"No," Andy admitted. "It's not exactly a restful environment."

"I've seen worse," Alex said.

Andy shrugged. "I don't like it here."

"In the hospital?"

"In this town." Andy glanced over his shoulder, as if New Haven were listening, as if it had snuck up on him.

But Andy was calm, his manner easy. Alex wondered if he was medicated.

Turner leaned forward and rested his elbows on his knees, interlocking his fingers. "I need you to talk to us about what happened, strictly off the record, no tape recorder, no notes, nothing can be used against you in a court of law."

"Why? I told you what I did."

"I'm trying to understand."

Andy Lambton's eyes shifted to Alex. "And she's supposed to help you understand?"

"That's right."

"She's covered in fire," he said.

Alex forced herself not to look at Turner, but she knew they were both thinking of the blue flame that had surrounded her in hell.

"I told you I did it," Andy said. "What else do you want?"

"I just need clarity on a few things. We had a good look at your computer. Aside from some pretty unremarkable porn, your search history didn't turn up anything to speak of. And nothing related to Professor Stephen or Dean Beekman."

"Maybe I cleared it."

"You didn't. And that's unusual too."

Andy shrugged again.

"How did you get into Dean Beekman's home? Professor Stephen's office?" Turner continued. "Did you follow them? Stake them out?"

"I just knew how."

"How?"

"He told me."

Turner practically growled in frustration. But Alex had the sense that Andy wasn't being stubborn. Something else was going on here.

"*Who* told you?" Turner demanded.

Now Andy hesitated. "I . . . my dad?"

Turner leaned back in his chair, appeased. "Did he know you planned to hurt these people?"

Andy's head snapped up. "No!"

"He just handed you his key card and rattled off their work schedules for fun?"

"He didn't rattle off anything. The ram told me." Andy smacked his lips, scraping his tongue over his teeth as if he didn't like the taste of the words.

Alex stayed very still. "The ram?"

Andy rolled his eyes. It wasn't a look of contempt. There was something wild in the movement, like an animal caught in a trap, straining to get free.

Even so, his voice was reasonable. "It wasn't a big deal to find them, to get them to let me in. I've spent most of my life at Yale, okay?" He jabbed a finger at Turner. "And don't try to bring my dad into this. You said we were off the record."

"I'm not going to get your dad jammed up. I'm trying to understand what happened here." Turner studied Andy. "Talk to me about Charles II."

"The . . . king?"

"Why did you open Marjorie Stephen's Bible? Why Judges?"

Now Andy's face flashed with anger. "She cost my father everything. And over what? Someone else's mistake?"

Turner spread his hands as if he was just laying out the evidence. "My understanding is he was the person in charge of the lab. Oversight was his responsibility."

"They went too far."

"He has tenure. He isn't out of a job."

Andy laughed, a harsh, serrated sound. "He could have handled losing his job, but he became a joke. A study on honesty that used falsified data? He couldn't show his face at conferences. He lost his reputation, his dignity. He was a laughingstock. You don't . . . You don't know what that was like for him. He doesn't want to teach anymore. He doesn't want to do anything anymore. It's like a part of him died."

"They judged him," said Alex. "They signed the death warrant and as good as executed him. You wanted revenge."

"I . . . did."

"You wanted to humiliate them."

"Yes."

"Knock them down off their high horses."

"Yes," he hissed, the sound curling through the room.

"But you didn't want to kill them."

Andy looked surprised. "No. Of course not."

Turner's eyes narrowed. "But you *did* kill them."

Andy nodded, then shook his head, as if he was a mystery to himself. "I did. He made it easy."

"The ram?" Alex asked.

Andy's eyelids fluttered rapidly. "He was kind."

"Yeah?" Alex pushed.

"Easy to talk to. He . . . knew so much."

"About what?"

Again Andy looked over his shoulder. "This town. The people here. He knew so many stories. He had all of the answers. But he wasn't . . . He didn't lord it over me, you know? He just wanted to help. To make things right. He was polite. A real—"

"Gentleman," Alex finished for him. Cold sweat had broken out over her body, and she struggled not to shiver.

The ram told me. Alex thought of Darlington's horns, curled back from his forehead, glowing behind the protection of the golden circle—his prison.

But maybe the circle had been an illusion. Maybe Darlington had let them believe it kept him at bay when it had been nothing more than fairy dust.

She had known there was something off about the crime scenes, elaborate stage sets steeped in New Haven lore. A game a demon might like to play.

Turner was watching her. "Something you want to share with the class, Stern?"

"No . . . I . . . I have to go."

"Stern—" Turner began, but Alex was out the door, striding down the hall. She needed to get to Black Elm.

Darlington, who knew everything about New Haven's history, who had "recognized" the quote from Davenport's sermon. What had he said that day? *I always admired virtue. But I could never imitate it.* Alex tapped the quote into her phone. The search results popped up immediately: Charles II. Darlington had said he was the hermit in the cave. And of course, he'd meant Judges Cave. Anselm had warned her: *Whatever survived in hell wouldn't be the Darlington you know.*

Demons loved games. And he'd been playing with them from the start.

PART II

So Below

35

November

W e're not alone," the Gray whispered, one finger held up to his lips like an actor in a play.

Alex had taken a car to the gates of Black Elm.

She had walked the gravel drive in long strides, her anger like an engine, a locomotive pushing her ahead of common sense.

She had slotted her key in the door, tidied the mail, washed her hands. She had seen the basement door, a gaping wound, an open grave.

There had been a thousand moments to think, to reconsider. She had stood at the top of the basement stairs, gazing into the dark, a knife in her hand, and still she had believed she was being cautious.

The fall had come swiftly. But it always did.

In the cold dark of the basement, Alex took stock of her mistakes. She should have stayed with Turner and finished the interview with Andy Lambton. She shouldn't have come to Black Elm alone. She should have told Dawes her suspicions, or Turner, or anyone. She should never have trusted her gentleman demon. But she'd wanted to believe that Darlington would be okay, that whatever he'd endured in hell wouldn't leave a mark, that she could be forgiven and order restored. He would be made whole and she alongside him.

But what if she was leaping to the wrong conclusions now? What if Not Hellie or one of the other demons had pushed her down the stairs, or some squatter who hadn't shown up on Dawes's cameras?

What if Eitan and Tzvi had trailed her here? Or Linus Reiter with his white umbrella?

Too many shadows, too much history, too many bodies piling up. *Too many enemies.* There was no way to fight them all.

At least Alex would be visible on the cameras. Someone would know where she had gone. If she didn't come back. The pain in her ribs made it hard to take a deep breath. She looked at the Grays in front of her. Not just any Grays. Harper Arlington and Daniel Arlington IV. Darlington's parents.

No one from Alex's long list of enemies had a motive to see them dead. No one but Darlington, little Danny left alone again and again. *Heaven, to keep its beauty, cast them out, but even Hell would not receive them.*

"How long have you been here?" she asked.

Daniel's eyes darted to the corner, as if he expected something to appear through the walls. "I don't know."

Harper nodded in agreement.

"You can't get out?" Alex asked. Grays never stayed with their bodies for long, not unless they had a reason. Like Hellie wanting to say goodbye. The real Hellie who had loved her.

"He told us to stay."

"Who?"

They said nothing.

Alex bent to look at the bodies. The cold had helped keep the corpses from rotting too badly, but they still smelled terrible. Gently, she rolled them over. There were gaping trenches carved into both of their chests. Claw marks. And they'd gone deep. Straight through the sternum, the ribs, leaving two dark, pulpy craters. He'd torn their hearts out.

"Who did this to you?"

Harper opened her mouth, closed it, like a marionette worked by a clumsy hand. "He was our son," she said, "but not our son."

Again, Daniel's eyes slid to the corner. "He left that there. He said it could happen to us too. He said he would eat our lives."

Alex didn't want to know what was in the corner. The shadows seemed darker there, the cold deeper. She swung the light from her phone in that direction, but she couldn't make sense of what she saw: A heap of wood curls? Scrap paper? It took her a moment to understand that she was looking at a body—the remnants of one. She was looking at someone who had been devoured, nothing left but a husk. Was that what Linus Reiter would have left of her? Was that what Darlington had started to do to Marjorie Stephen, leaving her withered and aged but still recognizable?

Alex knew it was pointless, but she tried calling Dawes. The screen hung on the number. Service at Black Elm was sketchy at best and nonexistent underground. She cast the light from her screen up the steps again. What was waiting for her up there? Had Darlington tucked her away for a midnight snack? Was he still somehow tethered to Black Elm, or had he been creeping through New Haven to set his little murder scenes? It made a kind of sense. Darlington had survived in hell as both demon and man. Some part of both of them had returned to the mortal world to sit in that golden circle. And some part of that demon boy still loved New Haven and its peculiar lore, would have known the story of the three judges, would have liked building a macabre scavenger hunt for her and Turner.

But did it really add up? Had his desperation all been an act? Was he more demon than man? Had he always been?

Whatever he was, he didn't really know what she could do, that she might be weak and injured but that the things he'd left to terrify her were going to be weapons in her hands. Her ribs ached every time she breathed, and her shoulder was throbbing where she'd connected with the stairs, but she'd had worse. Even so, the door up there was heavy enough that she wasn't going to be able to kick her way through on her own. She touched her wrist where the salt star marked the place the snake had entered her. She could only hope it was ready to strike.

"Who wants to help get us out of here?" she asked the Grays.

"You can bring us back to life?" Daniel asked.

So the Arlington brains had skipped a generation.

"No," she said. "But I can at least make sure you don't spend eternity in a basement."

"I'll go," said Harper.

"Don't leave me alone down here!" Daniel cried.

"Fuck it," said Alex, though she had no idea if what she was about to do was even possible. "Everybody into the pool."

She held out her hands and Darlington's parents rushed into her. It felt like she was standing in a crowded party, a hundred voices shouting, the noise unbearable. She tasted crisp champagne on her tongue, smelled clove, tuberose, amber. *Caron Poivre.* The name of the scent arrived in her head, the vision of a bottle on a dressing table, a glass grenade. She saw her lean face in the mirror; a little boy was playing on the floor in the reflection, dark hair, serious eyes. He was always watching her, always needing something from her, the longing in him exhausted her.

Then she was walking the grounds at Black Elm. They were tidier, green and lush in the heat of summer. She was watching an old man walk with that same little boy, a short distance up the path. He loved them both. He hated them both. He hated his own father, his own son. If he could just get a foothold, if he could just find his way to a little luck, he wouldn't have to feel like this, like a nobody, when he was an *Arlington.*

Alex gave her head a shake. She felt like she was drowning in self-loathing. "The two of you really need to think about how you want to spend your afterlife. I recommend therapy."

She glanced at the corpses on the ground. She remembered Darlington in the dream, human and heartbroken. *I don't know how to not love them.* Apparently he'd figured it out.

Then she was racing up the stairs. The sense of strength in her was almost too much, as if her body couldn't contain the force. She didn't feel the pain in her shoulder or her ribs anymore. Her heart beat loudly in her ears. She took the stairs two at a time, threw her arms up to protect her face, and crashed through the bolted door.

Alex heard someone scream and saw Michael Anselm crouching by the open back door, his face white, his eyes wide with terror.

"Alex?" he squeaked.

"What are you doing here?" Alex demanded.

"I . . . What are *you* doing here?"

"Black Elm isn't Lethe property. And someone has to take care of Cosmo."

"That's why you just knocked the basement door off its hinges?"

Alex was glad Anselm hadn't been turned into demon food, but that didn't mean she trusted him. "What do you want? And where have you been?"

Anselm stood and dusted himself off. He straightened his cuffs, attempting to regain some dignity. "New York. Living my life, going to work, playing with my kids, and trying to forget about Lethe. I met with the board this morning. I came to talk to you about their ruling."

"Here?"

"Dawes said this was where you were. She's supposed to be here too. I don't want to make this speech twice."

Dawes must have seen Alex on the security cameras. She might have even called to warn Alex that Anselm was on his way, but Alex had been stuck in the basement. The Grays in her head were so damn loud she couldn't think, but she wasn't willing to give up their strength yet. Could Anselm have shoved her down the stairs? What possible reason would he have? All she knew was she had to get rid of him. Darlington might be in a murdering kind of mood, but she didn't intend to let Anselm decide what happened to him.

"Let's get out of here," she said. "It's cold and creepy."

Anselm narrowed his eyes. "What is going on?"

There are two dead bodies in the basement, probably three, and I'm juiced up on Grays because I'm pretty sure the gentleman of Lethe thought it would be cute to commit multiple homicide and eat someone.

"A lot," she said, because even she couldn't sell *Nothing*. "But you're out of the business of solving my problems, right?"

"Not if those problems become Lethe's." He looked around and rubbed his arms. "But you're right. We'll find some other place to talk. This house should be knocked down."

Boom.

The sound shook the walls, as if someone had detonated a bomb on the second floor.

"What was that?" Anselm cried, gripping the kitchen island like a drowning man.

Alex knew that sound: something banging on a door that should never be opened, trying to get into the mortal world.

Boom.

Anselm was staring at her. "Why don't you look scared?"

She was scared. But she wasn't surprised. And she'd made the mistake of letting it show.

"What the hell did you do, Alex?" He was angry now, and he stormed past her, stalking through the dining room, toward the staircase.

"Stop!" Alex said, catching up to him. "We have to go. You don't know what you're dealing with."

"And you do? I have clearly underestimated your ignorance and arrogance."

"Anselm." She grabbed his arm and spun him around. It was easy with the Grays inside her, and he blinked at her strength, staring at her fingers gripping his arm.

Boom. Plaster gusted down from the living room ceiling. They were directly beneath the ballroom now, beneath the circle of protection.

"Take your hands off me," he insisted, but he sounded frightened.

"Anselm, if I have to drag you out of here I will. It's not safe and we have to go *now*."

"You could do it, couldn't you?" Anselm said, his terrified eyes searching hers. "I outweigh you by what? Nearly one hundred pounds? You could haul me right out of here. What *are* you?"

Boom.

Alex was saved from answering by the ceiling caving in.

KITTSCHER: There's a theory that all magic is essentially demonic, that every ritual both summons and binds a demon's powers.

Have you never wondered why magic takes such a toll? Our brushes with the uncanny are encounters with these parasitic forces. The demon is feeding even if its powers are contained. The bigger the magic, the more powerful the demon. And the nexuses are little more than doorways through which demons may, for a brief time, pass.

NOWNES: What you suggest is perverse in every way.

KITTSCHER: But you do not say I am wrong.

—Kittscher's Daemonologie, *1933*

36

Alex and Anselm fell backward as the ballroom floor collapsed from above in a cascade of plaster and wood. Darlington crouched in the wreckage, his horns glowing, his golden eyes like searchlights. He looked bigger than he had before, his back broader.

He growled, and in the sound she heard a word, maybe a name, but she couldn't make sense of it.

Alex put herself between Darlington and Anselm. "Darlington—"

Darlington roared, the sound like the thunder of a subway train. He slashed at the floor, leaving deep trenches in the wood. She thought of the claw marks in his parents' chests.

"Run!" she shouted at Anselm. "I can hold him off!"

Anselm was pressed against the wall, plaster on his suit, his eyes big as moons. "It . . . he . . . what . . ."

Darlington stalked toward them.

She licked at her wrist, and the salt snakes leapt from her body, hissing and snapping. Anselm screamed. Whatever Darlington had become halted as the snakes slithered across the floor toward him.

Anselm whimpered. "That's . . . that's Daniel Arlington?"

The rattlers lunged at Darlington, jaws closing on his legs and arms. He howled and tried to shake them off, stumbling back toward the stairs.

"This is . . . this is an abomination," Anselm gibbered. "Stop him now! You have the advantage."

"Just get out of here!" Alex shouted over her shoulder.

"You can't possibly think you're going to save him! He could bring down Lethe, all of us."

Darlington slammed one of the salt serpents against the banister, then pinned it there with his horns.

"Look at him," Anselm demanded. "For once in your life, think, Stern."

Think, Stern.

"Don't let him get to the circle!" Anselm cried. "Send that monster back to hell and I'll find a way to get you back into Lethe!"

But why would Darlington want to go back to his prison? And how did Anselm know about the circle of protection?

Think, Stern. To Anselm she'd always been Alex. Miss Stern when he was angry. It was Darlington who called her Stern. She hesitated, an impossible notion fighting its way through her muddled thoughts. She remembered when Anselm had told her the story of the three judges, how much he'd reminded her of Darlington.

Darlington without magic, without Black Elm. Without a soul.

She remembered how surprised she'd been when he had asked about her mother. *Does she embarrass you?* The wave of shame that had overtaken her, how exhausted she'd felt after that meeting. She remembered Anselm stretching in the sunlight like a well-fed cat. *I feel almost human.*

Alex knew she shouldn't turn her back on a wounded demon, but she had the feeling she'd already made that mistake. She moved slowly, cautiously, trying to keep both Darlington and Anselm in her sights.

Anselm was pressed against the wall in his rumpled suit.

Alex slid her tongue over her wrist. Her salt snakes uncoiled. They knew a demon when they saw one. Even if he was dressed up in human skin and the authority of Lethe. They leapt.

Anselm held up his hands and a ring of orange fire swept forward. The salt snakes seemed to pop and sizzle in the heat, exploding in a hail of sparks.

"Well," he said, dusting himself off for the second time that day.

"I had hoped you'd do the killing. I wanted to watch you torment yourself over the murder of your beloved mentor for a while."

Does she embarrass you? The question had hit her like a punch to the gut, left her shaken and tied up in guilt. He'd been feeding on her. She remembered him standing in Sterling, shaking his head like a beleaguered dad on a television show. Like he was performing being human.

"You're his demon," Alex said, understanding coming on in a flood. "You hitched a ride when we tried to bring Darlington out of hell the first time. When Dawes and I botched the ritual at Scroll and Key. And you've been fucking with us ever since." *He was our son but not our son.* "You killed Darlington's parents."

Anselm rolled his shoulders, his body seeming to shift beneath his skin. "They showed up at Black Elm when I was trying to figure out how to get my lesser half out of that cursed circle."

Whatever I am will be unleashed upon the world. Darlington hadn't just been using the force of his will to stay inside the circle; he'd called on the remainder of his humanity for restraint. It was that same humanity that had fought to give them clues, even to try to warn her. In the dream, there had been two of him: demon and man. *There have to be*, he'd said. *The boy and the monster.*

But Anselm hadn't been able to feed on Darlington in the mortal realm, because he was protected by the circle. So the demon had needed to take on another form.

"You killed Michael Anselm too," she said. That was the husk in the basement. The demon had fed on Anselm, stolen his life. When Alex had lunch with him by the water, she'd even noted how different he seemed—young, at ease, handsome, like he was having a damn fine time. Because he was. He was sated on human misery. She'd shaken his hand. Made a deal for her mother's life. How he must have laughed at her desperation.

On the stairs, Darlington snarled, still besieged by Alex's serpents, but she had no idea how to call them off. And why was Anselm so much better at fighting her salt spirits than Not Hellie or Not Blake or the other demons?

"The murders," she said, "all of that about the judges and Professor Lambton, they were just distractions."

"A game," Anselm corrected with a gentle smile. "A puzzle."

To keep them from finding and using the Gauntlet and freeing Darlington's soul from hell.

"Two people died and Andy Lambton is in a psych ward."

"It was a good game."

The night of their disastrous ritual at Scroll and Key, it had been the real Michael Anselm at Il Bastone—fussy, cold, determined to keep Lethe trouble free. The first campus murder had happened later that very night. The demon had fed on Marjorie Stephen, aging her like a terrible poison, but he'd stopped before he'd made her a husk. He didn't want to assume her form. It was of no use to him. Besides, he'd just been there to construct a little tableau. He'd been more careful when he'd killed Dean Beekman, kept his demon hungers in check, used Andy Lambton to do the dirty work.

"I needed to sever Darlington's tie to the mortal world before you bumblers got his soul free and united it with his body," Anselm admitted. "But while he was in the circle, he was protected. And yet the lure was right in front of me all along. I just had to put his damsel in distress. Of course he came running." Anselm raised his hand. "And now the task is simple."

A blazing orange arc of fire burst forward. Alex felt it sizzle past her shoulder singing the flesh. It struck Darlington dead-on.

"No!" she cried. She rushed at Anselm, letting the strength of the Grays flood her. She slammed him against the wall and heard his neck snap. The Grays shrieked in her head. Because Anselm was a demon. Because he was their killer. Because she was a killer too. Harper and Daniel Arlington shoved their way out of her body, leaving her weak and breathless.

Anselm's head lolled on his broken neck, but he only grinned and raised his hand again, fire leaping forward. Alex dug in her pockets and hurled a cloud of salt at him, savoring his yowl as his flesh bubbled. At least he was susceptible to that. She unloaded the rest of her salt store on him, but she knew there was no way for her to actually destroy Anselm. Not without a stake or a salt sword—and maybe even that wouldn't do the trick. This demon was not like the others.

Alex's serpents leapt forward and piled onto the quivering, bubbling mass of Anselm's body. "Hold him!" she begged, though she had no idea if they understood.

She ran toward Darlington. He lay naked on the stairs, the glow from his markings dimming, the jeweled yoke bright against his neck. The burn was black and cut across his chest. Her snakes lay in charred, wriggling heaps, scorched by Anselm's fire.

Alex slid to her knees on the stairs. "Darlington?" His skin was hot to the touch, but she could feel it cooling beneath her fingertips. "Come on, Danny. Stay with me. Tell me how to fix this mess."

Darlington's golden eyes opened. Their glow was fading, turning milky.

"Stern . . ." His voice sounded distant, a bare echo. "The box . . ."

For a second Alex didn't know what he was talking about, but then she nodded. The Arlington Rubber Boots box was in her coat pocket. She kept it with her always.

"I'll hold on as long as I can. Get to hell. Bring my soul back."

"The Gauntlet—"

"Listen, Wheelwalker. The circle is a doorway."

"But—"

"*You* are a doorway."

Hellie had described Alex the same way, the night of her death.

Why wait? That was what Darlington had asked her when she told him they were going to attempt the Gauntlet. What if he'd been trying to explain she didn't need to walk the path, that there was a portal right in front of her, a crack between worlds that only she could slip through? *As you like, Wheelwalker. You choose the steps in this dance.*

"Stay alive," she said, and forced her body up the stairs.

She was slow without the Grays, the pain making her clumsy. But she had the keepsake box in her coat pocket, and it felt like a second heart, a living organ, beating against her chest. She didn't know if

Anselm was following. He had no reason to. He had no idea what she intended, and his focus would be on Darlington, on destroying him. If she didn't hurry, he would burn Darlington's body alive before she ever had a chance to retrieve his soul. If she even could. If this wasn't another mistake that would get them both killed.

She lurched down the hall and saw the shimmer of the circle, dimmer now, broken in places. But where it was brightest, she glimpsed the other Black Elm, the one she'd seen in hell, a ruined heap of rocks.

In this world, in her world, there was nothing but a gaping hole in the floor. If she fell, she would break her legs, maybe her back. There was no time to second-guess. *All worlds are open to us.*

"I hope you're right about this, Darlington."

Alex shoved off from the doorway. One step, two steps. She leapt.

Heat flashed through her as she crossed the circle. But she never hit the floor. Instead she found herself stumbling over dusty, rocky ground. She could still see the flicker of the circle around her, but now she was in the demon realm.

"Darlington!" she shouted and yanked the box from her pocket. "Danny, it's me!"

She didn't need the old man's voice this time. He remembered her. He knew she'd tried to bring him home.

He looked up at her, a rock still in his hands. "Alex?"

She held the box open. "Trust me. One last time. Trust me to get us out of here."

But the look on his face was one of terror.

Too late she realized it was a warning.

Something slammed into her back. The box flew from her hands. It was like watching movement underwater. Time slowed. The box arced through the air and struck the ground. It shattered.

Alex screamed. She was on the ground scrambling toward the broken pieces. She felt something grab the back of her shirt and flip her over, the force driving the breath from her body.

A rabbit was standing over her, six feet tall and dressed in a suit—Anselm's suit. It placed one of its soft white feet on her chest and

pushed. Alex shrieked as her broken ribs shifted. But none of it mattered. The box was broken. There was no way to bring Darlington
back and reunite him with his body. He would die in the mortal
world, and his soul would be trapped forever in hell.

The rabbit leaned down, its red eyes twitching. "Thief," it sneered.

She had let them die one after another. Babbit Rabbit, Hellie,
Darlington. And maybe now she was going to die too, crushed by a
monster. If she died in hell, would she stay here forever? Move on to
some other realm? The blue fire that crawled over her body caught
on the rabbit's fur, but it didn't seem to care.

"How did you cross the circle?" the thing demanded, shifting its
weight, pressing down harder.

Alex couldn't even draw breath to scream. She turned her head
to the side and saw Darlington watching, his face sad, a rock in his
hand. He wanted to help her, but he didn't know how any more than
she did. She had no Grays to call on here.

"How did you cross the circle?" the rabbit demanded again. It
flexed its paw and Alex shuddered. "Not so tough now, hmm? Not
so scary. What are you without your stolen strength? An empty little
cipher."

She thought of Darlington's burned body on the stairs, the old
porcelain box lying in pieces, the demons they'd set free. Her ribs
hurt; her shoulder throbbed. The thing crushing her beneath its foot
was right. She did feel empty. She'd been hollowed out. A cipher, an
empty cup.

A shattered box.

Except she wasn't broken, not where it counted. She was bruised
and battered, and she had a bad feeling that rib was poking one of
her lungs, but she was still here, still alive, and she had a gift Anselm
didn't know about—in either realm. *You cannot imagine the vitality
of a living soul.* That was what Belbalm had told her. Alex had only
ever claimed the dead. But what if she claimed the living?

She remembered Darlington leading her up the stairs at the
Hutch, into the hall at Il Bastone, down haunted streets, and through
secret passages. He'd been her guide, her Virgil. How many times

had he turned to her and said, *Come with me?* He'd promised her miracles and horrors too, and he'd delivered.

She held out her hand, just as she once had to Hellie, just as she had to countless spirits, just as Darlington had to her again and again.

"Come on along," she whispered.

Darlington dropped the rock. His soul flooded into her like golden light. New-leaf green. Morning bright. The sweet vibration of the cello's bow. The ringing, triumphant sound of steel on steel. Her body erupted into white flame, searing, blinding.

The rabbit shrieked, high and helpless, as the fire burned through its body.

Alex's pain was gone. She leapt to her feet, and before Anselm could recover, she was running toward the glimmer of the circle. She hurled her body through it. The world went white. She closed her eyes against the brightness, then gasped as she realized she was falling.

The floor of Black Elm was rising up to meet her. But she had Darlington's spirit inside her and it was nothing like the power the Grays bestowed. If the strength of a Gray was a candle lit inside her, this was a thousand searchlights, a bomb blast. She struck the ground on soft feet. She was light, graceful, and the world was ablaze with color. She felt the cold on her skin from a draft somewhere in the house. She saw every bit of broken wood and fallen plaster borne aloft on the air, lovely as a snowfall. She saw Darlington's body on the stairs, the yoke still gleaming against his neck, though the rest of him was scorched black. He was curled on his side, trying to hide from Anselm, who had followed Alex into hell and back out again.

The monstrous rabbit was gone and Anselm was a man once more, though he was singed where Alex's fire had burned him. He leapt over her toward Darlington, orange flame streaking from his fingertips—but fell into a crouch, hissing, held at bay.

By Cosmo.

The cat had come yowling down the stairs, his fur on end, aglow with white light. Darlington's protector. How long had that cat been watching over the owners of this house? Was he a salt spirit or something else entirely? Anselm shrieked, rocking back and forth on his heels and hands. He had never looked less human.

Alex could hear that singing steel sound, could feel Darlington's spirit inside her. She knew now the pleasure that Belbalm had felt when she'd consumed the spirits of the living. *Greed is a sin in every language.* Darlington's voice, chiding, bemused. She could *hear* him, the thoughts clear as if they were her own. She didn't want to relinquish this feeling of power, this elation. He tasted like honey. But she knew better than to get used to a drug like this. She could only hope she wasn't too late.

"Go," Alex made herself whisper.

He coursed out of her, a river of gold. She could still taste his soul on her tongue, hot and sweet. He flowed into the body on the stairs.

"Thief!" screamed Anselm, and Cosmo howled as the demon let loose a torrent of fire that engulfed Darlington.

Alex ran at Anselm, not thinking, just desperate to get him to stop. She should have felt weak in the wake of all that power. But there was no pain. Her ribs weren't broken. Her chest didn't hurt. This was what the power of the living could do. She crashed into Anselm, knocking him to the ground, but he was on top of her in a breath, his hands clamped around her throat.

"I'm going to burn the life out of you," he said happily. "I'm going to eat . . . you . . . up."

His teeth were growing in his mouth, long and yellowing. On the stairs beside them, Darlington's body was a charred hulk. He looked like the pictures of people in Pompeii, curled in on themselves as the world turned to ash. Too late. No one could come back from that.

But then she realized the jeweled yoke was gone.

His markings began to glow, light shining through the cracks of his burned flesh. Again Alex tasted honey on her tongue.

Anselm hissed, and she saw blue flame racing up his hands, his arms, engulfing him in fire. Her fire. Hellfire. How? It had only existed in the demon realm before.

He shrieked and drew back, seeming to flicker before her, his shape shifting, and she knew she was glimpsing his true form, something clawed and strange, its bones set at odd angles.

"*Golgarot.*" That growl from Darlington again, but this time she understood the demon name.

The thing that towered over her on the stairs was both more and less like Darlington. His voice sounded right, the echo gone, but horns still curled back from his temples, and his body looked too big, not entirely human. His markings had changed too. The symbols were gone, but there were golden bands around his wrists and neck and ankles.

"Murderer!" shouted Anselm, as his body twitched and pulsed beneath his suit. "Liar! Matricide! You—"

He didn't get another word out. Darlington seized Anselm in his massive hands and lifted him off his feet. With a single, furious snarl, he tore Anselm in two.

The demon's flesh gave way as if it were paper, dissolving into a mass of wriggling maggots.

Alex sprang back.

Darlington's body seemed to shift again, retracting. The horns vanished, the golden bands. He looked mortal. He stood there for a moment, gazing at Anselm's remains, then turned and started up the stairs.

"Darlington?" Alex stammered. "I . . . Where are you going?"

"To get some clothes, Stern," he said, climbing the steps and leaving bloody footprints behind. "A man can spend only so much time without trousers on before he begins to feel like a deviant."

Alex stared up at him, one hand on the banister. The gentleman of Lethe had returned.

Doom Sparrow (also Bloodfinch or Black-Winged Harbinger);
family Passeridae
Provenance: Nepal; date of origin unknown
Donor: St. Elmo, 1899

Whether these sparrows were bred or enchanted, or developed their unique traits in the wild is unknown. The first were identified circa 700 when a sparrow colony took up residence in a mountain village, the population of which subsequently poisoned themselves in an act of mass suicide. World population of the bird is also unknown, but at least twelve exist in captivity.

Notes on care and feeding: The sparrow is kept in a state of magical stasis but should be fed weekly, at which time it should be allowed to fly or its wings will atrophy. It prefers dark, cold spaces and will become lethargic in sunlight. When tending to the sparrow, keep your ear passages blocked with wax or cotton. Failure to do so may result in listlessness, depression, or, in the case of prolonged exposure, death.

See also the Tyneside Canary and Manuscript's Queen-Moon Nightingale.

Gifted by St. Elmo, who believed they were acquiring a Cloud-Beaked Harbinger, notable for its ability to predict storms in its flight patterns.

—from the Lethe Armory Catalogue as revised
and edited by Pamela Dawes, Oculus

Has no one noticed that the societies "gift" Lethe with all of the magic they deem too unsafe or too worthless for their own collections? The leavings, the disasters, the mistakes, the worn-out artifacts and unpredictable objects. Though our armory may represent one of the greatest repositories of magic housed at a university, it also has the dubious distinction of being the most hazardous.

—Lethe Days Diary of Raymond Walsh-Whiteley
(Silliman College '78)

37

Darlington had been asleep and in his dreams he'd been a monster. But now he was awake and brutally cold. And maybe a monster still.

He made his way up the steps, dimly aware that he was leaving a trail of bloody footprints behind him. His own blood. Anselm had no blood to leave. He'd broken in half as if he were filled with sawdust, a facsimile of a man. Each step made a drumbeat: anger, desire, anger, desire. He wanted to fuck. He wanted to fight. He wanted to sleep for a thousand years.

Darlington knew that at some point he would have been embarrassed that he was naked. But maybe he'd spent so long in two places at once that his modesty had gotten lost somewhere in between. He didn't want to see the damage he'd done to the ballroom. In fact, after so long in captivity, he wasn't sure he ever wanted to see the ballroom again. Instead he headed directly to his bedroom on the third floor.

He felt as if he were viewing it through thick glass, or one of those old View-Masters, click the button, turn the slide. The colors seemed wrong, the books foreign. He had loved this room. He had loved this house. Or someone had. But now it gave him no pleasure.

I'm home.

He should be glad. Why wasn't he? Maybe because Alex had freed his soul, but some part of him would forever be trapped in hell, carrying rock after rock, setting stone upon stone, begging to stop, to rest, but unable to. There'd been no boredom, no sense of repetition. He'd been desperate the whole time, a man trying to revive a corpse, trying to breathe life into a body gone cold, looking for some sign of hope, sure that every single stone was the one that would bring Black Elm back to glory. There was more, of course. He had been many things in hell, jailer and jailed, torturer and tortured, but he wasn't ready to think about that and he was only relieved that there were some secrets he could still keep from Galaxy Stern.

He could sense her standing at the bottom of the stairs, hesitant, and he was ashamed of the thoughts that entered his head. Could he blame the demon for these visions of carnality? Or was he just a man who'd been in jail for a year? His cock didn't much care about the debate and he was glad he was alone. And that his erection wasn't glowing like a New England lighthouse anymore. He pulled on jeans, a sweatshirt, his old coat, waited patiently for the tide of want to recede. He packed a small overnight bag—his grandfather's old leather satchel. It was only then that it hit him.

His parents were dead. And in a way, he had killed them. Golgarot had fed on his soul in hell, dined on his shame and hopelessness. He'd eaten Darlington's memories and the worst of his sadness and need. He had killed Michael Anselm for the sake of his plans, an expedient means to an end. But killing Darlington's parents would have delighted him, not just because Anselm drew satisfaction from pain, but because some shriveled, bitter part of Darlington wanted them to die and die badly—and Golgarot knew it. The boy who had been abandoned to the stones of Black Elm had no care or clemency to give his mother and father, only violence.

Darlington sat down on the edge of the bed, the knowledge of everything that had happened crashing into him. If he let his mind alight on any single thought for too long, he'd go mad. Or maybe he was already mad. How was he supposed to be human again after what he'd seen and done?

Nothing had changed. Everything had changed. His bedroom

looked just as he'd left it, and aside from the giant hole in the ball-room floor that he could never afford to repair, the house seemed to be intact.

His parents were dead.

He couldn't quite get the fact to take on weight and settle.

So he would keep moving. Think about the bag, pick it up. Think about the door, open it. Think about each step he was taking down the hall. These were safe things to gather around him.

Darlington descended the stairs. The patch of squirming mag-gots Anselm had left behind should have repelled him, but maybe it was his demon skin that refused to crawl. Alex was waiting in the kitchen, eating dry cereal from a box. She was the same too—skinny, sallow, ready to take a swing at anything that looked at her wrong.

She's a killer. That had seemed important once, a dark revelation. He remembered her standing in the basement of Rosenfeld Hall, how still she'd been in the moment when he'd needed her to act, a silent girl with black glass eyes, her gaze as steady and as wary as it was now. *I have been crying out to you from the start.*

They watched each other in the quiet of the kitchen. They knew everything about each other. They knew nothing at all. He had a sense that they had entered into an uneasy truce, but he couldn't quite name the war. She was more beautiful than he remembered. No, that wasn't true. It wasn't that she had changed or that his vision had sharpened. He was just less afraid of her beauty now.

After a long moment, Alex held out the cereal box. An odd peace offering, but he took it, dipped his arm in, tossed a handful of puffs into his mouth. Immediately he regretted it.

"Good God, Stern," he gasped as he spat into the kitchen sink and rinsed the remnants away. "Are you eating pure sugar?"

Alex crammed another handful of garbage into her mouth. "Pretty sure there's some corn syrup too. And real fruit flavoring. We can stock up on your nuts-and-twigs stuff . . . if you want to stay here."

Darlington wasn't ready to make any decisions about the house. About anything. "I'll sleep at Il Bastone tonight." He didn't want to say what came next, but he made himself form the words. "I need to see their bodies."

"Okay," Alex said. "Their car is in the garage."

"Golgarot must have put it there." The name felt wrong on his human tongue, as if he was speaking with a tourist's accent.

"I only knew him as Anselm. His— The real Anselm's husk is down there too."

"You don't have to go with me."

"Good."

Darlington was tempted to laugh. Alex Stern had gone to hell twice for him, but the basement was a step too far. He dug in a drawer for a flashlight and headed down the steps.

The smell struck him, but he'd known that was coming. He wasn't prepared for the way the bodies had been mutilated.

He paused on the stairs. He'd meant to . . . He wasn't certain what he'd intended. To close their eyes gently? To speak some words of comfort?

He'd spent three years studying death words, but he still had nothing to say. All he could think of were the words emblazoned on every piece of Lethe House ephemera.

"*Mors vincit omnia,*" he whispered. It was all he had to offer. He'd been washed up on a familiar shore, but the sea had changed him. Grief would have to wait.

He turned his flashlight on what had been the body of Michael Anselm, a man he'd met only briefly when he was a freshman being inducted into Lethe as the new Dante. Exactly how were they going to explain a dead board member? That would have to wait too.

He climbed the stairs. The basement door had come off its hinges, and he leaned it carefully against the jamb, the boulder at the door to the tomb.

Alex had returned the cursed cereal to its cupboard and was leaning on the counter looking at her phone, her hair a black sheaf, a dark winter river.

"I need to know what to tell Dawes," she said. "Anselm avoided her cameras, but she knows I'm here and she knows the ballroom camera is offline. Are you ready to be back?"

"I don't know that it matters. Perhaps it would be best to explain in person." He hesitated, but there was no reason not to ask. "Did you see them? My parents? After . . ."

She nodded. "They helped get me out of the basement."

"Do they think I killed them?"

"Sort of?"

"Are they here now?"

Alex shook her head. Of course not. He knew better than that. Grays rarely returned to the scene of their deaths. Contrary to most popular fiction, ghosts didn't come back to haunt their murderers. They wanted to be reminded of places and people they loved, human pleasures. It took a vengeful and dedicated spirit to haunt someone, and neither of his parents had that kind of drive.

And they would have wanted to be far from Golgarot. The dead feared demons because they promised pain when the pain should be over. They'd been very frightened of Darlington indeed.

Alex drew her coat more tightly closed. "The old man is here."

"My grandfather?"

"I can hear him. I can hear all of them now."

Darlington tried not to show his surprise, his curiosity, his *envy*. How could this scrap of a girl have so much power? How could she see into the hidden world that had evaded him for so long? And after a year in hell, why did he still give a damn?

"They never shut up," she added.

She's trusting me, he told himself. Alex was handing him knowledge that he knew, with complete certainty, Lethe didn't have. Another offering. He found he was as greedy for her trust as her power. He pushed those thoughts away.

"What is he saying?"

Now Alex's eyes shifted uneasily to the toes of her boots. "He says to be free. That you've given up enough blood to this place. It's yours to take or leave. It always should have been."

Darlington snorted. "You're lying. What did he really say?"

Alex shrugged and met his eyes. "That Black Elm needs you more than ever, that this is your home by right of blood and treasure, and a lot of rambling about the Arlington legacy."

"That sounds much more like him." He paused, studying her. "You know what happened here, don't you? What I did? Why I survived the hellbeast?"

Alex didn't look away. "I know."

"I always wondered if I'd done the right thing."

"If it makes you feel any better, I'd smother him right now if I could."

Darlington was startled by his own abrupt laugh. Maybe Alex could have stopped him from being eaten that night in Rosenfeld Hall. Maybe she'd wanted his discovery of her crimes to die with him in that basement. He supposed she had betrayed him. But in the end it had taken this monstrous girl to drag him back from the underworld. There was nothing he could say that would shock her, and that was powerful comfort.

"I'll be back," he said, in the hopes that his grandfather would understand what he was about to do. "*Better to flee from death than feel its grip*," he quoted, letting the death words cast the old man out, a peace offering to Alex of his own.

"Thanks," she said.

"I don't know what to do about . . ." He couldn't quite manage to say *their bodies*. He bobbed his chin toward the basement instead.

"We have bigger problems," Alex said, rising from the counter. "Come on, I called a car."

"Why don't we take the Mercedes?" She winced. "Stern, what happened to my car?"

"Long story."

She locked the kitchen door behind them, and they started down the gravel drive. But after only a few steps, he had to stop, put his hands on his knees, breathe deeply.

"You okay?" she asked.

No, he certainly wasn't. The sky was heavy, low, and gray, thick with clouds that promised snow. The air was mossy and sweet, blessedly cold. Some part of him had believed there was no world outside of Black Elm, no street at the end of the drive, no town beyond. He had forgotten how big things could feel, how crowded with life, how beautiful it could be to know the season, the month, the hour, to simply say, *It is winter.*

"I'm fine," he said.

"Good," she said, continuing on. Practical, merciless, a survivor who would keep walking, keep fighting no matter what God, the devil, or Yale threw at her. Was she a knight? A queen? A demon herself? Did it make any difference? "I have good news and bad news," she said.

"Bad news first, please."

"We have to go back to hell."

"I see," he said. "And the good news?"

"Dawes is making avgolemono."

"Well," he said as they reached the stone columns that marked the end of Arlington property. "That's a relief."

He did not look back.

38

Dawes was standing on the front steps of Il Bastone when they arrived, her headphones around her neck, her hands twisting fretfully in her sweatshirt sleeves. Turner stood beside her, leaning on one of the smoke-stained columns. He was in jeans and a button-down, and the sight of him out of a suit was almost as distressing as watching a ceiling cave in.

"Who are these guests I don't recall inviting?" Darlington asked as the demons moved out of the shadows across the street.

Slowly, Alex opened her door and climbed out, wondering what the driver thought about the odd group of people standing in the road at twilight.

"Demons," she said. "We brought them back."

"As an exchange program?"

"It was an accident," she said as their ride pulled away. "They set fire to the house."

"Why am I not surprised?"

"We were trying to rescue you, Darlington. There were bound to be hiccups."

"I'm not sure I've ever noted your gift for understatement, Stern."

"Demonic hiccups."

"Alex? Mija?" Alex's grandmother was standing on the sidewalk, her dark hair shot through with gray, dressed in a soft turtleneck and a long black skirt that brushed the ground. When Alex was small, she'd loved the sound of the fabric trailing over the floor. "But doesn't it get dirty, Avuela?" Her grandmother had winked and said, "What's a little dirt when the devil can't find me?"

Alex knew this was not her grandmother, but her heart twisted anyway. Estrea Stern had been afraid of nothing, determined to protect her strange granddaughter from her flighty daughter, to shelter her with prayers and lullabies and good food. But then she'd died and Alex had been left with nothing but her mother's dollar store magic, her crystals, her whey smoothies, her boyfriend the acupuncturist, her boyfriend the capoeirista, her boyfriend the singer-songwriter.

"Who is feeding you, mija?" Estrea asked, her eyes warm, her arms open.

"Alex!" Dawes shouted, but her voice seemed far away when home was so close.

Darlington leapt in front of her and snarled. His shape altered before Alex's eyes, his golden horns curling back from his forehead.

Alex tasted honey. Her body burst into blue flame and the grandmother demon squealed, losing its shape, seeming to slide back into the form of a young woman, a hybrid of Hellie and Alex and something unnatural, one shoulder lifted too high, head lowered as if to hide its leering mouth, its many teeth.

Darlington charged forward like a bull, slamming into the demon and pinning it to the sidewalk. He rammed his horns against it as it shrieked. The other demons cringed back into the shadows between the houses.

"Darlington!" Alex said. It was almost dark and people were coming home from work. If they drew a crowd, they were going to have even more problems.

But he wasn't listening or the monster in him didn't care. He rammed into the demon with a snarl, severing its torso. Its legs dissolved into wriggling maggots, but it just kept on screaming.

"Darlington, enough!"

Her flame unfurled in a crackling blue wire, snapping around the glowing golden band that had appeared on his neck where the yoke had been. It snaked around Darlington's throat and yanked him away from Not Hellie. The rest of the demon's torso dissolved into squirming grubs.

Darlington fell back on his haunches with a growl. Like a hound brought to heel.

"Shit," Alex said, batting at the blue flame leash, watching it recede. "I'm sorry, I didn't—"

But Darlington's horns had faded with the fire. He was human again, kneeling on the sidewalk.

"I'm sorry," she repeated.

His gaze was dark and assessing, like he was studying a new text. He rose and brushed the dust from his coat. "Best we get inside, I think."

Alex nodded. She felt nauseated and tired, all the gleam of carrying Darlington's soul within her siphoned away. She'd let the demon feed on her like some kind of amateur. And what the hell had just happened?

"Is it really dead?" she asked, stepping over the maggots and trying not to gag.

"No," said Darlington. "Its body will re-form and try to feed on you again."

"And Anselm?"

"Golgarot too."

Alex wondered what that meant for a creature like Linus Reiter.

In the doorway of Il Bastone, Mercy released a nervous laugh. "The demons don't like him, do they?"

"Not one bit," said Turner, the leaves of the oak clustered around him. He'd called to his salt spirit. To help Darlington or to put him down? Maybe Turner was having doubts about the whole soldier-for-good thing after seeing those horns come out. "How was Spain?"

Darlington cleared his throat. He was human again, but the shape of the demon seemed to linger over him, a memory, a threat. "Hotter than expected."

"Anyone want to explain how he got here?" Turner asked. "And why Alex just caught fire?"

But whatever spell had bound Dawes frozen on the steps had broken. She descended the stairs slowly, then stopped.

"It's . . . it's not a trick is it?" she said quietly.

She was wise to ask, when friends and parents and grandparents and members of the Lethe board might all be monsters in disguise. When Darlington had just crushed a demon against the pavement. But this time the magic was kind.

"It's him," Alex said.

Dawes sobbed and lunged forward. She threw her arms around Darlington.

"Hey, Pammie," he said gently.

Alex stood awkwardly to the side as Dawes wept and Darlington let her. Maybe that was what she should have done, what someone without so much blood on her hands did. *Welcome home. Welcome back. We missed you. I missed you more than I should have, more than I wanted to. I went to hell for you. I'd do it again.*

"Come on," Darlington said, his arm over Dawes's shoulders, ushering them all back inside, slipping into the role of Virgil as if he'd never left. "Let's get behind the wards."

But when he set foot on the steps of Il Bastone, the stones trembled, the scorched columns shook, the lantern above the doorway rattled on its chain. Beneath the porch, Alex could hear the jackals whimpering.

Darlington hesitated. Alex knew this feeling, the fear of being banished from a place you'd called home. What had Anselm said? *Are you so eager to be cast out of Eden?* Another little joke for the demon, another puzzle she'd failed to solve.

The door creaked softly on its hinges, a high whine of anxiety, as if it was deciding whether there was danger on its doorstep or not. Then the house made up its mind. The steps went still and solid, the door sprang wide, every window came ablaze with light. Even the house could say what Alex could not: *Welcome back. You were missed.*

You are needed. Part demon or not, the golden boy of Lethe was back, and human enough to pass through the wards.

"Where's Tripp?" she asked.

"He's not answering his phone," said Dawes.

Alex's stomach turned. "When did he last check in?"

"Three hours ago," said Turner as they shuffled into the dining room where someone had set the table. "I went by his apartment, but no answer."

Darlington looked skeptical. "I suppose this is a reasonable time to ask why you brought Tripp Helmuth, of all people, to hell?"

Alex threw up her hands in annoyance. "You try putting together Team Murder on short notice." She had left Tripp on the New Haven Green. She'd seen him set off toward downtown. Could he be late? Scared of returning to hell? He knew another descent was the only way to be rid of their demons. They were the bait. Their misery. Their hopelessness.

"We never should have left him alone," she said.

"He had the seabird," Turner noted.

"But the salt spirits can only do so much. I don't know about you, but I could tell Not Hellie was adapting. She was less scared of those snakes the last time I used them. She wasn't frightened out on the sidewalk a minute ago."

"You're all forgetting he could just be a coward," Mercy said as they settled around the table.

"That isn't fair," Dawes called from the kitchen.

"What?" Mercy demanded. "You saw how freaked out he was. He didn't want to make the descent a second time."

"None of us do," said Turner. "And you wouldn't either."

"I'll go," Mercy said, her chin lifting. "You're down a pilgrim. You need someone to fill the gap."

"You're not a killer," said Alex.

"Yet. Maybe I'm a late bloomer."

Dawes returned to the dining room with a big tureen of steaming soup. "This isn't a joke!"

"Let's try to remember that not being a murderer is actually a good thing," Darlington said. "I'll take Tripp's place. I'll be the fourth."

Dawes set the tureen on the table with a loud, disapproving *thud*. "You will *not*."

Alex didn't like the idea either. The Gauntlet wasn't meant to be used as a revolving door. "I'm not giving up on Tripp. We don't know that Not Spenser got him. We don't know anything yet."

"We know the math," said Turner. "Four pilgrims to open the door—four to make the journey, and four to close it all up at the end. The full moon is tomorrow night, and unless Tripp suddenly slinks out into the open, the prodigal demon is our only option."

"We'll find another way," Dawes insisted, ladling soup into bowls aggressively.

"Sure," Turner replied. "Should we just have Mercy stab someone?"

"Of course not," Dawes snapped, though Mercy looked scarily game. "But . . ."

A faint, sad smile touched Darlington's lips. "Go on."

Now Dawes hesitated. "Look at you," she said quietly. "You aren't . . . you aren't completely human anymore. You're bound to that place." She glanced uneasily at Alex. "You both are."

Alex crossed her arms. "What do I have to do with it?"

"You were on fire," said Dawes. "The same way you were in the underworld." Dawes dipped her spoon into her bowl, then set it down. "We can't send Darlington back, and I . . . if Tripp's demon . . . if something happened to him, it's our fault."

No one could disagree. Dawes had said that Alex and Darlington were tied to the underworld, but the truth was that they were all bound together now. They had seen the very worst of each other, felt every ugly, shameful, frightening thing. Four pilgrims. Four children trembling in the dark. Four fools who had attempted what should never be dared. Four shoddy heroes on a quest who were meant to survive this reckless endeavor together.

But Tripp wasn't here.

"I'll go back to his place tomorrow," Turner said. "Reach out at his job. But we agree right now, no matter what, we make the descent tomorrow night. We can't let those things keep feeding on us. I have seen some shit in this life and been through it too. But I won't make it to the next full moon."

No one was going to argue with that either. Alex didn't want Darlington back in hell, but they were out of options. If what he had just done to Not Hellie couldn't stop these things, nothing in the mortal realm would.

"All right," said Alex.

Dawes gave a short nod.

"How exactly did you get Darlington out?" Turner asked a little too casually.

Alex was tempted to ask if he wanted her to write up a statement. But Dawes and Mercy and Turner were owed an explanation, or whatever answers they could patch together.

So they ate, and they talked—about Anselm who was no longer Anselm, the bodies they'd left at Black Elm, the murders of Professor Stephen and Dean Beekman, and the third murder that would have been committed if Turner hadn't arrested Andy Lambton.

When they were done, Turner pushed his empty bowl away and scrubbed his hands over his face. "You're telling me Lambton is innocent?"

"He was there," said Alex. "At least for Beekman. Maybe for Marjorie Stephen. I think Anselm enjoyed making him an accomplice."

"That's not his name," Darlington said.

"Well, whatever you want to call him. Golgarot, the demon king."

"He's a prince, not a king, and it would be unwise to underestimate him."

"I don't understand," said Mercy. "The . . . demon prince or whoever . . . he ate Anselm. Shouldn't he be a vampire now? Why is he messing around with getting some guy to commit random murders?"

"They weren't random," said Darlington. His voice was bleak, cold, something left at the bottom of a lake. "They were a puzzle, steeped in New Haven history, a custom lure for my mind, for Alex, for Detective Turner. A perfect distraction. He was having fun."

"But not drinking blood?" Alex asked. She'd tussled with Not

Anselm, and aside from being able to create fire out of thin air, he'd been physically weak, nothing like Linus Reiter.

"Golgarot is not like your demons or the demon that devoured Lionel Reiter. He tortured me in hell. He had already fed on my misery, and when I tried to come through the portal you opened at Scroll and Key, he was able to follow."

"When the circle bound you to Black Elm," Dawes said.

"But not Golgarot. He hadn't fed enough on me to be trapped by Sandow's spell."

"And the horns?" Turner asked.

"You were all travelers, moving between this world and the demon realm while your bodies remained here. That wasn't true for me. I walked right into the mouth of a hellbeast, and when I entered the demon realm, I split." He kept his words steady, but his gaze was faraway. "I became a demon, bound in service to Golgarot, a creature of . . . appetites. I became a man who fed his keeper with his own suffering."

"Right down the middle, huh?"

Darlington's smile was small. "No, Detective. I think you well know that one can be both a murderer and a good man. Or at least a man who tries to be good. If only the evil did terrible things, what a simple world it would be. Both demon and man remained in hell. Both demon and man were bound by the circle of protection."

"Anselm followed me into hell," Alex said, "when I crossed the circle."

"He had to in order to fight you. Golgarot is both more and less powerful than your demons. As long as I was bound to the circle, he could move freely, consume victims as he chose, but he remained weak. He couldn't enter this realm completely, not without killing me or pushing me back into hell forever."

"But . . . but he's dead now, right?" Mercy asked.

Darlington shook his head. "I destroyed his mortal body, the one he'd constructed. But he'll be waiting for me in hell. For all of us."

Dawes frowned. "Did he know we'd found the Gauntlet?"

"No," said Darlington. "He knew you were searching, but he had no idea you'd found it or that you were trying the ritual to free me on Halloween night."

"He said he came to Il Bastone and saw our notes," said Mercy.

"He told us that," Alex said. "But it's impossible. He's a demon. He couldn't get past the wards. It's why he didn't take us to the Hutch the night he banished us from Lethe."

Darlington nodded. "He'd set up an early-warning system. Hell is vast. He couldn't guard every entry. But he knew where you were headed, and once the alarm was tripped, he knew you'd found me."

Turner drew in a breath. "The wolves."

"That's right. He'd set them to watch over Black Elm."

"They were demons," said Alex, the realization like a slap. "They became our demons."

Four wolves for four pilgrims. They'd all drawn blood when they'd attacked, all gotten a taste of their human terror. Alex remembered the wolves burning like comets as they'd fled hell. The demons had followed them into the mortal realm.

"Golgarot stopped the ritual," Mercy said. "He made me turn off the metronome."

"But he didn't step into the courtyard." Alex remembered him hovering beneath Dürer's magic square. Maybe he hadn't wanted to risk seeing it or getting caught up in the puzzle.

"He wasn't going to let you take me out of hell," Darlington said. "He intended to strand you there with me."

"But Alex got us out," Turner said.

Alex shifted in her seat. "And left the door open for our demons to follow us through."

"I don't understand," Dawes said. "Why are there no warnings about the Gauntlet in the Lethe library? Why are there no records of its construction, of what happened to the first pilgrims who walked it, of Lionel Reiter?"

"I don't know," Darlington admitted. "It wouldn't be the first cover-up in Lethe's history."

Alex met Dawes's gaze. They knew that well enough. Lethe's members, its board, the few in the Yale administration who knew the true occupation of the secret societies, had a long history of sweeping all kinds of atrocities under the rug. Magical casualties, mysterious power outages, strange disappearances, the map in the Peabody basement. Everyone had believed Daniel Arlington was in Spain for most of last semester, and almost no one knew Elliot Sandow had turned out to be a murderer. There were no consequences, not if you just kept finding new places to bury your mistakes.

Mercy had set her red notebook next to her soup bowl and she was drawing a series of concentric circles in it. "So they covered it up. But Lionel Reiter became a vampire. We don't even know what happened to the other pilgrims or their sentinel. Why leave the Gauntlet intact if they knew how dangerous it was?"

There was silence then, because no one had the answer, but they all knew the truth couldn't be good. Something had gone wrong on that first journey, something bad enough that the Gauntlet had been wiped from the books and Rudolph Kittscher's diary had been hidden or destroyed. It might just be that Reiter had been followed by a demon, that Lethe was responsible for creating a vampire. But then why not hunt him? Why leave him to prey on innocent people for nearly a hundred years?

"Could I go alone?" Alex asked. She didn't want to say it. She didn't want to do it. But they might be down one pilgrim, and the longer they waited, the worse it was going to get. "I don't need the Gauntlet. Why can't I just walk back through that circle and find some way to drag our demons with me?"

"That's awfully self-sacrificing," said Turner. He glanced at Darlington. "She fall on her head?"

"I'm not doing it to play hero," Alex said sourly. "But I already got Tripp killed."

"You don't know that," protested Dawes.

"I can make an educated guess." She hoped it wasn't true. She hoped Tripp was safely tucked away in his fancy loft apartment, eating bowls of vegan chili, but she doubted that was the case. "I roped him into this, and there's a good chance he's not coming back from it."

"You can't just walk in by yourself," said Darlington. "You might pull your own demon with you, but you'll all have to go through to get rid of the others."

"What about Spenser?" Mercy asked. "Uh . . . Not Spenser, Tripp's demon?"

"If the demon consumed Tripp's soul—" Darlington began.

"We don't know that happened," Dawes insisted.

"But if it did, then the demon would be able to remain in the mortal world and feed on the living."

A new vampire could be preying on people in New Haven right now. Another bit of misery Alex had helped to create. Mercy had every right not to trust Tripp, to suspect he was a coward. But Alex liked Tripp. He was a dumbass, but he'd tried to do his best for them. *I like being one of the good guys.*

"We're going to have to create a tether," Dawes said. "Open the doorway and pull them back through."

"The vampire too?" asked Mercy.

"No," said Darlington. "If Tripp's demon really did become a vampire, it will have to be hunted on its own."

"Mercy and I have been searching the armory and the library for a way to lure our demons," said Dawes. "But there's only so much we can do if we need to be in the right position to open the Gauntlet."

"They're drawn to us when things are bad," said Alex.

Turner shot her a look. "So every hour of the day?"

"There's the Doom Sparrow," Mercy said, consulting her notes. "If you release it in a room, it sows discord and creates a general sense of malaise. It was used to disrupt meetings of union organizers in the seventies."

"*Have you heard that silence where the birds are dead yet something pipeth like a bird?*" Darlington quoted.

"I really missed having no idea what you're talking about," Alex said. And she meant it. "But I'm not sure we want to start a trip into hell feeling completely miserable and defeated."

"There's the Voynich," said Dawes. "But I don't know how to get hold of it."

"Why the Voynich, of all things?" Mercy asked.

Even Alex had heard of the Voynich manuscript. Aside from the original Gutenberg Bible, it was probably the most famous book at the Beinecke. And it was certainly harder to get a look at. The Bible was always on display in a glass case in the lobby and one page was turned daily. But the Voynich was very much under lock and key.

"Because it's a puzzle," said Darlington. "An unparseable language, an unsolvable code. It's what it was created for."

Mercy shut the cover of her notebook with a loud *snap*. "Wait a minute. Just . . . You're saying the Voynich manuscript was created to trap demons? Scholars have been speculating on it for centuries!"

Darlington lifted his shoulders. "I suppose it traps academics too. But Dawes is right. Accessing anything other than a digital copy is nearly impossible, and taking it out of Beinecke? Forget it."

"What about Pierre the Weaver?" asked Mercy.

Turner leaned back and crossed his arms. "This ought to be good."

But Dawes was tapping her pen against her lips. "That's an interesting idea."

"It's brilliant actually," said Darlington.

Mercy smiled.

"Does anyone want to tell me and Turner who Pierre is and what he weaves?" asked Alex.

"The Weaver was acquired by Manuscript," Dawes said. "It was used by a series of cult leaders and false gurus to lure followers. Pierre Bernard was the last, and the name stuck. The trick is making sure the Weaver spins the right emotional web."

"And it will trap the demons?" Turner asked.

"Only for a short time," said Dawes. "It's all . . . very risky."

"Not as risky as doing nothing." Alex didn't want to talk anymore. They couldn't wait until the next full moon. "I'm not going to let those things chase us around and eat at our hearts until they pick us off one by one."

"They're only going to get stronger and more savvy," Darlington said. "Personally, I would prefer not to see you all eaten and then have to deal with a bunch of vampires wearing your faces."

"Okay," said Turner. "We use Pierre the Whatever. We trap them and drag them down with us. I still have a murder suspect who was . . . encouraged, if not coerced, into helping to commit two horrific crimes and planning another. I can't get them to ease up on his sentence because demons were involved."

"He was driven mad," Darlington said. "That's how you'll get him leniency. Whether his monsters were real or imagined, the result was the same."

"Let's say I let that slide," Turner continued. "There are the remains of three missing persons in the Black Elm basement, and someone is going to come looking for those people eventually. I have to believe Anselm's wife is wondering why he hasn't come home, even if that demon was out and about, wearing his suits and using his credit card."

Bag the bodies. Switch the plates on the rental to transport them. Cremate them in the crucible after hours at Il Bastone. Wipe the car. Dump it. Alex knew what they should do. So did Turner. But she also knew he wasn't going to talk about it. He might have killed Carmichael in cold blood, but he was still police and he wasn't going to be involved in covering up a crime.

"We'll take care of it," said Alex.

"I won't clean up your mess."

"You won't have to."

Turner didn't look convinced. "I'm going to take you at your word. Now for all your talk, you haven't explained what happened out there on the sidewalk in front of this house. I saw a demon tear another demon in half. I saw you covered in fire that shouldn't exist in our realm and I saw you use it to keep him in check. Anyone want to explain all that?"

Darlington shrugged and reached for seconds of soup. "If we could, we would."

Alex could tell from Turner's look that he thought Darlington was lying.

Alex did too.

39

The house was big enough that there was room for everyone to sleep behind the wards. Darlington was back in the Virgil bedroom on the third floor. Dawes would sleep on the couch in the parlor, and Turner had claimed the floor of the armory.

Alex and Mercy set up camp in the Dante bedroom. But before Alex turned out the light, she tried texting Tripp once more. It wasn't safe to go looking for him at night, but she and Turner would try in the morning.

"I wasn't very nice to him," said Mercy.

"That's not what got him in trouble. And you don't owe everyone nice." She lay back on her pillow. "I need you to be ready tomorrow. Dawes said the descent could be different this time. I don't know what that means for you on the surface, but there's at least one vampire running around out there. I don't like putting you in danger again."

Mercy wriggled under the covers. "But we're always in danger. Go to a party, meet up with the wrong person, walk down the wrong street. I think . . . I think sometimes it's easier if instead of waiting for trouble, you go to meet it."

"Like a bad date."

Mercy laughed. "Yeah. But if anything terrible happens to me—"

"It won't."

"But if it does—"

"Mercy, if anyone fucks with you, I will teach them a new word for violence."

Mercy laughed, the sound brittle. "I know." She sat up, punched her pillow, leaned back on it. Alex could practically see the wheels turning. "To be a pilgrim . . . you all killed someone?"

Alex had known this conversation was coming. "Yup."

"I know . . . I know Dawes killed Blake. I'm not sure I want to know about everyone else, but . . ."

"Why am I qualified to be on Team Murder?"

"Yeah."

Alex had told Mercy about Lethe, about magic, even about the Grays, and that she could see them and use them. But she'd left her past good and buried. As far as Mercy knew, she was a kid from California with some gaps in her education.

There were plenty of lies Alex could tell now. It was self-defense. It was an accident. But the truth was that she'd contemplated killing Eitan that very morning, and if she'd been able to get away with it and find a place to stash the bodies, she would have done it and never looked back. And she'd promised she wasn't going to lie to Mercy again.

"I killed a lot of people."

Mercy rolled over on her side and looked at her. "How many?"

"Enough. For now."

"Do you . . . How do you live with that?"

What truth was she supposed to offer up? Because it wasn't the people she'd killed who haunted her. It was the people she'd let die, the ones she couldn't save. Alex knew she should say something comforting. That she prayed or cried or ran laps to forget. She hadn't had many friends and she didn't want to lose this one. But she was tired of pretending.

"I'm just not made right, Mercy. I don't know if it's remorse or conscience that I'm missing or if the angel on my shoulder decided to take a long vacation. But I don't lose sleep over the bodies on my scorecard. I guess that doesn't make me a great roommate."

"Maybe not," Mercy said and turned off the light. "But I'm glad you're on my side."

Alex waited until Mercy was snoring, then slipped out of bed and padded upstairs to the third floor. The door to the Virgil bedroom was open, and there was a fire blazing in the hearth beneath the stained glass windows depicting a hemlock wood. Darlington was sprawled in a chair by the fire. He'd changed into Lethe House sweatpants and an old robe—or maybe it was called a dressing gown. She wasn't sure. She just knew that she'd been looking at him without a stitch of clothes for weeks, but that something about seeing him this way—feet propped on the ottoman, robe open, bare chested, a book in his hand—made her feel like a Peeping Tom.

"Something you want, Stern?" he asked without glancing up from his reading.

That was a complicated question.

"You lied to Turner," she said.

"I imagine you've done the same when necessary." He looked up at last. "Are you going to hover in that doorway all night or come in?"

Alex made herself enter. Why the hell was she so nervous? This was Darlington—scholar, snob, and pain in the ass. No mystery there. But she'd held his soul inside her. She could still taste him on her tongue.

"What are you drinking?" she asked, picking up the tiny glass of amber liquid from the table beside his chair.

"Armagnac. You're welcome to try it."

"But we—"

"I'm well aware my Armagnac was sacrificed for a worthy cause—perhaps along with my grandfather's Mercedes. This bottle is far cheaper and less rare."

"But not actually cheap."

"Of course not."

She set down the glass and settled herself in the chair across from him, letting the fire warm her feet, acutely conscious of the hole forming in her right sock.

"You sure this is a good idea?" she asked. "Going back to hell?"

His eyes returned to the book he was reading. Michelle Alameddine's Lethe Days Diary.

Was he wondering why she hadn't been the one to stand sentinel? "Find anything interesting in there?"

"Yes, actually. A pattern I hadn't seen before. But a demon loves a puzzle."

"She did help," Alex said. "She told us you believed the Gauntlet was on campus."

"She doesn't owe me anything. I told myself I would never look at her diary, that I wouldn't go hunting for her opinions on her Dante and give in to that particular vanity. But here I am."

"What did she say?"

His smile was rueful. "Very little. I am described as fastidious, thorough, and—no less than five times—eager. The overall portrait is vague in its details, but far from flattering." He closed the book, setting it aside. "And to answer your question, returning to hell is an abominable idea, but I don't have any others. In my more futile moments, I'm tempted to blame Sandow for all of this. It was his greed that put this series of tragedies in motion. He summoned the hellbeast to devour me. I suppose he thought it would be a quick death."

"Or a clean one," Alex said without thinking.

"Fair point. No body to dispose of. No questions to be asked."

"You weren't meant to survive."

"No," he mused. "I suppose you and I have that in common. Was that almost a smile, Stern?"

"Too early to tell." She shifted in her seat, watching him. He had always been indecently appealing, the dark hair, the lean build, the air of some deposed royal who had wandered into their mundane world from a far-off castle. It was hard not to stare at him, to keep reminding herself that he was truly there, truly alive. And that somehow he seemed to have forgiven her. But she couldn't say any of that. "Tell me what you wouldn't talk about in front of the others. Why do you still have horns—"

"Occasional horns."

"Fine. Why did I light up like a blowtorch when you used them?"

Darlington was quiet for a long time. "There are no words for what we've done. For what we may yet do. Think of the Gauntlet as a series of doors, all meant to keep the unwary from strolling into hell. You don't need those doors, Stern."

"Belbalm . . . Before she died—"

"Before you killed her."

"It was a group effort. She said that all worlds were open to Wheelwalkers. I saw a circle of blue fire around me."

"I saw it too," he said. "On Halloween. A year ago. The Wheel. I don't think it was coincidence. And I don't think this is either."

He rose and crossed the room to his desk and removed a book of New York landmarks. He moved with the same easy confidence he always had, but now there was something sinister in those long strides. She saw the demon. She saw a predator.

He flipped through the book and held it open to her. "Atlas," he said, "at Rockefeller Center."

The black-and-white photo showed a muscular figure wrought in bronze and poised on one knee, bent beneath the weight of three interlocked rings resting on his colossal shoulders.

"The celestial spheres," Darlington continued. "The heavens in their movements. Or . . ."

Alex traced her finger around one of the circles emblazoned with the signs of the zodiac. "The Wheel."

"This sculpture was designed by Lee Lawrie. He's also responsible for the stonework in Sterling." Darlington took the book from her hands, returned it to the desk. He kept his back to her when he said, "That night at Manuscript, it wasn't just a wheel I saw. It was a crown."

"A crown. What does that mean? What does any of it mean?"

"I don't know. But when you crossed into hell through the circle of protection, you broke every rule there is. And when you carried me out again, you found another one to break." He settled himself back in the chair across from her. "You stole me from underworld. That was bound to leave a mark."

Alex could hear Anselm—Golgarot—screaming *thief*. She saw the wolf's lips pull back to form the same word.

"Is that what those things are?" she asked. "Around your wrists and neck? Marks?"

"These?" He leaned forward, and the change in him was instant, the glowing eyes, the curling horns, the broadening of the shoulders. Without meaning to, Alex found herself scooting back in her chair. He was man and then monster in the space of a breath. The golden bands glowed at his wrists and throat.

"Yeah," she said, trying not to show her fear. "Those."

"These marks mean I am bound in service. Forever."

"To hell? To Golgarot?"

He laughed then, the sound deep and cold, the thing at the bottom of the lake. "I'm bound to you, Stern. To the woman who brought me out of hell. I will serve you 'til the end of days."

40

Her face went very still. Darlington had learned that this was what Alex Stern did when faced with uncertainty. Fight or flight? A survivor's move was sometimes no move at all. He could see her in the basement on that night so long ago, a girl wrought in stone.

She raised a brow. "So . . . are you going to do my laundry?"

Fight, flight, or sarcasm. "What a horrid girl you are."

"Ma'am. What a horrid girl you are, *ma'am.*"

Now he laughed.

But Alex's brows had drawn together. Her jaw was set. She looked like she was squaring up for a fight. "There are too many mysteries. I don't like the way they're adding up."

"I'm not certain I do either," he said, and he wasn't lying this time. "You can see the dead, hear them, use them for your own ends—and unless I'm very much mistaken, were it not for certain scruples that Marguerite Belbalm lacked, you could use the living in much the same way."

All he got for that assessment was a short, sharp nod.

"As for me . . ." He wasn't sure how to finish that sentence. As a man he had suffered in hell. But as a demon he had doled out suffering with ease and ingenuity. Sandow had come to them, murdered by Belbalm, his soul already consumed by her. He would never pass beyond the Veil, but hell was happy to claim him. Darlington's demon self had enjoyed finding new ways to make Sandow miserable, to pay for the anguish he'd caused.

Darlington had been frightening to the shades of the Veil and even to himself. It had been . . . If he was honest, it had been exhilarating. He had been a creature of the mind since he was a boy—languages, history, science. The rest of it, the training he'd put himself through—fighting, swordplay, even acrobatics—had all been in service to the future adventures he'd been sure he would have. But the great invitation had never come. There had been no noble quests or secret missions. There had been rituals, glimpses of the world beyond, schoolwork, reports to write, and that was all. So he had kept honing himself like a blade that would never be tried.

Then Dean Sandow had sent him to hell. Darlington shouldn't have survived, but he'd managed to hold on until at last rescue had come.

And now? Was he human enough? He had been able to sit at the table and hold a conversation. He hadn't growled at anyone or broken any furniture, but it hadn't been easy. Demons were not thinking creatures. They operated on instinct, driven by their appetites. He had prided himself on being nothing like that. Never rash. Guided by reason. But now he wanted in a way he never had. He had been tempted to bury his face in his soup bowl and lap at it like a greedy animal. He wanted to place himself between Alex's legs now and do the same to her.

Darlington drew a hand over his face and gave himself a little shake, praying for sense to return. He was her mentor. Her Virgil. He owed her his life and he could do better by her. He was not some slavering beast. He would pretend to be human again until he was.

Darlington had been surprised by the way that the others had come together to work and plan. He almost hadn't recognized the command in Alex, the confidence in Dawes, all of it born of his absence. *They would have gone on without me. They would have grown stronger.* Sitting there, watching them hatch their schemes with Turner and Mercy, he'd felt like a stranger in a place he'd once known he belonged. His understanding of his own lack of consequence had been both slow and sudden in its cruelty.

"As for me, I don't know what I am," he said at last.

"But you can control"—she waved a hand as if casting a spell over him—"whatever that demon shit is."

"I certainly hope so. But I think it would be wise for you and anyone else near me to keep a ready supply of salt at hand. We might consider putting prohibitions on Black Elm too, or wherever I wash up, so that I can't leave without escort."

How reasonable he sounded. It wasn't so hard to playact the man he'd been.

He considered the strange and terrible girl before him. Her eyes were black in the firelight, her hair shining as if it had been lacquered. Undine the water spirit, risen from the lake in search of a soul. Darlington hated to think of that night at the Halloween party at Manuscript. He'd been out of his mind on whatever they'd used to drug him. But when he had looked into the great mirror, he had seen that Alex was something more than her mortal self. And he'd understood that he wasn't the hero he'd always dreamed of being. He'd been a knight, and what was a knight but a servant with a sword in his hand? For the first time he had known himself and his purpose. At least it had seemed that way at the time. All he had wanted was to serve her, to be seen and desired by her. He hadn't known he was looking into the future.

"You are a Wheelwalker," he said. "I know that only because you know that, only because Belbalm and then Sandow knew it. I'm going to have to dig deeper than the Lethe library to find out what that truly means. But I do know this: Not all of us will return from the underworld tomorrow night."

"We made it out before."

"And you brought four demons with you. One of whom may have taken up permanent residence in our world to feed on people until it's vanquished. But we won't all be coming back this time. As long as hell is short a murderer, the door will remain open, and your demons will keep coming through. Hell's price must be paid."

Alex scowled. "Why? How do you know that?"

"Because I was one of them. I was a demon feeding on the suffering of the dead." He'd meant to say it easily, casually. Instead the words emerged haltingly and stinking of confession.

"Am I supposed to be shocked and horrified?"

"That I engaged in a kind of emotional cannibalism to survive? That I ate pain and enjoyed it? I'd think even you might be troubled by that."

"You've been in my head now," she said. "Did you get a look at the things I did to survive this life?"

"Glimpses," he admitted. A string of bleak moments, a deep and desperate ocean, Hellie shining like a golden coin, her grandmother glowing like a banked ember, her mother . . . a disaster, a cloud, a tangle of frayed yarn, a mess of pity and longing and anger and love.

"We do what we have to," Alex said. "That's the only job of a survivor."

A strange benediction, but one he was grateful for. He folded his hands, debating his next words, unwilling to let them remain unspoken. "What if I told you that some part of me still hungers after suffering?"

Alex didn't flinch. Of course she didn't. It wasn't in her repertoire.

"I'd tell you to keep your shit together, Darlington. We all want things we shouldn't."

He wondered if she really understood what he was. If she did, she might run from this room. But it wouldn't be a worry for long, not after the descent. Until then, he could make sure the demon didn't slip its leash.

"You need to accept that hell is going to try to keep one of us," he said. "It will be me, Stern. I was never meant to leave."

He wasn't sure what he expected: Laughter? Tears? A heroic demand that she take his place in hell? He had lost track of who was Dante, Virgil, Beatrice. Was he Orpheus or Eurydice?

But all Alex did was lean back in her chair and cast him a skeptical glance. "So after we fought and bled to drag you out of hell, you think we're going to just bring you back like a foster dog who shit on the carpet?"

"I wouldn't put it—"

Alex rose and tossed back his glass of his expensive Armagnac like it was a dollar shot on ladies' night at Toad's. "Fuck off, Darlington."

She strode to the door.

"Where are you going?"

"To the armory to talk to Turner. Then I have some calls to make. You know your problem?"

"A predilection for first editions and women who like to lecture me about myself?"

"An unhealthy respect for the rules. Get some sleep."

She vanished down the dark hall, there and gone, like some kind of magic trick.

41

Alex didn't fall asleep until the early hours of the morning. There was too much to plan, and her time with Darlington had left her buzzing at some uncomfortable frequency that made sleep impossible. She had been talking to him in her head so long, it should have been easy to sit and hold a conversation. But they were not the same people anymore, student and teacher, apprentice and master. Before, knowledge had flowed one way between them. Power had rested in his hands alone. But now that power was in motion, constantly shifting, bumping up against their understanding of each other, confused by the mysteries that remained, falling into the shadowed places where that understanding failed. It seemed to fill the house, a coil of hellfire that ran through the halls and up the stairs, a lit fuse. Yale and Lethe had belonged to Darlington, but now they were playing on a wider stage, and Alex wasn't yet sure what role either of them were meant to fill.

She had barely dozed off when she was woken by Dawes shaking her shoulder.

At the sight of her panicked face Alex bolted upright. "What is it?"

"The Praetor's coming."

"Here?" Alex asked as she leapt out of bed and pulled on the only clean clothes she had—Lethe sweats. "Now?"

"I was making lunch when he called. I told Mercy to stay upstairs. He wants to go over preparations for the wolf run. Didn't you email him?"

"I did!" She'd sent her notes, links to her research, along with a four-hundred-word apology for being unprepared at their last meeting and a declaration of her loyalty to Lethe. Maybe she'd overdone it. "Where's Darlington?"

"He and Turner went to Tripp's apartment."

Alex drew her fingers through her hair, trying to make it respectable. "And?"

"No one answered the door, but the salt knot at the entry was still undisturbed."

"That's good, right? Maybe he's just hunkering down with his family or—"

"If we don't have Tripp, we won't be able to lure his demon back to hell."

They would have to face that problem later.

They were halfway down the stairs when they heard the front door open. Professor Walsh-Whiteley entered whistling. He set his cap and coat on the rack by the door. "Miss Stern!" he said. "Oculus said you might be late. Are you . . . in your pajamas?"

"Just doing some chores," Alex said with a bright smile. "Old houses need so much maintenance." The step beneath her creaked mightily as if Il Bastone was joining the charade.

"She's a grand old thing," said the Praetor, strolling into the parlor. "I was hoping to find Oculus had stocked the larder."

Oculus. Whom he hadn't bothered to greet. No wonder his Virgil and his Dante had hated him. But they had more serious worries than a throwback professor with no manners.

"Call Darlington," Alex whispered.

"I did!"

"Try again. Tell him not to come back until—"

The front door swung open and Darlington strode in. "Morning," he said. "Turner—"

Alex and Dawes waved frantically at him to shut up. But it was too late.

"Do we have guests?" the Praetor asked, craning his neck around the corner.

Darlington stood frozen with his coat in his hands. Walsh-Whiteley stared at him.

"Mr. Arlington?"

Darlington managed a nod. "I . . . Yes."

Alex could lie as easily as she could speak, but at that moment, she was at a loss for any words, let alone believable fictions. She hadn't even thought about how they were going to explain Darlington's reappearance. Instead she and Dawes were standing there looking like they'd just been doused with ice water.

Well, if she was already playing shocked, she might as well lean into it. Alex summoned all her will and burst into tears.

"Darlington!" she cried. "You're back!" She threw her arms around him.

"Yes," Darlington said too loudly. "I am back."

"I thought you were dead!" Alex wailed at the top of her lungs.

"Good God," said the Praetor. "It's really you? I'd been given to understand that, well, you were dead."

"No, sir," Darlington said as he disentangled himself from Alex, his hand at the small of her back like a hot coal. "I had just slipped into a pocket dimension. Dante and Oculus were kind enough to petition Hayman Pérez to attempt a retrieval spell on my behalf."

"That was most inappropriate," Walsh-Whiteley scolded. "I should have been consulted. The board—"

"Absolutely," Darlington agreed as Alex continued sniffling. "A terrible breach of protocol. But I must confess, I'm grateful for it. Pérez is tremendously gifted."

"That I can agree with. One of the best of Lethe." The Praetor studied Darlington. "And you just . . . reappeared."

"In the basement of Rosenfeld Hall."

"I see."

Dawes, all but forgotten on the stairs, cleared her throat. "Something to eat, perhaps? I've made cheese toasts with smoked almonds and a pumpkin curry."

Walsh-Whiteley's eyes traveled from Dawes to Alex and on to Darlington. The man might be pompous and prudish, but he wasn't a fool.

"Well," he said at last, "I suppose most things are best explained over a good meal."

"And a good glass of wine," Darlington added, shepherding the Praetor through the parlor.

Alex glanced through the window to where she could see the glittering eyes of the demons, gathered in the shadows between the houses across the street. At least they were keeping their distance. Darlington's attack on Not Hellie must have spooked them.

"Should I poison his soup?" Dawes whispered as she passed.

"You've had worse ideas."

The lunch was long, and Darlington and Alex could only pick at their food. They needed to fast for the descent. The conversation revolved around Sandow's death and Darlington's disappearance and the particulars of the supposed retrieval spell Pérez had performed. Alex wondered if Darlington had been such an excellent liar before he'd become part demon.

"Aren't you hungry?" the Praetor demanded as Dawes set down a warm apple crostata and a pot of crème fraîche.

"Portal travel," Darlington said. "Terrible on the digestion."

Alex was famished, but she just sniffled and said, "I'm too emotional to eat."

Walsh-Whiteley jabbed at the air with his fork. "Maudlin nonsense. There's no room at Lethe for delicate sensibilities. This is why the Ninth House is no place for women."

Inside the kitchen a loud crash sounded as Dawes made her feelings known.

"Are you up to attending tonight's wolf run?" the Praetor asked Darlington.

"Certainly."

"I think you'll be pleased with the way our Miss Stern has progressed. Despite her dubious background and lack of education, she's acquitted herself well. I can only assume as the result of your tutelage."

"Naturally."

Alex resisted the urge to kick him under the table.

When Walsh-Whiteley had finished the last bite of his crostata, and downed the last sip of his Sauternes, Alex walked him to the door.

"Good luck tonight, Miss Stern," he said, cheeks rosy from the wine. "I'll expect your report by Sunday at the latest."

"Of course."

He paused on the steps. "You must be relieved Mr. Arlington has returned."

"*Very* relieved."

"It's fortunate that Hayman Pérez was able to manage such a complicated spell."

"*Very* fortunate."

"Of course Mr. Pérez has been searching for lost Nazi bunkers in the Antarctic for the better part of a year. A pointless endeavor, I suspect, but he got the funding, so I suppose the board must see a purpose. He's been quite unreachable."

Alex wasn't sure if the Praetor had really caught them out or if he was bluffing. "Has he? I guess we got lucky."

"*Very*," said the Praetor. He tucked his cap onto his head. "Lethe sees me as a nuisance and a pedant. It has ever been so. But I hold the Ninth House to a higher standard than those who make a pretense of governing it. I believe in the institution that Lethe might be, that it should be. We are the shepherds." His gaze found hers, his eyes a rheumy indeterminate brown. "There are places we were never meant to trespass, no matter that we may have the means. Be careful out there, Miss Stern."

Before Alex could think of a reply, he was walking down the street, whistling a tune she didn't recognize.

Alex watched him go, wondering at who Raymond Walsh-Whiteley really was. A young genius. A reactionary curmudgeon. A student still in love with the boy he'd met on some seaside idyll, the boy he still mourned.

Alex shut the door, grateful to be behind the wards. Dawes was in the dining room with her blueprints and her notes, walking Darlington through what to expect from the descent. Alex was happy to leave them to it. She didn't want to think of Darlington as he'd been last night in front of the fire. *A predilection for first editions and women who like to lecture me about myself.* A joke. Nothing more. But that word kept sticking in her thoughts—*predilection*, precise and filthy at the same time.

She headed straight for the Dante bedroom. She had work to do.

"Baby!" her mother exclaimed when she picked up the phone, and Alex felt that familiar rush of happiness and embarrassment that always came with her mother's voice. "How are you? Is everything okay?"

"Everything's great. I was thinking about coming home for Thanksgiving."

Mercy and Lauren were planning a trip to Montreal with a couple of theater people Lauren had met working at the Dramat. They'd invited Alex, but Alex wasn't swimming in cash, and if she made it through the second descent and everything it entailed, she was going to use what money she did have for a trip to Los Angeles.

A long pause. Alex could imagine Mira pacing in their old living room, fear descending over her. "You're sure? I'd love to see you, but I want to make sure this is a healthy step forward for you."

"It's okay. I'd just come to see you for a few days."

"Really? That would be perfect! I've found a new healer and I think she could do wonders for you. She's great at purging negative energy."

How about demons? "Sure. That sounds nice."

Another pause. "You're sure everything is okay?"

Alex should have protested the healer more.

"I really am. I love you and I'm excited to see you and . . . Okay, I'm not excited to eat tofurkey, but I can pretend."

Mira's laugh was so easy, so light. "You're going to love it, Galaxy. I'll have your room all ready."

They said their goodbyes, and Alex sat looking at the window, at the stained glass moon glowing in a bank of blue glass clouds, never waxing, never waning. When she was small, she'd searched her mother's features for some hint of herself and found nothing. Only once they'd been sitting side by side on the bed, barefooted, and she'd noticed that they had the same feet, the second toe longer than the big toe, the pinky crowded in like an afterthought. It had reassured her. She belonged to this person. They were made of the same stuff. But it wasn't enough. Where was the shared sense of humor? A talent like sewing or singing or picking up languages? Alex thought of her mother walking down the street, shining with hope. But Alex was always in shadow.

She wanted to tell her mother to go away for a few days, to go stay with Andrea, but she couldn't do that without panicking her. And if she failed tonight, none of it would matter anyway.

Alex checked her phone. Still no message from Turner. She wasn't going to call, wasn't going to risk tipping the scales the wrong way. What she'd asked him to do wasn't exactly criminal, but it also wasn't anywhere close to honest, and Turner's virtuous streak was too wide for her comfort.

"Just what are you planning?" he'd asked when she'd found him in the armory the previous night.

"Do you really want to know?"

He'd taken a long moment to consider, then said, "Absolutely not." Without another word, he'd lain back down and pulled the blanket over his head.

"But you'll do what I asked?" she had insisted. "You'll make the call?"

"Go to bed, Stern," was all he said.

Now she looked down at her phone and dialed Tripp's number for the twentieth time that day. No answer. How many people would be dead before this was over? How many more bodies would float in her wake?

Alex hesitated, the phone in her hand. The next call might save her or quite literally damn her.

Eitan picked up on the first ring. "Alex! How are you? You go to see Reiter?"

Alex kept her eyes on the glass moon. "This is a courtesy call. I'm done being your errand girl. I'm going to work for Linus Reiter."

"Don't be silly. Reiter is no good. He—"

"You can't stop him. You don't have a weapon in your arsenal that can."

"What you say is very serious, Alex."

"I'm going to tell him every last thing about your organization and your associates."

"Your mother—"

"Mira is under his protection." Or she could be.

"I'm in New York. Come see me. We talk. We make a new deal."

Alex had no doubt she would not return from that meeting.

"No hard feelings, Eitan."

"Alex, you—"

She hung up. *Hell is empty, and all the devils are here.* Shakespeare again. One of the strippers back at the King King Club had the quote tattooed above her pubic bone. Alex had been jumping to do Eitan's bidding for months. It was time for him to be afraid. It was time for him to come running. Reiter was the devil the other devils couldn't best, the one they warned each other about.

"You're up to something, Stern," Darlington said as they packed for the wolf run later that night. "I can tell."

"Just keep your head down and don't let anything try to kill me."

"It's my price to pay," he warned her.

"It's Sandow's price. You didn't end up in hell because you did something wrong."

"But I did."

Alex took stock of the contents of the duffel: salt, silver rings, and a silver dagger for good measure. "We can debate this when we're done. Dawes will take notes. We can bind them up and put them in the Lethe library. *Stern's Daemonologie.*"

"*Arlington's Daemonologie.* Aren't you going to valiantly offer to stay in hell in my place?"

"Fuck off."

"I did miss you, Stern."

"Did you?" She hadn't meant to ask, but the words were out before she could stop them.

"As much as an unholy fiend without human feeling could."

That almost made her laugh.

No, Alex wasn't about to volunteer for an eternity of anguish. She didn't have the makings of a hero. But she wasn't leaving Darlington down there again. *Hell's price must be paid.* All that meant was hell was no different from any other place. There was always a price and someone to pay it. And someone was always on the take.

When they left Il Bastone to meet with the Wolf's Head delegation at Sleeping Giant, she felt a kind of ease, as if the thread that bound them now had drawn tight, as if no demon would dare to face them together.

I will serve you 'til the end of days. Had that been a dream or some kind of prediction? Had Alex, like her grandmother, somehow looked into the future to this moment? Even if she had, that gave her no greater insight into what it meant, or those golden shackles at Darlington's wrists, or the disturbing comfort it brought her to know she could call and he would come running. Gentleman demon. A creature even the dead had feared.

A ship sailed from New Haven,
And the keen and frosty airs
That filled her sails at parting
Were heavy with good men's prayers.

"O Lord! if it be thy pleasure,"—
Thus prayed the old divine,—
"To bury our friends in the ocean,
Take them, for they are thine!"

—"The Phantom Ship,"
Henry Wadsworth Longfellow

My last entry as Virgil. I thought I would never wish to leave this office, but instead I find myself counting the days until I can close the door of Il Bastone behind me and never darken the doorstep of this house again. I leave with my fortunes secured, but I know I will see hell again. How Nownes would laugh at me if he knew the extent of our folly. How he would weep if he knew the extent of our crimes. But why do I write? I will hide this book and in it our sins. I wish only that I believed in God, so that I might beg for His mercy.

—Lethe Days Diary of Rudolph Kittscher
(Jonathan Edwards College '33)

42

By 1 a.m., Alex and Darlington were back on campus, shivering with cold, their ears still ringing with howls. They waited for the others by the Women's Table. The shadows seemed too thick, as if they had weight and form. She was nearly faint with hunger, and the terrible possibilities of all she'd set in motion were gnawing at her thoughts.

Alex made sure her phone was on and sent a last text to her mom, just in case.

I love you. Stay safe.

Absurd, a ridiculous message from a girl who had crashed through life like she was charging through a series of plate glass windows. She'd cut herself to ribbons, then patched herself up, only to do it again and again and again.

You too, little star. The reply came fast, as if her mother had been waiting. But Mira had been waiting by the phone a very long time. For a call from the hospital, the cops, the morgue.

Alex knew they needed to get started, but when Dawes let them into the library, she went to check on Mercy in the courtyard first.

The air seemed colder by the basin, as if they'd truly left a door open and a draft was blowing through. There were no stars visible in the gray November sky, but Alex found herself drinking in the feel of the weather, the winter chill on her skin, the dim yellow light from the library windows, the textured gray of the stone. Hell had been like a vacuum, dead and empty, all color and life leached away, as if some demon had fed on the world as much as the souls that inhabited it. If this was her last look at anything real, she wanted to remember it.

She helped Mercy into her salt armor and they talked through the plan. They still didn't know what might be waiting for them—in this world or below. Mercy was armed with death words, bone dust, and a salt sword, but Alex had retrieved another item from the armory. She handed the jar to Mercy.

"I wouldn't open—"

But Mercy had already lifted the lid. She gagged and hastily shut the jar. "Alex," she coughed, "you have to be kidding me."

"Afraid not." Alex hesitated. "Vampires hate strong smells. It's where the garlic myth came from. It's not too late to back out of this." She needed to offer this chance at escape, at safety. Mercy had walked this path without hesitation, but did she really know what she was moving toward with such happy momentum?

"Pretty sure it is."

"It's never too late to make a run for it, Mercy. Trust me on that."

"I know." Mercy looked down at the sword in her hands. "But I like this life better."

"Better than what?"

"Better than what I was living before. Better than a world without magic. I think I've been waiting my whole life for the moment someone would see something in me that wasn't ordinary."

"We all are." Alex couldn't keep the bitterness from her voice. "That's how they get you."

Mercy's eyes glinted. "Not if we get them first."

Maybe because Mercy was so sweet, so smart, so kind—Alex forgot how much fight she had in her. She couldn't help but think of Hellie, what it had cost her to fall into Alex's orbit. What might it cost Mercy to be Alex's friend? But it was too late for that calculation. She needed Mercy in this courtyard tonight.

"The phone is on," she said, handing over her cell. "Leave it that way."

Mercy gave a rapid nod. "Got it."

"Stay close to the basin. Don't forget the balm. And if this turns ugly, you run. Find a room in the library to lock yourself in and stay there until daylight."

"Understood." Now Mercy hesitated. "You're coming back, right?"

Alex made herself smile. "One way or another."

Once the metronome had been set ticking in the courtyard, they waited for quiet on Cross Campus. Then, in front of the library's main entrance, they made their cuts, each to the left arm. Alex looked at Darlington in his dark coat, at Dawes in her sweats, at Turner standing at attention, ready for battle, even if he wasn't quite sure the war could be won.

"Okay," she said. "Let's go to hell."

One by one they daubed their blood on the entry columns. Alex felt a sudden nausea, like a hook had lodged in her gut and was pulling her forward, like the force that had drawn her across the city on bare feet to Black Elm. They entered, passing beneath the Egyptian scribe, and through that cold darkness, the door that was no longer a door.

All of them had taken on the same titles, in the same order. All but Tripp. Alex entered first as the soldier, followed by Dawes as the scholar, then Turner as the priest, and finally Darlington—the prince. Alex couldn't help thinking the title took on a different meaning with him in the role instead of Tripp, and that made her feel guilty. She wondered which part Lionel Reiter had taken when he'd made the descent nearly a century ago.

They continued in single file to *Alma Mater*, then on to the arches beneath the Tree of Knowledge that they once again marked with blood. Down the corridor, past the soldier's door, past the stone student unaware of Death at his shoulder, and into the vestibule full of those odd windows that looked like they belonged in a country pub.

"Just a man," Darlington murmured, and Alex knew he was

remembering his fight to give them clues to the Gauntlet, his demon wiles at war with his human hope. But she saw delight in his face as they made their way through Sterling, wonder and bemusement. Despite all that had happened, he couldn't help but thrill at the secrets lurking beneath the stone, left behind for them to discover. There was something reassuring in the way his eyes shone, the eager muttering over quotations and symbols. *It's still him.* Lethe's golden boy might not look quite the same to her, might have seen and done things no man should, but he was still Darlington.

"Here," Dawes said softly. "Your doorway."

Darlington nodded, then frowned.

"What's wrong?" Alex asked.

He bobbed his head toward the stonework. "*Lux et Veritas*? Did they run out of ideas?"

Leave it to Darlington to be a snob about a hidden gateway to hell.

They anointed the stone with their blood and that black pit appeared. An icy wind ruffled Darlington's dark hair. Alex wanted to tell him that he didn't have to do this, that everything would be okay. But there were some lies even she couldn't sell.

"I . . ." Dawes began. But sputtered out, a candle guttering.

"Do you know the story of the Phantom Ship?" Darlington asked in the quiet. "Back when the New Haven colony was struggling, the townspeople got together and packed a ship with their best wares, samples of all this brave new world had to offer, and their leading citizens set off to try to convince people back in England that it was worth investing in the colony and maybe coming over themselves."

"Why do I think this story doesn't have a happy ending?" Turner asked.

"I don't think they manufacture those in New Haven. The honorable Reverend John Davenport—"

"*Hide the outcasts* John Davenport?" Alex asked.

"One and the same. He says, 'Lord, if it be thy pleasure to bury these our Friends in the bottom of the Sea, they are thine, save them!'"

"Go ahead and drown them?" Turner said. "Quite the pep talk."

"The ship never made it to England," Darlington continued. "The whole colony was left in limbo, with no idea of what had happened to their loved ones and all the wealth they'd stuffed into the hold. Then, a year to the day after the ship set out, a strange fog rolls in off the sea and the good citizens of New Haven all walk down to the harbor, where they see a ship emerging from the mist."

He sounded like Anselm that day by the water, telling the tale of the three judges. Had Anselm been imitating Darlington? Or had it simply come naturally, Darlington's demon, fed on his suffering, speaking with his voice?

"They made it back?" asked Dawes.

Darlington shook his head. "It was an illusion, a shared hallucination. Everyone on the docks saw the phantom ship wreck before their very eyes. The masts broke, men went overboard."

"Bullshit," said Turner.

"It's well documented," said Darlington, unfazed. "And the town took it as gospel. Wives who had been waiting for their husbands were now widows free to marry. Wills were read and property disbursed. There's still no explanation for it, but the meaning has always been clear to me."

"Oh yeah?" said Turner.

"Yeah," said Alex. "This town has been fucked from the start."

Darlington actually smiled. "I'll be listening for the signal."

They moved on to the next door and the librarian's office. When Alex looked back, Darlington stood framed by darkness, his head bowed, as if in prayer.

Turner took up his post by the sundial door. "Keep your head straight," he said, the same words he'd used on their first descent. "And don't drown."

Alex thought of Tripp clinging to the railing of the boat, of the phantom ship sinking to the bottom of the sea. She met Turner's gaze. "Don't drown."

She followed Dawes through the secret door to the Linonia and Brothers reading room.

It was quieter in this part of the library, and Alex could hear every scuffle of their shoes on the carpeted floor.

"Darlington thinks he's not coming back," Dawes said. Alex could feel her eyes on her back.

"I won't let that happen."

They stopped in front of the original entrance to the courtyard emblazoned with Selin's name in gold letters.

"What about you?" Dawes asked. "Who's looking out for you, Alex?"

"I'll be fine," Alex said, surprised by the wobble in her voice. She'd known Dawes couldn't bear the thought of losing Darlington again, but it hadn't occurred to her that Dawes might give a damn if Alex came back too.

"I'm not leaving you down there," Dawes said fiercely.

Alex had said the same thing to Darlington. Promises were easy in this world. So why not make another? "We're all coming back," she vowed.

Alex slapped her bloody palm on the archway, and Dawes daubed her blood over it. The door dissolved, and the gold letters of Selin's name unraveled, replaced by that mysterious alphabet.

"I . . ." Dawes was staring at the writing. "I can read it now."

The scholar. What knowledge had Dawes brought with her from the first descent? What new horrors might she learn when they walked the road to hell this time around?

"What does it say?" asked Alex.

Dawes pressed her lips together, her face pale. "None go free."

Alex tried to ignore the tremor that passed through her at those words. She had heard them before, during the first descent when she'd seen Darlington's demon half, the torturer in his element.

Alex hesitated. "Dawes . . . if this doesn't go the way we planned . . . thanks for taking care of me."

"I'm fairly sure you've almost died several times since we met."

"It's the *almost* that counts."

"I don't like this," Dawes said, her eyes darting again to those golden letters. "It feels like goodbye."

Was I ever here? Alex wondered. Had she died alongside Hellie? Had she ever been more than a ghost passing through this place?

"Don't drown," she said and made herself walk on, back down the nave where she studiously avoided looking at the *Alma Mater* mural, then to the right where the circuit had begun. It was time to close the loop.

She studied the stained glass image of Daniel in the lions' den. Was she the martyr this time? Or the wounded beast with a thorn in its paw? Or just a soldier after all. She couldn't get her cut to well, so she slashed her arm again and smeared blood onto the glass. It vanished, as if the library was happy to be fed. She was staring into the empty.

She waited, and in the silence, Alex felt as if she could sense something racing toward them. A moment later, she heard the soft hum of the pitch pipe. She took her first step into the courtyard.

This time she was ready for the way the building shook, the shuddering of the stones beneath her feet, the hiss and bubble of the water overflowing the basin, the stink of sulfur. Straight ahead she could see Turner marching toward her, Dawes to her right, Darlington to her left.

They met at the courtyard's center and Dawes held up her hand for them to stop. But they didn't grasp the basin. Instead Darlington nodded at Mercy and she came forward, holding up a slender silver spindle. Pierre the Weaver. She pricked her finger on the tip, like a girl in a fairy tale, ready to fall into a hundred years of dreaming. Instead the silver cracked, revealing a sticky white mass inside. An egg sac.

"Have I ever mentioned how much I hate spiders?" Turner asked.

A slender leg poked through the cocoon of webbing, then another, so tiny they almost looked like hairs. Alex heard a soft snuffling sound, and then Mercy gasped as the egg sac gave way, a wave of tiny baby spiders cascading over her hands. She shrieked and dropped the spindle.

"Get in there," Darlington said, crouching down. He sounded calm, but it took all of Alex's will to stay still as the spiders flowed over the ground like a spreading stain. Darlington placed his palm on the paving stone and let them course over his fingers. "Let them bite you."

Turner cast his eyes skyward and muttered something under his breath. He dropped into a crouch and dipped his hand in, Dawes followed, and Alex forced herself do the same.

She wanted to scream at the feel of all those slender legs whispering over her skin. The bites didn't hurt, but she could see her skin swelling in places.

Thankfully the spiders moved on quickly, pouring up the trunks of the trees, casting silk strands into the air, letting them catch on the wind.

The previous night they'd all taken turns weaving with the spindle, the skein of spider silk falling in a lumpen mass. It wasn't beautiful, but it was the act of the weave that mattered, pouring their focus into it, a single phrase again and again: *Make a trap. Make a trap of sorrow.* In the past, the spindle had been used to create charisma and love spells to bind groups together, to make them loyal, to steal their will. This was a different kind of bond.

High above them, the spiders had begun to weave, seemingly in rhythm with the metronome. It was like watching mist form, a soft, soundless blur spreading from the gutters and corners atop the roof, until they stood beneath a wide canopy of spider silk, the web like spangled frost, turning the night sky into a kind of mosaic. Alex could feel sadness radiating from it, as if the strands were weighted with it, making the web bow at the center. A sense of hopelessness filled her.

"Just ride it out," said Turner. But he had his hands pressed to the sides of his head, as if he could squeeze the misery out of it.

Somewhere in the library, Alex heard glass breaking. Mercy drew her salt sword.

"They're coming," said Dawes. "They wouldn't—"

She was interrupted by the sound of breaking glass.

"No!" Dawes cried.

"The stained glass—" said Darlington.

But the demons didn't care. They'd been drawn by a beacon of utter hopelessness, and their only thought was to feed.

"Hands on the basin!" Alex yelled. "On three!"

Alex saw the demons racing toward them. There would be no time for last words or fond goodbyes. She counted down fast.

As one, they seized the edges of the fountain.

43

Alex had tried to prepare herself for the fall—the fingers clawing at her, choking her, dragging her down—but this time, she splashed backward into water. The sea was warm around her, and when the reaching hands never came, she made herself open her eyes. She saw bubbles rushing past, and saw the others—Darlington's dark coat behind him, Turner with his arms tight to his body, Dawes's red hair like a banner of war.

She glimpsed light ahead and tried to kick toward it, felt herself rising. Her head broke the surface and she gasped for air. The sky above was flat and bright, that murky shade of nothing. Ahead, she saw a swath of what might have been a beach. Behind her, a wall of dark clouds blanketed the horizon.

Where were the others? The sea was almost unpleasantly hot, and the water smelled wrong, metallic. She was afraid to put her head back under. She didn't want to see something with scales and snapping jaws undulating toward her.

She swam for shore, her limbs moving gracelessly. She'd never been a strong swimmer, but the current was nudging her toward land. It was only when her feet touched bottom, when she was able to stand, that she really looked at the water. It had left her skin stained red. She'd been swimming in a sea of blood.

Alex's stomach seized. She bent double and retched. How much of it had she swallowed?

But when she looked down, the blood was gone and her clothes were dry. She turned back to look at the horizon and the sea was gone too. She was standing on the sidewalk outside of her old apartment building. Ground Zero. She had plastic grocery bags in her hands.

Alex felt that horrible sense of vertigo, real life sliding away, coming apart like a dream—Darlington, Dawes, all of it. Just a day-dream. Her mind had been wandering, spinning out stories, but already the details were fading. *This* was real life. The pebbled texture of the stairs. The thump of bass coming from someone's apartment, the crash and gunfire of *Halo* from their own place.

Alex didn't want to go home. She never wanted to go home. She liked to linger at the supermarket, sailing down the clean aisles on one of the big carts, even though she never filled it, listening to whatever awful music they were playing, skin pimpling in the air-conditioning. But inevitably, she had to go back out into the parking lot, heat steaming up off the asphalt, and wriggle into the cramped little Civic if she was lucky—if Len wanted to be an asshole about it that day, she'd have to go wait for the bus.

Now she climbed the steps with her bags of Doritos and lunch meat and the big boxes of cereal she had found on sale, and pushed open the front door. It was better when Hellie came with her, but Hellie had been in a mood today, tired and cranky, giving Alex one-word answers, her head someplace else.

Someplace better. Hellie came from a different life from the rest of them. Real parents. Real schools. A real house with a backyard and a pool. Hellie was vacationing here. She'd gotten on the wrong train, ended up on a terrible field trip, and she was making the best of it. But Alex understood that, one day, she would wake up and Hellie would be gone. She'd be done. Alex even wished it for Hellie on her more generous days. But it wasn't easy to know that maybe Hellie thought she was too good for the flimsy balsa-wood life Alex had managed to stick together. Shelter, food, weed, friends who didn't always feel like friends. It was the best she could do, but that wasn't true for Hellie.

Alex bumped her hip through the door and entered the apart-ment, the smell of pot heavy, the air hazy with smoke. The noise

from the TV was overwhelming, the ceaseless pound of *Halo*, Len
and Betcha and Cam shouting at each other on the couch, Betcha's
pit bull, Loki, asleep at his feet. A bag of Cheetos was open on the table beside a blue glass bong, an empty baggie, Len's vape pen. Hellie
was curled in the big papasan chair with the taped-together cushion,
wearing a long T-shirt and underwear, as if she hadn't bothered to
get dressed, just rolled right out of bed. She was staring at the TV
listlessly and didn't even glance at Alex when she started unloading
groceries in their tiny kitchen.

Alex was unpacking a jar of Ragú when she saw the bloody mass
of fur near the sliding glass doors that led to the balcony. The jar slid
from her hand and shattered on the linoleum.

"The fuck is wrong with you?" Len said over the noise from the
game.

This couldn't be right. She was seeing things. She was misunderstanding.

Alex knew she should get down the hall and check the cage, but
she couldn't quite make her legs work. There was a piece of glass
lodged in the side of her foot, tomato sauce on her flip-flops. She
slipped them off, brushed the glass away, made herself take one step,
then another, felt the wiry spring of the carpet beneath her feet. No
one's head turned as she passed, and she had the eerie sense that she
hadn't walked into the apartment at all.

The hallway was quiet. They'd never hung art or photos on the
walls, except for a Green Day poster they'd taped up after someone
put a fist through the drywall during a party.

Their bedroom looked the way it always did. The battered old
TV stand she'd stuffed with paperbacks, mostly sci-fi and fantasy.
Anne McCaffrey, Heinlein, Asimov. The futon mattress on the floor,
the old blue-and-red bedspread crumpled up. Sometimes it was her
and Len in the bed, sometimes all three of them, sometimes just
her and Hellie. Those were the best times. And by the windowsill,
Babbit's cage. It was empty. The door was open.

Alex stood with her back pressed against the wall. It felt like she
had cracked down the middle. She and Hellie had gotten the little

flop-eared bunny at a pet adoption outside of Ralphs. They'd lied on the application, about where they lived, how much money they made, everything. Because once Alex held that soft white body in her hands, she'd wanted it more than anything. When they'd brought him home, Len had just rolled his eyes and said, "I don't want to smell that thing. I don't like living in shit."

Alex had been tempted to say she had bad news for him, but she was so grateful he hadn't gone into some kind of tantrum, she and Hellie just scurried down the hall and shut the door. They'd spent the whole day playing with the rabbit. It didn't do much, but there was something about being near it, about feeling its heart rate slow in her hands, knowing that this living thing trusted her, that made Alex feel better about everything.

They'd started calling him Babbit Rabbit because they didn't have a name for him, and then it just stuck.

"That thing looks like bait," Betcha had laughed once.

"Cheapest way to keep a bitch happy," Len had replied. He got annoyed when they talked about Babbit Rabbit or crooned at him. "Better than getting one of them knocked up."

Bait.

Alex walked back down the hall. Nothing had changed. No one had moved. She had become a phantom. The heap of fur and blood lay unmoving on the carpet. It was unmistakable now that she made herself look, really look. A little dead body. There was blood on Loki's muzzle.

"What happened?" she asked.

No one seemed to hear her.

"Hellie?"

Hellie turned her head slowly, as if the effort cost her something. She lifted her golden shoulders. Always she looked like a sunburnished bit of treasure, something precious. Even now, slack and dead-eyed, her voice flat when she said, "We wanted to see if he and Loki would play."

Alex knelt by the little body. He had been torn open, and there was almost nothing left inside him. His fur was still soft in the places it wasn't sticky with blood. Alex had loved to stroke his ears with her thumb. They were mangled now, the cartilage exposed in stringy lines. His one remaining pink eye stared at nothing.

"Don't be shitty about it," Len said. "It was an accident."

Betcha looked guilty and said, "We didn't think Loki would get so excited."

"He's a dog," Alex said. "What the fuck did you think he was going to do?"

"He couldn't help it."

"I know," said Alex. "I know he couldn't."

She didn't blame Loki.

Alex scooped up Babbit Rabbit's remains and went to the kitchen. She cleaned off her flip-flops and shoveled the sauce and glass into a corner.

"Oh, come on," said Len. "Rabbits are basically vermin. You're crying over a rat."

But Alex wasn't crying. Not yet. She didn't want to cry here. She took Len's keys off the counter without asking. She could pay that tab later.

She tucked what was left of the rabbit's body into a Ziploc bag and went out to the Civic. She hoped Hellie would follow. All the way down the steps, across the patch of dry lawn, the sidewalk, the street, she hoped. She sat in the driver's seat a long time, still hoping.

Then, at last, she turned the key and drove. She took the 405 through the valley, past the Galleria and Castle Park with its batting cages, climbing the hill. That was what they'd always called it, "the hill." Alex didn't even know the name of the mountain range she was crossing, only that it was the great divider between the San Fernando Valley and the west side. You could stand on Mulholland and look west to the dream of the ocean, museums, mansions. Or east to the valley and the consolation prize of smoggy days and cheap condos. The California dream for people who couldn't afford Beverly Hills or Bel Air or Malibu.

She got off at Skirball and took the winding road up to the crest of Mulholland Drive. She didn't really know where she was going. She just wanted to be up somewhere high.

It wasn't until she was parked in a big lot next to a church, gazing down at the hazy basin of the city with that little plastic-wrapped body in her hands, that she cried, big bawling sobs that no one but the oaks and the greasewood bushes could hear. She wasn't going to bury Babbit Rabbit here. She was afraid some coyote would dig him up and have a last go at him. But she'd needed to be someplace beautiful, someplace clean, where there was no history for her to stumble over.

Alex couldn't name what she felt. She only knew she never should have brought Babbit Rabbit home. When Hellie pointed him out in the cages, she never should have picked him up, never should have held his small body against her heart. He should have belonged to some kid who lived in Encino, who would have given him a real name and brought him to class for show-and-tell, who would have kept him safe. Alex had stolen from her mother. She'd lied and cheated and broken a lot of laws. But she knew that bringing Babbit Rabbit home was the worst, most selfish thing she'd ever done. Nothing good belonged with her.

She watched the sun set and the lights spread across the valley.

"You could go anywhere," she said to the night air. But she wouldn't. She never did.

She wiped her eyes and crossed the road and buried Babbit Rabbit in the pretty landscaped yard beside the gate that belonged to some private school. She shook him out of his plastic bag so that his body could decompose and feed the roots of the eugenia hedges.

Alex thought about lying down in the middle of Mulholland, right across the white dashes that split the road like a spine. She thought about some mother driving home with her kids in the back of the car, what she would see in her headlights in the moment before impact. She found herself floating, up over the pavement, the empty grid of the parking lot, the Civic idling with its driver's-side door still open. She was drifting over the chaparral, the white sage and ancient oaks, over the houses built into the mountain, fearless on their stilts, their swimming pools glowing in the dusk, then higher still as the lights grew smaller, a garden of bright flowers, laid out neatly in their beds.

How long did she remain there, untethered and safe from feeling? At some point, the sun began to rise, blotting out the stars in a wash of pink light. But the city below was not one she knew, not one she understood. She smelled autumn leaves and rain, the mineral smudge of wet concrete. She saw a wide-open park, paths crossing it in star-shaped patterns, three churches, their spires like lightning rods in search of a storm. The grass was green, the sky gray and gentle with clouds; the leaves rustled red and gold in their branches.

A breeze sighed through the trees, carrying the scent of apples and fresh bread, of any good thing you could want. Every surface, every stone, seemed to gleam with soft light.

She saw figures approaching from the corners of the park—no, the green. She did know this place. Was she dreaming again, or had she woken? She knew those people, found their names in her memories. Dawes, Turner, Darlington. Tripp hadn't made it. That was her fault. She remembered that too.

As they drew closer, Alex could see something had changed in their pilgrim raiment. Dawes still wore the scholar's robes, but now they gleamed golden like the loris's eyes. Turner's cloak of feathers was woven with coppery oak leaves. The prince's white armor suited Darlington better than it had Tripp, but now he wore a horned helm. And Alex? She held out her arms. Her steel bracers were emblazoned with snakes.

She knew where they were meant to go. Back to the orchard. Back to the library.

Slowly, they made their way down the street that would have been Elm, past Hopper and Berkeley. There was no sense of the sinister now, no Yale scraped clean of beauty. Instead it was as if the university had been rendered by some hack painter, a scene from a snow globe, a dream of a college. She could see people eating and chatting and laughing in the amber warmth behind the thick leaded windows of the dining halls. She knew that, should she choose to enter, she would be made welcome.

The library didn't look like a library anymore, or a cathedral, or an orchard. It rose in gleaming silver spires, an impossible castle, a palace of air and light. She met Darlington's eyes. These were the places they'd been promised. The university of peace and plenty. The magic of fairy tales that demanded only wishes, not blood or sacrifice. The Women's Table shone bright as a mirror, and Alex saw Mercy in it, pacing back and forth.

"Are we . . . are we in heaven?" Dawes whispered.

Turner shook his head. "No heaven I know about."

"Don't forget," warned Darlington. "Demons feed on joy, right alongside pain and sorrow."

The doors to the palace opened and a creature emerged. It had to be eight feet tall, and it had the head of a white rabbit but the body of a man. Between its ears, a crown of fire blazed red. It was as naked as Darlington had been in the golden circle, but the symbols on its body glowed ruddy like banked embers.

"Anselm," Alex said.

The rabbit laughed. "Call me by my true name, Wheelwalker."

"Asshole?" Alex ventured.

The creature shifted, and he was Anselm again, human in appearance, clothed. He wasn't in a suit this time but his casual weekend best—jeans, a cashmere sweater, an expensive watch on his wrist, a picture of effortless wealth. Darlington without Black Elm. Darlington without a soul.

"I liked watching Darlington kill you."

Anselm grinned. "That was a mortal body. Weak and impermanent. I cannot be killed because I do not live. But I will."

Alex saw there was a leash in his hands, and when he tugged on it, three creatures crawled forward on hands and knees. Their pale bodies were emaciated, a clattering of bones barely held together by sinew. Alex couldn't quite tell if they were human, and then the wretched details locked into place—one older, flesh sagging, hair cut in a gray crew cut; one young and frail, his curls patchy in places, his gaunt features haunted by the memory of beauty; and one woman, breasts shrunken, sores around her mouth, her yellow hair matted and clumped.

Carmichael, Blake, and Hellie. Around their throats they each wore a golden yoke like the one that had circled Darlington's neck, each attached to a golden chain held by Anselm.

How harmless they looked, how frightened, but they were demons just the same.

"Such sorry hounds," Anselm said. "They will starve until they feed on the suffering of the dead. Or until they pass back through the portal to pursue you once more. Then they will eat until they are full and feed upon your friends and companions. This is the demon's dream. A land of plenty. I would be glad to grant it to them." He paused and smiled, the expression tender, beatific, Jesus on a birthday card. "Unless hell's price is paid. Daniel Arlington's soul was rightfully claimed by this place. He is one of us and must serve his eternity here."

"I'm willing," said Darlington.

"For fuck's sake, at least try to negotiate," said Turner.

"There's nothing to negotiate," said Dawes. "He doesn't belong here."

Anselm dipped his head in agreement. "That's true. He stinks of goodness. But not all of you do."

"You don't need to be cute about it," said Alex. "They all know you mean me."

Anselm's teeth were white and even. "You've heard their hearts. You've seen through their eyes. They're all riddled with guilt and shame, but not you, Wheelwalker. Your only regret is for the girl you couldn't save, not for the men you murdered. You have more remorse in your heart for a dead rabbit than for all those boys you beat into nothing."

It was true. Alex had known that from the start. She'd said as much to Mercy the night before.

"No," said Dawes. She cut her hand through the air. "No to all of it. You can't have Alex. Or Darlington. No one stays."

None go free. Alex felt an ache in her throat. Courageous Dawes, who only wanted her family whole. And Alex was glad to be part of that family. Even if it couldn't last.

"You've been brave enough," Alex said. "This isn't your battle to fight."

"You don't belong here either. No matter what that . . . that thing says."

"You're so very certain, scholar," Anselm said. "But the Gauntlet was built to bring her here, a bloody beacon, a signal fire."

Alex kept her face impassive, but risked a glance at Mercy in the reflection. What was Anselm talking about? Some new trick to delay them, some new strategy?

"You fought to keep me out of hell," Alex said. "All of us." He had done everything he could to prevent them from discovering the Gauntlet and rescuing Darlington.

"I didn't understand what you were, Wheelwalker. Oh, I understood your appeal. An interesting plaything, a collection of parlor tricks, an infinite capacity for pain. But I didn't see the truth of you. I couldn't understand how you escaped my wolves. Not until you took his soul into your body."

"He's lying," said Dawes.

Turner shook his head. He could always tell the difference, even in the underworld. "He isn't."

"You know you aren't the first pilgrims to walk this path," said Anselm.

That was when Alex understood why the Gauntlet and those who had dared walk it had been scrubbed from the books, why they'd made sure no one knew about the extraordinary gateway built into the library's walls. For the first time since Darlington had returned, Alex felt real fear creeping in.

"They made a deal, didn't they?" she asked.

Anselm winked. "The only thing a demon loves more than a puzzle is a bargain."

44

Anselm's pets mewled as if sensing his pleasure. The thing with Blake's haggard face pressed its head against his leg.

"What is this?" Turner demanded.

Anselm let his fingers trail through Not Blake's hair. "The men of Yale built a Gauntlet and called their journey one of exploration. But exploration is just another word for conquest, and like all adventurers, once they had seen the riches they could attain, they had no reason to return empty-handed."

"It's Faust all over again," said Darlington.

Anselm hummed. "Except Faust paid for his sins himself. Not so your pilgrims. They claimed money, fame, talent, influence. For themselves and for their societies. They just left someone else to pick up the bill."

Skull and Bones. Book and Snake. Scroll and Key. Alex thought of all the money that had flowed through their coffers. The gifts given to the university. All bought at the expense of a future generation's suffering. And Lethe had allowed it. They could have investigated the provenance of the table tucked away in the Peabody basement. They could have at least lobbied to shut down Manuscript after what happened to Mercy, or gone after Scroll and Key after what happened to Tara. But they didn't. It was too important to keep the alumni appeased, to keep the magic alive no matter who got caught in its workings.

"Oh God," said Dawes. "That was why they erased the journey. To hide the deal they'd made."

"The Gauntlet wasn't a game," said Darlington. "It wasn't an experiment. It was an offering."

"A very fine one," said Anselm. "They walked away with wealth and power, stores of ancient knowledge and good fortune, and they left the Gauntlet in place, marked with their blood, a beacon."

"The Tower," Dawes whispered.

"A beacon for what?" asked Turner, his face grim.

"For a Wheelwalker," Darlington said quietly.

"I didn't really understand what you were, Galaxy Stern. Not until you passed through the circle of protection at Black Elm. Not until you stole what was rightfully ours. We had no idea the wait would be so long for one of your kind."

Now Alex laughed, a joyless sound. "Daisy got in your way."

Daisy Whitlock was a Wheelwalker, and she'd stayed alive, disguised as Professor Marguerite Belbalm, by eating the souls of young women. Her preferred prey was her own kind: Wheelwalkers like herself, inexplicably drawn to New Haven. Drawn to the Gauntlet.

"It didn't matter that you'd built your beacon," Alex said. "Because every time a Wheelwalker showed up, Daisy ate her."

"But not you, Galaxy Stern. You survived and you came to us, as you were always meant to. It is *your* presence in hell that will keep the door open, and you will remain here. One killer is owed to us. Hell's price must be paid."

"No," said Darlington. "It's my sentence to serve."

"It has to be Darlington," said Turner. "I didn't come here to make a deal with the devil, but if Alex stays, he said the door to hell remains open. That means demons coming and going, feeding on the living instead of the dead. We aren't letting that happen."

Anselm was still smiling.

"Stay," he said to Alex. "Stay and your demon consort returns to the mortal realm untainted. Stay and your friends go free. Your mother will be protected by the very armies of hell." He turned to the others. "Do you understand what I can do? What a demon's favor means? All you want will be yours. All you've lost will be restored."

Alex swallowed a wave of nausea as her vision shifted. She was sitting at the head of the table at a dinner party, candlelight gleaming off the dishes, the music of a cello playing softly beneath murmured conversation. The man at the end of the table lifted his glass. His eyes shone. "To the professor." It took her a second to understand it was Darlington seated there.

"To tenure," said the woman to her right, and everyone laughed. Alex. Older now, maybe wiser. She was smiling.

Pam turned and saw her face in the mirror. She was herself but not herself, confident and relaxed, red hair loose down her back. Everything was easy now. Getting up in the morning, showering, choosing what to wear, what to tackle next. She moved through the world with grace. She had cooked this meal for her guests. She had published. She could teach. Every day would be like this one, a series of tasks accomplished instead of an endless loop of indecision. The possibilities had been ruthlessly pruned, leaving a single, obvious path to follow.

She drank deep from her glass. *All is well.*

"You did good," said Esau.

Turner threw an arm around his brother. "*We* did good. And we're going to do more."

They were standing in Jocelyn Square Park, gazing out at a cheering crowd—cheering for him, for the jobs he'd brought to their city, for the possibility of a different future.

He lifted his arm above his head, pumped his fist. His mother was weeping with joy. His father was alive beside her. His people were around him. He wasn't the hall monitor anymore. He was a hero, a king, a damn senator. He was allowed to love them and be loved by them in return. His wife stood to his left, her smile radiant. She caught his eye, and the look they shared said it all. Better than anyone she knew how hard he had worked, how much they'd sacrificed to get to this moment.

There were no mysteries anymore, no monsters but the ones you had to have lunch with in DC. He would take a little rest. They would go down to Miami, or they'd treat themselves to a trip to the Caribbean. He would make up for every moment he'd been absent or distracted in pursuit of this goal.

"We did it," she whispered in his ear.

He drew her close. *All is well.*

Darlington sat in his office at Black Elm, looking out at the bor-ders lush with flowers, the neatly trimmed hedge maze. As always, the house was full of people, friends who had come to visit, scholars staying to make use of his extensive library or give seminars. He heard laughter floating through the halls, lively conversation from somewhere in the kitchen.

He knew everything he wished to know. He need only touch his hand to a book and he grasped its contents. He could pick up a teacup and know the history of anyone who had ever held it. He visited travelers and mystics on their deathbeds, held their hands, eased their pain. He saw the scope of their lives, absorbed their knowledge through his touch. The mysteries of this world and the next had been revealed to him. Not because he'd undergone some ritual, not even through rigorous study of the arcane, but because magic was in his blood. He'd almost given up hope, abandoned childish wishes. But it had been there all along, a secret power, just waiting to awaken.

He saw Alex in the garden, a black-winged bird, night gathered around her like a silken shroud shot through with stars. His monstrous queen. His gentle ruler. He knew what she was now too.

He returned to his writings.

All is well.

Alex stood outside of a freshly painted bungalow—white adobe, trimmed in blue. Wind chimes hung from the porch. A stone Buddha held court in the garden, lush with lavender and sage. Her mother sat sipping tea on a daybed heaped with colorful cushions. This was her house—a real house, not a lonely apartment with a balcony that faced the wall of another lonely apartment. Mira rose and stretched and went inside, leaving the door open behind her. Alex drifted after her.

The house was tidy, cozy; crystals crowded the fireplace mantel. Her mother rinsed her cup in the sink. A knock sounded. A blond woman stood at the door, a rolled yoga mat slung over her shoulder. She looked familiar, but Alex wasn't sure how.

"Ready?" the woman asked.

"Just about," Mira said.

They couldn't see her.

"Do you mind if my daughter joins us? She's home from school."

Hellie stood behind the woman in the door. But not a Hellie Alex had ever known. She looked brave, utterly confident, her arms lean and muscled, her bright hair in a neat ponytail.

"This place is so cute," she said with a smile.

Alex watched as Hellie and her mother idled in the living room, waiting for Mira to change and get her mat.

"That's her daughter," Hellie's mother said, gesturing to the photograph Hellie was peering at. A photo of Alex in a denim jacket, leaning against their old Corolla, barely smiling.

"She's pretty," Hellie said.

"She wasn't a very happy girl. She passed a few years back. Only seventeen. A drug overdose."

She passed.

Incense had been set before the photo, a white feather tipped in black. Another photo stood in a frame tucked behind the picture of Alex. A young man with curly black hair that tumbled over his tan face. He was standing on the beach, arm around the surfboard propped beside him. There was a pendant around his neck, but Alex couldn't make out what it was.

"That's so sad," Hellie said. She'd moved on to a deck of cards set out on the coffee table. "Ooh, does Mira read tarot?"

She plucked a card off the top deck and held it up. The Wheel.

For the first time, Alex felt something other than love and regret well up in her at the sight of Hellie, perfect Hellie with her ocean eyes.

"You shouldn't have let them kill Babbit Rabbit," she said. "I wouldn't have let him die."

Alex watched the Wheel spin, alight with blue fire that consumed first the card, then Hellie's hand, then Hellie, her mother, the room, the house. The world swallowed by blue flame. *All is well.*

She was standing on the steps of Sterling, surrounded by fire, and the others were looking at her with pity in their eyes. Alex wiped her tears away, her gut twisting with shame. She'd felt no sorrow at her own death, only relief to see the world wiped clean. She knew her mother had wept over her, but how many more tears had she wasted on a living girl?

And Hellie? Well, that was the worst of it. If Alex hadn't been with Len that day on the Venice boardwalk, maybe Hellie never would have gone home with them. Maybe she wouldn't have stayed as long. She would have made the trip back from hell and returned to the world of softball games and college transcripts and yoga on Saturday morning. She never would have died.

"I'm going to make this easy for you," Anselm said gently. "Take your place here, Galaxy Stern. Live in splendor and comfort, never want for anything, and see all the damage you've done in the world erased. Everyone gets what they want. All will be well."

What would it mean to become a ghost?

Darlington grabbed her arm. "It isn't real. It's just another kind of torture, living with something that isn't real."

He wasn't wrong. She'd known Len's love wasn't real. She'd known her mother's protection wasn't real. That knowledge ate at you every day. You lived on a tightrope, waiting for the moment the rope would vanish. It was its own kind of hell.

"I can make it easier still," said Anselm. "Stay or your lovely friend dies."

In the shimmer of the fountain that would have been the Women's Table, Alex caught a flicker of movement.

She recognized the man approaching Mercy in the courtyard. Eitan Harel.

As if from a great distance, she heard him ask, "Where is that bitch? You think this is a joke?"

He'd found her.

"He's going to hurt her," Anselm said. "You know that. But you can stop it. Wouldn't you like to save her? Or will she be one more girl you failed? One more life taken because you're so determined to survive?"

Another Hellie. Another Tripp.

Alex met Dawes's eyes and said, "Find a way to shut the door behind me. I know you can."

Turner stepped in front of her. "I can't let you do that. I'm not unleashing a tide of demons to feed on our misery. I'll kill you before I let you doom our world for the sake of one girl."

He wasn't much of an actor, but he didn't have to be.

"Stand down, priest," Anselm said with a laugh. "The Wheel-walker has my protection. You have no authority here."

Darlington gripped Alex's arm. "This was your plan? To give yourself up? This isn't meant to be your sacrifice, Stern."

Alex almost smiled. "I'm not sure that's true." Her life had been built on lies and stolen chances, a series of tricks, and evasions, and sleight of hand. She already knew the language of demons. She'd been speaking it her whole life. A little magic. The stones to take a beating.

"Come forward and meet the punishment you deserve," Anselm said. He held up the yoke. It was different from the one Darlington had been forced to wear, inlaid with garnets and black onyx. It was beautiful, but there was no mistaking what it meant.

"Alex," Darlington said. "I won't let you do this."

She let fire bloom over her body and Darlington yanked his hand back, his horns emerging. "It's not your call to make."

"I liked our game," Anselm crooned. "There are so many more to come."

But Alex was only half-listening. She was watching the reflection in the mirrored fountain. Tzvi stood behind Eitan. He had taken Mercy's salt sword. Eitan had a gun in his hands.

And Mercy had a bottle in hers. Datura. She hurled it at Eitan. The bottle of oil smashed against him, and before he could recover, Mercy shoved him toward the basin.

Alex seized the yoke from Anselm and leapt toward the water, jamming her other hand beneath the surface.

She heard shouting around her. Anselm was lunging at her and he wasn't in his human form anymore. She didn't know what he was—a goat with spiked horns, a red-eyed rabbit, a hairy-legged spider. He was every horror all at once. But Dawes and Darlington and Turner had arrayed themselves around her.

"Protect her," Turner shouted. "No one gets through!" His feathered cape looked less like a costume than actual wings, spreading wide. Dawes had raised her hands and words had appeared on her scholar's robe—symbols, scrawl, a thousand languages, maybe every language ever known. Darlington's horns glowed golden and he drew his sword. They had enacted their little play for Anselm's benefit and now they were ready to defend.

She had baited Eitan, telling him she was going to work for Linus Reiter, that she knew his secrets, that she would share every one in return for the vampire's protection. She'd had Turner call him up with all of the authority of the NHPD to question Eitan's connection to her, to make it clear she was talking, becoming a liability. Alex knew Eitan would move to deal with her himself. After all, he knew exactly how to locate her. She'd realized that when he'd sidled up to her outside of Blue State Coffee. She'd made sure her phone was on and left it with Mercy in the courtyard so that he could find her tonight.

Now she could feel his soul fighting her, slippery and screaming, scared for the first time in a long time, struggling to remain in the mortal realm. She thought of Babbit Rabbit's heart pounding against her palm.

She pulled his spirit to her, just as she drew Grays, just as she had drawn Darlington's soul to her to bring him home. He fought, but

Alex had hold of him. Eitan's spirit rushed into her. She saw a city of skyscrapers and sun-bleached stone, tasted bitter coffee on her tongue, heard the roar of the 405 in the valley below.

She spat him out.

"You want a murderer?" Alex said as Eitan emerged, gasping, his clothes wet, his body ablaze with her blue flame. "Here."

"It's not for you to decide who breaches the doors of hell," Anselm sneered. "You cannot—"

"I'm the Wheelwalker," Alex said. "You have no idea what I can do."

"What is this?" sputtered Eitan. The Chai around his neck disintegrated to ash.

Alex yanked the golden yoke over his head and watched the jeweled clasps fasten. The emaciated demons leashed to Anselm shrieked and whimpered.

"Heretic!" Anselm seethed. "Whore!"

Now Alex laughed. "I've been called worse in line at Rite Aid."

Anselm had dealt too long with the genteel, blundering boys of Yale. He didn't know how to recognize one of his own kind.

"Go!" Alex shouted, keeping her hand in the water. One after another they leapt into the fountain, passing through her to the mortal realm—Dawes, Turner, Darlington last. She was the Wheelwalker, the conduit. She felt them all, bright, terrified, furious, alive. Dawes like the cool, dark hallways of a library; Turner, sharp and glittering as a city at night; Darlington, gleaming and triumphant, ringing with the sound of steel on steel.

"What is this?" cried Eitan. "You try to fuck with—"

"You get to take your own beatings now," Alex said. "Hell's price must be paid."

She leapt into the water. But Anselm seized her arm.

"You are destined for hell, Galaxy Stern. You are destined for me." He bit down on her wrist, and Alex screamed as pain lanced through her.

Blue flame erupted over her, over him. But he didn't burn.

You are destined for hell.

He was drinking from her in great gulps, his cheeks hollowing with every draw. She could *feel* her blood being pulled out of her, feel her strength lagging.

You are destined for me.

"Okay," she gasped. "Then come with me." She tightened her own grip on his arm. "Let's see how you fare against us in the mortal realm."

She reached out to him with her power, drawing his spirit into her. It was like sludge, a river of misery oozing into her, a profound agony coupled with obscene pleasure, but she didn't stop.

Alex saw fear in his eyes and it was like a drug to her. "All is well."

Anselm released her wrist with a furious roar. She could see her blood coating his chin. Alex thrust the dreck of his spirit out of her and plunged into the water, terrified that at any minute she would feel his grip on her ankle, dragging her back.

Her lungs ached for air, but she kept kicking, kept swimming, desperate to see light ahead. There—a spark, then another. She was soaring upward through a sea of stars. She burst through the surface and breathed in the cold air of a winter night.

Alex tried to get her bearings. They were in the courtyard at Sterling. Tzvi was gone—probably chased away by the sight of Darlington in full-horned demon glory—and Eitan's body lay facedown in the mud. She heard the ticking of the metronome come to an abrupt stop.

Something was blurring her vision—flurries of white. It had started to snow. She counted her friends—Mercy, Turner, Dawes, and Darlington, her gentleman demon. Their ramshackle army, all of them soaked and shivering, all of them safe and whole. Above them the Weaver's web glimmered still, fragile in its architecture, weighted with frost and sorrow.

Dunbar dragged a tramp in from the railway station last night, sooty as a coal can and dressed in clothes so dirty they could stand on their own. Claimed he had the Sight. Rudy said it was a waste of time and I was inclined to agree. The man stank of cheap gin and had all the markings of a charlatan. He babbled on about long journeys and great wealth, the fortune-teller's usual stock in trade. His speech was so slurred I could barely make his words out, until at last Dunbar got bored and put us out of our misery.

I wouldn't even remark on the whole sorry business, only—and I put this down so that I may laugh at my own milk-livered hand-wringing later—when Dunbar told him it was time to go and slipped a fiver in his pocket, the tramp claimed he'd not yet said what needed saying. His eyes rolled back a bit—base theatrics—and then he said, "Beware."

Rudy laughs and asks, quite naturally, "Beware of what, you old fraud?"

"Them that walks among us. Nightdrinkers, moonspeakers, alls them that dwell in the dead and empty. Best watch for them, lads. Best bar the doors against them when they come." He wasn't slurring then. His voice was clear as a bell and it boomed through the hall. Raised the hair on my arms, I'll tell you.

Well, Rudy and Dunbar were done with it. They hauled him outside, and sent him packing, and Rudy gave him a kick for good measure. I felt badly about it and thought I should slip him another fiver. No doubt we'll laugh about all of it tomorrow.

—*Lionel Reiter, Skull and Bones*
Commonplace Book, 1933

45

Darlington couldn't quite put together the moments after the descent. He remembered snow falling, the dreary weight of his sodden clothes on his body. They were all tired and shaken, but they couldn't simply drag themselves home. There was too much evidence to dispose of. When he'd stepped into the mouth of the hellbeast, he'd been a man who followed rules, who believed he understood his world and its workings. But as he was not quite human any longer, he supposed a more flexible approach to morality was called for.

There were books scattered around the Linonia and Brothers Room. One of the tables had been knocked over. The demons had crashed through the eastern-facing windows, destroying an image of St. Mark at work on his gospels in the process, then smashed straight through the windows leading to the courtyard. There was nothing to be done about the damage. There was restoration magic they could use, but all of it was long and painstaking. It hurt Darlington to leave Sterling in such a state, but when the university reported the vandalism, Lethe could offer use of the crucible and whatever else they could find in the armory. For now, they just had to remove any sign of the uncanny.

It was easy enough to return the spiders to the spindle with another prick of Mercy's finger, but the web above the courtyard still hung thick with melancholy. It took them the better part of an hour to pull it down with a broom they borrowed from the janitor's closet, and transfer it into the waters of the basin, where they watched it dissolve. They were all weeping uncontrollably by the time they were rid of the damned thing.

They had left the body for last. Eitan Harel lay facedown in the mud and melting snow.

Turner retrieved his Dodge and waited for them by the York Street entrance. The tempest Dawes had brewed was still hot enough to manage the cameras, but there was nothing magical or arcane about the act of putting a corpse in a trunk. It was a cold act, ugly in its transformation: the body made cargo. Mercy hung back, clutching her salt sword, as if it might ward against the truth of what they'd done.

"You said you weren't going to help clean up our messes," Alex noted when the work was finished, and they piled into the Dodge, damp and weary, dawn still hours away.

Turner only shrugged and gunned the engine. "This is my mess too."

The door to Il Bastone sprang open before they reached the top of the steps. The lights were on, the old radiators pumping heat through every room. In the kitchen, Dawes had lined up thermoses of leftover avgolemono that they drank in greedy swallows. There were plates of tomato sandwiches and hot tea spiked with brandy.

They stood at the kitchen counter, eating in silence, too tired and battered to talk. Darlington couldn't help but think of how rarely the dining room at Il Bastone had been used, of how few meals he'd shared with Michelle Alameddine or Dean Sandow, of how few conversations he'd had with Detective Abel Turner. They'd let Lethe atrophy, let its secrecy and ritual make them strangers to each other. Or maybe that was the way Lethe had always been intended to function, toothless and powerless, bumbling along with a sense of their own importance, a sop to the university while the societies did as they pleased.

At last, Mercy set her mug down and said, "Is it done?"

The girl was brave, but tonight had been too much for her. The magic, the spells, the strange objects had all been a kind of play. Now she had helped to kill a man, and the weight of that was no easy thing to carry, no matter the justification. Darlington knew that well.

Alex had warned them that there would be a moment when she needed their defense, when she would ask them to fight for her without question. They'd done it—because they were desperate, and because for all their noble protestations, none of them wanted to suffer for eternity. Mercy had been eager to go along with the plan, to wear her salt armor, to face a very human monster. Maybe she regretted that now.

But this was not the time to be gentle.

"It's not over," he said. "There are more demons left to kill."

Maybe there always would be.

Alex was weak from all the blood she'd lost, so Dawes applied balm to the wound Anselm had left at her wrist, then took her upstairs to drop her into a bath of goat milk in the crucible. They had a kind of easy routine of caretaking that Darlington didn't quite understand and that made him feel like a child left out of a game. So he would make himself useful instead.

He went with Turner back to Black Elm.

"I can't believe I'm a wheelman for a demon," Turner muttered as he pulled out of the Il Bastone lot.

"Part demon," Darlington corrected. They drove without talking for a while, but eventually he asked, "How did Alex get you to go along with this anyway?"

"She came to see me last night," said Turner. "I didn't want to do it. She was asking me to use my badge to set up a murder. Then I took a look at Eitan Harel's record."

"That convinced you?"

He shook his head. "No. I'm actually very fond of due process. But you know Alex—she sees an opening, she's going to wiggle through it like a window."

"An apt description." *We do what we have to. That's the only job of a survivor.*

"She told me Eitan was a soldier for evil."

Darlington cast Turner a disbelieving glance. "That doesn't sound like Alex Stern."

"She was quoting me. Soldiers for good, soldiers for evil. I know you won't agree, but as far as I'm concerned, this was always about keeping the devil down. She kept telling me it was bullshit. Until last night."

"And then?"

"Then she said, 'But what if I'm wrong?'"

Now Darlington laughed. "*That's* Alex Stern."

Turner tapped the steering wheel as he navigated the near empty streets. "I'm going to be honest with you. That's not really what changed my mind either."

Darlington waited. He didn't know Turner well, but it was easy to see he wasn't a man who liked to be rushed.

"I picked her up in Darien," Turner went on at last, "the night Harel sent her to take on Linus Reiter. She was . . . I've seen her trade punches with a guy twice her size. I've seen her nearly get her skull split by a frat boy looking for revenge. But I've never seen her scared like that."

When they reached Black Elm, Darlington unlocked the kitchen door and they rolled Eitan's body down the stairs into the basement. The home he loved had become a tomb. He wondered what his grandfather made out of the carnage, or the fact that his grandson had abandoned this noble pile of rock. For the time being, at least. He wasn't sure what they were going to do with all of those corpses, or what kind of burial he owed his parents. What would it mean if they just disappeared? And what about Anselm's family?

It was too easy to vanish. He'd done it himself. And who had there been to seek him out? Dawes and Alex, Turner and Tripp. What life could he put together from what was left?

Darlington called to Cosmo, hoping the cat would make an appearance and he could offer some gift of gratitude, tribute in the form of tuna fish. But it seemed he would just have to be patient.

Like all cats, Cosmo would arrive when he wanted to and not a moment before.

Turner helped Darlington lean the basement door against the jamb once more. Then there was nothing to do but turn their backs on the dead.

Darlington slept for the first time since he had been restored to this world, for the first time in over a year. He had never been allowed to sleep in hell or to dream. *No rest for the wicked* had turned out to be a very literal proposition.

He dreamed he was back in hell, a demon once more, a creature of appetite and nothing else. He knelt again at Golgarot's throne, but this time, when he raised his head, it was Alex who gazed down at him, her naked body bathed in blue flames, a crown of silver fire at her brow.

"I will serve you 'til the end of days," he promised.

In the dream she laughed. "And love me too."

Her eyes were black and full of stars.

He woke at noon, his body aching. Sluggish and miserable, he showered and dressed in the jeans and sweater he'd packed in his grandfather's old leather bag. He couldn't seem to get warm.

"Hell hangover," Alex explained when she saw him. She was sitting in the parlor, one leg curled beneath her, still in Lethe sweats, a book of Hart Crane's poetry open in her lap—reading for one of her classes, he presumed. It pleased him too much to see her there, easy on the velvet couch, hair tucked behind her ears. "Dawes made breakfast soup."

From scratch, of course. The perfect cure. He ate two bowls of changua with fresh cilantro, little toasts topped with poached egg floating in the milky broth. His mind was beginning to clear enough to think of something other than survival. He supposed he'd have to reenroll. Lethe would help him. Assuming he was still considered a member of Lethe.

"Where's Mercy?" he asked.

Alex kept her eyes on her book. "I walked her back to JE this morning."

"Is she okay?"

"She wanted to talk to her pastor and have lunch with Lauren. She needs a little normal."

Unfortunately, normal was in very short supply.

After breakfast, he went to the armory and spent an hour digging through the drawers and cabinets. They needed to deal with the bodies in the Black Elm basement. He considered trying the library, but he couldn't quite bear to find the right phrase for the Albemarle Book. *How to dispose of a body. How to dispose of your mother's remains.* It was all too bleak. What he really needed to know was how to grieve for people he had done his best to stop loving years ago. His parents had come and gone from his life like unexpected gaps in the clouds, and if he had spent his days waiting for those brief hours of sunlight, he would have withered and died.

Briefly he considered the Tayyaara, a "magic carpet" that really could take you anywhere by simply opening a portal beneath it. But the destination had to be woven into the design, and anyone who had the skill for such things was long gone, so the weave had remained unchanged, and the carpet could take you only one place: a catacomb beneath Vijayanagar. For several hundred years, it had served as a kind of unofficial dumping ground for unwanted objects and people. He didn't know if what he felt for his parents was duty or love or the memory of love, but he couldn't toss them on some ancient garbage pile.

Alex and Dawes found him sitting on the floor of the armory, surrounded by glittering artifacts and bits of ephemera, stuck. The boy with the rock in his hand, forever trying to build something that had long ago been lost. They helped him put everything back in its proper place, and then they drove to Black Elm.

The whole house was beginning to smell. Or maybe he just knew what was waiting for them as they shuffled the door to the basement aside and stared down into the dark.

"Do you . . . want to say anything?" Alex asked.

He wasn't sure. "Is my grandfather here?"

"He's in the kitchen with Dawes."

Darlington glanced over his shoulder, the kitchen empty to his eyes except for Dawes clutching a wooden spoon like a weapon. Golgarot had offered him a life of revelation, of knowledge, the unseen made seen. That would never be.

"You can talk to him, you know," said Alex.

"I know you liked Stevenson's 'Requiem,'" he said, hoping his grandfather was listening, feeling foolish all the same. "But I'm afraid it doesn't suit."

If Darlington was honest, his grandfather wouldn't like any of it. A eulogy was nothing but death words.

"Go on," he told Alex.

She took a step down the stairs, then another. Darlington followed. The smell was worse here.

"That's enough," he said, and he saw her shoulders slump in relief. The heaps of his parents' bodies were visible now, the scraps that had been Anselm, Eitan Harel slumped against the wall. How could this be his life? His home? What had he allowed for want of skill or knowledge or grit? "I am struck by the profound depth of my failure."

Alex looked back at him from her place on the stairs. "You didn't let the demon in the door. Sandow did. The societies did. When the time came, you stood between the living and the dead. *Hoplite, hussar, dragoon*, remember?"

"You've been paying attention. I'm both delighted and unnerved." There was nothing for this but to see it done.

He laid his hand on Alex's shoulder and reached for the demon. It was an easy thing, like flexing a muscle, like taking a deep breath. He felt his body change, a rush of strength. All fear dropped away; his grief and confusion faded. He felt the curve of Alex's shoulder beneath his palm. If he curled his fingers, his claws would sink deeper. He would hear her gasp. He restrained himself.

Blue flame had blossomed over her body. She glanced back again, looking for a signal from him. He saw the will in her gaze, the way she had shoved her fear down. *I will serve you 'til the end of days.*

He nodded once and she lifted her arm. Blue fire spun from her hands, an arc of flame that became a river, coursing down the stairs and over the bodies. He'd been prepared to speak, a quote from . . . His demon mind couldn't manage it. He remembered Alex with her book of poems. Hart Crane. He grasped at the words.

"And if they take away your sleep sometimes they give it back again." It was the best he could do. He watched the bodies burn.

Part of him wanted to tell Alex not to stop there, to let the whole house burn down to nothing, to let them burn with it too. Instead they stood together in the dark shadows of Black Elm, until there was nothing left but ashes and the old stones that might stand forever but would never mourn.

46

The Mercedes was parked in the Black Elm driveway.

For a long minute, Alex couldn't make sense of what she was seeing. She was still back on the basement stairs, looking down into a crowded grave. When the fire had finished, the walls had been charred black and there was nothing left—no boxes or old clutter, no bodies, no bones. Anything that burned that hot should have consumed them too. But this was no ordinary fire.

When Darlington had spoken for his parents, Alex wondered if she should say something for Eitan. She knew the right prayer from her grandmother. *Zikhrono livrakha.* Let his memory be a blessing. But as Darlington would say, that didn't quite suit.

"*Mors irrumat omnia,*" she had whispered to the flames. It was all she could offer a man who had been willing to send her to her death for the sake of a little more profit.

The car shouldn't be there. It looked freshly washed, its burgundy paint gleaming in the late-afternoon light. *Reiter.* Alex's heart stumbled into a gallop.

"You left it in Old Greenwich?" whispered Dawes.

"It's daytime," Alex managed. "The sun is out. How did he bring it here?" And why now? Had he been watching them? Following them?

"He has a familiar," Darlington said. "Maybe more than one."

Alex remembered the person walking beside Reiter in the JE

courtyard, holding his white umbrella, keeping him safe. She scanned the trees, the cloudless sky, grateful for the harsh winter sun.

"We should get somewhere warded," said Dawes. "Regroup."

Alex wanted nothing more than to do just that. Her body had broken out in a cold sweat, and she was struggling to breathe. But they weren't done here.

She made herself walk toward the car.

"Alex, don't!" Dawes said, grabbing her arm. "It could be a trap."

Alex shook her off.

The driver's-side door was unlocked and the interior was spotless. He'd left the keys tucked in the glove compartment. They were heavy in Alex's hand.

"Give them to me," Darlington said.

Alex wished she had the balls to argue, but she was too scared. She dropped them into his palm.

They gathered around the trunk, and Darlington slid the key into the lock. The trunk popped open with a sigh. He nudged it upward.

Dawes released a high, helpless cry.

Michelle Alameddine lay curled on her side, her hands tucked under her chin as if she'd fallen asleep praying.

Alex took a step backward. Another death to lay at her feet. Michelle, who had warned them not to use the Gauntlet, who had fought her way back from death for this.

"I'm sorry," she said, gasping for air. "I'm so fucking sorry." She lost her footing, sat down hard on the gravel.

I'm sorry. She'd said the same thing to Mercy when she'd left her at the gates to JE early that morning. Mercy had been eager to wash away the sulfur stink of the night, to slip back into her crochet and corduroy. She hadn't mentioned Thanksgiving plans again.

"You're okay?" Alex had asked at the gate, and when Mercy had just looked down at her boots, she added, "You saved my life last night."

"You rescue me. I rescue you," Mercy said. But she didn't meet her gaze.

Mercy had wanted adventure, a chance to see beyond the ordinary world. And Alex had turned her into a killer.

"I thought it would be different," Mercy said, and Alex could see she was fighting tears.

"I'm sorry."

"Are you?"

"No," Alex admitted. She had needed a way out and she'd taken it. "But I'm grateful."

"Thanks," Mercy said as she passed through the gate.

"For what?"

"For not lying to me."

Mercy had a conscience. She believed in a just God. She wouldn't be able to walk away from death without it leaving a stain on her heart. But that hadn't stopped Alex from using her. It never did.

And now Michelle Alameddine was dead.

Alex felt Darlington's hand on her shoulder. "Put your head between your knees. Try to breathe."

Alex pressed her palms against her eyes. "I brought him here."

"Reiter was here already," Darlington said. "Michelle was his familiar."

"What?" Dawes exclaimed.

Alex stared up at him. "What are you talking about?"

"I think he recruited her while she was an undergraduate. I put it together when I was reading her Lethe Days Diary. There were probably others before her."

"She knew where the Gauntlet was?" Dawes asked.

"I don't know," Darlington said. "I don't know what he shared with her. Reiter knew about the societies. He'd stolen the life of a Bonesman. He knew about Lethe. But he couldn't enter warded spaces, so he had to find someone to keep an eye on the Gauntlet."

Alex thought of Michelle sitting in the parlor, always on her phone, keeping removed from their research but never stepping away completely. She remembered Michelle's shock when Alex had told her they'd found the Gauntlet, her insistence that Alex shouldn't use it. Had she been warning Alex or speaking for Reiter? Michelle, who had lied about why she was on campus, who had followed Alex and Mercy to class. Michelle with the jaunty scarf at her throat, the turtleneck sweater. Had he been feeding on her?

"She wouldn't do that," Dawes said. "She wouldn't work for a demon."

But she might. For the right price. Michelle had been to the other side when she'd tried to take her own life. She'd told Alex clearly enough: *I am never going back.*

Alex understood that kind of vow. "He promised her immortality."

"That doesn't make any sense!" Dawes was almost shouting now, tears on her cheeks. "He's a demon. He would have to eat her soul. He—"

"Pammie," Darlington said gently, "she wanted to believe she could live forever, and that's what he told her. Sometimes the story is what matters."

"We aren't putting her in the basement," Alex said as she pushed to her feet. "Or in the ground."

She wasn't going to bury Michelle Alameddine the way that Reiter buried his other victims. The way he would have buried Alex if she hadn't run far and fast enough that terrible night.

Alex forced herself to walk back to the trunk, to look at that body, at the puncture marks at her neck, the tattoo at her wrist. She hoped Michelle had found some kind of peace beyond the Veil, that her soul was safe and whole.

"He made a mistake," Alex said. She could feel her fear changing shape, forming claws and teeth, becoming anger. A welcome alchemy. "If he'd been smart, he would have kept Michelle alive to spy for him."

"Pride," Darlington said. "Reiter was too eager to hurt us, to make us feel his power."

"Cunning, not smart," Alex said, and Dawes nodded, wiping the tears from her eyes.

Darlington gazed down at Michelle's body. "You deserved better," he said softly.

So had Mercy. And Hellie. And Tripp. So had Babbit Rabbit and every other sorry creature who had made the mistake of crossing Alex's path. It hurt to know that Reiter hadn't just fed on Michelle's blood, but on her pain. He would have sated himself on her desperation, her sorrow, her longing for a life that would never end.

I'm going to punish him, Alex promised as they laid Michelle between the elm trees, as Darlington spoke the words of an old poem over her body, as she called the fire once more. *I'm going to hurt him the way he hurt you.*

"*This is the forest primeval*," Darlington recited. "*The murmuring pines and the hemlocks, bearded with moss, and in garments green, indistinct in the twilight, stand like Druids of eld, with voices sad and prophetic . . .*"

She would teach Reiter what real pain tasted like. It was all she could offer this girl she'd barely known. Vengeance that came too late, and prayers spoken in fire.

47

It had taken Alex a few tries to remember exactly where Tripp's apartment was. Turner could have helped, but he was back at work, trying to figure out where his conscience lay on the matter of a man who had helped to commit two murders under demonic influence.

"No more favors," he'd warned her the last time she saw him at Il Bastone.

"They're not really favors, are they?" Alex asked as they sat on the front steps in the cold, breath pluming in the air. The snow had melted away, a false start to true winter, and the sky above them looked hard and bright as blue enamel, as if you could reach up and knock on it. The leaves still clung to their branches in trembling clouds of red and orange. "Not anymore. You don't get to go back to not returning my calls."

"Why not?"

Because I think Mercy may have changed her mind about rooming with me next year. Because I don't have many friends left and I need to know you're one of them.

"Because you're a part of this now. You've seen through the Veil, past it. You can't go back to pretending."

Turner rested his elbows on his knees, clasped his hands. "I don't want to be a part of it."

"Bullshit. You like this fight."

"Maybe I do. But I can't be a part of Lethe, that fucking map, everything this place and these societies stand for."

"You do realize you're a cop, right?"

He shot her a glance. "Don't start with that shit, Stern. I know who I am and I know who my people are. Do you?"

Turner was trying to rile her. He couldn't help it. She was the same way, poking and prodding, looking for the angle. But nothing like a couple of trips to hell to get your priorities in order.

"My people are right here," she said. "You. Dawes. Darlington. Mercy, if I didn't scare her away. You're the ones who fought for me. You're the ones I want to fight for. Lethe has nothing to do with it."

"It isn't that simple."

Probably not. But she'd been in Turner's head. When the moment came to choose a path, he'd made his own—with a bullet. That was something she understood.

Turner rose and Alex did the same. No aches and pains thanks to the magic of Lethe.

"What do you want at the end of all of this, Alex?" he asked.

Freedom. Money. A weeklong nap. "I just want to be allowed to live. Maybe . . . maybe I want to see this whole place undone. I don't know yet. But you can't go back to the way things were. No matter how much you might want that. You can't walk through hell unchanged."

"We'll see," he said, heading down the steps. He paused on the walkway and looked back at her. "It changed you too, Stern. You may not care about good and evil, but that doesn't mean they don't exist. You stole a man out of hell. You beat a demon at his own game. You'd better think about what that means."

"And what's that?"

"The devil knows your name now, Galaxy Stern."

Alex had expected Turner to try to vanish back into his own life, to put distance between himself and Lethe, but when they finally arrived at Tripp's place, there he was, bundled up in an Armani overcoat, leaning against the Dodge. He was reading a newspaper that he folded neatly away when he saw Alex, Dawes, and Darlington.

"Surprised to see you," Alex murmured as they headed into the lobby.

"Not as surprised as me."

"Do you think he's alive?" Dawes asked as they crowded into the elevator and Turner punched the button for the top floor.

"No," she admitted.

Alex wanted to believe Tripp had simply been too scared to return to hell and that they'd find him watching TV and eating ice cream, but she didn't really believe that and they were taking no chances.

Dawes and Darlington had laid down fresh barriers of blooded salt in knot patterns at the entry to the building, the elevator, and now the door to the stairs. Alex had Mercy's salt sword. If Tripp's demon was still here, they'd have to find a way to contain and destroy it. If it had fled, they'd have to find a way to hunt it. More work, more trouble, more enemies to fight. Why did that excite her? She should be spending her nights studying and writing papers. If only those things came as naturally as violence.

"Do you smell that?" Darlington asked as they approached Tripp's door.

There was no mistaking it, the stink of something left to rot.

"That's new," Turner said. He rested his hand on his gun.

The door was unlocked. It creaked on its hinges as Alex gently pushed it open. The loft had a huge wall of windows that had been blacked out with blankets and duct tape.

In the gloom, Alex saw the galley kitchen was littered with dirty dishes and a couple of old pizza boxes. There wasn't much furniture— a massive flat-screen with a gaming system, a couch, and a recliner. A second later she realized someone was in the chair, huddled in the dark.

Alex raised the salt sword, but the thing moved quickly, with the same horrible speed she'd seen in Linus Reiter. *Vampire.* Her fear rose up to choke her. The monster hissed and knocked the sword from her hands.

But then the vampire was on the floor. Darlington towered over it, horns out, the bands at his neck and wrists glowing. Alex was alight with flame. Turner had his gun drawn.

Darlington seized the salt sword, then hissed as it burned his palm.

"D-D-Darlington?" said the monster. "That you, man?"

Darlington hesitated.

Alex yanked one of the blankets down from the window. The thing shrieked and shrank back. "Tripp?"

"Alex! Guys, oh God, don't look at me, I'm so gross."

Tripp was in the same dirty polo shirt and blazer he'd worn to their first descent, a backward Yale sailing cap on his head. He was shockingly pale, but other than that he looked like Tripp. Well, that and the fangs.

Alex stood back, still wary.

"Is that Tripp?" Dawes asked. "Or is it his demon?"

Turner kept his weapon raised. "He's definitely not human."

"Shit," said Tripp, taking off his cap and running a hand through his dirty hair in a gesture Alex had seen countless times. "I knew something was wrong. I haven't taken a shit in . . . I don't even know how long. And every time I try to eat, I have some kind of seizure. And . . ." He looked up guiltily.

"I think he wants to drink our blood," said Dawes.

"No!" Tripp cried. But then he licked his lips. "Okay, yes. I just . . . I'm so hungry."

"Can we get him some rats or something?" Dawes suggested.

"I'm not going to eat rats!"

Alex peered at him. "If this is the demon, Tripp's body has to be somewhere. Or what's left of it."

Not Tripp's eyes darted guiltily to the corner of the kitchen, to what looked like a pile of rolled-up pieces of paper. A husk. Just like the one she'd seen in the Black Elm basement—the husk of the real Tripp Helmuth's body.

Darlington's demon form hadn't receded. He was still on high alert, his eyes glowing gold. "That thing sucked Tripp dry. That's all that's left."

Tripp—or the demon—backed away, baring its fangs. "I couldn't help it."

"You're a killer," Turner said.

"We're all killers!"

"I'm not arguing semantics with a vampire," Darlington snarled. "You know what we have to do."

He was right. Alex had tangled with one vampire, and that was more than enough. But this demon didn't seem like a threat. It seemed feral, weak, and . . . a little dopey.

Her eyes scanned the apartment; aside from the husk of the body in the corner, it looked messy but ordinary—laundry on the floor, dishes in the sink. The only part of the loft that appeared clean or well organized was the big chair and gaming setup. Photos of Tripp's family and friends had been arranged carefully around it, some figurines from games she didn't recognize. She thought of Linus Reiter's vases and bottles of liquor and bouquets of hyacinths. Did all vampires like to nest?

"Darlington's right," said Turner. "This thing is a menace. And we're responsible for its presence here. We need to put it down. It's dangerous."

"I don't think he is," Alex said slowly. "What have you been doing for the last week, Tripp?"

"Just playing video games. Watching old episodes of *Ridiculousness*. Sleeping a lot."

"What have you been eating?" Dawes asked, her voice strained.

"Bugs mostly. But they're a delicacy in some countries, right?"

"What if we didn't kill him?" Alex asked.

"You have to be kidding," Turner exclaimed. "He's a loaded weapon."

"He's barely a squirt gun."

"It could all be an act," Darlington growled.

"Should I put on some tunes?" Tripp asked. "I have this amazing Red Hot Chili Peppers double album—"

Maybe they *should* kill him.

"He's . . ." Alex wasn't going to say *harmless*. "He's Tripp. Maybe he got the personality right along with the life force."

Darlington shook his horned head. "Or it's all an act and he's contemplating killing us all."

"Are you?" Dawes asked.

Tripp winced. "A little bit?"

But an idea had taken root in Alex's mind. "Tripp, call your seabird."

Tripp licked his knuckles, and a silvery albatross rose from behind him, circling the room, with a bright, piercing cry.

"It's still there," marveled Dawes. "How can that be?"

The bird dove straight for Darlington. Alex slid in front of him, dragging her tongue over her wrist and letting her snakes snap out.

For a moment the rattlers and the albatross seemed to face off, and then they receded.

"Tripp's salt spirit did what it was supposed to do," said Alex. "It tried to protect his life, and when it couldn't do that, it stayed with him. It protected his soul."

Darlington still didn't look convinced.

"Look," Alex said, "we did this to him. We took him to hell. We put him in harm's way. He's our responsibility. Without him we never would have gotten you back."

"Didn't you say he did it for cash?"

"Well," said Tripp, "I didn't want to mention it, but my rent is—"

"Not the time, Tripp."

"Alex is right," Dawes said. "He's . . . still him. And he might be useful if we're going to go after Linus Reiter. We could find a way to place him under some kind of prohibition if we're worried he's going to . . . act out."

After Michelle, after Anselm, after Darlington's parents, they needed this, a small victory to carry out of this nightmare.

Darlington threw up his hands, claws receding, a handsome young man in a fine wool coat once more. Alex felt her own flames recede. Their powers were connected now. Bound by hellfire.

Turner holstered his gun. "If he murders someone, I'm not taking the heat."

Darlington jabbed a finger at Dawes. "You've gone soft."

Dawes only smiled. "Come on," she said to Tripp. "We'll get you to Il Bastone and I'll see what I can find to feed you."

"Oh man, thank you. Thank you."

"But you're going to have to change," Alex said.

"Of course. I know I haven't been the most responsible member of the team, but I believe in transformative growth—"

"Clothes, Tripp. You're going to have to change your clothes."

"Shit, man! Absolutely. What did I say? You're all right, Alex." He put up his hand for a fist bump. "I just really want to eat you."

Alex nudged her knuckles against his. "I know, buddy."

He disappeared into the bathroom with disturbing speed and returned in clean shorts and a fleece.

As they walked out into the falling night, Alex felt wildly hopeful. Eitan was dead. Anselm was banished. They would find a way to break the enchantments on the Gauntlet so no one would ever be able to use it again.

The churches on the green shone like stars in their own constellation, and the Harkness bells began to ring. The tune was sweet and familiar, though her brain couldn't quite place it.

Come on along. Come on along.

Fear, hard as a stone, settled in her gut.

Let me take you by the hand. Up to the man. Up to the man. Who's the leader of the band.

Alex peered up at Harkness. As she watched, a dark shape detached itself from the stonework high atop the tower. It spread its wings, a black shadow against the gathering dusk, its eyes glowing red.

"Oh God," Tripp moaned.

"Is it Reiter?" Dawes rasped out.

"I don't think so," said Darlington. "He can't shake his human form."

Turner was staring up at Harkness, at those eyes gazing down at them. "What else could it be?"

"A demon. A monster under his command."

"No," said Dawes. "That can't be. We trapped those demons back in hell. We closed the door."

It is your *presence in hell that will keep the door open.* The wound at Alex's wrist throbbed.

"He bled her," Darlington said.

Golgarot. He hadn't been trying to kill Alex or even keep her in hell when he bit her. "He used my blood to prop open the door."

The thing perched atop Harkness launched itself into the night.

"We have to track it," said Dawes. "Capture it or—"

"That thing is the first," Darlington said. "It won't be the last. We have to find a way to shut the door for good, to seal the Gauntlet before the demons figure out how to keep it open."

"Would that be so bad?" Tripp asked innocently.

"Demons feeding on the living?" Turner snapped. "Hell on earth? Yes, Tripp. That would be bad."

Alex watched the creature circling above. She was done being used by Lethe and men like Eitan.

"You don't get to prey on us," she said to the thing in the sky, to Linus Reiter and Golgarot, and to every hungry thing that might be hunting them. "You don't get to use me to do it." She faced Turner. "Find Mercy. Warn her. Make sure she's safe. Dawes, get Tripp to Il Bastone—and don't let him eat you."

"Alex," Dawes said warningly, worry in her voice. "What are you going to do?"

"The only thing I'm good at."

Alex set off across the green, daring the monster above to follow. She drew her salt sword and called to her hellfire, letting it bloom over her body. If Reiter wanted a target, she'd give him one. Darlington had already fallen into step beside her, matching her stride, his horns glowing, a low growl rumbling in his chest.

A little magic. A talent for taking a beating. A demon at her side. That was all she had, but maybe it was all she needed.

"Come on, Darlington," she said. "Let's give them hell."

Acknowledgments

Thank you for once more making the descent with me. As in *Ninth House*, almost all of the buildings and structures in this book are real and can be found on the New Haven map—except for Black Elm, which was inspired by some of the homes in the Westville area. Sweetwell is also imagined, but I don't recommend cruising Old Greenwich looking for its likeness. At least not at night.

Every inscription and piece of decoration described at Yale, in New Haven, and in Sterling Memorial Library is real, including the University Librarian's secret door. I did take a small liberty with Dürer's magic square, which is a few feet from the Daniel and the lions' den entrance to the Selin Courtyard, rather than directly above it. (James I was referring to the Bodleian, but if I had to choose a library for a prison, Sterling would be a very fine one.) The collection of pond water in the basement of the Peabody Museum is also real (though I'm sure it has been packed safely away during the renovation). The amethyst map is not, but it should be noted that many Yale students and faculty owned enslaved people, including Jonathan Edwards—the fire-and-brimstone preacher for whom Alex's residential college is named. For more on the relationship of the Ivy League to slavery, consider Craig Steven Wilder's *Ebony and Ivy: Race, Slavery, and the Troubled History of America's Universities* and the research of the Yale and Slavery Working Group (https://yaleandslavery.yale .edu).

I would like to say a special thank you to Camila Zorrilla Tessler, whose help accessing and unraveling the mysteries of Sterling was invaluable. Thank you for answering my strangest questions and for sharing your many insights about Yale and the library. Thank you also to Tina Lu and Suzette Courtmanche of Pauli Murray College, who hosted my most recent research visit to campus; and thank you to David Heiser of the Peabody Museum, who was kind enough to tour me through a small fraction of the museum's extraordinary collection during my first visit. Thanks again to Michael Morand, Mark Branch, Claire Zalla, and the brilliant Jenny Chavira, who connected me to so many wonderful people and resources. D, thank you for sharing your experiences on both sides of the law.

Many books contributed to the world of *Ninth House* and *Hell Bent*, but I'd like to specifically highlight *Visions of Heaven & Hell Before Dante*, edited by Eileen Gardiner; *Yale: A History* by Brooks Mather Kelley; *Yale in New Haven: Architecture and Urbanism* by Vincent Scully; (as always) Patrick Pinnell's *Yale University: An Architectural Tour*; *Model City Blues: Urban Space and Organized Resistance in New Haven* by Mandi Isaacs Jackson; *The Plan for New Haven* by Frederick Law Olmsted and Cass Gilbert; *The Great Escape of Edward Whalley and William Goffe* by Christopher Pagliuco; *The Public Artscape of New Haven: Themes in the Creation of a City Image* by Laura A. Macaluso; and *The Streets of New Haven: The Origin of Their Names* by Doris B. Townshend. If it's still running, I highly recommend the New Haven Museum's fantastic exhibit on the New Haven Clock Company Factory. If it's not, I hear Gorman Bechard is working on a documentary.

At Flatiron, I'd like to thank Bob Miller, Kukuwa Ashun, and my editor, Megan Lynch, who approached this novel with ingenuity and care. Thanks also to my genius marketing and publicity teams: Nancy Trypuc, Katherine Turro, Maris Tasaka, Erin Gordon, Marlena Bittner, Amelia Possanza, and Cat Kenney; Donna Noetzel, Keith Hayes, and Kelly Gatesman, who made this book look so good; and Emily Walters, Morgan Mitchell, Lena Shekhter, and Elizabeth Hubbard in production. I am forever grateful to Jenn Gonzalez, Malati Chavali, Louis Grilli, Kristen Bonanno, Patricia

Doherty, Brad Wood, and everyone on the Macmillan sales team for supporting my stories.

At New Leaf, huge thanks to Veronica Grijalva; Victoria Hendersen; Jenniea Carter; Emily Berge-Thielmann; Abigail Donoghue; Hilary Pecheone; Meredith Barnes; Joe Volpe; Katherine Curtis; Pouya Shahbazian, who has helped me walk through the valley of the shadow of development; Jordan Hill, who is a fantastic reader, strategist, and co-conspirator; and, of course, Joanna Volpe, who has been my champion for over ten years and who somehow sees a way through the storm when I'm ready to wreck the ship.

Many thanks to David Petersen and Justin Mansfield for their help with Latin and Arabic, to Sarah Mesle for introducing me to Shell and Bones, to Amie Kaufman for her expertise on sailing and her help shaping Tripp's story, to my college roommates Hedwig, Emily, Leslie, and Nima for sharing their memories with me, and to my generous and wise critique partners Daniel José Older, Holly Black, Kelly Link, and Sarah Rees Brennan for their creativity, intelligence, and good humor. Thank you to Melissa Rogal for being a diplomat and a general, to Peter Grassl for doing the math and putting out many a fire, and to Morgan Fahey for always coming through with quality arcana. Jeff, thank you for being so fun to scheme with. Adrienne, thank you for delivering cocktails, kindness, and wisdom when I most need them. Alex, thank you for lending me your marvelous writing and marketing mind. Sooz, thank you for your help on everything from flap copy to my weird input brain. Thanks also to Noah Eaker, who first took a chance on Alex and her journey.

Chris, Sam, Ryan, and Em, thank you for keeping me laughing. Mom, thank you for raising me on poetry and common sense. E, thank you for building a place of comfort and ease and beauty with me. I am so happy to be home with you. Fred, all hail Ball.

As always, a final thank you to Ludovico Einaudi, whose music guides me through every draft.

About the Author

Leigh Bardugo is the #1 *New York Times* bestselling author of *Ninth House* and the creator of the Grishaverse (now a Netflix original series), which spans the Shadow and Bone trilogy, the Six of Crows duology, and the King of Scars duology—and much more. Her short fiction has appeared in multiple anthologies, including the Best American Science Fiction and Fantasy. She lives in Los Angeles and is an Associate Fellow of Pauli Murray College at Yale University.

About the Type

This book was set in Garamond, a typeface created by and named for Claude Garamond, a sixteenth-century Parisian engraver and type-founder. A perennial masterpiece of old style serif, Garamond is distinguished by its graceful irregularity among individual letters and contrast between light and heavy strokes, which give the sense of a calligrapher's handwriting. This version of Garamond, Adobe Garamond Pro, was designed by Robert Slimbach, who captured the gracefulness of the original Garamond typefaces while creating a typeface family that is well suited for contemporary digital printing.

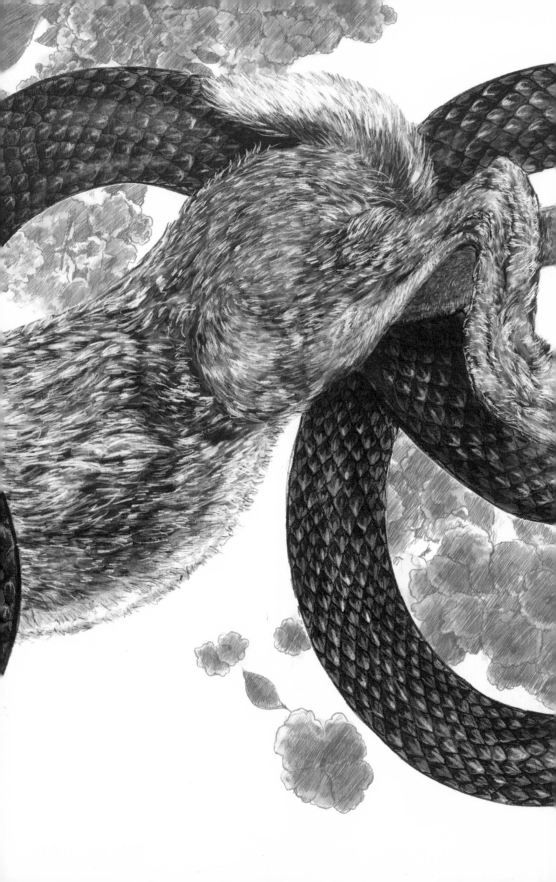